As recollected by one Campbell Crabbe:

AN AMERICAN
DESCENDENTALIST WESTERN

One of the strangest of episodes in the history
of the cattle country and the open range
at the height of the free grass era

Written in and to these

YOU,
KNIGHTED STATES

Jack Kohl

The Pauktaug Press
Pauktaug, New York

ISBN: 978-0-69207-025-3

Cover illustration: Freiman Stoltzfus
www.freimanstoltzfus.com

Interior design: Gary A. Rosenberg
www.thebookcouple.com

Printed in the United States of America

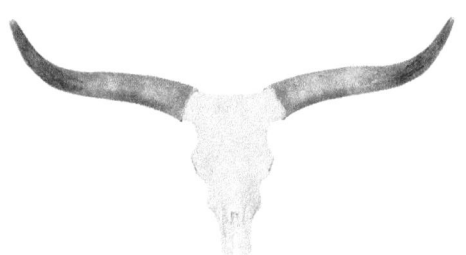

Contents

PART I

The Eve of Things

I.

The spaces between things are what ultimately cause us so much grief.

My trip had been three hard weeks according to plan—and several days longer according to disaster.

Late in the spring of 1883, I was thirty-four years old, and I stumbled into Pauktaug in early evening. Though I had been close to death once before in my life, I had never been so near to demise as on that night. I was struggling with my strongest bout of consumption, but also with the end of a stretch of three terrible days on the plains: without food, with very little water, and with several of my ribs cracked. Having no food during a three day march across grasslands did little to help the dreadful figure I already cut because of my advanced illness; and having cracked ribs only made me more terrified of my habitual, bloody, coughing. I ran out of water completely on the third and final day.

But despite all I had been suffering from my illness and injuries, I do not recall any pain as I took my first steps into my first wondrous hours in the town of Pauktaug.

And I must ask, would it not be most wondrous for anyone, having traveled nearly two-thousand miles in one direction, to discover, as it appeared then to me, that one had merely returned from whence they came? I am at considerable risk of lapsing into a cliché when I say that upon first setting foot upon Main Street in Pauktaug I suspected I might be dreaming all that I saw—or at least seeing some waking vision or mirage. But that suspicion did not last for very long, for despite my condition, there was no mistaking what was before me.

As I took my last steps off of the range, I set foot into a de facto replica of the north shore Long Island village I had left nearly a month earlier. Now I should remark that I had known the names of the two towns were the same. I had known that I was leaving one Pauktaug—that first and ancient one founded by Dutch settlers in the mid-seventeenth-century and named for the tribe that had haunted its woods and beaches—and that I was bound for a new one on the high plains. But nothing could have suggested to me— no description, no photograph, no warning—that I would step into a new town which by virtue of its exactness as a recreation would seem to abnegate all of the spaces that had been crossed to reach it.

Very much as I had done when a child, when I would rise from dreams and take to my toilette basin to restore trust to my senses, I took to the trough that lay right at the north foot of this new Pauktaug's Main Street. I braced myself as much for the cool sting I sought as for the brine and filth I expected in such a dubious source, but, to my surprise, the trough was remarkably clean.

I dared not drink even though the water was remarkably cool, clear, and seemingly clean. I scrubbed my face with that horse water—chilled in the evening's dry, Western, air—and concluded that the only taste of filth I detected was coming from my own soiled mouth and skin. I managed to stand after a minute's worth of this hasty bathing, and it was then that I took in the full sweep of the Main Street before me.

It might as well have been the ten-thousandth time I was doing so, however; for there, exact unto almost every detail was the Main Street I had known from back home in New York, comprehensive and unyielding in its realization. In the critical, blue, moonlight I extended my hand before me and affected to hold in my palm the first building ahead and to my left (the town theater). I could find no flaws in the rendering I pretended to hold in my hand; the theater was an exquisite likeness of the original.

I took an astonished step back and smacked the trough with my heels. I reeled a bit then and felt very dizzy. But I did not feel so unsteady as to refrain from taking the same measure—this time with my right hand instead of my left—of another building. This building was a longer structure, that of the Pauktaug Hotel—this hotel that appeared to match, at least at a distance, the one I knew from home in every respect.

I looked past the hotel, and in the full moonlight that shone upon the broad emptiness of grass that lay to the west I saw no harbor there as was to be expected at home. No, this was indeed a new, different, place. I looked left and to the east once more. And there, too, beyond the theater—and beyond the whole line of familiar buildings on the east side of Main Street—was nothing known to me. No familiar ascent of wooded hills (wherein my family's home could be found) as there was back East. On both sides there was only an immense, boundless, stretch of brown grass.

With my heels and lower legs still braced against the trough behind me, I took a slow look over both shoulders and confirmed one last time that back there, as well, was no familiar sight of home—even though I had just spent days traversing the ground in that direction. No Long Island Sound to be seen, and thus, of course, no Connecticut looming across the water as at home. Again: just grass, and the young, tenuous, stage road, pulled thinner and thinner into that wondrous, smoky, horizon line.

I turned and faced the trough once more. It was at this point that I recall catching the scent of freshly hewn lumber, the scent as surrounds any new frame building, any new house or barn, any crisp and splintery young fence or sidewalk. It seemed to permeate all of the air: that scent of lumber coupled to the novel and dry odor of the prairie grasses. I thought it odd that I smelled nothing of cows.

I realized that the strongest scent of new wood was coming from the trough. The carpentry of the trough could not have been more than a few days old; the source of such fresh wood scent could be traced down to the tender new splinters that had yet to wear away by use. The evident newness of the trough, the beautiful clarity of its water, all this conspired—despite the fact that I would never otherwise drink from a vessel meant for livestock—to take away any last strength I had to refrain from drinking all I could right away. Even with the town so near at hand, I dropped to my knees and slaked my thirst with an animal's desperation.

The water tasted as sweet and clean as it appeared. I believe now that nothing had touched the trough since it had been filled, but perhaps a mad thirst makes for the sweetest water. I drank my fill, caught my breath—despite the coughing and profound pain this deep breathing caused—and then drank again. This second bout of drinking left me desperate for air, and I repeated the process of breathing deeply, coughing, and clutching my rib cage in a useless effort to stave off great pain. I stood up during this second recovery. There had been nothing really wrong with the water; nor did standing up suddenly leave me more faint or dizzy. But as I looked back north over the forbidding empty prospect through which I had marched for three days, I suddenly fainted.

2.

When I came to, all that had transpired for the previous three weeks seemed likely to have been merely a dream. In fact it did not even occur to me that I might have been dreaming, for I woke up in such familiar surroundings that at first I looked about me with an almost cozy indifference and sense of routine. Nothing but a comfortable present came to mind as I awoke on the long settee in the main parlor of the Pauktaug Hotel.

Why should such a public room seem such a customary place to me for sleeping and casual waking? The Pauktaug Hotel, which had been built only a few years after I had been born in 1849, was not only known to me as an occasional site from childhood, youth, and early manhood—where, in company with my family, and later just my father, calls were paid on the exulted lecturers my father had commissioned or persuaded to visit Pauktaug—but also as a place where my father, in the early time of his declining years, would linger inordinately long in the dining room with his contracted visitors, over elaborate late suppers and cigars. And I, always close by in attendance of my increasingly brittle and feeble father, would often retreat to the parlor and doze—and, even, on occasion, stay through most of an entire night—all the while waking from time to time to the sound of my father's affected voice, his strains hoping desperately to be heard with, and above all connected to, the sometimes modestly celebrated men of letters enduring the late hours in his company.

When I awoke on the settee in the new hotel's main parlor, adjoining the lobby (and thus I lay just two rooms away from the large dining hall), all seemed as it often should have been back home during the routines of my early manhood in the late 1860s and early 1870s.

It was nighttime, but the hour was unknown. All seemed well. Yet all seemed well *and* strange at once. Though I had always thought the hotel—the Pauktaug House was its formal name—a clean, respectable establishment, I opened my eyes to it as if in a state of renaissance, in a state of incredible repair, in a state that suggested not the Pauktaug House I knew but one I *had* known, the one I had known through late youth. Nothing seemed demonstrably different in outward detail, but all seemed firmer, unworn, untouched by even the expected use of weathering hands repeatedly grazing against door handles and the arms of chairs. On further inspection—after my eyes made out what they could by the glow of a single, low, lamp—I could see many things subtly incongruous with the Pauktaug House I had known as a child: colors of drapes, shades and patterns of carpet, shapes and styles of chairs—all close but nothing quite exactly right.

This seemed the likely makings of one of those odd dreams of a sleep's ending, but then a sudden fit of coughing—violent, bloody, and protracted—wrested me from any doubts that I might be awake, and I was forced to sit up and ride out the fit. My cracked ribs ached and jabbed pain all about my chest; memories of the fall that had broken those bones began to return at that moment, but then subsided.

As soon as I was sure I was out of my fit, I reached for the spot where I expected an ancient, low, table to be—the place where I usually placed my spectacles before dozing. A table was there, in the customary place, but it seemed a bit lower than usual and of slightly different finish to the touch. My spectacles were on that table, but they were on the far side, away from the settee, as if someone else had placed them there.

I took a great sweep of a look around the parlor; everything was indeed as I had suspected—ever so close a match, but nothing quite right. But it was not until I performed a ritual I had formed after taking so many impromptu nights' sleeps in the Pauktaug

House that a shocking confirmation of the reality of the last three weeks of travel became apparent. This Pauktaug House was *not* the Pauktaug House of Pauktaug, Long Island of 1883; nor was it the Pauktaug House of Pauktaug, Long Island in the years when my father was still living—when it was common for me to wake in its parlor, having passed the time waiting for my father to finish entertaining his guests.

What was the shocking confirmation I saw? It had become my custom upon waking and rising from the settee over the course of many years to pay my respects and to bid goodnight or good morning to a trophy moose head that hung on the north wall of the hotel's parlor. It had been shot by Mr. Joseph Whisker, Sr., my father's main partner in business, on a hunting trip in the Adirondacks during the early years of my childhood, and the head of that moose had hung in that parlor ever since. Some remarked that it had a mournful air and an especially melancholy eye. But I always found it reassuring—a comforting, nearly personifiable symbol of something that refused to change or disintegrate in any way throughout all the years of my life. Even by the time of my journey west—save for trace bits of dust in certain unreachable crevices and twists of fur, and except for a few inexplicable tears in the hide and slight wear on the enormous antlers where presumptuous fellows had taken to hanging their hats—that moose hardly changed since I was a little boy.

As I have observed, it was my custom to acknowledge the bust of this mammoth trophy that presided over the parlor. I instinctively began to motion to the great head where I expected it to be, began that motion with the expectation of saying a few words, as well.

I completed the motion, but I was stopped from saying a word even before my lips began to part. A great trophy head was indeed in the expected spot—in the exact spot, in fact. But it was not the moose head I had known since boyhood. This was certainly not

Pauktaug, Long Island, New York, for in the place of the moose was a colossal head, the largest I had ever seen: a prize bull, certainly by any standards of civilization, but even by the standards of a race of giants.

The bull could not have been mounted any later than a year or two earlier. Perhaps it had been slain and prepared even more recently than that, for the closer I was able to stagger toward it with my uncertain steps, the more clearly I could see the freshness of the taxidermy. There was not a trace spot of dust on the bull's head, nor was there the slightest sign of fading from sunlight.

My focus upon this perfectly preserved, once animate, and living thing was so intense that for an instant I was led to believe that it was not merely a half-rendering of a dead animal but a sentient still life unto itself—or even the actual subject for a still life and not the resultant sculpture. For in that moment of focus upon the muscled head and bust I was compelled to believe that it answered my attention with a salutation to me in return.

"Mr. Crabbe?" spoke a cautious voice.

In the bull's black, glassy, eyes I detected movement that seemed to support my suspicion that this inanimate mass of trophy lived—until I realized the movement was the reflection of a living man coming toward me from the hotel's lobby.

"Mr. Crabbe?" the voice asked again in a careful, polite, tone.

I turned away from the bull—but slowly, for I was weak and unsteady on my legs—and faced the young and slender man who had addressed me. He was nattily dressed and very clean—surprisingly so when compared with many of the men, of any business, I had encountered on my three week journey west. His solicitude toward me seemed motivated by far more than that for an ill stranger's welfare. That mysterious part of his intense solicitude was dispelled in part almost immediately when I realized I had heard him correctly: he was calling me by name.

"Mr. Crabbe? How do you feel now, sir?"

"Is this—? Pardon me, but is this Pauktaug Village? Where is this? Where am I?"

Whilst keeping to a peculiar style of deference and slight, affected, formality that was foreign to my Eastern ways, this fellow at the same time became slightly more relaxed and condescending after I spoke. Perhaps it was that type of condescension that some feel they must invoke with the ill, when the ill wake from a long or troubled sleep; or perhaps he was generally an underling and therefore pleased to have the upper hand in anything when that rare hand presented itself—as in knowing where one was when another did not. Whatever the case, he took all the steps but the final two or three paces to me, smiled in a childishly patrician yet somehow still ingratiating way, and spoke to me so that I felt for a time like a new Rip Van Winkle.

"Well, Mr. Crabbe. Well. Well, well. You sure don't sound like no Englishman to me. And I never heard tell of Pauktaug as a *village*. Ain't that kind of quaint, though? Come along. Why don't you come sit with me in the lobby?"

He extended his arm, yet he seemed afraid to commit to touching me. I took his arm quickly, for I had been ill too many times in my life to refuse the help of strangers when I was unsteady on my feet. He led me into the lobby and sat me down on an ornate chaise that was flush against the wall opposite the hotel's front desk. This room, as well, was an eerie match for the Pauktaug House back home—save for many small details that my increasing wakefulness began to note. Even my mysterious host was not unlike the clerks I had known back East in small hotels. He was dressed in the bright colors and rich patterns that characterize my memories of men's styles from that time, in the evening of the Victorian Age; but his color scheme was even more complex and bright than customary. Yet he was an innocent in his choices, evidently, and was sure, despite the comedy of his appearance, that he had quite dandified himself.

"Yes, sir, why don't you just rest right there. Lay down if you like!" he said.

"This is Pauktaug?" I asked once more.

"Yes, it is Mr. Julius. You've arrived. Yes, you have. And just about when we expected—but not *how* we expected, of course."

I was so grateful to have another human being confirm again my whereabouts, make them certain and plain so that his inexplicable address to me now as *Mr. Julius* instead of *Mr. Crabbe* was not of immediate concern.

"This is not New York? This is not Long Island?" I asked.

"Certainly not, Mr. Julius," replied my host. "This is *Pauktaug*," he continued, "and we're certainly not New York. This is Pauktaug, indeed—and in some of the finest new country in the land. This is Pauktaug all right—fresh as a new brand, smoke and hiss and everything! There couldn't be another, now could there?"

"As a matter of fact there is," I replied, as I caught a first glimpse of myself in the large mirror on the wall between the front desk and the dining room doors.

"Now, really!" the man answered, and he took a seat on a stool that was set inexplicably in the middle of the lobby. He seemed to be settling in, as if I were about to lead a session of storytelling. "Really! Are you tying knots in my tail?" he asked.

"I'm thirsty—very thirsty," I said.

"I don't think we ever saw a man drink so much water as you did before we set you to sleeping in the parlor there. Don't you remember?"

I shook my head in the negative.

"I'll be right back—and with more cool water than you'll be able to stomach!"

My caretaker vanished into the dining room of the hotel. Soon my host—still resplendent in his bright red waistcoat and green, striped, pantaloons—returned with water. And he brought coffee, as well, which was very welcome. But I had to take long draughts of the water to quench my thirst lest I impulsively do so with the coffee and burn myself.

After I took my fill—an entire pitcher's worth—of water, I settled back on the chaise and let my head rest against the wall. My host was keen, then, to offer me the coffee which I had resisted until then. I was eager to accept, yet as I leaned back with the steaming cup in my hand, a severe fit of coughing overtook me. With this fit my ribs ached something fierce.

My host offered me a clean, white, handkerchief, and even in the midst of my convulsions I took discreet looks at the cloth and could see traces of my blood staining the material. I was accustomed to such sights; but I was astonished when after I blew my nose into the handkerchief I found that the cloth was blackened whenever I blew, by the dust from the last three days on the range.

It was then that I stole a good look at myself in the mirror which hung between the front desk and the entrance to the dining room. When I looked in that mirror, what did I see? Since childhood I had been accustomed to seeing my family's (paternal side) trait of high cheekbones augmented in an extreme way by my inordinately sunken cheeks, but my appearance then was even shocking to myself. Through the gentle steam tendrils of that cup of coffee I saw how hunger and illness had pulled the skin dry and tight around *all* the distinguishing bones of my face and jaw— tight to an unprecedented degree, for not a trace of softening fat remained to gentle my appearance. My aquiline nose had taken on a sharpness that shocked me, for it seemed to have extended and sharpened itself, the bridge to tip looking like the lengthened nib of a new steel pen, in consequence of my cheeks having surrendered so much claim on my face. My cheeks: they were not sunken; they were, instead, truly pitted, and I looked deeper into the mirror to see with shock that I could make out the suggestion of the contours of my skull. During the long, silent, pause in which I tried to reconcile myself to my appearance, I could see, as well, that my host took advantage of my distraction to fathom the extent—and perhaps danger—of my appearance.

I endeavored to distract him, and myself, from the subject of my face: "Thank you, sir, for the coffee."

"It *is* good. Isn't it? Some of the best that money can buy, I hear!" he replied. But all the while he said this, and for quite some time after, he marveled at my condition, as if I were one of the new wonders of the frontier. I deeply regretted that notion, for this man—despite his oddly colored and genteel clothes—had the air of a frontier native, and it had been my hope to be struck by wonders in the West and not to impress them myself upon anyone of that country.

"How do you feel, Mr. Julius?"

I decided to let this mysterious appellation of *Mr. Julius* pass one more time, and I decided that I would assert something of my accustomed social dominance, at least as I had enjoyed it back East when I was very young, by choosing to ignore any questions I chose. I deemed this question the first of such, and I thought, too, that it would be a good thing to set a precedent of behavior and standing in this new place with even the very first person I had met. *I* resolved to ask the questions, and I decided to learn obliquely if this man was indeed the first and only person I had encountered since reaching town. I could recall nothing of the time between my losing consciousness near the water trough and waking up in the eerily familiar hotel.

"How was I found? Who found me?" I asked with as much authority in my voice as I could conjure without triggering another coughing fit.

"Mr. Davis and I first saw you right out that window over there. We saw you fall over not long after we had our first sight of you. We both went out and helped you into the parlor there. Couldn't get you to say much. But you did answer to the name of *Crabbe*."

"That is my family's name," I muttered without caution.

"We'd been expecting the stage to come in about three days ago—that is if they made a run on account of having anyone or anything to carry. It was said that there might be a man with the name *Crabbe* on one of the stages this month. But we supposed after a time that they had no one to carry into town from the railroad, since three days ago the stage didn't show up at all," said my host. He said nothing, however, about where he got the name *Mr. Julius.*

"There was indeed a stage—carrying just myself and one other man. Did another man come into town yesterday or the day before?" I asked.

"No, no one," my host answered quickly, and then he got to the real point that just then was obviously gnawing at him. "We didn't think there'd been a run of the stage this week. If there was, and you was on it, then what happened to it?" he asked, a bit suspiciously.

"The coach lost a wheel, and the coach wrecked itself—violently. I believe I cracked several ribs in the crash. The driver said he thought the wheel had been thrown by something hidden in the road. Then he said he was certain there were Indians watching us from a distance, as if a trap had been set," I ventured.

"Injuns!" my host grunted and laughed with disbelief. Can't say that I thought any of that kind of thing's been going on in this country for some time!" My host paused and then grunted again. "Injuns! You don't say?"

"Yes, I do," I answered.

"Injuns! You don't say!" he said yet again.

"I do indeed," I replied with pride and with an effort to appear strong. But that effort sent me into another fit. This time my host took my coffee cup and spared me from having to place it on the tray.

He offered back my coffee cup after refilling it, and then made bold to ask, "What happened next, after the driver said he saw Injuns?"

"The man I had been traveling with by chance in the coach proposed we continue on foot," I said. "The driver said we were mad to leave."

"He'd be right," added my host.

I ignored this remark and continued: "We had neither food nor water, and my fellow traveler convinced me we were closer to our destination than to the place we had started from, the end of the railroad. I trusted him in this, but after some hours on the road he proposed moving cross-country. He said it would be more direct and that any Indians, if in pursuit, would look for us first on the stage road. But I did not wish to leave the road, despite my concerns about Indians."

"Injuns!" grunted my host.

I ignored this interruption, as well. "We parted ways," I said. "The other man went onto the range. I stayed with the road for a night, a day, another night, another day—and then into nightfall of today when I reached, I believe, the spot where you found me."

"I along with Mr. Davis—" my host added pointlessly.

With this latest interruption my body's voice suddenly broke in on my mind's narrative: "I'm hungry!" I exclaimed involuntarily.

"Well, of course you are, Mr. Julius. Of course you are," answered my host, and with that he disappeared into the darkness of the dining room and likely went into the kitchen just beyond.

In a matter of a minute, the man—who had still not introduced himself—returned with a plate of cold meat and hard bread.

"There you are, Mr. Julius. We can fix you better things come morning, but I brought you this now rather than make you wait."

I had to take great care to prevent myself from inducing another coughing fit as I combined my impulse to eat along with my desire to speak at the same time so as to resolve my host's inexplicable habit of addressing me as *Mr. Julius.*

"Why do you call me *Mr. Julius?*" I asked him—also showing care and caution in the way I put my question, for I felt that if I refrained at first from revealing that I was not this *Mr. Julius*, he might give me more information about this other man. I knew there might be an interesting answer. For, again, I also noted he had called me by my correct surname at least once. I had suspicions, then, as to what the answer might be, but at that point I could hardly have believed it on my own.

"Well, you are Mr. Julius Crabbe? Aren't ye?" asked my host.

My suspicions were thus confirmed. I did have a cousin, an Englishman by birth and residence, by the name of Julius Crabbe. But surely, I thought, my host's reference to this name was merely an unlikely accident, for I had had no contact—nor had anyone in my family as far as I then knew—with that cousin since I had been a boy. And even if my host had heard some passing reference to such a name at some point, surely still, I tried to believe, his use of the name remained some sort of remarkable accident.

"No," I replied with calm indignation, "I am Campbell Crabbe, of Pauktaug, New York."

"Really? You don't say! Well, what do you know! *Our* Mr. Crabbe never said that we should be expecting two other Crabbes at the same time. Well!" exclaimed my host as he straightened his vest.

"In this case by *Mr. Crabbe* you don't mean a Mr. Ellsworth Crabbe?" I asked carefully.

"I most certainly do mean Mr. Ellsworth Crabbe. He and Mr. Whisker—they're the founders of Pauktaug here. There weren't a thing here t'all of a town not three years ago but prairie dog holes—not even a town for them dogs at that! And in the last year, more than in any other time, Mr. Crabbe built this entire town. He done built this place right out of the big old empty that was all that was here before. Mr. Crabbe—Mr. Ellsworth Crabbe—he's kin of yours?"

It was already clear that my host would never have dared to have called Mr. Ellsworth Crabbe merely *Mr. Ellsworth*—even in a humble, respectful, intimate servant's third person reference. He was clearly *the* Mr. Crabbe to him.

"Yes, I am his brother," I answered.

My host eyed me for a silent moment. I believed him to be taking stock of my condition again, but soon I realized he was meditating something else.

"Really? You don't say? You look kinda young to be a brother of his."

My response to his impertinent suspicion was swift and firm, and I was pleased that taking a deep, angry, reflexive breath in preparation to respond to this did not trigger one of my coughing fits.

"My brother is nineteen years my senior, yes!"

From the force of my indignation he could tell that what I said was true.

"Yes, Mr. Crabbe. Of course. Yes, certainly. It's just that we were told to expect a Mr. Julius Crabbe at any point this month. Mr. Davis himself went out to our Mr. Crabbe's place to tell him of your arrival—or of Mr. Julius's arrival, if you take my meaning."

"Mr. Davis?" I asked.

"Mr. Davis runs this here hotel. I just work for him and work in the kitchen—and do other odd such things. He left some hours ago. He should have reached Mr. Crabbe's place by now. But I doubt they'll be back much before dawn. How's the food, sir?"

I was pleased to have been settled as a *sir.*

"It's quite fine," I replied.

I did not wish to share any more personal details with my host, even though my instincts suggested he was harmless. But I could not resist asking two more questions myself.

"You're sure it was a Mr. Julius Crabbe that was expected?" The answer was a firm nod in the affirmative.

"Why did you think I was that man?" I then asked. "I didn't appear here from on the coach—not in the customary way, anyway."

"You answered to the name *Crabbe* is all when we carried you in," my host answered plainly.

All this seemed sound—as sound as anything could seem under the circumstances. However, I could not begin to fathom why my cousin, an Englishman, would be making his way to the frontier Pauktaug at the same time I had resolved to travel there. I knew, of course, of the understanding between my brother and myself—of my pledge of an indefinitely imminent arrival for that spring—but the introduction of a nearly forgotten foreign relative into the manifold mysteries of that night confounded me.

My host retreated to the hotel's front desk, just opposite from where I continued to sit and work on my cold supper. He realized that I was through talking for a spell, and though he offered to give me a room of my own upstairs on family credit, I resolved to remain in the lobby for the final dark hours of that then early morning.

Standing in a slightly different place than did its counterpart in the Pauktaug House back home on Long Island, a large clock marked the time as it stood against the wall between the front desk and the inner doorway of the hotel's vestibule. It read just before four in the morning after my host and I ceased speaking. Dawn was still some hour or so away at that season of the year, and as I meditated on the subtle differences between that clock and its near twin back East I must have lapsed into a profound doze, for after seeming to blink for only an instant, I was awakened by loud voices—loud but sounding from afar—and I looked at the clock face to see that it had leaped to four-thirty as if in a moment's time.

3.

The distant voices brought me to my feet. The water, coffee, and supper—as well as my brief rest—had worked an astonishing bit of recovery upon me. But even more remarkable was that I felt I knew precisely from where the sound of the voices came.

My host spoke first in reaction to the rowdy noise that carried to us from up the street: "Sounds like something's up at the—"

"At the tavern on the east side of the street," I said before he could finish.

"You don't say?" my host answered as he attempted to conceal his surprise, but then he continued as if he had not heard my interruption: "Seein' as how I've been around since near the time they broke ground on most everything here in town, I'd say it was comin' from the *saloon* over there," he added with condescension.

My old family custom of keeping a certain distance from humble characters like my host made me precise in my next choice of words. I said, "You're not wrong."

"What do you mean, Mr. Campbell?" he asked. He was quick to correct himself:

"Mr. Crabbe?"

"I mean that we're both speaking of the same place. Could that noise down the street mark the return of this Mr. Davis you spoke of?" I asked.

"He's no stranger to the saloon. But I think he'd come back here first with any news from our Mr. Crabbe's place," said my host.

He could see that I was eager to investigate the commotion up the way for myself; he added some valuable native caution: "Besides, that racket doesn't sound like any funnin' goin' on—not at this hour, at least. And though we hardly have any right now, Mr.

Davis wants me to remain here for what guests we got upstairs. He wants me to stay here and see to you, too. We'd best stay inside."

My host did not realize that despite my nearly two-thousand mile journey, and my illness and weakness, nothing could stop the surge of energy and resolve that welled within me at this first sign of human sound—save for my host's, of course—since my arrival in that disturbingly familiar town. I had come too far in my voyage to remain a passive traveler at the every end, even though my host's advice seemed wise.

"You really should stay here, Mr. Crabbe. You ain't well. Let me get you something more to eat? How's about something even stronger than coffee if that suits you? Besides, Mr. Davis would bring your brother right here, or your brother would come right here first, if he was in town."

Despite my host's veteran and native status—which likely made all of his advice valuable—I was able to shoot him a look of determination that all but silenced his warnings, save for one last entreaty from him.

"Please stay here, Mr. Crabbe. No disrespect, sir, but this ain't your country. I tell you it ain't safe right now. I can tell by the way that noise out there sounds. This ain't your country."

I made my way to the door. My legs were not only weak from sickness; they were also sore from my march to a degree I had never experienced before. I felt weakness and fatigue all over, and my cracked ribs still ached. But I took a cautious deep breath, inhaled the robust and dry air drifting in through the open windows, and then responded with a masculine depth and brevity with which I surprised myself.

"Sure looks just like my country."

"You don't say?" my host muttered as I left him in the hotel lobby and stepped out in the darkness of Main Street.

There was still no sign of dawn at that hour, but the brilliant fraction of the moon gave enough light for me to make my way in wonder up the familiar course of the Main Street of a town in which I had never been before. The tavern, the saloon, was less than fifty yards to the southeast of the hotel's front entrance. Even with my cautious, unsure stride, I reached it with relative speed and ease. I might have reached it even more quickly had my eyes not been fascinated by the magical appearance of the utterly familiar placed on unfamiliar ground.

4.

I stepped into the saloon. Before me was another stunning recreation—for there was a near match of the long, dark, wood bar of the tavern at home, with its great mirror (only this mirror was new, and it bore no trace of the flaky, spidery cracking that had fascinated me back home). But the pattern of the tin ceiling was surely a close match, probably only failing to serve as a twin if a patch of its pattern were held up against the original in very close inspection.

Below the four or five most pronounced smoke stains on the ceiling, at tables in the back corners, and below the three or four most pronounced smoke stains above the long, dark bar, sat sodden, stoic cowmen—they evidently indirect or unrelated parties to the scene unfolding at the dead center of the saloon, for they seemed almost indifferent to all that I was about to witness. But their eyes were rapt upon the scene—the eyes of these smoking men of the back tables and the bar—as if, in being slightly older in appearance than the men standing in the center of the room, these more veteran cowmen were there to leave a testimony in tobacco smoke on the ceiling, an oblique but simple transcript of events.

Though I have no doubt that the men in the center of the room, those who were standing and most engaged in the noise and the action, were no strangers to tobacco, these younger men were all too engaged to be busy with smokes. They stood with their backs to me, focused on something or someone seated in a chair in front of them, but out of my view.

I moved quietly to a place at the bar. Behind that bar was a thin, bald, aging but hale looking man. He was not entirely unlike the barkeepers I had known in the old Pauktaug since my boyhood errand days, (but I noted in him a degree of fear about the then present situation unlike anything I had ever seen, or heard tell, back home in New York).

From the bar, I was now able to see the fronts of the five men whose backs—forming an opaque wall of duster coats—had made the central focus of the room's excitement impossible for me to see when I had first entered the saloon. It was they who had brought the room to the agonized pitch that one could sense in the bartender's eyes. The five men had adjusted their half-circle into almost a straight line—a line running perpendicular to the length of the bar.

The line came to a slight salient where the center man of the five stood. He was evidently the leader of this group. Though the two men on his right and the two men on his left were of varying degrees of formidable appearance, they all demonstrated a nearly equal degree of deference and attention to the man in the center. He was tall, powerfully built, and likely in the latter half of his fourth decade. He clenched a large, dark, hat—decidedly in the Western style—and clenched it angrily in his left hand. Two of the other men gripped similar hats in their hands, as well; and the two remaining men held weathered bowlers that at one time—perhaps not long before in that rough country—had meant to follow the dapper and spotless style of gentlemen's headwear back East in that decade. But these bowlers could not have looked new for very long in their line of work. They could only have looked new as long as a Sunday collar could have looked new amidst the routines of such men. Yet none of these men clenched their hat brims with anything like the rage and intensity as did the man in the center.

"What can I get you, mister?" whispered the barkeeper.

I was astonished when he spoke, for I had been certain that no one had noted that I had entered the saloon. I scrambled to think of what to request.

"Best keep still, stranger," whispered the barkeeper—in such a way that his question seemed to have been retracted. "Rutledge is set to be one son-of-a-bitch tonight," he added in another whisper.

Before this Rutledge, the man in the center of the standing group of five, sat an unconscious man in a straight-backed chair. Somehow he had been pitched into this chair with a perfect combination of callous force and chance balance so that he was seated after the manner of a relaxed but wakeful man. Had it not been for his closed eyes and his oddly parted lips—from which streamed a trickle of bright blood—I would have thought the man awake and still in the midst of an active exchange with the line of five men who faced him. Because he was a short man, his head had been propped up at an angle by the upper knob on one of the sides of the chair's back. He appeared to have his head cocked in preparation to make an answer to the leader of the five, this fellow named Rutledge. But the seated man only appeared to be awake.

A cowhand to the right of this Rutledge, one of the men clutching meekly to the rim of a distressed bowler hat, leaned into his leader with words of encouragement: "Pitch into him again, Mitch," he said to Rutledge. "He still ain't said why he was there. We've got a right to an answer."

"*Mr. Whisker's* got a right to an answer," replied Rutledge with the kind of exasperation one reserves for a supportive fool.

"Yeah, of course. Pitch into him again, Mitch. Find out why he was on Mr. Whisker's spread," the meek man with the bowler rejoined.

"*I'll* pitch into him when I say so, when I'm ready for it," Rutledge shouted to the man on his right. He was correct in this assertion, for his mien emitted an authority given by a fusion of his confidence with a tacit code. What temperance he displayed seemed guided by either some implied limitations of that tacit Western code or by some then still unrevealed state of lieutenancy he occupied in the order of the town.

Rutledge's eye caught mine for an instant, and in that moment I could see the animal part of him quickly assessing my unfamiliar appearance and my potential power of threat. But something in his expression dismissed me as insignificant for the time being, and he began to fix once more on the unconscious man in the chair. Before Rutledge could turn entirely away from me, however, the bartender—perhaps overestimating the significance of Rutledge's pause in regard to me—aggressively called out Rutledge's name, yet it still sounded more as a *please* than as a warning.

"Shut up, Bootz," was the easy and confident reply from Rutledge, and then he stepped forward and took hold of the unconscious man's face by the chin. Rutledge then shook the man's head roughly several times.

"Hey, you!" shouted Rutledge, "You skulking dog! What say you tell us—you tell *me*—why you was loping around uninvited in the middle of the night on Mr. Whisker's range? Huh? You ready to answer me now?"

He gave the head a hard slap, and the man's eyes finally popped open, and his head assumed a slightly different angle in the low, amber, light of the saloon. It was then, to my great shock, that I saw the first face I recognized in this new Pauktaug. Sitting in that chair—his eyes glaring back at Rutledge, animated as much by indignation as by desperation born from helplessness—was a man named Kettle. He had traveled with me in the coach up until it had been wrecked and stranded. Again, the driver of the coach, and his man, had elected to stay with the coach to protect its cargo until the arrival of the next coach or a relief party—which he expected to arrive, at the latest, in a matter of days. Kettle, a man made penniless after paying his fare for the coach to Pauktaug, was set maniacally in his desire to reach town in his quest for work. An experienced cowman he said he was—notwithstanding a notably puny frame—and he was certain that a town rumored for its recent and miraculous levels of growth and prosperity would hold an opportunity for him if he only walked right up to one or the other of its two barons and asked for a situation.

Kettle, a man native to that country, he claimed, was sure that Pauktaug could be reached with only a half day's hard push on foot. Despite the driver's cautioning that I would be safer waiting for relief with him and the coach (where there was a limited but reliable source of food and water), and despite the ridicule the driver leveled at Kettle's estimation of the distance between the site of our stranding and the new town of Pauktaug, I too—moved by a host of internal drives and hopes—decided to make my way on foot. The driver reluctantly wished us well, offered us one canteen of water and one unsaddled horse released from the team, and warily remained with the coach in hope of relief—I say warily, for it was in no way certain, he said, that a wave of unaccountable renegades were not making their presence known, in closing circumference, on the visible horizon. In fact, it was because of that possibility that I was further persuaded by Kettle to move on. I do not know why it did not occur to me that Kettle and I might be equally—if not more—vulnerable as we slowly marched under full sun along the new freight and coach road toward the only slightly older town itself.

After a mere six hours of that first day of three, my seemingly expert cowman and I had exhausted our meager supply of water. It was not long after that point, nearing late morning and the greatest light and heat of the day, that I began to suspect that though my companion was directly harmless to me, and though perhaps indeed with some kind of history in that new country, he was best characterized and first recognized as a man quite touched in the head. The maniacal repetition of his intentions, that he had made even whilst we had been still safely driving along in the coach, seemed the sad, false hope of a petty charlatan when seen under the ceaseless white light of the road—of a road, mind, in a country where there was not so much as a sapling tree or a rudimentary boulder from which to make some shade: no, merely an ocean of grass, intersected only by that tender, new vulnerable, road.

At each rise he would assure me—this through the hour after the canteen went dry—that the town would surely come into view after ascending just one more rise. But this never happened. And, then, to my dismay—for I would be alone if I did not give into his firm resolution (and, too, to my relief, for his increasing display of intense but gentle madness made me crave his departure)—Kettle declared that he would be leaving the road and making his way cross-country to where he was certain the town would appear: a mere three or four miles distant, as per his as-the-crow-flies reckoning.

We shook hands, and I encouraged him to take the horse; we parted ways. I thought though *I* was the stranger to this raw, blank country, it was he that was most certain to meet a swift demise. The presence of the road reassured me, and notwithstanding the fact that I found only one, sickly, miasma-painted water hole along the way, on the night of the third day I reached the trough at the north end of the new Pauktaug's Man Street.

So, again, to my astonishment, my shock, it was this very man, this Kettle, who sat as a sort of prisoner in the chair before that row of five intimidating cowmen—his lower jaw and neck in the clutches of the interrogator.

Rutledge pulled Kettle forward in the chair by the force of his grip, squeezed Kettle's face until it was distorted and comprehensively puckered, then released it with a dismissive throw to the side—to Rutledge's left, Kettle's right (so that Kettle's eyes were turned in my direction for the first time)—and it was clear that Rutledge had lifted Kettle to a great degree by that choking hold, for one could hear the thump of Kettle's haunches as they landed on the seat of the chair. In my mixture of shock and shame—the latter feeling emerging even before I was certain of Kettle's innocence from any transgression—I was relieved to sense that his first look in my direction did not seem to conjure any recognition or allow him yet to spot me.

"All right, you son-of-a-bitch," Rutledge began again, and he emphasized his new opening with a pronounced spitting upon the floor—as if he were asserting the terms that obtained between them now that he had the full attention of Kettle.

"All right, boy," Rutledge said (I might observe that Kettle and Rutledge seemed about the same age), "you wanna tell me *now* why you was walking across that range land in the dead of night? Who you working for? Looking to do some scoutin' before you do some stealin'? You a brand artist?"

Despite Kettle's weakened state—and he had been beaten, to boot, far beyond the pummeling from nature he and I had endured for the previous three days—he had always in reserve, it seemed, an ability to focus the energy of his gently crazed soul into powerful and frightening defensive rages, even when placed under formidable duress. I was compelled to replace the impression I had of a completely meek and feeble-minded fool with the awe I felt for a mad and snapping badger.

To my astonishment, it was clear that Kettle had every intention to speak, and to speak violently (the veins bulged in his low forehead as if that was how he loaded the old flintlock of his toothless mouth), but before he said a word, he too spat on the floor. He then made a motion to stand, whereupon Rutledge placed his boot heel on Kettle's knee and pushed him and the chair backward and over so that he struck the rear of his head upon the hard floor with a terrific thump.

"You son-of-a-bitch!" he screamed from the floor.

As Kettle tried to wrangle himself into a posture to rise, Rutledge presented his full, awesome, strength by walking over to where the wiry Kettle still squirmed and shouted and picked up the man with ease—as if Kettle were merely a pasteboard manikin in a haberdasher's shop window. The babbling cowman with the bowler hat righted the chair, and Rutledge dropped Kettle back into the seat.

"There's only one man here in the dog's place, boy, and that's you—you sneaky lookin' little bastard. Who you workin' for?" There was a pause, a silence—even though Kettle's veins continued to load. "I said: Who you workin' for, boy?" repeated Rutledge.

There was no answer. As if by rehearsed choreography, a cowman to Rutledge's left, almost equal to Rutledge's height and brawn (but he never spoke a word) went behind Kettle's chair and braced its back. He then braced the legs of the chair with the tips of his boots. When this motion was completed, Rutledge spoke again.

"You didn't hear me, boy. I said: Who you workin' for?"

"Rutledge!" called out the barkeeper at this point, but Rutledge was already in a full swing, and he landed a perfect right upon Kettle's jaw. If Rutledge had even heard his name called, I believe he was thereby compelled to land a harder blow—so that he could make unspoken statements to two men at once: a blow to draw an answer from Kettle, and that same blow intensified as a message for the barkeep, communicating Rutledge's freedom to do as he pleased.

Kettle righted his head from the turning action of the blow, and though he maniacally shouted all he said, the veins on his forehead continued to throb, as if nothing could unload them.

"I told you already! I'm not workin' for anybody! I'm just a good hand *lookin'* for work. I was on my way to speak to Mr. Crabbe, you son-of-a-bitch!"

I had never told Kettle my surname, or my business in hoping to reach this new Pauktaug, so it surprised me to hear him reference what was likely my brother's name.

Rutledge punctuated the start of his reply with a lighter blow, with only the base of his open hand to Kettle's small forehead.

"You wasn't even on Crabbe land; you was on Mr. Whisker's place—and remember, you puny, nothin', *you're* the dog here!"

Somehow Kettle's veins continued to bulge as he shouted back.

"I didn't know if it was Mr. Whisker's or Mr. Crabbe's! I just knew that there were two big new places out this way, and those were the names of the men in charge! I told you, when you found me, I'm just a cowhand by trade, hard up for work, and I was making my way as directly as I could, to either man, to ask for a situation!"

Even in his most placid moments, Kettle had a malady of mind about him that could wear on the most Christian soul. He had a way of being just sane enough at first to make one regret any later alliance formed on that first impression—for his subtle ticks were revealed during any sort of challenge, be it even in a mild and friendly debate. Thus I pitied Kettle then, in that saloon, for no matter the honesty of his professions, I could not imagine there being limits to the rages of an unfettered man like Rutledge when he had cause to see—even when Kettle had been given the provocations that might turn even a perfected man into a monster—the odd, inappropriate angles, postures, and aggravating wrinklings that Kettle's face would assume during any kind of tension. Those looks had tried my tolerance on the road; I did not suspect there was much tolerance in Rutledge at all.

Rutledge took away the last step that he had maintained between himself and Kettle's chair. The cowhand behind the chair reinforced his grip, such that one could hear the joints squeak in the chair's back. In his left hand Rutledge started to roll the wide brim of his dark hat, as if it were a scroll, an angry letter he was about to post without any further proofreading or hesitations.

"If you're such a cowhand, you mean to tell me you didn't think what might happen if you went wandering around on a stranger's range, long, long, after midnight? That's next to dismounting before being invited, you son-of-a-bitch!"

"Rutledge!" the barkeeper uttered again—but now with less volume, yet with a greater earnestness from its hoarse intensity.

Rutledge held up his left hand—the hand holding the increasingly rolled hat—and did not turn his head to look at Bootz, the barkeeper.

"I told you, Bootz, to shut up! Now I'll say it once more," Rutledge said as he focused his voice upon Kettle again, "if you're such an old hand, you didn't expect to find, as you was wandering about a stranger's range, the likes of us riding back to the bunkhouse on Saturday night: tired of the liquor, tired of riding, just itching to come across a little fool like you? Now tell me! If you're such a cowhand, you didn't think to wait till morning from fear of that? You don't seem to know the ways a' your trade, boy!"

I astonished myself when at this point I said with some force, "Now listen here, Mr. Rutledge!"

I was accustomed back East, especially in my home village of Pauktaug, to an immediate pause of deference, if due only to my father's reputation of nearly a half-century's duration. However, I felt a new respect for the paralysis the barkeeper suffered after Rutledge then turned to face me and leveled his left arm in my direction, freeing his forefinger from its tight grip upon the scrolled hat brim.

"Hey, stranger!" Rutledge rasped. "You best keep your health by keeping your silence. We'll find out about you soon enough!"

Rutledge tossed his hat onto a nearby table, causing the men who were sitting there—half-drunk with liquor and encroaching sleep as the first rays of morning light came through the lattice of the front doorway—to rise and yield the table, as if Rutledge had claimed it and was about to seat himself there. And I should remark that these were formidable, armed men who yielded so quickly to Rutledge.

But Rutledge did not take a seat. Instead he reached for his holster and removed a hefty revolver with a long barrel.

"I'm tired of hurting my working hands on you, you little cow thief," Rutledge said as he reversed his grip upon the gun from handle to barrel. "So tell me now, long rope," Rutledge muttered with an enraged hush, as he tapped the gun's handle in the open palm of his left glove, "what were you doin' out there wanderin' around in the dark?"

"I told you already!" hissed Kettle.

"Who you workin' for?" roared Rutledge, and he lifted the pistol high in the air with his right arm. "Some newcomer's been buyin' up entire herds from ranchers in the neighboring counties. Perhaps they're thinking of stealin' themselves some new stock, as well! Who you workin' for?"

"I know I'll never be workin' for you," Kettle hissed again, revealing an even more prominent network of festering veins in his tiny forehead—they bristling like the roots of an upturned tree after a storm.

"Oh, yeah? Why's that, brand blotter?" Rutledge asked, nearly knowing the answer that would come so that he would have cause to feed the energy behind the great blow he was itching to deliver.

"Because I won't be following you to hell," screamed Kettle, and then he planted a strong strike of spittle right upon Rutledge's boots.

This gesture pleased Rutledge, for it gave him incentive to bring back his right hand a bit farther—so as to cock his arm and set delivery of the gun handle against Kettle's skull—and then Rutledge muttered some raw obscenity as a mark of his satisfaction.

Yet as he spoke, a shot resounded out from just outside the open front door of the saloon.

5.

The shot had been fired by one of two men, both of whom held rifles pointed to the sky. But after one focused on their guns for a few moments, it became clear that the shot had been fired by a one hardy looking cowman who was dressed not unlike Rutledge and some of his men. But it was clear that he was not one of them; his dress and appearance were tidier, cooler, though it was evident that he, too, was accustomed to countless hours on the range and under the sun and moon.

The smoke from this man's shot drifted across the brow of another man, slightly smaller, of nearly fifty years of age. He, too, had a formidable bearing; yet he was dressed almost as a man of business—perhaps even as an undertaker might be dressed in those parts, in that country: all in black, a frock coat and a dark gentleman's hat (both powdered finely with trail dust). Part of me also thought he looked rather like a minister without a collar, and as the smoke tendrils passed away from his eyes—eyes that fell short of the confidence to deliver a sermon—I followed his secure but highly specialized look of deference toward the man who had fired the shot. That man had taken a step forward into the doorway. He was a powerfully built man, of advanced middle age, several inches short of six feet—yet this failure to reach intimidating height did not compromise the look of power demonstrated by his tendency to width. Perhaps someone may have described him as stocky, and perhaps in a very plain sense of expression that word was suitable. But even on first sighting this man suggested to me the physical authority of the most imposing livestock, an aging bull, perhaps.

The powerful outline of the man's face—he appeared to me at first utterly shadowed in the early morning light—was presented to me in profile. His head had been turned to the side so as to nod to the man who was with him. Thus after I heard the shot that must have come exactly with the nod, I looked to see this man slowly begin to turn his head from the right and directly aim his eyes toward Rutledge and Kettle.

As soon as he faced forward, this stock-like man took three confident steps into the saloon and thus into its low amber light. His accompanying man took a set of steps from the outside until he, too, was inside the saloon. Other men by then were visible behind them, standing outside of the door.

Smoke from the fired rifle coiled slowly from the upturned barrel and rose lazily in a definite tendril over the shoulders of the evident leader of this new group of men—floated over his shoulders in such a way that it appeared to wave from side to side like an indolent bull's tail, only this tail hinted at swattings heavenward instead of toward the ground. That smoke proceeded to the ceiling and surely wrote over the more casual markings of the men who smoked in that saloon merely for decadent amusement.

I had not seen this man—at least not for certain—for almost thirty years. But I was certain that my long voyage was over: this man was Ellsworth Crabbe, my brother.

Everyone in the room had been jolted by the sound of the shot, but no one turned about with greater intensity than Rutledge. I was touched to see expressions of relief flash across other men's eyes when they recognized Ellsworth Crabbe. He did not bring greater tension to the scene into which I had stumbled; he brought a certainty of immediate resolution that only a trusted authority seems empowered to bestow. It was clear to me from that very instant that my brother had that kind of sovereign role in this new Pauktaug.

It was with all the unreleased aggression of his final but still deferred blows upon Kettle that Rutledge turned upon this new presence in the room. Yet it was as if his anger, his petulance—no, it was more: one should say his sense of unquestionable right to these emotions—vanished at the sight of Ellsworth Crabbe. But this did not stop Rutledge from radiating that he still had in reserve his own significant and not altogether secret expectations of power.

"What's this, Mitch?" my brother asked of Rutledge as the last bit of gunsmoke made its way to the ceiling.

Rutledge took an astute step forward that also took him a bit to the side, so that his body, he imagined, would eclipse my brother's sight of Kettle in his chair.

"Well, Mr. Crabbe!" exclaimed Rutledge, affecting the powerless mockery that a truant schoolboy invokes when he is about to be apprehended by the schoolmaster.

Ellsworth Crabbe in that year was fifty-three, and, again, Rutledge was in the latter half of his fourth decade. But it was by some other power of personality or hierarchy that allowed Ellsworth to reign over this scene—even though, as I could soon tell, Rutledge was not even one of my brother's men. Ellsworth was altogether above, it became clear, even checking Rutledge in the latter's childish and petulant swagger. In fact, he allowed it to him—as if it were an unavoidable condition with which Rutledge was forced to contend—and thus the intelligence in Rutledge was cut by this, far more than by any traditional reproach. One might ask by what means Ellsworth carried out such a sophisticated level of condescension against Rutledge. The means were likely not an affectation but a true invocation of tolerance for rabble. But when a rabble mind has its own shrewdness, nothing can offend its pride more than tolerant condescension.

"Mitch," my brother said to Rutledge, "I came here with word delivered by Mr. Davis—he rode all the way out to my place himself—that my cousin has arrived in town, on foot—without benefit of the stage."

Ellsworth took a few steps farther into the saloon. The smoke from the rifle was by then completely dissipated, so that my brother appeared to lose his tail as he continued to speak.

"When we arrived at the hotel Mr. Davis's man said that my cousin had wandered over here to investigate some commotion that he had hoped was a sign of my arrival. You can imagine my concern."

Ellsworth took the last step he could afford to take without stepping so close as to threaten or initiate violence. His followers took an equal last step—and then one additional step, so that they were all parallel to Ellsworth, covering his flanks, and facing directly Rutledge and his line of men.

Unlike my brother's men, Rutledge's men had not reinforced their leader's few forward steps. In fact, they had moved slightly off to the sides, giving cause for Ellsworth's men to suggest that their final position was less one of challenge than a block to any exit. The man who had been bracing Kettle's chair had faded toward the back of the saloon and into a shadow.

Rutledge and Ellsworth stood face to face.

"And you can imagine my further consternation, Mitch, when we rode over here—and I don't mean to give offence—and we saw the night horses of you boys outside."

Rutledge broke in at this point with seemingly untroubled confidence.

"Well this certainly ain't no cousin of yours, Mr. Crabbe," he said as he nodded back toward Kettle. It was difficult to say if this statement had been a compliment to the Crabbe family character or if it had been an arch remark upon what seemed my brother's excessive concern about the situation.

"Let me see the man you've got here," Ellsworth commanded.

Rutledge stood aside, doing so in such a manner that one did not feel he had yielded any important ground.

"I do not know this man. This man is not my cousin," Ellsworth mused as he contemplated the lean and beaten face of Kettle.

"I told you he was wasn't no kin of yours," added Rutledge—somehow with a tone that maintained a subtle, skulking, liberty.

"Who are you, boy?" Ellsworth asked Kettle with warmth and cordiality.

"Oh, Mr. Crabbe! I am the man what come so far only to see either you or Mr. Whisker. Oh, Mr. Crabbe! Kind sir!" exclaimed Kettle, as his former maniacal looks of defense gave way to these exuberant professions of ingratiation for my brother. It was clear to me that Ellsworth was already aware that Kettle was not altogether right in the head. It was evident to Rutledge, too, that my brother had sensed this in Kettle; thus he said nothing, and he seemed to relax—and to wait as if for a polite interval to pass before he and his men could simply slip away and ride off.

Ellsworth would not allow Rutledge the liberty of silence, however: "Come on, Mitch. Tell me what this is all about."

"It's simple, Mr. Crabbe. Me and the boys here were riding back to Asharoken."

I would learn later that *Asharoken* was the name of one of the only two ranches surrounding the town; the other, *Mattinecock*, was Ellsworth's.

"And we were riding after two in the morning—just after a little funnin' here in town—and we came across this skulking dog wandering around on Mr. Whisker's range. He started talking crazy, and he said he would only answer Mr. Whisker's questions, that he had to see Mr. Whisker right away."

"That's right! That's all I did!" exclaimed Kettle, hardly supporting his case as he leapt up from his chair and revived the strained veins in his forehead. "I'm just an honest cowboy looking for work. Everyone in this country knows there ain't no more prosperous new place than Pauktaug. I heard they was lookin' for good men here!"

"You're just a liar!" shouted Rutledge. "You're so puny, who'd ever have had you workin' on their place before? You'd rate a wrangling boy at best in the remuda. Besides, word ain't been put out that Mr. Whisker's hiring! Spring roundup's over. Hell, we're letting men go soon. Mr. Crabbe, this fellow is just making all this up! And what's a man with any experience doin' pretending not to know what might happen if he wanders onto a stranger's range and won't answer for himself—especially in the middle of the night! Answer me that!"

"That's a fair question," Ellsworth said. And then he asked Kettle his name: "Mr.—?"

"Kettle, good sir," replied the beaten man, with no temperance of his ingratiation.

"That's a fair question, Mr. Kettle, that Mr. Rutledge has put. I'd like to hear its answer," Ellsworth said calmly.

"I just got a little desperate—and lost, too," answered Kettle.

"Lost!" interrupted Rutledge. "He was right on the Asharo-ken trail from town to Mr. Whisker's main house. It's certain: he was out there to take a count for his outfit. They're probably out there now while we're in here doing exactly as they hoped we'd do! Damn me for not thinking of that till now!" Rutledge shouted this reproach to himself and slapped his thigh with his hat. "We wasted a loop on this son-of-a-bitch!"

Ellsworth replied, "No, Mitch, I don't think he's any rustler. I'd know if that kind of trouble had reached us. You would too. The spring count was almost perfect. You know that. I think he's what he says he is: desperate—and maybe a bit touched in the head."

This blunt appraisal seemed reinforced when Kettle made no objection to it; he merely continued to follow my brother's words, no matter what they were, as if his imminent salvation were attached to every phrase.

Ellsworth continued: "But you're no veteran hand, Mr. Kettle; otherwise you would know how foolish it was to wander around out there on foot."

"Mr. Crabbe," Kettle replied, "it's all over this country how you've built your place up and the town—and how Mr. Whisker's place is prosperin' too. I just need me some work! Surely you got something for me! I'd be a good man for your place. Or could you put in word for me to Mr. Whisker? What do you say, Mr. Crabbe?"

Ellsworth paused a moment before answering, as if affecting to give the question due consideration would temper the reaction Kettle might display upon hearing a disappointing answer.

"No, Mr. Kettle, I think not. And I know for a fact that Mr. Whisker has all the men he needs, and I—"

"But you, sir? What about you, kind sir?" inserted Kettle.

"—I have no real need for you myself either." Then Ellsworth took a long, odd, pause, and he looked over his shoulder as if seeing past his men, to the vast range that belonged to Whisker. This pause seemed to fill the sadly broken Kettle with hope; but it caused no reaction in any of the other men in the room, as if such a silence upon inexplicable beats was but an expected custom of my brother's. Soon Ellsworth realized the phrase he had molded from that silence, though it remained cryptic.

"Mr. Kettle, we do things pretty much the same way on my place as they do on Whisker's; but we *do* things differently on my place. Rutledge had no call to give you such a rough time."

Kettle's disturbed senses made him misapprehend the meaning of this; or perhaps he only pretended misunderstanding, using a degree of affected madness to get what he wanted.

"Oh, thank you, kind sir! Mr. Crabbe, I knew you'd be a good man, that you'd treat me kindly, that you'd surely have some place for me."

Kettle's forehead veins continued to bulge as he made this last plea. "If I wasn't just a bit lost on coming into town, I'd have made my way to your place first. Everybody knows that though Whisker is said to be a good man, *you're* the good man behind all of this place."

Despite all that would immediately follow in the exchange between my brother and Kettle, Kettle never quite let go of the delusion that Ellsworth was then set to be his particular benefactor—even as my brother's patience with the man wore increasingly away.

"You're failing to understand me, son," Ellsworth said. "But I suspect what understanding we now have is a good as it will be. No matter."

Kettle continued to beam in Ellsworth's direction, oblivious to the fact that my brother's interest in his situation was nearly at an end. Ellsworth lingered a bit longer only so as to ask a few questions in regard to his own original business in town.

"Mr. Kettle, you came to town via the stage?"

"Yes, I did," Kettle boasted, as if he had in his keeping information that would imminently earn him reward and praise.

"The stage that wrecked and may have been attacked, the one that is still out there?" my brother asked.

Again, Kettle swelled with an obtuse pride, and the veins on his small forehead coursed with a pitiable degree of expectation: "Yes, I did, sir!"

"What happened to the other passengers?" Ellsworth asked.

"The driver wanted to stay behind, and so did his shotgun man," said Kettle. "And there was only one other man in the coach with me. He and I left on foot to make our way here, but he wouldn't listen to me. I knew the best way here, and I got here. But he didn't want to leave the road. I tried to make him come with me, but he wouldn't listen. I don't know what became of him. He should have come with me, he—"

"What can you tell me about this man? Anything?" my brother asked eagerly. "What did he look like?"

"Well, kind sir, I can't say as I could tell you too much about him. He was a young man, I think—but kinda pale, kinda sick."

"Sick?" mused my brother. "What did he sound like?" he then asked with increasing volume, as is often customary in speaking with someone who proves himself soft in the head.

"He didn't say much. Coughed a lot. Was dead-set on getting here," smiled Kettle.

"When I ask what he sounded like, I mean: Was he a foreigner? Was he an Englishman?"

"Can't say I've heard what an Englishman sounds like. They talk different? Anyways, he sounded like most any other man, but kinda book-learned, maybe—kinda sounded like you, Mr. Crabbe. I don't think he was from these parts."

Kettle then paused and affected a scholarly squint. My brother was ready to turn away at this moment when Kettle added a last observation:

"He sure was dead-set on getting here—*and* on finding you. Said his name was Crabbe, too!"

"You damned fool, that *is* my cousin you're describing. For you to stand there and grin like a Bedlam freak and think I'd find a situation for you at my place! You left my cousin in a strange country. If I didn't know you were so soft!"

And then a great calm came over Ellsworth. He tempered his voice: "Still, Mr. Kettle, I can see you have limits—and troubles that are in excess of your due punishment. Again, Rutledge here didn't have the cause to mete out the likely end you were about to receive before I walked in here. We're all spent from the spring roundup. But, still, they had no cause."

"Oh, thank you, kind sir!" exclaimed Kettle with another grin.

Ellsworth turned away, completely finished with Kettle, and about to march out of the saloon.

"You and your boys should go on back to Asharoken, Mitch," my brother said to Rutledge. Rutledge furrowed his angry brow, but he and his men made their way toward the door.

I ran my fingers through my hair and rubbed my face to prepare to present myself to my brother. At the same time, Kettle was smart enough to realize he had been utterly dismissed. He looked desperately about the room, and that is when Kettle's eyes alighted on me. He ran to me and grabbed my shoulders and called out to Ellsworth, who was already being followed to the doorway by his men.

"Mr. Crabbe! Mr. Crabbe! Why, here's your cousin right 'chere! Mr. Crabbe! Why here's another Mr. Crabbe!"

Ellsworth turned around, and in his approach he had to work his way past the exodus of men who had heeded the command of the bartender that the saloon was then closed.

Soon Ellsworth was standing right before me, narrowing his eyes as he examined a face he not seen since it was a child's face—a face he had not seen since 1855, when I was six years old. It was evident that he was puzzled, and unsure of something that was revolving in his mind as a possibility.

"Mr. Kettle, this is *not* my cousin. But you say *this* is the man who was on the coach with you, who claims to have my name, who you left alone on the road to town?"

"Why, yes!" Kettle continued to beam—and now, too, with a touch of false humility—as if readying himself to receive the bounty on a lost prince. "And I—"

"Leave us! Now!" my brother commanded. Something in Kettle's last confirmation exhausted any vestige of my brother's tolerance. Ellsworth endeavored, in fact, to temper a rage he was cultivating for this unstable man.

My brother took a brief pause from his scrutiny of my face and from consultation of innumerable inner histories and called out one last time, as if in warning, to the meek form of Kettle before he may have vanished.

"Mr. Kettle, we indeed do things very much the same way on my place as they do them on Whisker's." I was puzzled and astonished to hear Ellsworth paraphrase, nay repeat, himself so quickly. He continued: "But we *do* things differently on my land." There was a pause at this point, ostensibly to allow Kettle to take a few steps back so as to better hear my brother's words, but I might

40

have sworn Ellsworth had paused solely so as to give some kind of cryptic emphasis to his next phrase.

"Rutledge had no *true call* to pitch into you as he did."

"Oh, thank you, Mr. Crabbe! Thank you, kind sir! You're too good!" said Kettle.

Ellsworth held up his hand to keep Kettle where he was—near the door. Then he made a quiet remark that was intended for only me to hear. With that first whispered confidence I was certain that Ellsworth knew who I was. It was a thrilling manner of reintroduction.

"That man cannot hope to understand me," my brother said in a whisper. He then placed his hand on my shoulder to reassure me that I should stand in place at the bar, and he took one step away and called out to Kettle as if Kettle were a small, defective, child.

"Mr. Kettle, go across the street and into the hotel, last building on the left as you go north back up Main Street. Tell Mr. Davis— or his man at the front desk—that I sent you for a room and breakfast under my name. Rest there for the day. And take these."

My brother tossed him several dollar coins over the course of several throws, keeping Kettle at a distance—almost as one tosses scraps to a strange dog that has proven its friendliness but one that snaps too hard in hunger at the handouts offered in pity.

"By tomorrow night," my brother said to Kettle, "pay someone to take you out of town and back to the railroad—again, by tomorrow night."

"Thank you, Mr. Crabbe. Thank you, kind sir! Thank you," exclaimed Kettle, and in his obtuse glee he made his way with sadly happy indifference past Rutledge and his men and the other cowhands as they climbed into their saddles. He vanished up Main Street on his way toward the hotel.

In complete silence, truly without saying a word, Ellsworth ushered me out of the saloon, over the plank sidewalk, and down the stairs to the level of the street. He found a clear, tightly packed patch of the ground and anchored the both of us there. With a nod from Ellsworth, all of his men mounted their horses and cantered away to the north end of Main Street, and there they took up quiet positions, seemingly in waiting for my brother's next command.

Seeing that his men were in their proper position, my brother turned and faced me, at last. I had so much to say; I had many questions. Yet in coming to the true end of my journey, even my joy in the completed voyage could not stave off the sudden recognition I then felt of a complete and terrifying bodily weakness. My brother could see that I wished to speak but could not. He placed a hand on both of my shoulders and tightly held me at arm's length, as if I had been placed in iron traces—he seemingly ready to pull me into some new state as if by the preternatural energies that lived behind his eyes and within his ponderous skull. Not realizing that my silence was not merely an emotional enthrallment but also a result of impending physical bankruptcy, Ellsworth gave me a shake of affection with his two arms.

"Is it really you, Campbell? Cam? Blazes, is it really you, my boy?" Somehow I was able to mutter a *yes* to this question and give a smile.

"You and I have been writing for years, my boy, but you wouldn't write me to say exactly when you expected to arrive? But I've been doing nothing but readying for you to arrive, Cam! And you're here now! That's what matters!"

Through an increasing fog of an increasingly light head, I hoarsely whispered, "I did write you, more than once, over the last two months, to say that I should arrive at this time."

"My boy! Those letters, they must have miscarried. We often fail to receive things out here. They may still be making their way!" he laughed. "But I did expect you at anytime. I just couldn't be sure of precisely when."

I could not reply to this. Light from the rising sun was breaking into the street through the alley next to the saloon, augmenting the sense of sickness that was at war with my elation, for I had to squint fiercely—and this made my head pound and my stomach bear an acute nausea.

"My boy, Cam, to think that I rode into town thinking it was Julius who had arrived first," my brother said.

Somehow this revelation gave me the mettle to speak again: "Julius—Julius Crabbe, our cousin from England?" I had not seen our English cousin since I was a small boy, but my memory of him was clear. I was astounded that my brother would have any contact with him—let alone conduct business with him in America and so deep in new country.

"Yes, my boy. Yes," my brother answered, and his face lost its light momentarily.

"He's due to arrive any time now." Then Ellsworth's face recovered its joy: "But it's glorious to find it was you instead. You couldn't remember Julius anyway; you couldn't remember back that far."

Through my squinting I could see that my vision was fading. Only my brother's great enthusiasm could have prevented him from seeing how ill I was, even from his first sight of me, to say nothing of the precipice I had then reached as the eastern sun began to sprawl first over my brother's vast range and then beyond to Whisker's equally immense holdings to the west of town.

Among the last words I heard from my brother were, "Cam, my boy! Aren't you well? Of course—"

I began to collapse, I believe, at this juncture, and then all I could hear him say, as if from afar, as he caught me in my fall was, "Of course! Blazes! Of course, you've been sick, my boy—!"

I felt a great peace and warmth pass over my body as I felt my brother gently rest my head atop his crumpled coat. I felt no fits of coughing, no aches in my ribs, no throbbing in my head. I merely felt great a glorious surrender to sleep, and the pounding that had crept into my head from the harsh sunlight seemed transferred as if to a trio of strong horses striking the earth and approaching at a full gallop to where I lay. Their stomping at the hard ground near my head and the breathy chortle from their wet lips and nostrils—and the gentle chirping of their bits—are the last things I recall from the close of that dawn. It had been the second time in less than a day that I had collapsed in that very same street—which only a few years before had never seen the tread of shod horses or the sole of a white man's shoe.

6.

When I awoke I was in an enormous bed in one of the upper rooms of the Pauktaug House. I forced myself to sit upright and to look about the room. My cracked ribs and my general weakness were accompanied then—as I moved my legs and arms in order to sit up—by a comprehensive soreness. I recognized the hotel room of the Pauktaug House of this new Pauktaug for what it was, and for when it was. From out of the shadowy corner where I almost imagined a figure like my older brother's in vigilant repose indeed emerged Ellsworth—older, of course, and more stout, but of a far more powerful and intimidating cut than I ever credited to him when I was a child.

"Cam, my boy! I'm glad you're home—at least I hope you will decide to stay with us for good and call this home."

For all his apparent strength, there was a touching deference in his manner—especially as he rose to his feet and held his wide-brimmed cowman's hat in both of his hands before his waist. I could not account for how the change had been affected in the interval of my sleeping, but it appeared to me that Ellsworth was in an entirely new and different suit from the one I had seen on him at dawn in the saloon. Even his boots appeared to have been brushed and polished.

"It would not be hard to call this place home," I said. "This place, Ellsworth, it's almost an exact replica of home, of Pauktaug. How did you—?"

My brother relaxed, and he took on that air of easy command he seemed to wield with such ease in the West—but slightly altered when we were alone, as if I were to feel a part of that command, a part of his council of war. I did not trust his star chamber's welcome at first, but there was little evidence to make such an invitation seem anything but sincere.

He relaxed when there were practical questions to answer.

"How did we build so much in only two years? I presume that's what you mean, dear boy."

That was not what I had meant. I was wondering how he could have remembered the model so perfectly. But I settled in to hear any explanations that might be offered freely.

"We were prospering here—both Whisker's place and mine—but I wanted a town once I knew you were coming, a familiar place to rise at a faster rate than our ranch's returns would allow. I borrowed quite a sum of money, and I set to building up the town and my place at a pace that no one in this country has yet to see. Whisker's place is growing faster, as well, on account of all I've risked on the town and on my ranch. But he's not accountable to the loan. I took that risk completely on my own."

I used his name again in my next question; this gave him a surge of satisfaction, and he tossed his hat aside to the chair behind him with a casual pride. He walked to the window.

"Ellsworth, from whom did you borrow the money?"

"Our English cousin, Julius," answered my brother, and then he repeated, "Julius. Yes, Mr. Julius Crabbe," in a quiet and sober way.

I felt I understood his need for dramatic repetition of the name. Julius Crabbe, a name I had not heard since my brother's departure from the old Pauktaug when I was a boy, had been present during my brother's last days in our family's home. I still could not believe my brother would, even after nearly thirty years, have any business with Julius Crabbe, much less be in his debt for a large sum of money. I knew that he had despised our Cousin Julius. Even in the soft repetition Ellsworth made of our cousin's name, I could still suspect that that same, though now ancient, enmity was intact.

"But, Ellsworth, why borrow from Julius?"

My brother did not turn his gaze from looking down upon the Main Street he had recreated. I could tell from his tone, despite the degree of the fraternal care and inclusion he hinted he wished to bestow upon me, that my rights in his star chamber had strict, inscrutable, limits.

"You'll allow *me* to worry about that," he said from a stern reverie. My brother suddenly heard himself in this phrase, and I think he realized that whilst the choice of words may have been sound, the tone had been inappropriate, at least for that occasion.

Ellsworth turned to me and smiled, hoping to let the moment pass without remark. Curiously, for all the unremitting power and easy authority my brother would always project to me in this new Pauktaug, I felt, for the first time, an impulse of great, though cautious, solicitude towards him—as if I could offer assistance that had never been requested but was still welcome and of use. Thus, when I let the matter of my cousin's loan drop and made instead a second effort to ask about the recreation of old Pauktaug there in the West, he seemed pleased. Even as I asked the question, he gave me a firm nod—as if he were bestowing figurative lieutenant's bars upon my shoulders as a reward of my first gesture of discretion.

"How were you able to build this town, this second Pauktaug, to look so much like our own back home?" I asked as I still lay, sitting up, in the bed.

"Did I come close, Cam? You were there not long ago—only weeks ago, likely. I haven't seen it in many, many, years."

"But that's what makes it so remarkable," I said.

"Then it *is* close; it is good. You would know best; and I only care if *you're* pleased in the match. Whisker had some hand in the remembering, but he didn't feel as I did—that the challenge of building our town here had much meaning. How did I do it? There was never a place I missed more, that I suffered more regret in leaving."

"But you never returned, never came back—not as far as I knew," I protested.

"I have a great deal I wish to explain to you. We will have the time for it; you're here now!" he said, and he clenched his right fist in great satisfaction and anticipation as he spoke his last phrase.

I had so many questions. "This Whisker. You mean young John Whisker, old John Whisker's son?"

"Yes, I do. We've partnered in more than one business venture in life, and then merely kept each other company in others, as in our separate cattle concerns here in Pauktaug."

It was clear to me from that moment that when my brother said *Pauktaug* he meant only the new one, the Western one. He made no qualifications before or after the name. As to the issue of John Whisker, the idea that my brother had kept another old Pauktaug citizen in tow throughout his life did give me jealous pause, for beyond my brother, I was not unique in my knowledge of the village that served as the model for this new Pauktaug of the West.

Carefully avoiding the idea of the loan my cousin had granted to my brother, I asked if it were merely a wild and improbable coincidence that Julius Crabbe should be headed for the new town at nearly the same time as my own arrival.

"Yes, insofar as I knew he was on his way here and due soon—but did not know exactly when you would be on your way. But, again, you and I have been discussing by letter your possible journey here for some time, and when I didn't hear from you I should have supposed that one strong possibility was that you were on your way."

My brother seemed slightly uncomfortable with the answer he gave. I was not sure if his answer gave answer to my question at all; it had not, really. Ellsworth then paused for a moment and looked out again into the brilliant midday sunshine.

"And, no," he continued, "it is not, at the same time, a coincidence at all. I first started to borrow from Julius when my hopes of your joining me here increased. He's coming, I am certain, solely because of the loan—to see this town and our place, to look into his investment and seek returns."

Ellsworth paused once more and turned to me.

"This is all for you, dear boy. I'm doing all of this for you." He swept his arm about as if to embrace the entire town.

"For me?" I asked. My brother quickly detected my discomfort and alarm. He tempered his words and gave me temporary relief.

"Well, I should say it all *will* be yours."

But part of me was suspicious that he still stood by some oblique and intense meaning with the words that accompanied his swinging, regal, right arm; whatever that meaning was, it remained, as yet, one of the growing list of private convictions which, despite my implied place at his right hand, my brother had no intention of revealing.

Ellsworth turned yet again and peered down upon the town that had been built almost solely upon resources that he had gathered, and from exquisitely preserved plans that he had carried in his mind for nearly thirty years. As was his wont, he folded his arms across his massive chest as he beheld an object of great pride: that Main Street. In this case, however, he was also shoring himself up to hear the answer to a difficult question.

"How is father?" he asked.

I found myself folding my arms myself as I prepared to answer the question. "Father is dead. He died just before the new year," I answered.

"That must have been in one of the letters that I did not receive," said Ellsworth.

"Yes," I answered. "I wrote you about it."

I did not know what to make of Ellsworth's next exclamation, whether with it he was assigning a kind of praise or blame.

"Eighty-two years of age!"

He turned to face me, but he did not look directly into my eyes until after he repeated once more, "Eighty-two years of age, then!"

After he spoke he took several steps toward me and placed both of his hands on my shoulders. Sensing one of those moments when I could tell he preferred no questions, he pushed me gently back and forth in a brotherly sort of way, and in praise of further discretion. He suddenly stopped the fraternal jostling and squeezed my shoulders fiercely, as if silently imparting to me his acceptance of the paternal mantle upon word of our father's death. So extreme was the force of my brother's spirit and the strength of his presence—and the strength of his actual person via his grip, as well—that I accepted Ellsworth's self-coronation as if it had always been intended, and that it would be just when it took effect, even though part of myself was somewhat embarrassed for him and his presumption of ascendancy and intimacy on many planes.

Ellsworth took a step back and folded his arms once more in what appeared to be his most characteristic mannerism of contented authority.

"I had my doctor look at you while you slept. How do you feel? Do you wish for me to summon him again?" Ellsworth asked.

"No," I replied. "I feel rather well this morning—today, I should say." Again, I was in earnest in this reply, for though I knew I was still profoundly weak and ill, I felt significantly better after my long sleep. I noted, too, that I had not felt even one impulse to cough since waking in that cool, dry, peaceful hotel room.

"Cam, my boy, let me ask you something. Did you really make

this entire trip without a weapon? We found nothing on you as we readied you for bed here. In respect to safety, Pauktaug here is not a match for the one into which we were born. This is not a place for a man to wander around unarmed."

I thought of Kettle and the incident in the saloon for the first time since waking. "I've seen that for myself," I remarked, and Ellsworth took my meaning.

My brother's thoughts seemed to move then to the plight of the wrecked stage coach Kettle and I had left behind—by that point for four days.

"Cam," Ellsworth said, "I've summoned as many of my men as I can spare to come in. But they are on the farthest reaches of my range at this point. It will take as long as until tonight to form up in any force and to ride out to see to this coach you rode in on. We've heard nothing of them, no word from the drivers—and they were due, of course, days ago. It's possible that they were rescued from the railroad end of the run, but I think we'd have had word from that end if that was the case. It's likely they wouldn't even have cause to worry yet on the railroad end, since the coach doesn't run more than once a week from here on its return trip. They'd only be due to leave here by tomorrow to go back."

Ellsworth uncrossed his arms and made his way to the chairs where he had slept and had kept his vigil over me. Though one might suspect I would have noted this before, it was only then, as he reached for his cowman's hat, that I registered the size of his ponderous, large, skull and muscular neck, for in that time of life—unlike in his youth—his head was altogether bald, save for two gray, closely cropped bands of hair that ran along the sides and then met just above the top of his neck. Curiously, his bald crown was nearly as tanned as the rest of his skin, even though he seemed to remove his hat only rarely when he was outdoors. But perhaps his air of authority made one recall him as a man who never failed to keep his hat in place.

His muscular neck seemed to suggest the dense, tightly packed, sinews that surely proliferated in the other wide parts of his formidable limbs. Yet he was not a sluggish muscular man. He moved well.

"Cam, you're to rest here and make yourself at home in the hotel until I return. We'll probably leave at dawn to find what we can of your coach. In the meantime, order anything you like and ask for anything you need from Mr. McCarthy downstairs. I've taken care of all of that."

"Thank you, Ellsworth, but I want to come with you in the morning," I said with resolve.

"You can't. You shouldn't. You're ill, dear boy."

"But, still, I want to. I cannot tell you how much better I feel already." I spoke adamantly.

This seemed to please my brother. With his large hat in hand again, he crossed his arms once more and struck a fierce, jolly, paternally bemused but also proud stance.

"I'll come for you in the morning, then," Ellsworth said with a grin and a shrug. "If you are indeed well enough to go, then I will consider it—but will only just consider it. I make no promises in this. The riders that will be going out on this ride will be entirely under me. And I would have to think about getting you your own good horse—you'll need a string of horses out here, in fact—and to getting you well heeled."

At first, when he spoke of seeing to it that I was *heeled*, I took it that he was referencing my health. With a few qualifying words surrounding an expression that was new to me, I soon understood that he wished for me to be armed as soon as possible. I told him that after he had left Pauktaug when I was a boy, I had grown into a man with a collector's passion for weapons, and that our father had supplied my passion with gifts that ranged from firearms of the past to fine contemporary guns. My father's generosity along those lines had dissipated in my later youth and then had vanished altogether in our last years together. Despite my reports that my father's gifts to me had slowed and then ultimately stopped, my brother appeared skeptical throughout the course of this story as to the likelihood of our father ever having lavished unnecessary items upon me.

"What happened to all of your guns, then? Why didn't we find you armed, Cam, when you came in?" my brother asked.

"I had to sell them. I took them into New York City last year and sold the collection for what money I could get," I said.

My brother unfolded his arms and opened the door, readying himself to leave. "You sold every last one?" he asked, and he smiled faintly.

"No," I recalled, and I began to stand as I spoke, as much from a sincere sense of feeling somewhat rested and recovered as from hoping to show my brother that I would be strong enough to ride with the rescue party set to leave for early the next morning.

"No, I kept one—a fine revolver from a set. I broke up the pair. Up until I left Pauktaug last month I still had constable duties, and I carried that gun for that purpose on rare occasions. I carried it all the way with me on my way here until I reached the end of the railroad line."

My brother gave an approving nod upon learning that I had had the foresight to carry a weapon with me for as long as I could into such new country, and then he pitied me that I was given cause to sell it just before the time when it would have been of most use.

"I needed it for the coach fare," I said, "and for any other needs I might encounter here—should you not have been here when I appeared—so I sold it at the outpost at the end of the railroad line."

It was now my brother's turn to impress and please with *his* discretion, his willingness to refrain from unnecessarily reflecting upon the obvious; he said nothing more, for the time being, of my ordeal, of my pitiable circumstances.

Instead, with grandly simple tact, he said quietly, as he shifted his weight from one boot to the other: "Constable? A constable! That's splendid! Splendid, dear boy! Let me think on that for a bit!"

Ellsworth began to march into the hallway and to close the door behind him when a simple practicality overtook his mind and he called back: "I'll return for you at dawn!"

7.

The door closed, and I was free from having to affect that I was altogether free from exhaustion. After watching, through the window, my brother ride off toward his range in the east, I lay down in bed and let the warm noon sunlight of that grassy, dry, new country lull me into a wonderful, careless, doze. I do not believe I ever committed to a sleep with a greater sense of ease and hope in all of my then thirty-four years. Despite a sense of hunger that accompanied the early moments of my dozing, I passed into an unbroken, dreamless, sleep that lasted into early evening. There was no sound coming from the town, not even from the saloon up the street that had been the setting of Kettle's trial. However, through the floor below me, I could hear pleasant noises rising up from the dining room and kitchen.

Though I was considerably sore and stiff as I dressed, my hunger was so strong, and the sounds emanating from below were so convivial, I could not resist making my way to the hotel's first floor as quickly as I could. When I appeared at the entrance to the dining hall the same clerk who had attended to me the night before approached me with speed from the front desk.

"Mr. Crabbe! Mr. Crabbe!" he exclaimed. In the most ingratiating and obsequious way I was now only *Mr. Crabbe* to him.

"You shouldn't be up, Mr. Crabbe!" the man insisted as he began to work the back of my coat with a worn tailor's brush. "I would've brought your supper to your room—anything and as much as you'd like. You shouldn't be up. You should be resting."

I replied that I preferred to take my supper in the dining room. The large room was nearly empty, save for a lone cowhand, dressed for Sunday, who sat in a far corner and paid me no mind at all.

The clerk, who served as my waiter for this supper, brought me an enormous steak—one that had come from the very range that surrounded the town. Though he could not say for certain, it likely had come from one of Mr. Whisker's cows, he said, for he was fairly sure that my brother had not sold any of his stock to the town butcher in some time.

"You just call out for McCarthy if you need anything—anything at all, Mr. Crabbe," the clerk, this McCarthy, assured me after checking for the third time after the quality of my steak.

"Perhaps you could tell me, McCarthy, if a man by the name of Kettle is presently a guest of the hotel?" I asked.

"He was, Mr. Crabbe. But he had his supper and left not long after you came downstairs."

"Left? For good? Where to?"

I was certain Kettle could not have found any conveyance for hire for the long journey back to the railroad as of yet, and certainly not at night. I also wondered where he might even find a man for hire—what with my brother enlisting all the men he could for the morning's ride to relieve the stranded coach.

McCarthy was dressed in an altogether different pair of colorful pantaloons from those he had sported the night before—and a bright and incongruously colored waistcoat (incongruous with the pantaloons, that is). He straightened the vest before answering my question—as if he were affecting the manners of a head waiter in one of the towns he had heard of back East.

"Well, Mr. Crabbe," said McCarthy, "this Kettle fellow, as I said, just took his supper and left. He said he had business with your brother, and he just took the small bag he had with him and started out on foot some time ago—maybe an hour, maybe two."

"I see," I said.

McCarthy attended then to the lone cowhand sitting in the back of the dining room. Soon McCarthy stepped through a door and vanished into the kitchen. I took that chance to allow myself to rise and depart without ceremony. I went out onto the front sitting porch of the hotel and took in the beautiful, gentle, and warm air of the Western night.

Notwithstanding my fatigue, a grand sense of security and hope compelled me to hold to as much time in that fading day as possible. I was in the eve of things, of great, stable, and good things I was sure, so I wanted to linger—to stand upon the precipice before prosperity, warmth, and good feelings, and hoard them by keeping them imminent but not yet used. I wished to linger in the last day connected to my past in the East, to all that had been connected to insecurity and the fostering of illness, but also hinged to the confirmation that all that would follow would be free of my long and habitual cares. Thus, despite the call of my clean bed and unlimited steak, I insisted to myself that I should walk. The town was empty, and the moonlight of late spring shone down upon a Main Street without a single horse.

I marveled that I felt so few impulses to cough as I walked north on Main toward the water trough where I had collapsed less than a day before. Out beyond the trough, to the north, lay the immense expanse over which I had trod until reaching Pauktaug. Out in that black, open, cosmos of grass still waited the coach and its men—vulnerable and pensive, surely, yet passively confined by their charge's value and the great distance that lay between them and any other place toward which the driver and his man could walk.

I made my way along a road that led out into the grasslands and up a slight rise. But after I crested over this rise, the grasslands revealed only more endless prospect, undulating ceaselessly to the east. Yet the road drew me farther, for about a mile, and in the darkness I finally came across what I had taken to be, at a distance, two anomalous trees. When I reached theses supposed trees, I realized I had come upon the western gate and frontier of my brother's range land. An endless wire and post fence stretched both north and south from that gate; it was the first fence I had seen since leaving the railroad. There was not a single animal in sight, however. I opened the gate and entered my brother's range.

Fatigue and a desire to sleep persuaded me I should soon turn back, but I resolved to push on just a bit farther, to where a slender stone appeared to glow with an ivory pallor under the climbing moonlight. It lay several yards off of the road, to the south.

I reached that supposed stone and found instead the body of Kettle—his clothes ripped from his body, his skull crushed (but his face still recognizable), and his torso bearing the mark of repeated stabbings or impalements. Around his body, imprinted in the dry soil, were signs of both shod and unshod hooves—of a horse or horses and one or more head of cattle. The prints were mixed together and difficult to read. Though the prints looked fresh, it was possible that Kettle had met his odd death sometime after they had been left in the ground. Perhaps the prints had nothing to do with his death. But notwithstanding the fact that in the old Pauktaug I had had cause, on two separate occasions, to appraise and handle the bodies of men who had passed suddenly during the course of my tenure as constable, I felt unable to touch or examine Kettle's body in any way. I did not have the nerve for such a thing. Thus I could not say whether the hoof prints were underneath him or merely surrounding him—the latter case, had it obtained, suggesting some hint, perhaps, as to the circumstances surrounding his death. The unshod prints scattered away from his body in wild, directionless circles; the shod prints doubled back over themselves and ran directly back to the road leading to and from my brother's distant ranch house, but blended imperceptibly there with innumerable other prints that obscured their ultimate course, whether east (toward my brother's home) or west (back to town and then toward Whisker's ranch).

I must have stood there in wonder for some time, for after an indefinite period of minutes passed, I began to feel something of a fundamental sadness for Kettle; yet as I breathed deeply before a reflective sigh, either the first odors of death or my own returning fatigue caused me a dreadful fit of coughing. I coughed so violently that it was one of my more scarlet spells. I seemed with my own blood to freshen what had congealed upon Kettle in the cooling night air, and fear at the return of my physical pain (mixed, too, with the horror of Kettle's blunt demise) caused me to begin a quick march back toward town.

The closer I returned to town the more quickly I moved. All of my conflicting thoughts then yielded to the one, to the fear and apprehension that surrounded Kettle's inexplicable death. I looked at my pale hands as I climbed the steps to the hotel's lobby, fearing that their own sickly pallor was also being roasted into an alabaster death by a sinister moon. I made quick work of reporting Kettle's death to McCarthy when I found that tireless fop of a clerk at the front desk.

McCarthy, seeing my distress and fatigue, volunteered, "Well, that's mighty odd! Mighty strange!" He still seemed more intent on resuming his solicitude toward my comfort, however, than in lamenting Kettle's demise. He began to ask what he could do for me, but I ignored his questions and interrupted him.

"Whom should we report this to? There is a dead man lying out there in the dark, in the open. Who is the law here?"

"The law ain't really arrived here yet, Mr. Crabbe. The county seat is more than a hundred miles from here, and this town is new. We ain't seen a sheriff or a marshal yet—any kind of what you'd call a policeman. But we have Mr. Crabbe, sir! And then there's Mr. Whisker, too! But I don't know if he's back from Texas yet. I guess we'll just have to tell whoever comes in first in the morning."

"By morning! What of the dead man lying out there? Someone must bring that body in at least!"

"I wouldn't feel right poking around on Mr. Crabbe's place at night looking for the stiff! Better to wait for morning!"

"Then bring the body in on my authority—on my authority as a Crabbe!" I ordered.

McCarthy seemed delighted by this thinking, for I had suddenly transformed an action that may have displeased one Crabbe into one that would placate another.

"Yes, sir! Of course, Mr. Crabbe. Now you just go upstairs and get your rest. I'll go out and see that the body's brought in nice and respectful-like in the buckboard and kept in the icehouse. Anything I can bring you before I go and before you turn in?"

"No, McCarthy," I replied. "I only need to rest now."

I climbed the steps to my hotel room and went immediately to bed. Sleep came on quickly. After a few last coughs, my body settled into a beautiful torpor, and my eyes closed with the reassuring view of an eternally youthful Pauktaug, the town's perfect rendering redeeming the critical white and blue light of the moon. I fell asleep to the sound of McCarthy keeping his promise: he driving a buckboard and team out into the darkness of the plains.

PART II

United States

I.

The possibly imminent arrival of my English cousin in the new Pauktaug at nearly the same time as my own arrival left me in wonder. I was left all the more in a state because, what with the possibility of the coach line incapacitated, it was a likely prospect that my brother and I would have to meet him at the railhead when we received word of his arrival. That would seem a remarkable journey to me, for it was on a trip to the railroad with my brother, long ago (when I was six) when began the one other episode in my family's life involving my English cousin.

My father was himself an Englishman by birth, but he had always cherished a fascination for someday visiting and perhaps even settling in the United States, notwithstanding the fact that his family's great wealth and powerful standing in the south of England obviated any need for him to displace himself and compel himself to forge a new existence in a new country. His family, however, had adopted the cause of charity on an ambitious scale, and because my father lacked the force of character to confess at close range his privately formed ambitions for himself (especially when the idealism of the family's charitable mantle was an obstacle to embarrass him), he decided to make his way to America in his twentieth year and to declare sometime afterwards his intentions to remain in the new country. He harbored a desire to be an entrepreneur—to emulate those of his forebears who had amassed the Crabbe family wealth through Eastern trade companies—and then to undertake the family course of largesse only after recreating for himself the original means that permit both an elevated standard of living and at the same time an ease in colossal benefaction.

My father would forgo the notion of making his fortune by trade with India and the Orient. Instead, he decided to join forces with an American from New York, one John Whisker, who, somewhat east of the whaling village of Cold Spring Harbor on Long Island's north shore, and just a bit further east beyond the shipbuilding village of Northport, had started for himself a promising but small factory dedicated to the manufacture of productions fashioned from whalebone: stays and umbrellas. The business was called The Pauktaug Stays Works, and Mr. Whisker, during a tour of London and later the countryside of the English south, chanced to meet my father. Though there was a decade between the two young men, Mr. Whisker easily persuaded my younger father to join him as a partner after my father expressed keen interest in both the United States and in Mr. Whisker's new business. Something in Mr. Whisker's free conscience, his unadulterated focus upon fostering the new business for the sole sake of personal prosperity, may also have appealed to my father—a man virtually besieged by family tradition, their belief that all excessive gain should immediately be slated for scattering amidst the bereft and ill-fated.

Thus, in 1820, when my father was twenty-years old, he made his way to Long Island on an ostensible visit to the United States for a tour of New York and New England. After three months of the alleged tour had passed, my father sent word back to his mother and father and uncles that he would remain in America and try his own hand at building up independent capital. Throughout the course of his first years in Pauktaug, my father was besieged by letters that expressed the disappointment of his family. And, remarkably, letters that contained faded strains based upon the same themes of disappointment continued to arrive from England even into the late years of my childhood. I saw that these letters plagued my father, and even as the expressions of disappointment were tempered over the decades, my father's reactions to even their mildest reproaches seemed to grow as time passed and as enormous prosperity attended the original gamble that Mr. Whisker and my father had played upon whalebone.

His guilt when reading these ever more mild letters nevertheless perpetually increased due, in great part, to the profound wealth that my father began to enjoy sometime just before his marriage to my mother, about ten years after his arrival in the United States.

Yet something in or about the distance between things—in this case the distance between England and America—allowed my father to recover from every blow dealt to him by such letters. The distance permitted him perpetually to defer giving his family any final answer as to his ultimate personal and financial intentions, and his ever spiraling affluence persuaded him to defer choosing the moment when he had reached the mark of appointed safety for carrying out the family tradition of representing professional philanthropy wherever a Crabbe was found to reside.

Though my father made one personally difficult voyage back to England two years after his first arrival on Long Island, he never left his adopted country after his marriage to my mother and the birth of my brother in 1830.

Though my father married Ellen Gull, the daughter of a Long Island farming family that had lost two of its sons to the lure of strong situations in my father's and Mr. Whisker's factory, he elevated her by marriage—and thereby her family—to instantaneous prominence via the power his touch had gained as one of the fathers of Pauktaug's most significant business forces. Yet there have been times in my later years when I have sometimes wondered if my father's choice of a rooted American wife and family was made, in part, so as to help facilitate his desire to refrain from ever returning home to England—on account of his family's appraisal of such a wife and on account of subjecting his wife and his children to such a dangerous voyage—home to a place where he would have had to meet the silent but no less withering reproaches which would have outmatched any direct censure he was enduring by letter at home. But those suspicions are not easy to sustain on at least one count, for I have no direct evidence that my English grandparents or granduncles and uncles would have opposed my father's union. On the contrary, their uniquely progressive stance may have regarded his choice as a sort of personal extension, perhaps, of their impulsive largesse—as a sort of perpetual, concentrated, charity via perpetual union.

In fact—though I suspect my father was earnestly in love when he proposed marriage to my mother—I have come to think that perhaps it was *he*, my father, who came over time to regard his alliance with the American Gull family as his gesture (but also his limit) of family obligation toward philanthropy. I have come to believe that by concealing perhaps from his English family as much as he could of my mother's family's rank (and this concealment not motivated by traditionally shallow shame, for the Gulls were highly regarded as prosperous though unassuming farmers on Long Island), my father may have hoped to give the impression that he had already alighted upon the full duties of his family sense of obligation toward the poor.

Or perhaps my father never gave his English family any passive impression of the standing of the American Gulls and hoped only to outlast his English family in this life before they could ever see for themselves the truth—that his largesse had *not* been deferred for want of a target, but nor had it found an appropriate target. He simply concentrated all his means into his own, young, secure family—a peculiar solution in which he could satisfy his own sense of charitable tradition without at the same time in any way failing to enjoy in a direct manner all which he lavished upon his new bride via his constantly accruing business wealth. My father's situation was exquisitely designed to suit a host of contradictory expectations—expectations of altruism put forth on the one hand by his family in England (they left constantly uncertain whether their reproaches of an errant son and nephew might always be just a bit premature); expectations put forth on the other hand by my father's own simple, raw, desire for material gain and its permanent accumulation and protection; and, lastly, internal, polarized notions embracing all of the preceding expectations, and countless more, as well, of an agonized subtlety, all wrangling within the tortured, simple, conscience of a highly limited man; his conscience tragically just below a perfectly, dramatically designed intellect— thus uniquely inadequate, as well, to recognizing fully any isolated facet of the contradiction if his simple conscience had permitted him to become a fully committed man for one cause or another.

Yet the distance between things utterly protected him, and with the Yankee tenacity of Mr. Whisker fully invested in the fate of the Pauktaug Stays Works, my father settled into decades of ease, tinged by only the most mild but constant sense of foreboding. Though my father himself was not a native species of Long Island, still he resembled in those years one of those vulnerable island animals of the tropics, carrying out a safe existence for untold centuries until the sudden introduction of some white man's dog, cat, pig, or rat makes quick work of exposing unsuspected vulnerabilities in an ostensible paradise. My father, however, always suspected these vulnerabilities, but in his case he never suspected any ship would ultimately touch down on our island and reveal them. He was more like an only mildly wise tortoise—one born without a shell—losing, year after year, his initially profound anxiety concerning his unprotected tender parts, losing his fear only after enough time had passed without anything or anyone robbing him of his safety upon his remote island.

But up until my sixth year I had no hints of the latent threats and conflicts that had roiled, not only in the nearly two decades before my birth, but also, again, through those earliest years of my own memories—which, outside of my intermittent struggles with burgeoning consumption, comprise nothing but a string of unbroken halcyon days in the company of my wealthy and seemingly powerful father, my gentle mother, and my inspiriting and significantly older brother, Ellsworth.

Thus it was somewhat puzzling to me when, in early 1845, my father received a letter that seemed to me to disquiet his mind to a degree out of all proportion to its contents. The letter was not one of the regular ones received nearly every month in either the hand of his father or mother but from one of his brothers (one of my uncles). The letter's contents were startling, for they would pose a threat to my father—he, again, that defenseless, island species—in a way perhaps never entertained even by the most talented regions of his anxious imagination.

It appeared that the East Indian trade business of my grandfather, his own brothers, and my father's brothers, had fallen upon hard times; the family was not only obliged to curtail its customary charitable activities, but it was also compelled to reach out to my father for *his* assistance on behalf of at least one of his brother's sons. Again, this turn of events was remarkable—on many counts. At first it may have seemed that these circumstances would have lessened my father's always latent fears that great altruistic things were ultimately expected of him; since now that his English brethren themselves could not undertake such causes, it might be thought that they would not demand as much from others in the family circle. But my father, I suspect, felt he knew better than this. His fears began to mount as he began to imagine that this letter was merely a veiled but direct passing of the family's philanthropic mantle to him. Yet he must also have been confident that with the great distance of the Atlantic between England and Pauktaug he could still maintain his American circumstances as they then still obtained.

Then I am certain that his fears led him to suspect that the letter might be in fact an oblique call upon him to make his entire English family the subjects of a charitable cause. But after further consideration, I imagine my father also put that trepidation aside, for his father, uncles, and brothers had too much of a business streak mixed in with their idealism to ever let themselves become entirely monetarily vulnerable.

However, the letter's actual request began to gnaw upon my father's imagination in the weeks after its receipt, for it asked if my father could secure a situation for my cousin, Julius, in the Stays Works. It had been a family custom in England to ask of its young men that they apprentice themselves in the family business under relatively humble clerical circumstances before they were permitted to ascend into its more exulted and relaxed executive concerns, and one of my uncles hoped that my father's American business could offer such a place whilst the family's concerns in Britain and India were under great distress due to the loss of an entire fleet of ships in a Ceylonese typhoon.

This request would present no challenge to my father's resources, nor would it be out of the question for him to create a situation for my cousin in the Pauktaug Stays Works. In fact, he and Mr. Whisker were often looking for young men for that very purpose.

But this request, if honored—and there was no way that my father could escape honoring it; it would have to be honored; it must be honored—would bring the young man to Pauktaug itself. He would be a witness to my father's life and circumstances—a witness to *all* of our very comfortable, nay extravagant, lives. My father might choose, at a distance, to refrain from honoring the family's long-standing request that he account himself yet another of its esteemed patrons of the poor and unfortunate, but there was nothing developed in his solitary, self-created, code that could protect his peculiar conscience if he refused this explicit request from his brother for the sake of a nephew. He would have to assent to this request, but in saying *yes,* what was he to do? The spaces between things could no longer protect him then.

It had to be conceded that my father's nephew, Julius Crabbe, was a young man—merely twenty-three years old at that point—and it could hardly be sure that he would carry with him the family's zealous, ceaseless, philanthropic credo. And because my Cousin Julius was so young, surely, even if he did serve as a new emissary and generational representative of the English Crabbe's cause, my father, then a well-established man of fifty-five, would have no trouble in either ignoring the preachings and conceits of such a considerably younger man or in perhaps bullying him instead into our untroubled, prosperous, ways—especially when the young Englishman would be isolated with us on Long Island and totally under our supervision and at our mercy whilst he enjoyed our hospitality and protection. Perhaps he might be persuaded to live among us after the style of my brother, who was then twenty-five—my brother, the most studious and sporting and respected young man of means amongst Pauktaug's few true gentlemen.

Yet nothing could be certain until my cousin was among us. After delaying an answer for as long as he could, my father finally wrote back to England, penning a letter that clearly professed a welcome for my Cousin Julius, and, as well, a pledge that a situation could be arranged for our cousin in the Pauktaug Stays Works— offered with the meek condition (characteristic of so many of my father's edicts from that point forward; the statement concealing, of course, an oblique hope) that my cousin would find an ample situation awaiting only if his new surroundings "met with his unalloyed pleasure" and if the position "offered the requisite challenges and meritorious attentions befitting a young man surely possessing all the character and grace as would suit a young gentleman bearing the name of his illustrious great-grandfather."

It was likely that my father, unless circumstances were very extreme, could not be counted upon to reject my cousin for employment unless, again, his failings were so egregious that to ignore them would only discredit my father amidst his fellow citizens and entrepreneurs. Thus it became my father's hope, surely, that my cousin himself would quickly reject a place in the Pauktaug Stays Works and leave my father to continue his happy ascent in business without witnesses or external family conscience. There was still the hope, too, that this newest Julius Crabbe would revel in our ways and be only a pleasurable addition—as a boon to my father's business and as a sympathetic new middle brother to myself and to my brother, Ellsworth.

Again, one would only know after they had met the man. But what, for instance, would this Julius think when he discovered, among countless other things, that my brother was not obliged to serve in any clerical apprenticeship? Instead, he was completely free to pursue his passions for horses, dogs, natural history—and his particular fascinations: fossils and ancient coins. Once more: there would be no telling until Julius Crabbe made his way west across the Atlantic.

At last an answer to my father's reply arrived. My uncle had accepted my father's gracious offer to the young Julius Crabbe, and my cousin would be sailing for New York by June of 1855. For a few days in that late winter of 1855, this news caused great distress for my father, for he was uncertain what preparations, if any, should be made—outside of the traditional preparations one makes for an extended house guest (and my father's lavish household was always ready for such events, for it seemed we were often entertaining interesting guests of all kinds from various parts of America, whom my father and Mr. Whisker had met through business).

It has even occurred to me that my father might may have entertained the notion of somehow arranging things so that our affluence and comforts would appear much less formidable than they actually were. Yet such a plan would have been impossible to carry out whilst still permitting us all to enjoy the level of existence to which my father was still strongly committed. But all these considerations which I am certain compelled my father to agonize privately during that late winter of 1855 were, by necessity, pushed aside by a more immediate threat—one left no empty voids, no spaces between things, behind which one might hope to hide and carry on in affected ignorance.

My mother, from youth, had always been mildly consumptive. In fact, that affliction was sometime whispered to have contributed (by perverse, cruel, means) in part to what was taken for my mother's singular beauty. A natural, porcelain complexion was somehow augmented into an even more rarefied yet lovely translucence by her affliction. And when some thought that my mother might be blooming into a last, Indian summer ivory brilliance of loveliness in her forty-fifth year, her small frame gave way to the strain of the most intense wave of that illness, which also seemed to have aided her lithe, pale, beauty to reach one last apotheosis before its sure descent into age.

As with my own struggles with consumption up until that point, my mother—perhaps from the boundless care and protections my father was able to afford—had merely suffered bouts, to my recollection, that only caused her to retire from her social and family rounds for no more than a few days at a time—and such rare retirements occurred perhaps no more often than every half year, if even that frequently. Whatever fatal tendencies my mother's constitution may have carried, my father would enwrap them in the soft and limitless protection of his means—the finest luxuries and the finest doctors and medicines that could be coaxed from New York City. My mother was like the most delicate china teacup amidst the settings in the dining cabin of a fine ship—appearing regularly at table, but always stored with the most elaborate wrappings and paddings should any disturbance seem imminent upon the sea (encased, then, to such a degree that even the most violent hurricane, whilst laying waste to the ship's deck, could do no harm to that protected, swaddled, brittle, but lovely cup).

Oftentimes I would enter into my own consumptive periods when my mother's would begin, but I remained unusually strong during the late winter and spring of 1855. While my father and brother brought all their powers and resources together in the pursuit of rendering unto my mother every possible comfort and resource intended for her health's restoration, I spent a rather typical span of months, under the guidance of my tutors by mornings and afternoon, and in a happy freedom amidst the flowering woods and warming shores of the Sound in the company of my brother's hounds.

As June approached, with the help of physicians from New York, my father managed to restore my mother to something like a vulnerable stability, and the combination of the effort required to maintain that stability along with the quiet ebullience that came to all of us with the tenuous prospect of my mother's recovered health, formed a fog of particularly good spirits and seeming confidence all about and within my father. This state of mind was established so strongly in my father that when the June date came for my cousin's arrival, my father joyfully delegated his best team and most trusted driver to take the American welcoming party (my brother and myself) to the railroad station so as to receive the young Englishman, Julius Crabbe.

The ride was a long one, and my brother and father, thinking to augment the sense of event that such a journey would bring to me, thought I would enjoy staying in the station town's hotel on the night before my cousin's arrival—and thus, as well, we would easily be up early and rested for my cousin's arrival on the early train from New York, and our horses and driver would be fresh for the return journey to Pauktaug.

Though my father's opulence and generosity toward us all always bordered on the nearly decadent, it was my brother, I am sure, who would have thought to propose the hotel—not only for its practical purposes, but for the sense of adventure and occasion it would provide to me. One must understand that though no little fellow could have been more content with his draw of mother and father from the hands of Fate, he could not have been more inspired and enthralled than by the choice the Universe had made for him in his sole sibling.

My older brother was indeed an *older* brother; he was, again, nineteen years my senior. He was the happy, late autumn consequence of my mother's and father's early winter marriage of 1830. They had hoped for more children, but as none were forthcoming after many years had passed, my brother provided my mother and father with that object of sole purpose and focus unto which they could pile all of their love, moderate and perhaps questionable wisdom, and resources—and thereby, too, with ease, realize my father's aspiration of raising his child lovingly and directly, and not at the affluent distance he himself had ostensibly enjoyed but really endured via the reticent gulfs created first by nurse, then by governess, then by tutors and other instructors. My father wished to link the loving, intimate, web he had witnessed in his bride's farm home—all the children and forebears happily entangled and endeared by their close quarters, limited means, and warm hearts (there had been autumn evenings in that home, my American grandparents' home in Commack, my father would often tell me before the fire as I listened, when in the last months before his marriage the dried, standing, cornstalks of the previous harvest swayed just outside of the windows, and seemed more glorious and regal under the supper moonlight than any vertical splendors of Man he had ever seen in his youth on the Tour); again, he wished to link all that had burned so brightly for him in that farmhouse, all that he had seen created with such seemingly simple ease (as if the ruddy glow of unaffected joy had been carved into the faces of both the youngest children and the most ancient eighteenth-century rebel granny faces with the same ease with which a fully earnest and happy grin had been cut into the jack-o-lantern that had met him on the cool, dry, porch before he had raised his hand to the door to announce his intentions to my American grandfather); again, wished to link all that he had seen in that golden autumn farmhouse to his own future family, but without the strain of limited means.

To my father's credit he would succeed in this for nearly a quarter of a century, perhaps because he was never tested, however, by limited means; or perhaps instead he always fell just short—ever so short (for there were never dried leaves or cornstalk shards blowing about our maze of servant-swept porches on October nights), ever so short not because he was never tested by limited means, but because he was never inspired and liberated by their company.

We would never be tested by limited means; no, other more oblique and sinister tests would have to arrive. Only then would the more tempered grin of our harvest jack-o-lanterns—those that I had suspected with wonder from my bedroom on October and November nights, as they, concealed below, would offer only their flickerings to me, flickerings down unto the front stairs during one of my mother's and father's crystalline autumn dinner parties—only then would those grins, carved by one of our Irish housekeepers, seem to expose a nearly imperceptible arch turn to the edges of their smiles.

But my father's efforts to wed warmth to means had its own measures of unique successes, the most representative and uncontested result best displayed in Ellsworth. I am compelled to observe once more that no little fellow could have been more proud, more exalted, more enthralled than myself in regard to his one and only sibling. In fact, it would suit the description best if, instead of styling him as a sibling, I revealed that his true role in my child-hood was that of a supreme, publicly conceded, expertly polished and princely third parent. He retained all the warmth, ardor, and physical grace of my Yankee grandfather's family, but experienced a life completely free of their frictions from the plow and the sandy Long Island soil. He retained, too, a lack of shame for all the priv-ileges we enjoyed, an unapologetic air that descended to him from my father.

But beyond what he retained in pure form from his antecedents, it was the glory of the alchemical mixtures that surfaced in him alone that seemed to make him *the* man of Pauktaug: a man of physical and material *and* native humility—but the resulting ulti-mate admixture of privilege emanating from him seemingly alto-gether free of the original ingredients used to assemble him. I never saw him ill-at-ease when my father and Mr. Whisker entertained even the most esteemed and encrusted of dinner guests; I never saw him condescend even to wandering vagabonds whom the village constable would push along until they were south of the Pauktaug Village line.

Ellsworth permitted my father lavishly and almost recklessly to augment his carefully selected collections of ancient and modern coins, of fossils, and of the finest esoteric books. Yet as soon as these items came into my brother's hands after my father would return from one of his frequent journeys to New York, each item received the complete attention and focus of Ellsworth's singular talent for care and protection—each item became as if it were his only item, as if it were the sole cornhusk doll or toy of one of my American aunts' youth.

He would use and admire his things, but he would carefully pre-serve them, as well. Never did one feel, as his suite on the house's third floor began to darken with the cabinetry as of the richest Victorian museums, that his room were the scenes of excess, of clean but evident neglect by surfeit, or of objects forced to remain anonymous and undervalued even when they numbered to a count wherein other collections they would suffer as supernumerary. No. Somehow his suite embodied the same clean grace as that of my American grandmother's nearly ascetic parlor in Commack. In his possessions and in his person and in his spirit Ellsworth did indeed embody the best of my father's hopes for his American experiment, that experiment my father had conceived during that October when he completed his courtship of my mother in her native home.

But my father never had the intellect to realize fully what experiment he only half-consciously formed in his mind and undertook; my brother, the subject and product of this experiment, however, most certainly did have the vast mind and soul to be not only the subject and product but also the conductor of the experiment. He was third parent not only to me but to himself—and thus, too, increasingly to my mother and father, for as they realized that my father's only half-conscious resolutions were being supplanted by the fully conscious and superior aims of my brother, my mother and father receded into a happy passivity (this augmented as my father's business began to grow of its own volition and with the happily greater attention given to it by Mr. Whikser).

My father never surrendered a sense of family dignity or responsibility, but he increasingly felt that such indispensable concerns were best represented and executed by the decrees of Ellsworth, who by even the simplest utterances, even on behalf of the business, could combine material wisdom and hungry simplicity of the most ardent, sober, conscious, capitalist with the ultimate tolerance and Christian kindness of our American grandfather—that farmer, a man fully conscious that kindness was his ultimate duty, for he was certain, because of the natural limits of his fields, never to prosper in realms were an anonymous and ruthless business philosophy would inevitably come into play.

Ellsworth was all things to me: revered older brother, ultimately trusted father, friend, and hero. I have often thought it a wonder that I grew into a strong walker and runner as a young boy, for it seems that I spent nearly all of my first six years straddling my brother's neck and sitting on his shoulders—and seeing most things for the first time from his level of view. He was less stout and muscular at that time of life, much more slender and lithe in frame than the man I would encounter twenty-eight years later in the second Pauktaug.

He had at that time a solid, smooth, shock of shiny black hair, and some of my earliest memories are of long walks in all seasons through the village, along the Sound shoreline, and through the then seemingly vast stretches of woodland that extended east of the great house that my father had built several years before his marriage to my mother—long marches astride my brother's shoulders during which, surely, as I held to his shiny hair as it if it were a frayed set of reins, I learned more of natural history, fairy tales, and other fables than I ever retained from long hours with my tutors, and more of a sense of security and of all the solid, material, earthy world being right with itself than almost any supply of resources and implied station granted to me via my father's supreme place in the business arena of Pauktaug Village.

2.

I remember the June morning of my cousin's arrival via the Long Island Rail Road very clearly. I was, even then, seated astride my brother's shoulders as we stood on the small plank platform of the depot. Most travelers from New York City to Pauktaug, at that time, as I recall, took a steamer from the city to Northport Village (just to the west of Pauktaug) and then only had to endure a brief coach ride from Northport to Pauktaug. A decade later the steamer would travel on to Pauktaug, as well. Yet for reasons that are now uncertain in my memory, my Cousin Julius elected to travel the last leg of his long journey by train; perhaps the attractions of first-class travel, even for such a brief ride by rail, outweighed the prospect of enduring the three-hour journey in the unsegregated cabin of the plebian day steamer.

Again, I recall sitting atop Ellsworth's shoulders as the east-bound train approached the station. My place around his neck was so frequent and certain that at times I wonder if he employed me as a yokefellow for some gentling purpose to his own mind—or if at those times that I was on his shoulders I was as the mind of the pair and he content to surrender all the burdens he normally shouldered on behalf of my father and our family.

Yes, I think he often carried me not so that I could merely enjoy, as a child, the simple thrill of such height and riding (though that is how I perceived it, certainly, at that time) but so that a Centaur's arrangement could be effected. I became as the clear, unaffected child mind at the top—unlearned, unburdened, content with the natural order of things, unmoved to dissect and to deter-mine either benign or sinister underlying and intangible causes, completely ignorant of all seething principles and abstractions, so that a leaf was grand for being a leaf, and needed thank no point of origin or creation—and Ellsworth was then content as the Centaur's base: another proud member of a happy standing order, separate from the leaf, but proud with and next to it, free from the risk of perceiving the similes and, worse still, the anal-ogies that haunt the spaces between things. Or perhaps he took pleasure in vertically antagonizing space, he realizing in miniature the mighty chauvinism of the skyscrapers of New York of the fol-lowing century, of a time that I alone was young enough to survive to witness. Or perchance Ellsworth may have thought me a sort of periscope, reaching upwards from his submarine depths, offering a view and subtle challenge to the voids above. If not in all of these ways, then at least in some, I am certain that my brother, as much as for my own sincere childish delight, also impressed my little form into service for some obscure but strictly designed purpose of reaction—if he was not doing so quite yet at that time of that year, then surely quite soon after, for it was to be a summer and autumn in which Ellsworth would be both compelled and besieged by ulterior motives.

Once more, I watched from atop my brother's strong and happy shoulders as the eastbound train puffed into the depot. I recall that it was a bright, cloudless day, and Ellsworth's spirits seemed as high as my own, and honed with an equal simplicity of focus and intensity of anticipation as I know I too exuded at the happy prospect of meeting another young Crabbe for the first time—and one from so far away, from our father's native England, to boot.

As the doors of the first-class coaches halted, Ellsworth waved back to my father's driver, who was standing close by with the carriage and team, waiting in readiness to carry any baggage that was not being shipped directly to my family's home in Pauktaug. The driver answered with a deferential salute, and Ellsworth and I strode as one, for only *his* legs were engaged, when a figure emerged from one of the coaches, a figure that in every way suggested it must be none other than our English cousin, Julius Crabbe.

Besides this cousin that I was about to meet, I was never again in my life to meet any of my father's family from England; nor was I to have, with the exception of my father, of course, any considerable time spent in the company of native Englishmen. Thus I cannot say for certain how much or how little in the way of representation was embodied by the personality of the young man whom we approached on the platform. I can say, however, that I feel I should reveal already that even then I suspected it would be naïve for me to rest upon any imagined national traits or surmised familial attributes in accounting for the strong first impression which coolly radiated from my cousin. Whatever qualities I ascribe to the man, I would have it understood that they were, at last, peculiar and unique to him.

Even after a host of nearly infallible and reliable immediate impressions flowed directly to both my brother and to me from the cool, shy face of our cousin, Ellsworth still offered a hearty wave and the broadest of smiles—the latter one to have broken almost any icy man, among the living or even from among the famous ranks of the past. But, again, we were met with not an aggressive haughtiness but an aggressive shyness, that kind of shyness that hopes to dominate obliquely whilst never surrendering its apparent and sincere meekness. So it was that Ellsworth's earnest and warm smile did not break a stoic's face into a strong smile, but my brother's smile rendered from a man of more mysterious resistance a wan, ambiguous, nearly imperceptible splinter of a grin—the kind of meek grin that fails to acknowledge that the warmth it often meets with in others is from their effort to minister to such ostensibly idealized, recalcitrant, gentleness.

His face radiated an aloof, passive, idealism to such an extent, that even to my child's powers of perception it appeared sinister.

My brother felt pushed back by the ambiguous condescension of our cousin's wan smile when we came to a halt before him, and Ellsworth decided to put me down to the ground even before a word was said by anyone. At times I have wondered if Ellsworth put me down onto my own legs simply so that he could safely extend his hand for a traditional handshake. Yet I ultimately think otherwise. Not only did no handshake come—one neither initiated by my brother nor one by my cousin—but I think my cousin's aggressive meekness was so palpable to both Ellsworth and me that not only do I believe my brother was resolved to refrain from offering his hand if none was given even before placing me on the ground, but I think his placing me down was also akin to going further than refraining from offering his hand; it was his only means of countering the intangible affront of the young man's demeanor and expressions of mouth and eye. Yet I feel strongly that Ellsworth also felt immediate regret in placing me down, as if it had been more the result of my cousin's push of cold spirit than my brother's effort to pull his own warmth back within himself.

Perhaps no observer of this scene—save the three active parties—would have noted that anything was awry in the first meeting between Julius Crabbe and his two American cousins. Yet Ellsworth—and I did, as well, in my own childish way—had felt slighted, if not just by our cousin personally, then by some principle or manner or aesthetic that my cousin happened then to represent or embody so well.

Once more, this would have appeared as no slight to virtually any other observer but myself. However, to Ellsworth it was a great slight that would have to wait for many imminent and demonstrable wrongs to come along to support it, to reveal it—but when those wrongs came they would transfer all of their insult back to that original passive act. The instinctive antipathy would have to wait for its support. And only then—after it was found and justice and reckoning put into their long, slow, motion—would Ellsworth have the power to figuratively lift me up once more, though for the rest of that summer I still often rode behind his neck in actuality.

My own sense of a slight or of any festering antipathy between my brother and my cousin vanished after they ultimately did tip their hats to one another and did shake hands briefly with an ostensibly adequate cordiality. The original moment had passed for the time being—again, at least, to my powers of observation— had passed without seeming of lasting impact, as happens when one passes and brushes against strands of poison ivy intermingled with traditional ivy that has been encouraged to climb a trellis or stone wall.

But I did note that my brother had crossed his arms tightly. I had never seen him do this to such a degree before, and it was at that moment that I feel Ellsworth acquired this action as a recognizable personal trait of motion under particular circumstances.

The driver soon had all of my cousin's bags and a few small trunks stowed out of our way in the carriage, and as the sleek, black, rested team trotted north to Pauktaug, my original perceptions of my cousin's inherent traits were masked by my fascination for the superficial sounds of his English voice and manners—these things, again, pushing aside the central and personal qualities of the man and taking their place, at least for me, for a time. In fact, as we rode north, I became somewhat convinced he might be a somewhat pleasant fellow and a valuable ally, for he produced for me a small box containing several large and perfect specimens of fossilized shark teeth he had collected when on a tour of Arabia. They were a gift to me, and as fossils were also an interest of my brother's, an hour or more of seemingly pleasant conversation ensued between the two young men on that very subject—interrupted only by Ellsworth's annotations concerning native trees and flowers which seemed to attract the eye of our cousin along the course of the drive.

3.

My recollection of that afternoon abruptly ends, leaving our uneasy trio still in the midst of our drive, but it resumes with equal suddenness with the memory of my father's principal housekeeper ringing the bell that called us all to our first dinner with our new extended houseguest.

When I arrived in the dining room, my father, brother, and cousin were already seated. My mother was not yet in the room, but as her health had remarkably improved, she—with the happy encouragement of my father and the guarded consent of her doctors—would use the occasion of my cousin's arrival as the first time she had appeared at table or before guests in many months.

As I took my seat, I saw my father—still in good spirits at the prospect of my mother's ostensibly recovering health; still in the good spirits that had pushed aside all the strange anxiety that had so long plagued him at the prospect of hosting a member of his English family in his American home—smiling and listening carefully to the superficially gentle, angular murmurings of his nephew. Ellsworth, who sat at the opposite end of the long table, seemed to counter my cousin's superficial control and placidness with his own efforts of superficiality, and he appeared to match the easy cheerfulness and solicitous cordiality of my father's manner in nearly every respect, as well. I suspect he did this in part for my father's sake (so as not to embarrass him in general, and so as not to reawaken his anxiety over his nephew's presence), and I suspect he did this for his own sake, as well, so as to attempt some delay in passing full judgment on our guest.

I should note that the anxiety my father had displayed in the first weeks after learning of my cousin's intended journey to Long Island from England was never something openly discussed. Yet my brother's sensitivity and my own powers of observation still made my father's dread quite evident, and its gradual decline in power was also equally palpable and equally traceable to the source: to apprehensions in regard to his life in America being called to judgment in respect to the original expectations held for him by his family in Britain.

So, again, in respect to my father's anxieties being kept at bay, and in respect to my brother attempting to keep his own instantaneous inclinations toward contempt for our cousin in check, I found Ellsworth in seemingly cheerful audience to my father's and cousin's conversation as we assembled for our first supper together with Julius Crabbe. But notwithstanding all the efforts my brother made to make his outward bearing cheerful and welcoming to our new houseguest, and despite all the sincere force of objective reconsideration' he was applying inwardly against the quick judgments he had formed at the railroad depot in opposition to my cousin, Ellsworth could not help but fold his arms tightly as the conversation paused upon the entrance of my mother into the dining room.

My mother's unusually strong recovery from her latest struggle with consumption would play a critical role not only in my memory of that evening, but in my memory of that spring, summer, and powerful autumn. She was, again, the last to enter the dining room for supper, and she appeared in her favored white camisole of complex and intricate lace, encased by an even more intricate white bodice. So much of her appearance and her very essence depended upon her reliance on—and her equanimity concerning and her acceptance of—paleness, of an ivory grip that had held her for all of her life since adolescence. As a sort of defiance against the unavoidable whiteness her body compelled her to present, or perhaps as an aggressive complicity with it, she favored white in nearly all of her clothes. Notwithstanding that she was into her forty-fifth year that spring, all of this unavoidable and agent whiteness combined to put her most powerful feature into profound relief—a head of long, dense, sable-black hair (which shone with all the natural richness of a haughty little girl's springtime mane), and this conspired with her unique, awful, pale blue eyes to seem as two voluble strokes of the soul's pen across the great blank sheet of the remaining parts of her person. Her hair and her eyes made their marks upon her as do brief lines of large-lettered verse on the otherwise blank pages of large gift volumes.

My existence at that time was relatively removed from other families' lives, so the intermittent bouts of my mother's great illness, normally followed by restricted, tentative recoveries, seemed like a matter of course to my child's mind. Having a beautiful, delicate, mother as the centerpiece of all care and concern seemed to me the natural way of things—and her recoveries appeared to be the equally natural result of my father's and brother's worries and ministrations and of my father's great means brought to bear in excess upon and opposition to her pain or even mild discomfort.

As was his custom upon my mother's entrance into the dining room, my father raced to the opposite end of the table, from his place at the distant head, and pulled back my mother's chair. She gave her customary abashed smile—mixed with a look of subtle entitlement to which she had long trained herself—and waited to be seated until my father carried out the introductions.

"Dearest Ellen, this is our nephew, Mr. Julius Crabbe, come to stay with us for the year—and perhaps beyond," my father began with a sincere but theatrical formality. My mother, long accustomed to feeling herself the most regal presence in tiny Pauktaug, nodded her head with a latent condescension befitting a pride ready to meet any manner and breeding boasted by an ancient empire. Such a condescension—all the more powerful because it was supported by a sincere, loving, warmth (a warmth fostered by her farm origin that created a glow of hospitality and love, warm and crisp as the autumn fields that stretched south to the ocean, which could match the means of any ruling class of antiquity)—such a nod from my lovely mother presented a rich challenge to even the coldest hearts that passed through our dining room and library and parlor during my childhood.

My cousin, however, was a peculiar man, and he took the challenge of that nod—which had been, in fact, no challenge, but an oblique embrace of a farm girl playing Victorian hostess for well nigh a quarter century by that point—as a challenge indeed, despite the fact that I am sure that at the same time he knew as well as anyone the circumstances, the warm circumstances, under which we were making our first overtures to him. A man of subtle, sinister, jealousies—masked by accomplishment and feints of hospitable reciprocations—is a dangerous man. The tragedy would be that my mother, father, and I were all too much children to mount a defense against the oblique force that my cousin would thrust against our paradise—my mother too much a child because of her ultimately constant illness and generous, unaffected, heart; my father too much a child because it would be his long neglected and happily deferred childhood conscience upon which my cousin would prey; I too much a child for I was child, and therefore helpless to cause real effect or offer genuine warning even when I made observations well beyond my six years. This scenario left Ellsworth to stand increasingly alone in that pivotal year in which my cousin was guest in our home, for my brother's intellect was no child's. However, at this early phase in my cousin's time with us, I suspect it was still unclear to Ellsworth just how much of a threat Julius might pose to our quiet Eden on Long Island Sound.

"My dear Nephew Julius, this is your aunt, Ellen Gull Crabbe."

I had never heard my father introduce my mother with the inclusion of her maiden name; my mother seemed to take no note of this. My father seemed to assign no conscious meaning to this gesture himself, for he placed his hand upon our mother's shoulders with the same loving grasp that characterized nearly all of the choreography of their gentle, ongoing, romance. In fact, what with our mother's especially strong recovery in this instance, my father seemed to glow with an even greater degree of pride in my mother and her beauty than was his wont. Ellsworth and I exchanged furtive glances at this moment, however. With my father and mother to be increasingly removed from Ellsworth over the course of that spring, summer, and autumn of our cousin's visit, my brother would steadily escalate his reliance upon me in moments of crisis—rely upon me, the only actual child in the scene, for a sober, mature, confirmation of things, things he could only suspect were unfolding.

Since my mother's entrance into the room, we had all been standing in her honor. But after my father's introduction of my mother to Julius—Julius then sensing perhaps some rarefied weakness in my father; or perhaps my cousin invoking a procedure he would have undertaken under any circumstance—Julius made his way to my mother's place as she began to sit, and he took her hand for a gentleman's kiss before she could take to her chair. Whatever his intention—and he did not seem displeased at the result—my mother appeared flattered by the gesture, enough so that it revealed that a veiled embarrassment of her origins could have been behind such pleasure. It was the veiled embarrassment that that seemed to please Julius most.

To Julius, my mother may have appeared the embodiment of health and middle-aged beauty, for, again, this particular recovery from her chronic illness left her at her best—somehow at her last and grandest best. Though my cousin came from a family and a style of existence that made our affluence appear relatively humble, one must recall that he came to us in a period during which his family's station and resources were both highly diminished, and vulnerable, still, to further extreme compromise. He came to us, then, with all these circumstances coupled to an exquisitely honed sense of sinister immaturity—a combination ripe for producing latent acts of the most elegantly passive belligerence. Somehow my mother—Long Island farm girl turned minor royalty of this Republic of villages and young industry—became the emblem for all that Julius would hold in contempt during his stay among us in America. Yet he was never to make a single gesture that could be detected as anything but sincere grace to his hosts, and they would embrace him with all of the power their hearts could offer—my mother honored seemingly to receive the blessing of a member of my father's family (a family she had otherwise never met at all); my father pleased in his bland obtuseness to receive what seemed the approval of his marital choice from this young emissary of one of his brothers. Again, only Ellsworth would be left, the one sole adult capable of quietly building a case against this sly and malicious invader in our midst. But the malefactor was only guilty of being suspicious thus far. What charges could Ellsworth yet level against our cousin in a report to my father?

"Thank you, dear nephew. May you feel that our home is yours," my mother said as my cousin relaxed her hand.

"I will endeavor to do so," replied Julius as he made his way back to his chair on my side of the table. I followed Ellsworth's lead at that point and took my seat once more. My brother sat opposite me, alone on his side of the long table. I watched him closely as he settled in once more to his chair and folded his arms again; in childlike admiration I emulated that pose. We did not wait for my father to reach his place at the head of the table opposite my mother; we were seated before he even passed my brother's chair.

My father was a man whose greatest pleasure and sense of moral satisfaction came from pleasing his immediate family. That goal, combined with a subtle obtuseness of intellect and conscience allowed him to pass behind my seated brother, as he (my father) made his way to his place at the head of the table, with a completely unaffected smile of good humor and contentment. My father was pleased with my cousin's greeting to my mother; my father was so pleased with my mother's ostensible good health and restored beauty that he felt at peace with her security. All was utterly well, he was sure. Because of my father's limited powers of appraisal, my cousin's superficially quiet and finished manner seemed to give reason to dismiss any remaining fears my father had entertained when he first received announcement by letter of my cousin's intentions to live with us as an experiment in America. My father could dismiss his last, lingering, fears, with great speed and ease. And my father's romantic love for our mother was so profound—and yet at the same time so routine—that this particular recovery of hers put her at a unique disadvantage.

It was good fortune for her immediate health; but it was unfortunate for her future stability, for her radiance reassured my father to such a degree that he felt his rose could be left unattended for a time. She had shown too much bloom on the eve of frost.

But to my father's credit, he was not entirely without powers of observation; or perhaps it was that Ellsworth's authority in our family—slowly and surely assumed as he left his adolescent years—was still clear enough to impress upon my father that something appeared gravely awry to both of his children.

As my father took his chair, the bright look of misguided contentment was lessened as he caught Ellsworth's subtle expression of reproach—eye contact directed straight to my father solely by the turning of eyes and not by the head. Ellsworth's arms also remained tightly crossed. My father's aquiline features, even in his fifty-fifth year, appeared sharp and defined, but when he had cause to feel deflated, or was checked in his figurehead reign by Ellsworth's de facto prime ministry, my father could appear slightly puffy and loose in the face and neck—so that one had a slight glimpse into the skin tone of his infant years and youth, before the time when his regal pointedness of nose helped him to assert himself to podiums of authority, upon which he really did not possess the inner magnitude to mount a defense should anyone have challenged his nose with a poke. But his rural Long Island industrial empire never provided him with challengers to his mediocre powers of ascendancy.

Ellsworth was the ultimate head of our family—and thus, too, an agent proxy for the family's business. But my brother, at least at this time of life, still retained a healthy and appealing skepticism against his own absolute authority; and my father's weaker powers of understanding mistakenly took Ellsworth's deference to him at times as a sign of true apprenticeship and not as the oblique and noble sublimation of better judgment that it really was.

It was this understanding, perhaps, that allowed my father to maintain his position of power with his business partner and employees during those last years of my brother's time on Long Island—for Ellsworth's conditioning of our father made him a courteous, mild, likeable, false tyrant in his place of industry (where, at the same time, there was no one who would have challenged him had he behaved otherwise). Ellsworth's conditioning helped my father to think he maintained the status quo at his place of work, but it weakened him in a unique way in his home, for Ellsworth's affected lieutenancy would reveal its ultimate insincerity when a challenge to my father would at last be necessary. Thus my father projected strength (in the factory) where, after many years of trust, it was not necessary, and subtle weakness in the very locale (his home) where he was also being given the impression that his decrees were utterly his own and final.

But this is not to say that my father did not regularly consult with and defer to Ellsworth. In fact, he was about to do so right at that very table. However, my father did not see that his consultation was taken as a discreet and oblique form of deference; and Ellsworth did not fully realize that his lieutenancy, his noble discretion of hiding true command, was in fact fooling the subject of that kindness and deception to a greater degree than ever intended. My brother had thought that the gentle charade—for my father's sake—was carried out by tacit agreement by both men, by both father and son. But my father was fooled by my brother's acting prowess; and Ellsworth was fooled in that he did not realize my father had assumed no counter role in the gentle charade. My father was playing no character; he was utterly himself in his dangerous obtuseness. Yet Ellsworth's delusion was based upon a son's creditable love and hope for his father. But perhaps there was discredit in holding out hope for so long. All that being said, Ellsworth was in command and knew it (as did everyone else); my father was not in command of his house but sadly believed that he was.

I must also remark that Julius somehow immediately understood the nature of this imperiled relationship between my father and my brother—imperiled by the misunderstanding between the older and the younger man, a misunderstanding which could survive interminably without affecting malignant result so long as the singularly apposite and dangerous third party never appeared, that third party who was uniquely designed to reveal and exploit that misunderstanding.

My cousin was, by exquisitely perfected design and by exquisitely dangerous timing, *the* man meant to serve as the belligerent puff of ill-wind against my family's half-known, half-unwitting, house of cards. Julius was suited perfectly to be the catalyst for tragic uproar in my seemingly endless childhood idyll, and he appeared at the point at which greatest vulnerabilities were about to be revealed.

Yet Julius would also require a unique catalytic moment to reveal his powers as destroyer. At this point—at this first supper of his first day in old Pauktaug—what was sinister in my Cousin Julius was only just detecting the potential for weakness in my family.

"We are ever so pleased you are finally among us, dear nephew," said my father as he took his chair.

I could see the warmth and simple sincerity in his eye. I followed this look to my cousin and then back to my father, and it was then that I noted my father's sudden, slight, childish look of deflation as Ellsworth exercised his first powers of principal command in lieutenancy in my cousin's presence.

Julius appeared to be aware suddenly of the same subtle censure of eye from senior son to father which I had observed, as well. At that moment, Julius realized the order of command in my family. But he could not yet have been certain, I am sure, as to the substance of the censure.

"The honor—being here in your fine home—is altogether mine, uncle," replied Julius as he made a first attempt to read the cipher of my brother's brow and his tightly crossed and folded arms. If my cousin read something of a caution to my father from Ellsworth about his suspected nature, Julius would have been correct, but only in small part. Ellsworth's silent communication was in greater part a reminder to my father of the anxiety that he himself had borne at the original announcement of the impending first visit of any of his English family to his home in America. My father was obtuse enough to have failed to realize that we, my brother and I, had noticed that original anxiety; or obtuse enough to have forgotten by then that we had noticed it; or obtuse enough, in the extreme, to fail to recall that he had ever had such extreme misgivings about the prospect of having witnesses from the English Crabbes in our home. But Ellsworth's silent communication was in greatest part a reproach to my father on an entirely different count.

My father brought not only a childlike hope to each period of my mother's recoveries from her consumption but, worse, a childlike forgetfulness. He seemed to meet her illness's remissions as if they were truly an end to her sickness. My brother and I, of course, entertained a similar hope, but my father seemed to demonstrate no expectation that my mother's cycles of health and sickness were part of an inescapable pattern.

Thus he was devastated each time my mother's ghostly pallor would completely return; devastated each time her agonized fits of coughing and weakness would compel her to confinement, and then compel him to respond as a child—with the angry retaliation as that of a little boy decrying for the first time the inequities of sickness and death. Yet perhaps it was, in part, this very pattern in my father—his meeting each of my mother's relapses as if it were the first time she had contracted such a physical misfortune—that compelled such an effective fight to be mounted against each of her bouts of consumption.

For when each time she descended anew into the darkest stretches of her bloody coughing, of her intensified pallor, of the strain and tightening upon her limbs and face (which, strangely, seemed at the same time to reinforce a childlike prettiness and fragility in her appearance), my father would employ all the finest physicians our family's considerable wealth could afford—all imported from New York City. Some were paid to stay in attendance at all hours. Whether it was from the effectiveness and intensity of these ministrations, or whether my mother's constitution naturally allowed her to have periods in which she could rally from her worst confrontations with her illness, is impossible to say.

However, at the end of each stretch of her illness, my father would dismiss the physicians and exult in the triumph of wealth and means against nearly any misfortune. And perhaps there was some justification behind the logic in such celebrations, but Ellsworth always regretted my father's naïve impulse to rejoice as if each victory were final and complete. This is not to say that Ellsworth did not share wholeheartedly in my father's faith in the power of wealth and the material; on the contrary, my brother's faith in them was comprehensive and unremitting. Ellsworth felt convinced that their power should never relent, that the doctors should be employed at all times, that all manner of treatments should be engaged in a constant, tireless, war—in a campaign that anticipated regressions. Ellsworth did not reproach my father for celebrating the power of our means, but for celebrating incomplete triumphs. My brother would have brooked the gaudiest celebration, had it been more in honor of the material powers that were still in excess and in reserve, so long as my father had made it clear that he would continue to operate the family business to such a degree that material gain was unlimited—so that material expenditure could also be unlimited. Ellsworth did not fear to use our arsenal—even unto a constant firing of even many unaimed and expensive rounds—so long as the magazine was restocked in a manner of exponential compensation and resupply. For every bullet fired a cannonball had to be procured to replace it for the future according to Ellsworth. Of course it was my father's original philosophies that had led to my brother's convictions. But if my father was a minor prophet and founder of a faith, Ellsworth was a builder of cathedrals, a monstrous architect of Romish pomp and solidness—all whilst living within an exterior aesthetic that only inspired pride and merely moderate resentment to our more humble Yankee neighbors and employees.

Yet my father was weak in a critical way; he undertook the American experiment only so long as it was pleasant—yet he had never been tested by unpleasantness. Somehow, unlike hundreds of other barons, he had ascended without conflict. He had become wealthy without ruthlessness, and thus his deeper faith in the material world was limited—or his faith in its remedial applications was limited—when he felt unsettled in his mind and spirit, for he had done no real battle to gain or possess it. And so his tender, ongoing, romance with my mother had somehow made him associate the means expended for use in the fight against her illness with the very illness itself, and thus he began to form dangerous and peculiar associations when she became well—as if her recoveries and the end of exorbitant financial and material hemorrhages were somehow united in a manner outside of mere cause and consequence. Sometimes the relapse of her illness would follow the cure so quickly that while he was still paying the cure's bill the disease would reappear. He connected all of this in a strange way. It was as if he began to believe that removing the cyclic cure applied to a cyclic illness might prevent its recurrence. It was as if he believed that though railings on the mountaintop of health prevented plummeting, they at the same time lure one to the edge. It was as if some deep, original, guilt made him believe that all prosperity led to dangerous figurative gouts. Though my father had exulted and triumphed in the experiment of a freely competitive economy of the American way, though he had made us exult in the process of gain and security and wild affluence, he had developed in those years just before my cousin's arrival, a tragic misconception that our wealth both stopped yet somehow perpetuated the agonizing process of my mother's sufferings.

In addition to his innate weaknesses, my father had developed this highly specialized vulnerability to its peak just at the time of my cousin's arrival, but he had not yet applied the most dangerous aspects of the peculiar associations which had formed in his mind concerning our great wealth and my mother's illness. Thus in addition to all that my made my father vulnerable before the judgment of my English relatives, my father displayed this peculiar belief of his in ways that made Ellsworth silently enraged—and in ways that would spark the most belligerent and predatory instincts of our new houseguest.

Thus it was on account of my father's foolish face of unjustified contentment that my brother delivered not only his subtle furrowing of brow, but also his demonstration of silent reproach via his crossed arms. To my father's general credit, and in credit to his sense of allegiance, he seemed to understand that Ellsworth's silent remonstrations not only checked him in this his most recent cyclical overestimation of my mother's health but also for the misleading impression and implications his demeanor might leave upon a visitor towards whom my brother was feeling increasing compunctions.

Though my father responded dutifully and subtly, the result of Ellsworth's efforts produced a change that appeared to any cunning outsider as only an increased awkwardness and vulnerability in my father. For now he appeared as a guard put on watch, but one who broadcast his ineptness to protect his charge after Ellsworth had had to give the subtle command to cease inordinate hospitality.

It was clear that my cousin sensed this much as the servants presented us with soup after grace. My father's attempt to appear suddenly more guarded and worldly played rather pitifully.

"Julius, would you share with me your account of the present state of things with my—our—family's enterprise back home?"

Both the words *our* and *home* offended Ellsworth; he raised his eyebrows with a critical flare.

"Dear uncle," replied Julius, "things are looking better for the company."

"I am glad to hear that," said my father. "Of course your welcome from us here does not depend upon my brothers' continued ill fortunes."

"You mean to say an offer of a place in your company here still stands, no matter if my father can soon afford to recall me?" asked my cousin, with a look that seemed to appraise the weaknesses beyond the superficial power of the offer.

"Why, yes, of course it—" began my father in reply. Before he could finish, he chanced to look again to the right. There sat Ellsworth with his reproachful, folded, arms.

"Why, yes, Julius! Of course it does!" interposed my mother with a laugh over the gentle ringing of the service at table. "Your Uncle Charles is so easily flustered! Charles!"

"Yes! Yes! I do beg your pardon, nephew."

My cousin insisted that not a single pardon was necessary. He was likely telling the full truth with that assertion; for a deep and nearly altogether secreted pleasure stole across his face during the latest episode between my father and Ellsworth. My mother's evident obliviousness also seemed to please him.

"Yes! Yes! A young man of your experience and concern in the company will be more than a match for the humble challenges we can present here and the true needs we have at the Stays Works, dear nephew," offered my father after he recovered with my mother's assistance.

Ellsworth presented an incredible range of reaction to my father's last statement. To the general phrase, *young man of your experience*, Ellsworth seemed to have no objection, as if it matched his openness to hiring any valid prospect into the family business if he knew nothing untoward about him (for my brother was a fair man, I was sure, despite the ponderous superiority of his intellect and station); to the phrase, *and concern in the company,* insofar as it referenced my cousin's particular character and investment in his time with my father's family's company in England, Ellsworth seemed to feel already that even that involvement must have been ruled by underlying principles that would excite his deepest suspicions and ultimate contempt; it enraged Ellsworth—this, again, I could see in the voluble stricture of his folded arms—to hear our generally kingly but softly regal father refer to the merely "humble challenges" our Long Island factory could offer to Julius Crabbe. This is not to say that humility—and even an affectation of humility—in my father was always thought to be out of my place in Ellsworth's eyes; but there was a sincerity in this new expression and a new degree of humility, offered suddenly and without any other kind of precedent, exclusively for the delectation or rejection of Julius.

For myself, though a mere child of six—happily accepting the silent reproaches Ellsworth orchestrated against a father who seemed suddenly powerless against a threat that another type of man would never have permitted—I began to take exception to certain turns of phrase and degrees of accent that *should not* have been held against my father by his children. I cannot say if Ellsworth also added these infractions to his growing list of complaints against our father, but I know I felt utterly disappointed to hear that my father's ostensibly unique accent and way of speaking were not peculiar to him. Julius made it clear that my father's British English, his array of words that had seemed for all my life peculiar solely to my father—words and phrases that even permitted us to gently ridicule him, as if that affectionate mockery only praised something singular in him, something that he almost allowed us to believe had sprung forth independently from him—again, Julius made it clear that there was a familial source to these hitherto alleged singularities.

"Indeed!" my father would often exclaim in wonder at the tales Ellsworth and I would share with him concerning our rides and walks with the family horses and dogs in the surrounding Indian woods.

"Indeed!" my cousin would also utter—along with dozens of other words, phrases, and mannerisms—in natural echo to my father's same tendencies.

Perception of this parallel struck my girlish mother as quaint and charming; it is hard for me to say how it struck Ellsworth, for he was already wrestling with and preparing a defense against far more subtle threats from Julius. For me this discovery was chilling. My father was highly unnerved—one could read this in his brow and in his sudden careful choice of words—that I (and, of course, likely Ellsworth) had detected this similarity of familial speech.

Julius was all delight in this perception, told through a telling grin of silence—not so much when he detected this between my father and himself, and not much more when he saw me (and, again, likely Ellsworth) discover this for ourselves, and not even much more, still, when he saw my father recognize the pattern between uncle and nephew. No. But he was utterly, sinisterly, gratified as he beheld the moment when my father first realized that his sons had likely noted the shared traditions of expression and language.

The most chilling moment of all on this count came some minutes after Julius made this last observation, for in echo of no one, and with no intention or result of causing an echo, my cousin—with an awesome, subtle, devious, yet cool utterance of directly unchallenged power—simply uttered, whilst pausing between a gentle ladling of his soup, "Indeed!"

There was a long pause. Just as it was made clear that it might be Ellsworth who might break it with too great an intensity, or that my father might obliquely reveal an even greater degree of shattering uncertainty and meekness in himself, my mother beckoned that the soup setting be removed and asked Julius to please reassure us that all would be well with the family concerns back in England.

"Again, I do believe that all signs indicate the imminent full recovery of our trade and its routes. But it is the loss of the cause—the loss of time for the cause—that the family so laments."

"The cause?" my mother asked with innocence.

"Surely, from my Uncle Charles here you are made too aware of our family's declared mission of charity?" Julius betrayed a subtle realization of an imminent advantage as he asked this question.

"My husband, their father," responded my mother, with a tone of mock scolding for my father, "tells us so little of his past life with you all in England. And I fear that he has made life so gloriously sweet and comfortable for us here that I have to confess I, too, have felt little desire to ask about it—until now, of course. Charity, though! The cause! That sounds so right, so admirable! I know we can rely on *you*, dear Julius, to tell us all we need to know—to relieve us of our selfish frontier ignorance. And, remarkably—for you, dear Julius, sound so much like my husband, their father—I somehow feel as if it would be nearly the same to hear this news from you as if it had been coming from their father, my husband, for all of these years.

Though my mother made few pretences in front of this finished young Englishman, that our station could pass for one of exulted exclusivity in America, several of the affected traits my mother had cultivated since leaving her girlhood farm were now so strong, that she made a good show to Julius, confusing him as to how sincere her modesty really was. Her deliberate manner of speech, for example—her penchant for redundancies (her *my husband, their father*)—made a man who founded his connivances upon precise and devious uses of language and manner quite cautious at first. But when my mother naïvely intimated that Julius deeply resembled my father in manner and speech—and that it gave her pleasure to hear him speak as if in personal historical proxy for my father—my cousin realized that his only likely challenger of serious power would be Ellsworth.

Julius had already realized it would only take time to wear down the weaknesses of my father; and now he had sounded the limitations of my mother. She was quite simple, merely an unaffected and lovely object by his standards. I was, of course, only a child. Ellsworth was left to stand alone. But he was not yet to be engaged in his full and desperate combat against this invader. That would come months later.

"Our family, Aunt Ellen, has a long tradition, dating back to my great-grandfather, of working to amass wealth through the graces of our Empire so that we might assist other Britons in their climb from indigence, despair, and darkness. Indeed!"

My brother almost perceptibly recoiled at Julius' sly inclusive invocation of the term *our family*, and my cousin's now apparent leitmotivic use of the mild exclamation "Indeed!" delivered a residual shudder to any initial reactions Ellsworth had when my cousin spoke. Ellsworth would dart discreet looks in my father's direction, but my father affected to be busy with his silverware whenever he was not being addressed or speaking himself. However tenuous the hold, Ellsworth, I could see, still felt assured, however, that he had my father in some degree of thrall. Thus Ellsworth still said little and kept his defensive focus on our new guest.

There was another brief silence in the conversation as the servants presented a new course. As soon as this was settled—as if something in the gleam of our rare china service inspired the remark—my mother exclaimed: "Charity! That is a grand idea. And we are all indeed one family. Think what we, here, might do!"

This innocent and sincere statement marked a moment of critical importance in my family's history. In that moment Julius became assured of his ability to divide and conquer a family, an entity—for which he had already formed his complete desire to introduce chaos and dissolution, this desire motivated by the overwhelming and nearly preternatural jealousy he felt toward all of us, even when merely suspecting our love and comfort and security from afar. My mother, sadly, by altogether misinterpreting the latent and sinister glee on my cousin's face at that moment, formed a tragic sense of warmth towards her nephew. For he would share in our comfort and happiness as an American family *and*, at the same time, instruct us in the ways—or reinspire my father in the ways—of enlivening the world's poor from our ostensibly excessive prosperity. Indeed! The moment was of course critical for Ellsworth, and for me, as well, for we saw the glee in Julius' face, but we knew it for the threat that it was. And, finally, there was my father—he, too, set irrevocably on a track by this moment—for he could not raise his gaze to oppose the glee he knew must reside in my cousin's face. Thus my father announced that his will was for sale to the man or woman who could compel his averted gaze.

5.

The remaining dining time was spent giving audience to my cousin's protracted description for my mother of the English Crabbe's long history of philanthropy—and of how that history had never been in jeopardy until very recent years, when crises within and without the family's trade company had made mere survival paramount to the greater cause. It was when descriptions of these crises were at their height, and when my mother's enthusiasm and sympathy seemed to be raised nearly to the point that she was close to insisting that the prosperous American Crabbe's should undertake a part in reestablishing the flow of the family cause that my father suddenly found the courage to interrupt and insist that Julius deserved a tour of our home and grounds before the evening light had altogether passed. It was late spring, and the day was a long one—affording us a clear light to conduct a tour through the house and down toward our beach and the Sound before it was time to retire for the night.

My father appointed my brother to lead the tour, and Ellsworth began by showing our cousin the rather commanding library my father had accumulated—one filled with an astounding collection of not only finely bound classical volumes, but also an impressive range of English and American authors. Of the American writers, my father's collection boasted a rarefied assembly of everything philosophical, theological, and speculative which could pour from that great Niagara of ink and thought: New England. For all my father's intellectual limitations, he seemed to pride himself on the completeness of his Transcendentalist collection, as if he felt that his patronizing of the American literary avant-garde was either a way to maintain one vestigial part of the old family cause or—possibly *and*—a way to elevate his intellectual perception by outsiders if solely by association with prominently displayed book spines.

It did please my father that Ellsworth began the tour with our library; little did he realize, however, that my brother gave that tour not as an indication of my father's prowess of mind, but as a warning to Julius of his own acuities. My father would not have been disappointed had he known this, for he was proud that Ellsworth did pore over the volumes of our library with an awesome intensity; he did not merely have a command over the newest of New England streams of thought, he could be said to utterly *know* them.

As well, my father already had formed a fear of Julius, but not having the strength or cleverness of mind to orchestrate a strategy for defense, he hoped that all of Ellswoth's gestures were undertaken for that purpose. Julius, however, only seemed to emerge from the first part of this tour with the confidence that my brother felt threatened enough to begin the display of his arsenal (and thus reveal the potential for his vulnerability). With that display came the oblique assurance that my father was the true lieutenant, one silly enough to hope that an external library was sound proxy for an absence of solid mind and character; and, too, my cousin further emerged with the confidence—should any of our family truly be engaged in reading—that only fools wasted their time on speculative matters that ostensibly only led to more speculative matters. There are book-learned gentlemen who acquire a sound contempt for bibliophiles; there are also book-learned men who take that contempt unto a dangerous level of presumption and self-confidence. Julius was among the latter.

We adjourned next to the second floor, where my father had set aside a suite for my brother's carefully acquired collections. Displayed on racks and mountings, on dark, richly paneled walls, in one room was Ellsworth's large collection of American, English, and Continental firearms. In the next two chambers—my favorite rooms—were my brother's collections of fossils and rare coins, acquired through years of careful correspondence and bartering with other affluent collectors.

My brother, despite all his sound suspicions concerning Julius, graciously lingered in his fossil chamber when our cousin confirmed that fossil and coin collecting were also passions of his own. With evident strain—evident, perhaps, solely to me—Ellsworth indulged my cousin's questions about the collection; and my brother, as well, perversely escalated his forced hospitality when he saw that the shared interest in collecting between our cousin and himself seemed to please our father, or at least permit our father unwisely to defer facing the conflict that was inexorably set in motion as soon as my cousin and brother met.

My mother was utterly pleased to observe the conversation between my brother and cousin concerning the fossil collection. She took this as a sign of a halcyon season ahead, and she led

Julius—they walking arm in arm—down through our back gardens and the slope to our beach along the Sound.

Our beach was among the objects of my mother's greatest vanity concerning our property and possessions, and on a nearly yearly basis my mother would command of my father that all of the walkways and trellises and gazebos that she had ordered built there were to see either the most elaborate of maintenance or utter replacement. The mere sign of faded or chipping paint or of corrosion from collected salt set my mother to setting legions of carpenters and painters to restoring the beach works to a nearly new appearance.

Out onto a perfectly finished boardwalk we all went in the last hues of the late spring twilight. My mother and father remained on the boardwalk above the sand with Julius. Ellsworth led me down to the water's edge where some abandoned garden tools I had commandeered as toys lay in wait at the water's edge. Two rusted shovels and a large garden hoe remained where I had left them, just out of reach of the high tide mark. I looked back at my mother and father as they swung their arms boastfully, so as to point out distant objects of possible interest to Julius—sights that faded from view as the evening advanced.

Ellsworth looked back upon that trio, as well, as he and I took up the shovels in anticipation of my favorite game of building canals and fragile creeks in the wet sand. He squinted back to the boardwalk in the dim light, and if it was not the lapping of the mild breakers creating a dull sibilance in the quiet air, then I might say my brother let out a nearly imperceptible snarl or growl as he uncrossed his arms and took up one of the shovels.

He softened his grim expression, however, as he looked down to me and gave my hair a rough rub. I was happy when he did that, for it was the same brusque gesture he gave to each of our hounds after they would return from running free in the east woods—often returning then with an astonished but unharmed tortoise or two clenched in their jaws.

"What should we play?" asked Ellsworth as he pushed the spade into the damp, slick, sand that met the very edge of the strongest small waves.

"Let's make the Hudson," I said, and I began to construct a river that led to the Sound—the Sound serving, then, as New York Harbor. My brother smiled, and then almost began to assist me in this. He suddenly stopped, however, and fell into a brief reverie as he looked north toward Connecticut across the Sound.

"No. What do you say we shovel against the sea tonight?" Ellsworth asked.

I enjoyed that game. We took several paces forward—so that the tips of our toes (we had taken off our shoes)—were lapped when the stoutest of the Sound's generally small waves broke on the slope of the wet sand. When we stood at the water's true edge—and could see from there the gentle, small, swarms of ancient horseshoe crabs gliding on the rocky bottom of the clear water; and could see around us, and just behind us, the tracks which their tails, like dry pen nibs, had drawn in the smooth sand—we began to each dig our own holes. The contest was to see who could keep his little ditch the driest for the longest time. At the water's edge, the challenge was posed not only by the water that would pour in from the mild surf itself but also from the sea water that seeped up from below—from where clams and mysterious sand worms liked to conceal themselves.

Ellsworth could always win at this game, and I liked to play if only to watch the fury with which he could shovel. We would often pause and laugh, and take no account of who appeared to be winning. I paused myself that night to laugh and wipe my brow. My brother continued to dig with passion that evening. I looked back to my mother and father continuing to show Julius the property from the vantage of the beach gazebo—showing it with an ingratiating manner that made it almost appear from a distance as if he were the prospective proprietor or holder of our deed—but my brother did not look back.

He shoveled against the unremitting sea—and I'll be blasted down to the dark reaches where those clams and worms lurk if he didn't seem to keep his little sand valley utterly dry for what seemed a nearly frozen but ultimately limited moment of permanence.

At last he had to stop, and we all retired up the hill and to the house; and, of course, the water erased our efforts, and the horse-shoe crabs continued to glide over the featureless sand like hawks at evening over the prairie.

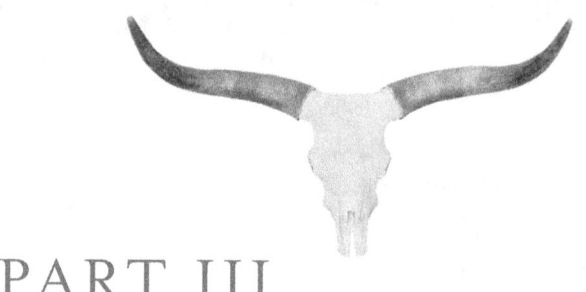

PART III

Shoveling Against the Plains

I.

I awoke on the morning of my second day in the new Pauktaug at half past three. Darkness and bright moonlight pervaded my room, but the sound of riders—and of many tethered horses stomping upon the ground in the cool, dry, night air—is what woke me from a deep sleep. Knowing that someone would soon be coming to wake me, I rose and washed quickly, and dressed myself for the ride that was ahead.

As I had expected, just as I was finishing with my boots, McCarthy knocked at my door. He had a splendid plate of steak and eggs for me, that somehow I managed to consume in the mere three to four minutes during which McCarthy described his ride out onto the land where I had said I had found Kettle's body.

"I drove out, Mr. Crabbe, to where you said I would find your dead man. And wouldn't you know it but his body lay just where you said it would. There's no proper law here! We need law here! No offense to your brother or to Mr. Whisker—for they're good, fine, law-abiding men—but we need a *lawman* here in town. Any real law is always days—weeks, even—away."

At this point McCarthy paused in his overly deferential way, sure in his expectation that a man of my station should be given room at such a juncture to say something severe. I could not bring myself to pause from the steak, eggs, and coffee for an instant. But after I took a few more aggressive heaps of food, I felt obliged to say something for the sake of McCarthy's pleading silence.

"So you say there is no law here? No constable, no marshal, no sheriff? Then things like this have happened before, or have been happening?"

"No, sir, they haven't! But I knew—I *knew*—they would! Things just couldn't keep on going so perfect-like all the time. And how—just how?—are we expected to grow if we don't finally gain some law?"

"Well, I am sure that a time comes when all new towns are required to make a formal appeal for law?" I asked.

"Mr. Crabbe, won't you use your influence with your brother— if I may dare to presume upon you with such a question—and tell him, insist to him, that the time has come for us to have a lawman in this town?"

"I will certainly see what I can do," I answered.

As my hunger was satisfied, my mind turned to things that under any other circumstance would have been foremost in my consideration. To begin with, as McCarthy's voice continued on concerning the arrival of lawlessness in the new Pauktaug, I suddenly realized that I had not felt the impulse to cough, not even once, since rising that morning. Despite the exhausting and disturbing events of the previous days, and notwithstanding the gruesome discovery of lonesome Kettle's ivory body under the moonlight the night before, I had slept deeply.

During sleep I still had to be cautious how I lay in bed on account of the pain and soreness of my cracked ribs (for they would be slow to heal), but when I realized I had not coughed even once that morning, I felt compelled to poke and prod at the sore spots just to make sure some kind of supernatural healing had not occurred.

The tenderness of my own ribs suddenly reinforced the horror of the memory of the porcelain whiteness of Kettle's mutilated and impaled body. My own comfort and returning health filled me with a surge of shame and wonder. I looked at McCarthy and saw him looking to me with an astounding degree of interest in anything I might say about the situation. Unfortunately, it was I who had been hoping that he might know how to explain such a death. In the awkward silence, I made reference to my experience as town constable in the old Pauktaug.

"Back East I spent the last five years serving as the village constable, and I've seen a few dead men in my time, but I have never seen anything like what I saw last night."

"Neither have I, Mr. Crabbe!" exclaimed McCarthy. "He was crushed and pounded—and stabbed by something that seemed too big and strong for any man to weld!" He had meant to say *wield*, I am certain. "I've heard tell of stampedes flattening a man, but there was no sign of anything like a herd, I'd say. But what do I know? I've always just been a town man!"

"Do you suspect he was killed deliberately?" I asked. "You know this country. Do you suspect some kind of foul play? Do you think, say, one or some of Whisker's men killed him? Perhaps this Rutledge fellow and his men?" All these question I asked in close succession.

"How can I say? I ain't never seen nothing like that. I'm just a town man. Had it not been you asking, I could never have touched that body the way it was, all gruesome and such!"

McCarthy paused for a moment and then exclaimed with real conviction, and not a little irritation and dependent pleading toward me, "That's why we need someone like you here. That's why we need you, Mr. Crabbe!"

106

"Need me?" I replied.

"Yes, as our lawman," said McCarthy.

I laughed and rose from my table, and I began the last efforts of dressing to go downstairs.

"I'm not a lawman for this kind of place. I don't know what it was I saw last night any more than you do!" I was immediately sorry that I said that, for I was vain of the deference that a man like McCarthy was already paying me in that new country, and I hoped to cultivate that further. But I could see that his decision to delegate authority to me was still undiminished. And I was vain, as well, of the fact that McCarthy did not seem at all inclined to suspect me of having had a hand in the killing.

"Sure, Mr. Crabbe, your brother and Mr. Whisker are good and powerful men, but they're businessmen—they don't have the time to see to such things. And now such things have arrived in our town. And everyone else is just bent on serving Mr. Whisker and your brother, sir."

"Such things have just arrived in your town, you say. I just arrived in town myself; how come you are sure that I have not brought this sudden death with me?" I exclaimed with a scoff as I made the effort to pull on my boots.

"You have the look of a man to be trusted, Mr. Crabbe. I trust the way you look. And, besides, you were a constable back East. We need you here, Mr. Crabbe. I heard tell that Mr. Whisker and your brother, sir, were given power by the governor to appoint someone to marshal when they felt they could make a choice. They are what you call practically the defactew mayors of Pauktaug, after all." I am sure he meant to say *de facto*.

McCarthy paused and then added: "And I am sure this death and your coming are what they call just a coincidence."

Hoping to deflect the nepotistic request that McCarthy was asking that I make of my brother, I returned to a few questions of my own once more.

"Again, you do not think it was the men from Whisker's place who might somehow have done this?"

"Mr. Crabbe, I say again: How could I really know? But I would think that Whisker's men would never carry out any business like that on your brother's land. But come to think of it, no matter how much Whisker's men—Mitch Rutledge and his boys—might rough up a fellow for trespassing, I haven't heard tell of any lesson being taught to such a degree—ever—by anyone in these parts. But Mr. Crabbe, who, what, do you think could have done such a thing?"

"I cannot say. It did not look like the work of a man, but nor did it appear to be the work of an animal. It seemed almost as if it had a precision and violence to it that would demand the agency of both."

"Can you twist that a bit simpler?" McCarthy asked. I did not answer.

Though I felt an urge to form an alliance with someone in town outside of my brother—and McCarthy seemed as likely a candidate as anyone since the demise of my traveling companion, Kettle—I suddenly felt as if I were entering into too much of an alliance too soon with Mr. McCarthy.

I made it clear I was ready to go downstairs to meet the rescue party that was assembling in the hotel lobby and just outside on the street. As McCarthy and I passed out of my room and made our way to the stairs, it was clear to me I should change the tenor of our discussion so as to ensure myself some distance from McCarthy as a confidante.

"That was a very fine steak, Mr. McCarthy. Might it have come from my brother's stock?" I had forgotten I had asked a similar question the night before, but for the second answering I received not only a repetition of the reply of the previous night, but also a bit more speculation on a further answer.

"No, Mr. Crabbe. Everything we've been serving for quite some time has been coming from Mr. Whisker's stock. I imagine your brother's stock would taste very much the same, coming, as it does, from the same original Texas stock, and running as it does on nearly the same kind of ground and grass and water as does Mr. Whisker's. But, again, no. Your brother has not sold to us, or anyone, I think, in maybe about a year—nothing from his increase, nothing at all, is the word, not even in the fall."

"To no one? Nothing? How can that be?" I asked as we reached the middle landing of stairs on the descent to the lobby.

"I have lived in this country, cow country, for nearly all of my life—though I came up here from Texas—and I can say that it strikes me as pretty odd, pretty strange—and it gives most other men here something to wonder about, too, I am sure. But then again I'm no cattle man, and as Mr. Crabbe is one of the most prosperous new men in this country, I—and nearly everyone else in this country—can't really say too much about it. He certainly brings new ways with him, Mr. Crabbe does."

McCarthy and I reached the lobby, and even though the first light of dawn was still some time off, the floor creaked under the weight of dozens of cowhands who were passing in and out of the dining hall, where breakfast awaited them as the assembly continued to grow in anticipation of the arrival of Ellsworth.

Before the power of the imminent day took hold, I was eager to ask a few more questions of McCarthy, especially as the noise of boots and spurs allowed for easy discretion.

"You say my brother stopped shipping stock to market last year. But what of the years before?" I asked.

"If I recall things properly, Mr. Crabbe, your brother and Mr. Whisker both arrived on the ground that would be Pauktaug with already sizeable herds they drove up from Texas. They were already wealthy men, and they built this town. And they seemed to know—even as Easterners—how to increase their stock by record rates. But as I said, about a year ago, I heard tell that nothing in Mr. Crabbe's stock was for sale. He seems to want to hoard it up for a spell, I imagine. It was about a year ago, as well, that he brought in men to start fencing in his entire range. That's the first I've heard of such a thing in this country. And after that you hardly saw any of his hands in town. But they did work on the spring roundup with Whisker's men on Whisker's range, along with a few other reps from this country, as small as that roundup was—very small, what with your brother's stock fenced in and Mr. Whisker having sold off nearly all of his herd last year. But everyone is still right neighborly here still and helps everyone else."

"Is that customary out here on occasion—to stop selling stock for a long period of time?" I asked.

"No," answered McCarthy, "I can't say as I ever heard of any such thing. But your brother built this town, built a fortune, built himself a great herd. I am sure he knows his business. Perhaps he's bringing a newer and better kind of business out here. Again, I'm not really one who could tell you. I'm a town man after all."

Amidst the noise I suddenly made an involuntary statement that I had not intended McCarthy to hear: "Strange, but it was also sometime last year that I told my brother I intended to come out here to him."

"I'm sorry, Mr. Crabbe, sir; I did not hear exactly what you said."

I made a quick recovery: "I said I hope you can direct me to my brother."

"Yes, of course, sir. I don't know that he has arrived yet, but he is due presently. Holy Moses! I've haven't seen so many Crabbe hands since last year. I don't know where you brother hides 'em all, but they sure is the best outfitted hands I've ever seen! But, yes, he's due presently."

McCarthy and I made our way through a lobby with cowhands who were still walking in and out of the dining room with scalding hot cups of coffee in their hands. We walked to the outside, to the hotel's front porch, and there I saw the familiar street of Pauktaug again, just as it would have appeared back East in the time before dawn on any given morning, but filled then with a strange and exotic scent of prairie incense and filled, too, with dozens of riders and horses who cluttered the air with equally exotic sounds.

The crowd outdoors was being augmented from all of the riders leaving the hotel. The sounds as that of dozens of orchestral triangles gently rang as rider after rider rose upward, as they mounted their horses, and from where I stood, slightly above that roiling mass of dark horses—that mass looking, then, like a swath of muddy range come alive—the scene of climbing men looked like a prairie dog village snapping to attention. Many of the faces of the riders were no less whiskery than so many prairie dogs.

Soon my brother, atop a strong, sinewy, ivory-colored horse, came clearly into view. The horse was indeed strong, for it demonstrated no sign of appearing disburdened in any way, as Ellsworth's swarthy frame dismounted from the saddle. As he climbed the two short steps to the hotel's porch, the crowd of men all fell into a concerted silence. Even the horses appeared to snap to attention in deference to Ellsworth.

The men, assembled now in the comfortable chill of the summer morning darkness, were all my brother's hands. Though I learned that a sizeable force of men had been left behind on Ellsworth's range with the great herd, this formidable group had been summoned for the rescue mission.

And when this crew of several dozen men fell to silence, it was not out of a soldierly obeisance, but nor was it from brotherly affection. Theirs was a cheerful compliance—completely unwavering, it seemed—based upon some unknown precedent or condition. Perhaps theirs was the extra compliance of normally faithful men augmented when their latent mercenary weaknesses were exploited. I could not say; all was still a mystery to me.

"Men!" Ellsworth was able to exclaim at a civilized volume, for all were so silent and attentive, "I thank you for this ride, this unexpected ride, you are about to make. I trust it will soon be over and all will be well for those we are hoping to relieve. In any event, you will all find my appreciation amply expressed when next you go to draw pay from Pope Pope!"

"Hell, it's just good to be back in town!" shouted a hand from the crowd. This met with a general laugh, including one from Ellsworth.

"We're all itchin' to go out to that coach for you, Mr. Crabbe!" shouted another hand. There was a beautiful tinkling of spurs and clatter of cold weaponry as general seconding murmurs followed the anonymous exclamation.

"Boys! Before we leave, an introduction is in order. This is Campbell Crabbe. He is my brother. You will all answer to him as you would to me. This is my sole living true relative, and I rejoice that he has returned himself to me and has come to this country!"

He embraced me as he finished this last phrase, and though I was pleased by the evident warmth and sincerity of his gesture, and though it was true that it was I who had traveled to him—I who had truly returned myself to him—I still found the remark somehow unsettling, for it had been Ellsworth who had originally parted from us all back East so many years before and who had vanished to parts unknown.

"Boys! I sent riders out yesterday as soon as I had word about the stage. They came in distant sight of it, but they could not get close. The stage is under siege, boys. Let's ride!"

"Ellsworth! Wait!" I shouted to my brother as the men made their last preparations to leave. "Mr. McCarthy and I have something we need to tell you."

"What is it, Cam?" my brother asked, and he folded his arms in a gesture that seemed to say he would halt the entire expedition for my sake if necessary.

"I found a body, last night on your land, not far from the entrance gate" I said.

"*You* found a body! What were you doing out on the range alone at night? That can get a stranger killed out here!"

"I can see that. But it was the man that made much of the trip with me from the railroad out here to this new Pauktaug. It was the man you helped yesterday morning when you found us in the saloon."

"Well, I warned him. And see what happened!" Ellsworth grunted.

"But he was on *your* land!" I said.

"Had he been shot?" Ellsworth demanded; he looked eager to get the ride started.

"No, it looked more like he had been stabbed, repeatedly—wildly. But I could not say what could have done such a thing."

"Where's the body?" asked my brother.

"It's out back, in the hotel ice house, Mr. Crabbe," said McCarthy. "I can show you," he added eagerly, and he began to step in that direction, as if Ellsworth and I were sure to follow.

"Not now, McCarthy. We'll have to resolve this later, after we get back."

"But Mr. Crabbe, sir, this kind of thing has reached our town now, *your* town, now. I've seen this kind of thing before in other places, and this is why we're going to need law, law and order, here, Mr. Crabbe, no matter how splendid you make it here for us."

I was impressed by Ellsworth's reply, for whilst losing none of the authority he appeared to command over McCarthy, he was able to make a quiet concession of significant sympathy.

"I agree with you, McCarthy. We do need a lawman for things like this—and for things generally. When I return from this ride, Mr. Whisker (if he has returned from Texas by now) and I will get down to the business of appointing someone until the county or state finally decides what it wishes to do with us."

"Oh, thank you, Mr. Crabbe! Thank you! You're such a good man to us all! What can I get you before you leave?"

"Thank you, McCarthy, but we are ready to ride now," Ellsworth said quietly.

"Yes, sir, Mr. Crabbe—and you, too, Mr. Crabbe—you all come back safely now!" said McCarthy to us both.

McCarthy went back into the hotel, and Ellsworth gave a signal to a cowhand at the north end of the crowd of riders, and that rider set the entire herd of men and horses into motion after him. After the last of Ellsworth's hands left their stirred dust behind in the early morning darkness of Main Street, Mr. Pope, my brother's foreman, emerged from the obscurity and made it clear he awaited Ellsworth's signal. My brother held up a hand to Mr. Pope, as if to ask him to wait for just a moment longer.

"Cam, how do you feel?" Ellsworth asked me.

"I feel splendid—strong. I really do. I don't need to stay behind."

My brother uncrossed his arms and took me by the shoulder. He gave me a mild, probational shake.

"Yes, indeed! Splendid! I think you are fit to ride. I am sorry these are the circumstances under which we are to have our first ride together, but at the same time I could not be more pleased. And we could need you out there—in case questions about the coach come up, questions that only someone on that last run could answer."

As I look back upon this exchange, I cannot believe I was permitted to ride. No matter how I must have felt, I am certain I looked near death, and I probably was. Yet I was glad of my brother's permission.

"Pope Pope!" my brother cried, and Mr. Pope gently goaded his horse to the edge of the steps on which Ellsworth and I stood. He led a riderless horse behind him, saddled and clearly ready for the mission of the morning. As a specimen of horse it was nearly a twin to my brother's own magnificent white mount.

"He's yours, Cam," my brother said as he nodded to the riderless horse. I could only think to nod back the enormity of my thanks and to approach the horse without hesitation. During the few moments I took to admire the sleek and muscled strength of an animal that Ellsworth had surely imported west at great expense, my brother followed the point of Mr. Pope's eyes to a particular saddle bag astride this horse.

From that bag he removed a new gun belt wrapped around two new, perfectly machined, ivory-handled Colt revolvers. "To make up for what the Constable of old Pauktaug lost on the trail in order to make his way to the new Pauktaug," my brother said as he handed me the belt. "Most men only carry one gun with them out here, so I'd be discreet about the second one," he added.

"I am ever so glad you're back, Cam!" Ellsworth said as he gave me one more brotherly shake of the shoulders, and then he mounted his own horse.

What was I to make of that phrase? *I* was not back. *He*, in a way, was the one who was back, for it was he who had left me and old Pauktaug so many years ago. But then, again, perhaps he did not make a distinction between the two Pauktaugs—indeed it was hard to do so in fact in the darkness before dawn—and perhaps felt that he had only left the old Pauktaug to make it to a better, or to *the* better one, and thus it was indeed *I* who had returned. I could not say, for what with the gravity of the ride ahead, and what with the sentimental trepidation I still felt around my brother, despite the warm and unquestionably loving though somehow vague welcome he gave me, I neither had the opportunity nor the sense of ease to gather any sure meaning from Ellsworth's words or gestures.

As I put on the gunbelt, my brother gave a nod to Mr. Pope to indicate that I was his charge for the time being, and Ellsworth set his horse into a gallop so as to overtake the main group—but not before relinquishing the look of pleasure and joy that had spread across his face during his last exchange with me. Had it not been that Ellsworth had to take the reins in order to guide his horse, and had to keep his arms free in order to keep his balance, I would have placed a bet that he would have crossed his arms again with a tightness to match the fixed stare and scowl he leveled against the challenging and morbid openness of the endless, dark, open range.

2.

After I was atop my new horse—and reveling in the creaking of an extremely fine new saddle (but of a style to which I was not accustomed)—Mr. Pope and I exchanged nods and were off in close pursuit of Ellsworth.

By the time the town was well behind us—and only appeared in vague, dark, miniature, over one's shoulder—an early dawn hue brought a blue dustiness to the range and sky. Ellsworth had caught up with the main group, and that wide, dense, train of men and horses sent up a constant tendril of dust as if an earthen, wild, rail-less locomotive was slowly making its way north then eastward toward the besieged coach and to the small rail terminus town that lay beyond.

Mr. Pope seemed content to remain with me for quite some time, we about a half-mile or more behind the main group. At some later date it occurred to me that not only had my brother appointed Mr. Pope to accompany me on that first active day and ride in the country of new Pauktaug, but also as a trusted storyteller of Ellsworth's place and achievements in the new country. Yet I did not find Mr. Pope's quiet narrative to have been forced upon him by any mercenary's obligations toward praise.

Despite a profound reticence between phrases, I felt that this Mr. Pope quite admired my brother—on both practical *and* on more inscrutable and speculative levels. I also suspected that this Pope may have welcomed anything I may have offered about my brother's Eastern past. Yet I quickly made it clear by reticence—if I was even correct in this latter suspicion—that I would offer nothing along those lines. I felt relatively certain that Ellsworth—at least among men in his employ—had developed no extreme confidences.

So I found it remarkable that Mr. Pope had been appointed to relay to me certain critical points of Ellsworth's history in the West, as I was being thrown suddenly and vigorously into that same West myself.

Mr. Pope—after we settled into an aggressive and constant trot—began by offering something of his own history. But it was that history's gray corners and unspoken mysteries that seemed to hint at Mr. Pope's apparent contentment to remain in his station, for perhaps he was always obliged to confront his gratitude towards Ellsworth's faithful employment of him before any individual ambition could fester into an agent unrest. At the same time, there seemed to be an intellectual profundity to the man that may have accounted, more than anything else, for not only his eerily quiet contentment, but also for his admiration for Ellsworth, an admiration based as if upon muted intellectual grounds that even between the two of them still remained entirely unspoken and only within the realm of suspicion.

Though this Mr. Pope—a lean, compact man, most likely a few years shy of fifty years of age—had grown up in Texas amidst cows and cattle, he had fostered and realized ambitions to go east and attend seminary. For some years he had returned home and had in fact served in the ministry, but was compelled to resign after an incident which later gave his own conscience no shame, but which dishonored the sensibilities of his parishioners, and made it impossible for him to remain in the church.

Whilst making it clear that he was reluctant to offer any more significant details to me, Mr. Pope conceded that though he understood why common men would think it impossible for him to return to service, it was still, he felt, a great shame that he could not, considering he was certain that both his clear conscience and God's judgment of his fitness for service rendered his loss to the church significant.

This mysterious and nameless shame compelled him to fall back once more for employment upon his original flocks: longhorn cattle. He soon became the supremely trusted man of Ellsworth's outfit from my brother's earliest days in that business. He told me that men in both Ellsworth's and Mr. Whisker's outfits—and most hands in the cow business—had thought it comical that a former minister should have had the surname of Pope, and thus, though he had never dabbled in Catholicism, he found himself branded (with no apparent chagrin, however) with the range name of Pope Pope. He never mentioned his Christian name; though surely no traditional Christian name could compare with the impression that his nickname and true surname delivered together.

Somehow this odd history, combined with what appeared to be a quiet and rarefied set of thinking powers—and, to boot, some of the best cowman's and foreman's skills in the territory—not only made him the perfect man to serve one of the fastest growing baronial concerns in that part of the new country in respect to business matters, but also somehow uniquely suited to be the witness and interpreter of Ellsworth's own great, unique, and obliquely paramount intellectual purposes.

After three hours of riding we caught up with the main group as it watered its horses at a small spring. We seemed to be riding a different route to the besieged stage coach than the stage road itself offered; I did not recall seeing the signs of such an oasis when I had made my grueling march on foot in the opposite direction.

Ellsworth and I did not exchange any words at this stopping point; instead, he passed by quickly and silently—seeming pleased to allow me to adapt without any mentoring or nursing from him.

Perhaps he even kept his distance so that I would grow accustomed to command in his absence, for his men already seemed to presume that my word was second only to Ellsworth's on the Crabbe range.

After all the horses were watered, I was told we would soon be no more than a half hour's ride from where a mild bluff or rise in the range would allow us to look down on the coach from two miles' distance.

Soon Mr. Pope and I were riding again—only in this instance we were now only yards from the tails of the last leading horses. But because there was still a fair amount of noise from all the animals, it was not hard for me to ask after a little more history to be shared discreetly.

"You were with my brother up here from the start?"

"Nearly so—give or take a few months of his setting the boundaries of his claim and Mr. Whisker's and my arrival with the first Texas herds for your brother in this country."

"How did my brother come to hire you in Texas?" I asked.

"I don't quite remember all the details and the times, young Mr. Crabbe, but I can say that it was your brother who would hire me when no one else in this country was willing to try me as a foreman—let alone even as a saddle horse wrangler for their outfits."

"What were the early days like up here?" I wondered aloud.

"The land looked about the same. But your brother—and Mr. Whisker (but mainly your brother, sir)—brought some real order and some real hope to a lot of men. There isn't a man here, you should know, that would talk against your brother."

Pope Pope only paused to dry his brow; the bright morning light was already hinting at a very warm day.

"I do not know where your brother learned his ways with cows, but he seems born to the business. Perhaps the best men of business, the best thinking men, are born ready to make even the thinnest, gnarled, old herd grow and prosper into something fat and sleek and numerous. Again, I do not know where he learned his business, but he seemed to wander out to Texas in the early seventies already knowing it. What he did not know he was gracious enough to permit me to suggest. And he had some formidable capital about him, for sure, with which to get started and expand. No one ever started in this business—no one I have ever heard of from here to California—the way your brother did. He had the means to start himself right off with one great bite of Texas country, a pretty fine herd, with less mavericks in a new concern than I've ever seen before. And then he had us make our way up here to Montana country in the late seventies. He built and financed that entire town himself; though I am forced to concede Mr. Whisker must have had some hand in that, too. But, still, wouldn't you know that he put all of that—and, again, that pretty town (like something, surely, you'd feel safe sleeping in back East)—put out all that and still met with no misfortune despite all he risked. He was turning in great profits after only a few years. There isn't a hand on his place that doesn't live as well as a king's prince, I'd say—each boy's got a full string of eight or more of the finest horses one can get in this country or have shipped out here from the East. And the boys want for nothing else if they work hard for him. He's got a purpose all right!"

"What purpose is that?" I asked.

"I don't know that I can really say," Mr. Pope replied soberly.

"How do you mean?" I asked with surprise.

"I mean I know he's bound to be the greatest cattleman this country's ever seen—maybe the *whole* country's ever seen, and will see—but I'll be bound to confess he's after something else, as well."

"And what might that be, Mr. Pope?" I asked.

"I couldn't say," he replied quietly, almost as if he suddenly felt he had volunteered too much.

I felt bold and made a slight demand that he qualify himself a bit further: "You mean *won't* say—that you won't, or *can't*, tell *me*?"

"No, young Mr. Crabbe. I do mean that I couldn't say, that I do not know. Please know that I am bound to speak to you as I would your brother. I do not know, indeed. I would not presume to ask him; your brother's a' prosperin' too well for me to presume any more than my daily duties. I only meant to imply that your brother knows his business—and then some."

I was not entirely satisfied with this answer, and I felt there was considerably more behind it, but I did not yet feel that my literal brotherhood with Ellsworth Crabbe was anything but a presumption of intimacy against the histories that he and his men had surely shared in the past decade or more—no matter what my brother or his foreman, or any other of his men, might insist.

I did, however, feel compelled to ask after something else that I suspected Mr. Pope could indeed answer. Surely, I thought, there was some simple cattleman's reason, some plain logic of animal husbandry, which would answer for a mystery that had begun to suggest itself to me since my arrival in this new Pauktaug.

"Mr. Pope, I had heard it said more than once back in town that my brother has sold none of his stock for almost a year, or more than a year. Is this true?"

Pope Pope looked slightly on guard for the first time since I had met him.

"Who told you that?" he asked in a plain enough delivery that one almost might have said he sounded stern.

"No one volunteered anything of the sort freely, I should tell you, Mr. Pope. It only came up when I asked McCarthy back at the hotel whether any of the steaks I had been served came from Crabbe stock."

"Whether McCarthy has meat or not from Crabbe stock from the town butcher would not tell him about your brother's business. And it *isn't* any of his business."

Again, Pope Pope was uncommonly plain in his manner when he spoke these last phrases, and his words appear to me now, in the reporting, to have been eerily harsh. I was able to surmise that the answer to my question was *yes*, even though Mr. Pope would not speak of it. He only reinforced my suspicions that the answer to my question was *yes* when he suddenly volunteered an assertion into a rather long silence.

"Your brother, sir, is the finest cattleman in this country. No matter what decisions he makes, no matter what experiments he undertakes, he is a man to be reckoned with. All of my many years in this business—and, again, they are many more than your brother's—are no match for his gift in making herds expand at a rate that no other man can match. *I* would never question him."

His very last sentence was rather odd, I thought, for his emphasis on *I* seemed to imply a great deal. That emphasis appeared to suggest that though he—a man with a long and thorough knowledge of cattle—could not or would not challenge Ellsworth, that perhaps I could (or should). I could not say with any certainty what I thought he was really suggesting. I did not feel bold enough to ask him; nor—despite mysteries of which Pope seemed certain, and despite the likely certainty with which he had been commanded by Ellsworth to divulge answers to nearly anything I might ask; and despite Ellsworth's hopes that I might do such bold asking—did I feel I could ask him anything more. Nor did I feel I could broach such subjects to Ellsworth. Notwithstanding a general sense of self-possession I felt I had earned by my thirty-fourth year of life, I felt alone in a land of intimidations—felt alone against welcoming men in my brother's employ, from whom I felt their Western nativity and expertise rendered any welcome and tolerance they offered to me tainted by a dangerously concealed condescension and resentment; and spoiled, too, most likely by a contempt for a sudden performance of nepotism. And I felt alone against a brother whom I had not seen for so long, one who had left with such silence that his very intensity of welcome and seeming penitence disturbed me.

I felt alone, as well, against his sheer expertness and command in such an open, empty, rugged and, again, intimidating land. And then, too, there was simply the land to feel alone against—none of it seemed mine, notwithstanding the eerie Pauktaug recreations that should have been reassuring to me. Despite those recreations, despite their solidness and density back in town, there was just too much land against it all. There was so much land, in fact, that it suddenly disturbed me to realize that though Ellsworth and Mr. Whisker were said to have some of the largest herds in that new country, I still had yet to see even a single cow.

So, again, though I did not have it from Mr. Pope in words, I felt I had it obliquely from this foreman that Ellsworth had not sold a single steer in more than a year. Mr. Pope would further reinforce my sense that unusual circumstances prevailed in this new Pauktaug when his kindly yet elusive mode yielded to a sudden instinct to volunteer bits of curious information. Something about me seemed increasingly to set him at ease.

"After we set right this business of the coach, young Mr. Crabbe, I know you brother will be to the railroad to see if your Cousin has arrived."

"Is that so?" I asked lightly, hoping a seeming casual interest would further encourage Pope Pope's sudden return to unguarded chattiness.

"Yes, it is. A little over a year ago, your brother confided in me that he had a true remittance man in an English cousin of his—and that he planned to apply for a loan from this cousin, a loan that would make your brother's place the biggest and best concern for filling this country with stock since the waters receded from Noah's keel. The loan came through early last year, and I suspect this cousin is finally coming over to check on his investment, as many of these English investors do eventually—many of them dressing for the part, too. He cannot fail to be pleased. We have the largest, sleekest, fattest, herd of animals here since this country was filled with buffalo. And who is to say how your brother plans to increase his holdings and stock in the seasons to come, once all those loan dollars are fully and finally applied—because your brother was well on his way to expansion based solely on his own independent profits even before the loan came in last year. I can't say what exactly he needed or needs the loan for. He may not know cows as I do, but however he knows business. Perhaps ceasing to sell stock for a time and taking out loans will learn us Texans something! I am man enough to concede that!"

Pope Pope paused for a few moments, perhaps tempering the flow of increasingly free talk. He countered the flow by posing a question to me.

"Is this cousin known to you, young Mr. Crabbe?"

I was surprised by the boldness of the question. Though I did not feel confident enough to exercise my station and interrogate my brother's help to my satisfaction, I did not wish to let slip away any cautions a man like Pope Pope felt in posing questions to me. I refrained from answering the question at all. I remained silent, and though an air of gentility and civility would remain between us, I had secured a situation for both parties which seemed to set compunctions about overstepping bounds with impertinent questions.

But somehow Mr. Pope's last question made me relatively certain that a strange set of circumstances had prevailed in this new Pauktaug only since about the time that Ellsworth received letters from me in which I began to hint that I would travel west to seek him out. At the same time that Ellsworth received his first indications of my intentions to travel west to him, he had stopped selling his stock and had not only made contact with Julius Crabbe but had also made an application to him for a reportedly enormous sum of capital, presumably for expanding the business.

Beyond the agonizing puzzle of all these events occurring seemingly together as part of some designed chain stood the remarkable fact that Ellsworth had sought out Julius Crabbe, of all of our cousins or remaining English or American kin, as someone to turn to for capital. I was baffled.

I also concluded with relative certainty that Ellsworth had accepted my warnings that I would come west at nearly the same time as he had sent for—or at least accepted the intended arrival—of a man that I knew I had come to despise in childhood, a man whom I could not imagine my brother failing to despise more than I did. And, once more, all this was framed, or put in motion, perhaps, by Ellsworth's mysterious resolution to cease selling any of his livestock for an indefinite period of time. Perhaps my cousin had resolved to travel to the new Pauktaug on account of that mystery. I could not say.

I must also repeat that I felt eager to protect my ignorance from complete revelation to native Westerners, so though it appeared that both McCarthy and Pope Pope thought it unusual that a man would cease to sell the very thing that made for his livelihood, I felt I should ask no more about such things. My sense of station also made me resolve that I should seek no confidences in Ellsworth's lower hands. And fearing to ask Ellsworth the same question and many others, I resolved to rejoice in the prospect of my rapidly returning health and in my resolution to permit Ellsworth to restore our brotherly intimacy on terms that would suit him.

The range seemed too vast and too empty—too much without any place of refuge save for the seductive replication of Pauktaug—for me to risk a misstep in any way. I had become too used in life to fearing that impulsive action would yield to my ultimate solitude, so I resolved that patience and comparative silence would best lead to the resolution of mysteries and familial peace for the two remaining American Crabbes.

3.

For a time, Pope Pope and I rode on in complete silence, and the main group of riders accelerated slightly and got ahead. But soon we overtook all of them, for they had stopped at the base of the predicted rise—the peak of which commanded a view of the stage road and the site where the coach was believed to remain in its wrecked and stranded, and perhaps even besieged, position.

The wreck had occurred about thirty miles out of town, and the stage road would have been the most direct route to follow to reach the coach and its stranded men. But as two scouts from our party climbed up the rise ahead of us, and then finished their ascent with a discreet crawl, I was told that as the riders Ellsworth had sent to the coach along the stage road the day before had been pinned down in a siege themselves, my brother and Pope Pope had thought it best to parallel the stage road via the open range to the east, and then to approach the site obliquely and slowly from the rise that we had then finally reached.

Those men who had made the failed but valiant rescue ride of the day before were then the intrepid quartet that insisted on being the first to climb to the summit to survey the wreck site from afar. Most of my brother's men dismounted and endeavored to soothe their horses lest they make too much sound. Though the stranded coach was nearly two miles distant, I was told that this fear of being heard was not unreasonable.

Ellsworth had left his reins in the charge of one of his men, and only a few moments before the leader of the quartet at the crest of the rise slowly waved his arm to beckon my brother, Ellsworth tapped Pope Pope and myself on the back and thus silently commanded that we follow him to the crest of the slope. The pat on the back drew out my first cough of the day, and it caused Ellsworth to flash a look of concern in my direction. I was astonished to say that the look seemed more inspired by his hope that my miraculous recovery in no way suffer any regression than it seemed a look to reproach me for making too much noise; one of the men at the crest looked in my direction with that latter reprimand in his eyes, however.

I stifled the cough as we three knelt down to finish the climb in a crawl, and I hoarsely whispered, "I'm all right. Do *not* mind me at all!"

As if to reinforce my assurances of good health, I thought it wise to ask a question if I could think of one, and I asked quietly how it was, after riding over such featureless terrain, that the riders were so certain that they were at the right part of the rise or even on the correct ridge at all, what with the coach road having remained out of sight for the entire time.

It was Ellsworth who answered that though he trusted his best men to find, for a second time, even a single blade of grass at the farthest reaches of the most featureless part of his rangeland, in this case circumstances did not demand that any of his men do more than fix upon the black, thin, tendril of smoke that rose like an attenuated and eroded column in the western blue of the sky. I was astonished that I had not seen this sign of fire before it was pointed out to me.

I took the spyglass that was offered and apprehended the distant, charred, mass of the stage coach. In that open country, it appeared like the smoldering end of a splinter amidst a ceaseless brown carpet of grass.

When I looked up from peering into the glass, all the other men were standing—and beckoning to the group below to mount. I stood up myself so that I could follow everyone back down the slope to our own horses. Ellsworth exchanged a few words with one of the men who had first scouted from atop that crest, and then he spoke aloud to us all as we descended the hill.

"My boys say there does not appear to be anyone down there, and the fellows who were here yesterday say whoever it was (Indians, they think) who had the coach pinned down in a siege seem to be gone."

When we reached the bottom of the slope, and after Ellsworth veered away from me so as to return to his horse, Pope Pope added, "Indians! We haven't had trouble like that up here for some years. But I suppose it's still possible."

Soon the entire body of men and horses—our prohibition against excessive noise lifted in favor of the impression our thunder would impart to any who might be in hiding below—moved with great speed up the rise and then down the long sloping plain that unfolded for more than a mile and a half until we reached the coach.

As we came to a halt before the wreck, our dust mixed with the smoke of the smoldering coach cabin; other scattered parts of the coach were still actively aflame. One of the men from the quartet my brother had sent the day before was the first to speak after he dismounted, surveyed the wreck, and walked back to where Ellsworth, Pope Pope, and I sat astride our horses.

"Hell, I ain't seen nothing like this in this part of the Territory for years, not since I used to work at the mouth of the Musselshell River, hell, ten years ago or more!"

"What do you mean, Roy?" Ellsworth asked.

"Hell, this is Injuns! Look at all the stubble in the ground and on all them boards! You ever see an Injun with a beard? Never! They always leave 'em behind!"

When the smoke would drift in such a way that we all, who had remained mounted, could see the coach itself, the *stubble* that this Roy had pointed out was very clear: arrows—many buried more than head deep in the boards and sides of the coach (including its roof, for the coach lay on its side); many others buried deeper along the lengths of their shafts, buried into the soil, on all sides of the coach. Those arrows buried in the soil seemed to have been lobbed as if from a distance, when the early part of the fight compelled the attackers to remain somewhat far off, sending their shots upwards in deadly parabolas, arching down in the hope of striking a blow from above. The arrows that brought stubble to the coach itself seemed to have been fired later, perhaps as the attackers contracted an encircling strike.

Via some silent signal, Pope Pope took an order from Ellsworth that he should take over the survey of the scene. With the foreman only a yard or two ahead, Ellsworth and I followed, on foot, as Pope, also dismounted, offered his surmise as to what had occurred, it seemed, not long before our arrival.

After circling a mild trail that surrounded the scene, Pope thought the attackers had indeed for a time engaged the wrecked coach via a contracting ring—described on horseback, all the horses appearing to have been unshod. Though prevailing local circumstances made it seemingly improbable, the probability, in fact, was indeed that this had been an Indian attack—Northern Cheyenne, likely, thought Pope, after examining and then dropping one of the arrows that had failed to lodge itself in the soil. But he was also certain, despite the evidence, that it seemed highly improbable that there might still be any active Northern Cheyenne left in that country.

Besides the horse that had been killed in the initial accidental crash of the coach, the remaining coach horses had been taken; most of the smaller cases and trunks had been stolen, as well; the two largest cases had had their locks blasted open by gunfire, and their contents had been entirely removed, with the exception of a few items of clothing and some books.

Despite Pope's warning—which he shouted back to Ellsworth after he (Pope) had gone around to the west side of the coach—I followed to where the bodies of the driver and his man lay. Their bodies gave the appearance to me of two charred, giant fish—for their flesh had been burned away, leaving behind, for the most part, only their skeletons, looking also like charred stays. But into any remaining flesh and into their spines—or perhaps this had been done before their bodies had been burned—a row of several arrows had been driven into each man's back. These arrows gave the appearance of the exposed, fine, skeleton of a fish's dorsal fin.

Again, whether the arrows had been driven in before or after the bodies had been set afire was hard to say. But as we got closer, Pope Pope knelt down beside one of the bodies and snapped away one of the burned arrows.

"I think these were planted before the fire," he ventured.

Almost as if in further effort to mark the scene as one of certain renegade depredation, a veritable Indian ghost had seemingly remained behind. Because the coach was on its side, the smoldering fire burning at the base of the belly of the wreck created enough heat to affect the rear wheel that was skyward and still free to spin. Somehow, the heat played upon the spokes in a slow fashion, as if they were the blades of a fan, and the wheel, eerily, continuously, slowly continued to spin, as if the echo and impact and force of the initial crash and then the subsequent later fight were still resounding. The ghost's presence seemed nearly tangible because the smoke that passed through the spokes was cut into shapes and strands, cut off from forming a constant stream. In short, it was as if an unseen Indian were sending smoke signals of his victory from the wreck of the coach.

I would not have been able to say had I been asked to swear to it, but I felt sure that the two burned bodies were those of the men (Buckle and Reg) I had ridden with to that point on the stage road. Their recognizable disparate sizes could be seen even in their burned, nearly altogether skeletal, remains.

Pope Pope noted several empty casks of lamp oil that were next to the dead men—which explained, in part, the degree to which the bodies had been reduced to bone by fire.

After we finished our walking circle, we three returned to our horses. Ellsworth and Pope Pope climbed into their saddles once again, and I followed their lead. Ellsworth then signaled to another group of his men, and after they approached he asked them quietly and soberly to see to the burial of the two stage employees. As if they had been expecting the possibility of death, each of these six men produced a small shovel that had been discreetly attached to his rig. Soon they were on the far side of the coach, hidden from view, interring the two men I had seen alive only two mornings earlier.

Pope Pope joined the men on the far side of the coach.. Perhaps he went to assist them in their labors; perhaps he went to guide them in the best possible disposition of Christian graves in a wild and empty country; perhaps he was still called on to officiate as a minister during such ordeals. I could not say for certain, for I did not venture to the grisly side of that wrecked coach again.

I was left, then, for a few awkward minutes in the company of just my brother. Before traveling west in that year, the last time I had seen him was on a night, that like this day on the range, called for officiation over the dead.

It was unclear to me if it was he or I who brought the greater part of discomfort to our relations at that point, but I had the distinct impression that it was Ellsworth—despite the formidable impression he gave—who at that moment felt the most ill-at-ease. I did not feel that he was embarrassed that I had so soon in a new country beheld such a ghastly scene, but I did believe I sat my horse before a man who appeared apprehensive as to where my thoughts might ultimately lead—as if, by the right or perhaps evident question put to him right then, but somehow having nothing to do with the catastrophe at that moment before us, still lead myself to some only seemingly remote conclusion that perhaps should have hovered before my mind's eye since arriving in the new Pauktaug.

It was clear that Ellsworth, though respectful of the disaster at hand, himself meditated some remote preoccupation. For some reason he seemed fixed upon this remote thing now that the distraction of the coach's mysterious fate had been revealed. I decided to risk asking him a question, however close to the private mark I feared it might have been.

"Do you think it was my place to stay behind with these men, to have helped in the fight?" I asked.

Part of me feared that the look I saw in Ellsworth was his concern for me in the eyes of his men in respect to this episode. Ellsworth suddenly smiled and brought his horse's flank nearly against mine. The relief in this smile was profound—profound for me, but even more profound for him (and thus mysterious to me, for it made it clear that any suspicions I might have about the nature of Ellsworth's preoccupied looks and expressions were far off of the mark).

Along with a second, even wider smile, Ellsworth extended his right arm to my right shoulder (our horses were facing opposite directions), and gave me one of the reassuring grips that I remembered from nearly thirty years earlier.

"No! No, Cam! You did the right thing. They did the right thing. You *should* have left; they *should* have stayed. They had to attend to their business, and you had to attend to yours. No, Cam, you should not have remained here. You would only be among the dead otherwise."

I realized then that the looks of preoccupations I could detect in Ellsworth did not register as vulnerability to the judgment of *any* of his men. No. No matter what transpired, even men as highly ranked in my brother's sphere as Pope Pope rarely, if ever, approached without being beckoned, and not a man present seemed to make furtive demonstrative appraisals of Ellsworth, ever, even from afar. And no matter what subtleties I felt privileged to see in Ellsworth's face, no other man would ever hint that any look but command pervaded my brother's brow.

Perhaps because I knew him from another place and time, I could see things—things that were further buried in his old man's face—that only one who had known the younger man could see. Ellsworth assumed a more relaxed, though no less preoccupied scowl, after I gave him the relief of my apparently simple question. But, again, somehow that scowl seemed part of the code of the past and not immediately connected to the ghastly scene of the wrecked coach—or perhaps the scene of the coach suggested some connection to Ellsworth from the past. Thus, my privileged view was baffled, perhaps, by the suggestiveness of the present; and the constant respect his men always accorded him left any facial expressions he made as inscrutable to me as the thoughts behind them. Ellsworth commanded respect and mystery and awe no matter what one's history or relation to him.

As most of the riders rested and as the burial detail was likely finishing their work, I chanced to catch another look creep across my brother's brow—this as he was reassuring me that the prospect of any kind of significant Indian problem returning to that country was highly unlikely. He was in the midst of relating to me what he knew of the supposed end and disposition of the Cheyenne's in that area when a look crossed the corners of his mouth and the corners of his eyes. It was that kind of warm, hospitable, squint that overtakes a man when he apprehends a select hale fellow from a distance—and in this case that great distance afforded by the immensity of the featureless range.

4.

Down from the same slope, whence we had ridden ourselves perhaps only a quarter of an hour before, rode another large group of riders. As they came closer I could see at their head an aging man—perhaps a few years my brother's senior, and of moderate height when gauged against the riders that surrounded him.

Pope Pope returned with speed from his burial duties as these new riders came to a halt where Ellsworth and I still sat astride our idle horses. None of my brother's hands seemed alarmed at the appearance of these men; in fact, quite a number of Ellsworth's hands saw men in the new group to whom they offered the warmest of waves and howdies. Pope Pope did not appear alarmed, but he seemed eager—as if by tacit agreement with Ellsworth—to be present for any significant encounters between men on the range.

This meeting prompted Ellsworth to dismount, as a way of inviting the leader of this new group to dismount, as well; Pope Pope remained on foot. The lead rider from the new group accepted the invitation, so I thought I should be on foot, as well. As I dismounted, I took note that I recognized the five men closest to the lead rider. It was the quintet of men I had encountered in the waning hours of darkness during my first morning in Pauktaug, and in particular I recognized Mitch Rutledge. All these men dismounted as the leader of this new group and Ellsworth approached each other.

In that instant of approach between Ellsworth and this man—this man who seemed utterly unknown to me in appearance, even though I would not have been surprised to have been told, even then, that there were things about him I should have recognized, even after decades—in that instant I noted a cautious but ultimately limited enmity between Rutledge and Pope. If just from the incident during my first dark morning in the new Pauktaug I would have felt an understanding for any dislike between them. But the strong temperaments of both men did not seem to be focused on each other as two men occupying the same position for different outfits, for different leaders.

Instead, the anger that one expected to seethe from such a man as Mitch Rutledge seemed aimed, vaguely, at the entire assembly uniquely gathered there at that moment. Again, he showed no love for Pope; his eyes then swept across the scene of the coach that continued to burn, and he showed no love for any of my brother's men; and, remarkably, he seemed indifferent to the fate of the coach. His eyes then landed on me; and then he looked between Ellsworth and myself and seemed to make some sort of calculation. It was clear by his eyes that for me he would never bear any regard.

Then I chanced—just as I watched Ellsworth and this new group's leader close the distance between them—chanced to watch Rutledge look right at my brother, and it was evident to me that if for any man this Rutledge held either jealousy, hatred, contempt, or profound fear, it was for Ellsworth.

But this flash of focus from Rutledge faded quickly, and in the sudden warmth of the meeting between my brother and the other reigning baron of that new country's range, Rutledge seemed to recede into the crowd as merely another common cowhand.

"Ellsworth!" exclaimed Whisker.

"John!" exclaimed Ellsworth. My brother's warmth was then the sort that I am certain he wished he could have casually extended to me. But Ellsworth was trapped by our history from feeling as much at liberty with me; and yet he was also trapped by some defining constraint with Whisker, this man he probably knew best of any, trapped by an ultimate loneliness that prevented him from adding to his dealings with this man the cool filial strength he could indeed still give to me. There seemed as yet to be no material or tangible being or entity to which Ellsworth could impart his full force and devotion. Ellsworth had virtually limitless resources, it seemed, but was entrapped by unclear circumstances into a peculiar emotional hoarding.

Still, to anyone present, these two men, my brother and Whisker, gave forth the warmth of gentlemen who met after mutually, stupendously successful business, and played generously and sportingly at cards or at other gentlemen's bets, absolutely certain not only of the other's security even in the event of a high stakes loss at such games, but also utterly secure in the security of their amicable fraternity in the event of such an outcome. They gave forth a warmth like that, even though I was relatively certain that Ellsworth likely never played at games.

But if the new country, if the northern range—fenced or open— had gentlemen, then I felt I beheld a convocation of two of its keenest examples at that moment.

"John!" exclaimed my brother once more as he took Whisker's hand and arm.

"Ellsworth!" returned Whisker as he vigorously shook that extended hand.

"John, when did you return?" asked Ellsworth with a cordiality that seemed to ignore the ghastly scene still smoking away behind us.

"Bad business, this!" said Whisker as he looked over Ellsworth's shoulder to the smoldering coach.

"Bad business, indeed!" echoed Ellsworth in concession to Whisker's adherence to the grimness of the scene. "Pope says it looks like wild and true Northern Cheyennes did it," Ellsworth added, almost lightly, as if the acknowledgement of the coach having been made, he could return to near levity by the novelty afforded by the scene. I must say that this was not a disrespectful levity; it was a frontiersman's levity—earned, I believe, after witnessing so many harsh scenes over so many hard years that an affectation of shock or grief or indignation would be just that: an affectation.

"You don't say?" remarked Whisker with a raising of his eyebrows and even, perhaps, a slight smile. The smile seemed in part a response to the color that such a report would still give to life in that country; the other portion of the smile was a sad grin suggesting that even if the story were true, the ultimate threat was well past amounting to anything more than a few more freakish scenes like this across the whole wide span of the American West—a few more colorful late rumbles of thunder before the Indian rain dried up for all time.

"Two boys were killed back there, though," Ellsworth added as he earnestly squinted and looked across the wide assembly of faces amongst Whisker's mounted hands.

"You don't say?" said Whisker once more; this time out of respect, with no latent grin at all.

My brother told Whisker the names.

"Yes, I know them," answered Whisker. "Good men. Should we pay some of our boys, give them a little incentive, to go after them that did this?"

"No, John, I think not," said Ellsworth as he gazed off to the north, along the course of the coach road as it reached to the railroad and the little depot settlement.

"Why is that, Ellsworth?"

"I think we're better off sending word to the army about this, and I think we'd be better off appointing some of our boys to just protect the road for the summer. I know I plan to make heavy use of it. I have a lot of shipments coming in for the rest of the season, due even now. The first of them are probably already waiting for me at the spur's end."

"Hell, Ellsworth, if you don't always know what's best for this country and for business!" Whisker assured my brother with another shake of the arm and hand.

Though I had hoped since coming to the new Pauktaug that this seemingly familiar name of *Whisker* might possibly have some connection to men of that name I had known in the old Pauktaug, in my distress on arrival, I had hardly given any more thought to this hope.

However, as I looked into this man Whisker's face, I saw my memory of a once very familiar young man of old Pauktaug emerge suddenly from beneath the dry and rutted bark of aging skin.

Something in my look of dawning recognition, as well as my status as a stranger, began to register on John Whisker's face as he glanced toward me. But his attention—this John Whisker Jr.'s (he the son of my father's original business partner)—was still engaged by the renewed levity and talk of Ellsworth.

"So, John, when did you get back from wintering in Texas?" Ellsworth asked Whisker once more.

"Rode in from the depot with some of my boys only two nights ago, but didn't see any of this since we went straight to my place and skipped going to town. And you're right. There's heaps of shipments waiting for you at the railroad spur, and wagon teams waiting to bring it in as soon as this business is cleared up and they get the word."

Whisker paused for a moment as the smoke from the fire shifted in the wind.

"Yes, sir. Spent the entire winter down in San Antonio. Still is nice country down there. But, damn, if those boys aren't jealous of us, Ellsworth!" This last phrase he said in a mock-discreet tone that only my brother and I could hear; as well, there was a great noise as the coach broke asunder and puffed new smoke, as do pieces of nearly disintegrated charcoal when they are poked and almost spent. "Yes, sir! 'Pushin' 'em up against the Black Hills' isn't something for a Texan to say with any satisfaction since we made what we made of this country up here!"

Whisker looked at the coach again as it continued to smoke and settle after its latest upheaval.

"Damn bad business here. Cheyennes! Really? You don't say! You sure I can't have at least some of my boys go after these red fellows for you? Least I can do after all the help my boys said you still were to us during the spring."

Whisker, though a year or two older than my brother, not only continued to display a brotherly and friendly rhythm with Ellsworth, but he also seemed to defer to him in a light and tacitly arranged manner. Signs of this deference would bring a look of slightly less than latent enmity out of the face of Mitch Rutledge. It was evident that he hoped himself for some sort of fraternal reward beyond increased pay and his foreman's standing for his service to John Whisker, Jr.

Ellsworth had turned his mind to the coach once more—or perhaps he had turned it to the northern horizon, to the direction of the rail town—so he did not appear for the moment to hear or register or react to Whisker's second appeal about going after the robbers of the coach, the killers of the stage men.

Whisker was not bothered by this. He took advantage of that circumstance to escalate in his expressions: "Hell! Indians! Hostiles! I don't think there's been that kind of trouble in this country since before we came to it, Ellsworth!"

Ellsworth looked with attention to Whisker again.

"Let me just have some of my boys trail these red sons-a-bitches and shoot the sons-a-bitches open, Ellsworth," Whisker added.

"No, John. We're not even sure—no one saw this with their own eyes—who the men are who really did this. Perhaps it was some old timer boys who just made it look like Indians did it."

"Why, Ellsworth, if you aren't always the picture of justice and fair play! Even with, you say, two men baking in the earth on the other side of that coach!" Whisker exclaimed.

"Mr. Crabbe is right! No one was here to see the real fight that took place," Pope suddenly interjected. I, too, was deeply impressed by my brother's sense of justice.

"That being said," Pope continued, "it still is a certainty, for all I have ever seen of Indians—as astonishing as it may seem. I suppose there's still enough room for a few of them to hide, even in an open country like this."

"It makes me certain of one thing, John," Ellsworth said. "We have to make good on the promise you and I made to ourselves last summer before you left for Texas at the end of the season."

"What's that, Ellsworth?"

John Whisker had a childish obtuseness to him, a carefree forgetfulness that came perhaps with great prosperity, which did not interfere with the overall impression of sturdiness of mind and memory he projected.

"We have to accept the governor's commission to appoint a deputy marshal until the territory can get around to making a formal appointment itself for this county."

"Law and order again, Ellsworth! You're completely right once more, old man!" exclaimed Whisker.

"Can you meet in town a week from today to discuss some nominees?" Ellsworth asked.

As John Whisker assented to this, my eyes chanced to observe how Mitch Rutledge continued to regard with scorn the fraternal conviviality between Ellsworth and Whisker.

By this time in the exchange, save for Pope and Rutledge standing by as lieutenants to their barons, all the other men had drifted back, somewhat away from the site, as much as to give Ellsworth and Whisker the privacy they must have customarily enjoyed during such parleys in the open as to move away from the coils of smoke that were starting to drift in our direction from the coach. One particularly dense stream of dark smoke finally compelled Ellsworth, Whisker, the two foremen, and myself to retreat in the same direction as the rest of the men—in the direction of the slope from which we had all recently descended. But before I could escape entirely, I inadvertently took in a deep draught of the smoke, and this triggered a reminder to me—and to all around me—that beyond looking as pale as ivory and as gaunt as a starving man I was indeed still much further from health and recovery than my surprisingly painless and placid morning had led me to believe. For several minutes I had to kneel on the ground in an attempt to exhaust one of my most violent fits of coughing. My ribs ached again with great pain.

Ellsworth, Pope, and Whisker (with Rutledge dutifully standing behind the latter's shoulder) all stood around me, then, on the weather side of that slope as I attempted to regain peace in my lungs.

"You ought not to drive your sickest boys so hard on a day like this," Whisker said to Ellsworth with a slight edge of scornful laughter. "Is he an Arizona Tenor?"

"This boy came in on this coach more than four days ago and then walked the rest of the way to town," Ellsworth responded with pride as he knelt next to me.

Whisker replied, "My boys here said they had a little trouble two nights ago with someone who said he walked into town—and that you, Ellsworth, broke that trouble up."

"Yes, I broke up that trouble, but the trouble was with another man," said Ellsworth. "John, this boy here is my brother, Campbell."

Ellsworth looked up with a great, sad, grin to Whisker—Whisker, the only man there whose memory could go back east and to the past of old Pauktaug.

Whisker knelt down and put a friendly hand on my shoulder; my brother still grasped the other. "Ellsworth! Why did you keep this from me?" he began with a smile. "Campbell Crabbe! Little Campbell! Little Cam! You don't say!"

Pope Pope knelt down at that moment, as well, but he did not presume to move in close as he spoke:

"The other man who walked into town from this coach, the one your boys were pressing so hard that we had to break it up, was just found dead."

Whisker turned and looked up to Mitch Rutledge, who was still standing by and scowling—his scowl having intensified as he watched the warm sentiment flow from his employer to me as recognition for me developed. Again, he stood whilst we all knelt, and stood apart at that. But he did not appear embarrassed or uneasy when Whisker shot a quick, reproachful sounding question to him.

"What do you know about this, Mitch?"

"Nothing, sir! Absolutely nothing! We press trespassers just as you ask us to—and just as everyone in this country does. Mr. Crabbe just saw fit to tell me when to stop pressing because he happened along—and felt like it."

"And Mr. Crabbe can do what he pleases, and you'll listen, Mitch!" said Whisker.

"Well, we did. We did, sir!" protested Rutledge.

"When was the man found dead, and what killed him?" Whisker asked. He looked to Pope Pope.

"It's hard—almost impossible, really—to say what killed him for certain. Beaten, impaled—all mangled up in some peculiar way. I've never seen anything like it. I looked at the body for a short time this morning."

John Whisker shot a questioning look to his foreman. Rutledge simply grunted dismissively.

Pope Pope continued: "Young Mr. Crabbe found him last night about a half mile up the road inside the place."

"My place," volunteered my brother.

"Your place, Ellsworth? You don't say?" said Whisker.

Rutledge interrupted at this point: "There! You see? What could I—or any of your boys—know about that then, Mr. Whisker. Not one of us has been on Crabbe range since he began to fence it all in last season."

"Quiet, Mitch!" shouted Whisker. This was both an acknowledgement of his foreman's point and alibi and a reproach for his speaking out of turn. "Mitch, get the boys together. We're going to ride home."

"Yes, sir!" Rutledge answered, with obliquely delivered

appreciation for his employer's understanding and with a scowl for me—because of the warmth I seemed to draw from John Whisker on account of our shared Eastern history.

Pope Pope retreated to his horse and to my brother's men according to some very tacit signal from Ellsworth. Mr. Whisker helped me to stand. My latest, violent, coughing fit had passed.

"Little Campbell Crabbe! You don't say!" said Whisker as he rubbed my hair. "You can't remember me! I only saw you once or twice—ever—before I left Pauktaug to follow Ellsworth into business, and you couldn't have been, before your brother left, more than—"

"I was six—six years old. But I do remember seeing you at our fathers'—yours and mine—on more than one occasion."

"You remember that? You don't say! Is your father still living? Is he in good health?" asked Whisker.

"No, he passed on this past winter, Mr. Whisker," I answered.

Whisker looked at Ellsworth, but my brother was looking off beyond the smoke of the coach, off into the distance in the direction of the railroad spur and depot and its little settlement. Whisker then looked to me and seemed to presume some of the circumstances that brought me at last back into my brother's sphere—some of those presumptions likely quite close to being correct. He smiled.

"When I left, *your* father was still well, Mr. Whisker," I said.

Whisker paused for a moment over what I had just volunteered, and then he insisted. "John! Call me *John* if you can, boy!"

"I'll try, sir," I replied, though I was confident that it would be nearly impossible for me to comply with this request.

"Yes, I had a little news from the old man just before I left San Antonio. I'm sorry he did not think to tell me you were coming," Whisker muttered as he removed his hat for a brief time and dried his brow with his sleeve.

"If he knew I left, he could not have known where I was going," I said.

"I see," muttered Whisker. "How's the old factory? Still money to be made in whalebone—in corsets and umbrellas?"

"When I left, they were still shipping such things out, sir," I replied.

"John! *John*, if you can, my boy!" insisted Whisker once more.

"Yes, I'll try," I replied. He was a genuinely warm and kind man, it seemed, and I resolved then that I would endeavor to make the effort to be more familiar with him if I could.

All the riders of both ranches sat astride their horses now, waiting at a distance for Ellsworth and Whisker to conclude their reunion. Even though they were nearly all very rough and independent men, Ellsworth and Whisker had them conditioned to wait for subtle signals to the same degree that my mother and father had trained our Irish servants to watch and wait over us at table when I was a child. Thus, John Whisker continued to talk to me in a casual, warm, and friendly manner—though we stood in the vast, treeless sunlight, with more than a hundred riders awaiting orders; and with a burning stagecoach standing in as an eerie fireplace in the midst of that open, unsettling, cattlemen's parlor.

As Ellsworth started to recover from his reverie, from looking intently across the plains to the north, a sudden, convivial thought flashed across John Whisker's brow, and he gave me a light slap on the back that almost reengaged my coughing fits.

"By the way, Little Campbell, you don't say you missed the new Pauktaug? Your brother rebuilt Pauktaug anew in this new country, brick for brick and shingle for shingle."

Ellsworth mildly smiled in response to this and then adjusted his hat—which seemed to prompt nearly all of his men and horses into a state of readiness.

"Well," continued Whisker with pride, "my memory contributed a few touches—but those, wouldn't you know it, are probably the only false ones."

The small bit of jealousy I felt upon learning that I was not the sole man who would have a share with my brother in the meaning of such a recreation—and thus, too, not the sole man to share exclusively in a great deal of personal history with Ellsworth Crabbe—that small bit of jealousy brought more relief than pain. John Whisker's confirmation took away the threatening aspect from the manifest display of memory I saw realized in the buildings and structures of the new Pauktaug.

We three made our way to our horses to remount. As I climbed atop my horse, Whisker added, "And to think most of those buildings were not even there as of the middle of last summer. It was virtually a tent camp as of last spring. I bet your brother—haven't you, Ellsworth?—I bet he even imported the trees and the missing Sound water while I was gone for the winter in Texas. Didn't you, Ellsworth?"

My brother only smiled.

5.

"Well, boys," Whisker said to both of us, "I will be sure to see what's been done when I come into town next week for our meeting concerning the appointing of a lawman. I look forward to that, for this here is a very bad business: these two fellows here who died with the stage—and that fellow who was killed on your ground two nights ago, Ellsworth! We don't need—shouldn't have—that kind of thing here anymore."

Ellsworth and Whisker then moved their horses close for a quiet final parley. I did not change my position, but I could still hear them speak. Ellsworth seemed to want this; Whisker seemed pleased to have me close, as well.

"Campbell, it sure is grand to see another face from the old days and the old place—and to add that face to what we've built here. Perhaps you're the first of many that will fill this entire place up with familiar ghosts. What do you know but that your brother will put the old gulls and dock up out here if he can? Did you bring any of that with you?"

"No, just myself," I replied, while still keeping a modest distance from their horses.

"Do you plan to stay with us?" Whisker asked.

I looked at Ellsworth and smiled latently as I replied, "Yes, I do."

"Well, you don't say! Splendid. I would welcome you to this country, which is utterly new to you; or I could welcome you home, since it is such a close replica in town. Both seem to negate the other a bit, so I will just say *welcome*."

It was clear, then, that John Whisker had a few more things he wished to say to Ellsworth. Again, it was not suggested by any signals that I should keep my distance, but some instinct compelled me to stay where I was, astride my horse, as Ellsworth and Whisker continued to speak.

I could not hear all of the details of their exchange. I could hear Whisker thanking Ellsworth for still having Crabbe men work the spring roundup even though only Whisker cows still grazed on open range. Ellsworth's stock was all fenced in by that spring. I could hear Whisker boast about the price he commanded and won for nearly his entire herd late last summer, when he sold most of his stock through proxies, including some help from Pope Pope, to an unknown buyer— likely a remittance man, he thought, who was new to the country. The herd was quickly driven off of Whisker range and was never heard from again. That sale happily compelled Whisker to buy two new herds of longhorns in Texas during the winter; they were being driven north, then, even as we continued to linger near that burning coach. The herds were still likely a week, maybe several weeks, to the south, said Whisker. I also heard him mutter that he was glad he had resolved to leave Rutledge behind and not make him one of the trail bosses. That had not sat well with Rutledge, said Whisker; still, he thought, he was a good foreman on the home range, despite his increasing displays of temper.

I could also make out questions from Whisker that were questions which he alone was bold enough to ask. If my ears did not deceive me I was certain that I heard Whisker ask my brother if it were true that Ellsworth had not sold a single cow in more than a year. Yes, I was almost certain that he asked that, for the answer seemed to fit such a question. However, the answer also fit what appeared to be Ellsworth's proud evasiveness—even unto the man I imagined was his closest friend in that country and, likely, even in life.

"Well, John, we've been trying some new ideas at my place. You're sure to find out how it all goes very soon; I have no doubt," Ellsworth answered.

"Where did you hear about these ideas? They aren't doing anything like it down in Texas, even if most men have fenced in their entire ranges down south," said Whisker.

"All these ideas are mine, John," Ellsworth said, and looked once more in the direction of the very distant railroad town to the north, and then he gave me a glance that seemed to beckon me nearer.

"You don't say! All your own ideas—well, I should say I'm not surprised, Ellsworth. All your own ideas! Not that I can say I really know, still, what any of them are." There was a slight pause as I decided to come abreast of my brother's horse. Whisker was on the far side from me.

"Well, that's probably just in the family now," smiled Whisker. I could tell that Whisker's last remark and smile were not mixed with latent resentment.

A shift of intimacies had been nobly acknowledged in a sub-tle way in that moment out in the open—but it was a shift that somehow did not damage the original and remaining confidences between John Whisker and Ellsworth. Whisker could have had no way of knowing, however, that Ellsworth's recent business practices were still utterly a mystery to me, so the shift was not really towards me, but merely to a degree away from Whisker.

Whisker was a generous and a seemingly confident and stable man and friend. Somehow he granted me this new place of osten-sible prominence with Ellsworth without in any way suggesting to me that it came at the cost of ending the lifelong history that Ellsworth and he had built since young manhood.

Perhaps the wind changed direction or speed in a subtle way, or perchance there was a sudden degree of accidentally concerted greater quiet amongst all the men some distance away, for I could then hear Whisker's next question to Ellsworth quite clearly. He asked Ellsworth if what he had heard about the Crabbe range fence being nearly completed were true.

"I haven't been anywhere but out here since returning home, Ellsworth, but many of my boys say you're nearly finished fencing in all of your range. Truly leaving the old ways behind?"

"Perhaps," muttered Ellsworth, as he looked back at Whisker after looking yet again in the direction of the distant railroad town. "We're going to try to finish them, finish the cows, in a new way. Yes. That's why I have got, in part, to keep this way between town and the railroad open. I've got an enormous amount of supplies coming in."

"You don't say!" laughed Whisker. "Hell, no matter what, we've got to keep that road open for the sake of everything. Again, Ellsworth, why don't you let me add the strength of some of my boys to at least looking around the length of the road until any threat has passed? I've got more idle cowhands around than I know what to do with—at least until the two new herds arrive. They're all good men; I haven't had the heart to send them away looking for work elsewhere, even after that easy spring roundup."

"All right. I suppose there is no harm in that," replied Ellsworth. "I suppose there is no harm so long as they *cause* no harm. Remember, tell them not to do anything but bring back reports. Again, I am pretty certain that this is a single occurrence. We can't have your boys shooting and killing just any Indian they see."

"You don't say!" exclaimed Whisker with a grin, and then he slapped my brother on his left shoulder.

I looked to both my brother and Whisker sitting astride their horses and facing one another as they sat side by side, this under a bright and critical but still cool late morning light. I had to shade my eyes—despite my already having a hat—so as to look at them then, and in that brilliant sunlight they appeared as sparsely featured granitic equestrian monuments. Their horses would shift weight and confirm the monumentalized to be living. The dime novels that I had read had accrued an interest in my heart as I had spent the recent years in circumstances that would compel my ultimate need to go West. That interest had grown and grown until it then appeared to me cashed and realized, minted under the sun (and the burning coach providing the smoke as from a kiln), and the figurative coins of interest jostled in the warm, grassy, parlor of the range: two living barons!

I prodded my horse forward several yards, and in closing that final gap the illusion of the equestrian statue vanished, and I was in the midst of their seemingly casual exchange once more.

"Here I returned," said Whisker, "to see as much of the spring roundup as I could only to find that my boys and yours have finished most of the branding. Landed a good amount of calves this spring, I must say—considering how small the remaining herd was after my great sale last season."

Whisker paused here—sure, I suspect, that Ellsworth would

counter. However, my brother was still intent on looking north. Whisker looked at me with a knowing smile, as if acknowledging that Ellsworth was prone to such inexplicable reveries.

"I say we landed quite a few calves this spring, Ellsworth. I suppose you already know that. And your place?" asked Whisker directly.

Ellsworth broke his silence: "Yes, we landed a good bunch this spring—a fine bunch."

"Going to pull your bulls for the summer?" asked Whisker.

"No, I'm thinking of leaving most of them in," replied Ellsworth.

"You don't say!" exclaimed Whisker, and then he gave me another knowing smile—as if to acknowledge that he knew Ellsworth must be pulling his leg—or tying knots in his tail, as men often said in that country. I had no way of knowing if this was so, however. I had no way of knowing what was routine in the cattle business. But everything that Whisker said suggested that Ellsworth was doing a great deal out of the ordinary.

"So, Ellsworth," continued Whisker, "You haven't sold a single cow for a year or more; your cows are dropping a good number of calves for the spring; you're going to keep your bulls in play for the summer; *and* you're completing the fence around what must be getting to be one of the largest herds ever seen on this range, if not in the country. Is that about the state of things?"

"Yes, that is about the state of things, more or less, at present."

"You don't say!" smiled Whisker.

Ellsworth beckoned to his foreman; Pope immediately galloped toward us. As Pope came alongside Ellsworth, Whisker remarked to me, "Either your brother is intent on clearing the market for my prosperity, or he's got something new in mind that will allow him to put everyone else in the business *out* of business. I can never tell with him."

Whisker laughed once more and then took leave of us:

"Ellsworth, I am going to trust you and leave this Indian

business alone for now. But we're going to ride—my boys and I are—back to my place by way of town. We'll take the coach road south and see what we come up with. Probably nothing, because the Indians'—or the killers'—trails seem to lead east, more or less in the direction of the north end of your place, Ellsworth."

"That's true, Mr. Crabbe," said Pope.

"Yes, leave it alone for now," replied Ellsworth as a final verdict. "But I'd be obliged if you keep some of your boys riding the road from here to town for the time being—a week or so, at least—until the stage line seems safe again. I myself will take word to the railroad spur so that the army can be notified about this incident by the telegraph."

"As you please, Ellsworth!" said Whisker.

"Thank you, John. And I'll keep some boys on the road from here to the north. It is likely that no one will hit it a second time if there are more men on it. But we have to start solving our law and order problems by officially bringing in law and order. Our boys shouldn't have to risk so much for our business concerns."

Again, Ellsworth seemed the paragon of reason and sound judgment as he made this last statement.

"Then we'll be leaving, Ellsworth," said Whisker. "Campbell, it is sure fine to have you among us. When we meet in town you are to be my guest at dinner, of course."

"Thank you, Mr. Whisker," I said.

"John!" insisted Whisker to me.

"I'll try," I replied, and as Whisker beckoned his men to follow him to the south and over to the stage road, Mitch Rutledge passed first, and his scowl seemed especially reserved for me—as if he had overheard his master's second insistence that I be on familiar terms.

After Whisker's large herd of men were well on their way south along the stage road, Ellsworth ordered Pope Pope to take most of the men back to the ranch and back to work for the end of the spring branding. Then he asked Pope to pick out six good riders that he could spare and to appoint them as escorts for the ride that Ellsworth intended to take toward the railroad.

Pope Pope quietly protested that such a ride might be dangerous. Ellsworth simply waved away these warnings, and within minutes I looked over my shoulder to see Pope leading the main body of men over the rise from whence we had all come.

Soon Ellsworth and I—and the six selected men who rode behind us—were moving with steady speed in the opposite direction. There was never any question that I was to remain with Ellsworth for this ride. My pride in this understanding obliterated any fears that Pope's warning may have stirred in me.

Ellsworth had us take right to the stage road for our route north, and it occurred to me more than once that myself of only two or three days before would never have imagined that I would so soon be back on the same road, but traveling in the opposite direction.

Though the area between the coach's disaster and the new Pauktaug had presented Kettle and myself with countless hard miles on foot without one sign of water, the area north of the wreck yielded several fine water sites for the horses—though knowing exactly where they were relied on the knowledge of my companions. This made me suspect that the area south may not have been as dry as it had appeared; perhaps I simply could not have been stuck with a more unfortunate yet ostensibly expert native companion than Kettle on that range.

Ellsworth said very little as we rode north, and the six men who accompanied us kept a vassal's distance at all times behind us. By early evening we reached the sole stage stop that lay between the railroad and the site of the stage's disaster. We were met there by the attendant and an agent of the stage company. The agent had made his way from the railroad town to the stage stop on that same evening; as of the morning of that day, the stage had already been overdue by an entire day. The agent had learned nothing of the fate of the stage from the stop keeper. It was Ellsworth who carried the news of the death of the driver and the shotgun rider, the loss of the freight and parcels from that run, and, of course, the complete destruction of the coach itself.

Whilst fretting over this news, the company agent remarked and lamented that beyond all the cruel and sad consequences of such a loss he had the further challenge of having many new passengers—and mountains of accumulating freight—waiting in town for the trip to Pauktaug.

One of the new arrivals, remarked the agent, was a particularly impatient and demanding Englishman who claimed to have special business with Ellsworth Crabbe.

"What is his name?" my brother asked as we passed the late spring night in the shelter of the stop keeper's cabin.

"Funny thing, Mr. Crabbe, but he gave your family name as his own. A relative?"

"Yes. If this is the man I expect him to be, the man you have waiting at the railroad depot is my cousin," answered Ellsworth. "I am going to need this road to be open and clear this summer. My men and Whisker's men will patrol it and see to its safety for some time. Until you can secure a new coach, I can have a buckboard fitted to help you make do in the meantime. And I'll have an entire train of buckboards hauling freight between the railroad and town this summer. But until the heaviest parts of the shipments start to arrive, which should be soon, I should be able to spare at least one for passengers. And I will escort these latest arrivals of yours back to Pauktaug myself."

"You would do that? Thank you, Mr. Crabbe. Thank you, indeed!"

We left early the next morning on fresh horses. We would pick Ellsworth's finer animals on the return trip. The stop man was so impressed by the fine, big, Eastern horses, that he thanked Ellsworth for trusting to stable them there. Everyone, with few exceptions, always seemed to be thanking Ellsworth.

The ride to the railroad town went easily and passed without incident—though I did notice that the six cowhands whom Ellsworth had trailing us suggested from time to time amongst themselves that we seemed to be pushing, to be keeping an undue pace. It was not in my power or experience to register such a thing on my own, but I could say, however, that after we were well into the second day of nearly ceaseless riding that my seemingly miraculous recovery to health began to slip away to a great degree. As I began to cough again and feel increasingly tired and weak—and to feel great relief when the first signs of the little railroad depot village came into view on the far away horizon—I felt it was rather odd that it was then that Ellsworth broached the subject of the deputy marshal position.

"Cam," Ellsworth suddenly began out of a period of long silence, and just after the brisk pace was increased even a bit more when the small railroad town's water tower came into view, "the governor appointed a new marshal for the territory some time ago. For towns that can't yet afford their own police force and sheriff, he's about all that one can count on in this country for law. Now we can afford it here—to have our own police and our own sheriff—but we haven't thought much about such things up until this point, and haven't had too much cause. But I can tell you that the last time the territorial marshal passed through Pauktaug, he asked John Whisker and me to appoint him a deputy for this county if we found the right man—a temporary appointment, that is, one that could stand until it was tested, the marshal approved it, or until he found the man he wanted to appoint."

Ellsworth paused; he evidently wanted some sort of reply from me. "I see," is all I could think to say. I had some idea of where his thoughts and words were heading, but I was uncertain—and my uncertainty was compounded, I was sure, by the impression given by my returning symptoms.

"When John returns to Pauktaug next week to discuss law for

our town, I am going to suggest you as my nomination for deputy—to serve so long, at least, until we can establish a formal sheriff for this county, or hire or put in an elected constable for the job."

I should have been moved, if not by the prospect of assuming such a position in the eyes of others in the new Pauktaug, then at least by the intimacy and confidence of such a gesture from an older brother who had been so long estranged from me.

Perhaps I was moved and flattered by the suggestion. But I was surprised by the boldness of my reply: "No one likes nepotism—no one, anywhere."

Ellsworth allowed another pause; in that silence he did not look at me; he only looked ahead at the water tower as it grew larger on the horizon. Then he made an answer that I found peculiar—peculiar as much because it seemed to have a cryptic, an internally contradictory, quality to it, as it also seemed to be made as a final statement on the subject. It sounded like an order. I was hearing in such a phrase a long cherished and hoarded intimacy my brother felt for me and at the same time I was hearing the coarse, intractable, command of a man who had had to reign and make judgments for himself without benefit of consultation or confidences for nearly thirty years.

But despite that assessment, which I think was close to the truth, the statement was still peculiar—peculiar in that it had, in addition to the polarized qualities I have already listed, some other, supremely peculiar intensity that reminded me that there were chambered parts of Ellsworth's mind before which I stood in complete remove and ignorance, if not even fear.

"I would not be able to trust anyone but you in a town over which I have so long presided," he said.

I did not know what to make of that statement. Somehow, however, the strength with which he had made the remark, combined with my increasing quiet—I refrained more and more from speaking for fear of triggering my returning coughing fits—made it seem as if I had tacitly accepted an appointment I know he had had the power and intention to make—even before he would bother, in a week's time, to confer seemingly with John Whisker.

Our seven companions (the agent rode back to the railroad town with us) closed the gap between themselves and Ellsworth and me as we finally came into the small depot settlement—which was merely a station for the train, a small warehouse, a depot for the stage company, a small hotel, and a small saloon (over which were several small rooms that were available for rent).

There was not a soul to be seen in the street, but there were mountains of supplies that had arrived since I had last been in the little town—piles upon piles of grain, much of it already loaded upon buckboards and other wagons, ready for shipment, it seemed, to the new Pauktaug.

We stabled our horses at the stage depot, and then Ellsworth led me and his men to the saloon. He bought drinks and food for his men, and then, with me in tow, he asked the saloonkeeper if there were guests in town waiting to go to Pauktaug.

There were several men sleeping in rooms upstairs, he said—men he thought were on the way to Pauktaug to answer the call that had gone out not long before: that able carpenters and laborers could find work there on the Crabbe fence.

"And, oh," added the saloon keeper as he wiped the surface of the bar with a dubious rag, "there's also a nervous English gent, probably just another remittance man new to this country—taken in by some booster writing, no doubt—taking a walk, probably out by the depot now or the tracks. He couldn't go far. There isn't anywhere to go."

The saloon keeper then looked at me.

Ellsworth saw this and said to the man, "Did you take weapons as payment from this man some days ago for coach fare to Pauktaug?"

"Why, yes, I did, sir, and—" the saloonkeeper began, already with an apologetic tone.

"Return them to him immediately," Ellsworth said.

"Yes, sir!" the saloonkeeper answered. As quickly as he might have retrieved mugs or glasses from under the bar, he produced two of my finest pistols and returned them to me.

"Mr. Crabbe, sir, what happened to the last run of the coach?"

Ellsworth did not answer the man. At that instant it occurred to me that Ellsworth was the owner of the stage line, if not all of the businesses in this depot town, as well. I met no one in this new country, save for Whisker, who did not seem to intimate that my brother was proprietor of nearly every acre and edifice in that part of the territory.

Ellsworth was eager to find this Englishman, this man that was likely our cousin, as quickly as possible. However, he made a mild effort to encourage me to remain in the saloon, to take some food, and to take a room and rest. It is easy to concede that I neither looked nor sounded nor felt well by that point, but I was not to be dissuaded from seeing that day's particular mission to its end.

Ellsworth wrote out a message for the barkeeper to take to the telegraph operator. The message gave details to the army about the attack on the stage.

Ellsworth and I walked outside and made our way to the depot. We were covered with dust and soil from the range, and our boots became even more soiled from walking instead of riding up the short, rutted, neglected little Main Street. We had neither carriage nor driver with which to approach the depot in this instance.

The south face of the depot had only a small, platform outside of the little station's entrance. No one was upon it. But the opposite side, where the trains ran by, was sure to have a longer platform. In fact, we could see the opposite sides of the far platform stretching off in two directions as we approached the depot, but they appeared deserted. Only the portion of the far platform eclipsed by the little station house remained hidden.

Ellsworth led us up the steps of the little depot and around to its rear.

And there, standing right in the stretch of the platform that had been concealed by the small frame structure of the depot, smoking and pacing in such a manner as to confirm the truth of the recent description of his impatience, stood Julius Crabbe. He looked thirty years older, but it was still the same man I recalled from my childhood. I would not have mistaken him under any circumstance.

He turned and faced us when he heard our footsteps. He withdrew his cigar from his mouth, but not in such a way as seemed preparatory to speaking or to drawing breath to shout a greeting. He had a manner that made one pause before rendering even a reluctant welcome. But I put my memories and associations of this man aside for a moment. I was going to look to Ellsworth, for surely he had good cause to bring about this meeting—if even only because he had good business cause to solicit Julius Crabbe as an investor. I looked to Ellsworth for some sign as to how to regard this second meeting with a man for whom I had only angry and painful associations. But looking to my brother relieved me of nothing, and told me nothing further.

Ellsworth had stopped advancing, as I had. He seemed to revel in some singular way in the space between our cousin and himself. Ellsworth stood at my side, regarding our cousin sternly as I regarded my brother for signs of the nature of this event. Ellsworth struck an almost militant pose. He said nothing for a long instant, and seemed to keep within him a thousand words, and even more words clutched and held safely amidst his own tightly crossed and knotted arms.

PART IV

The Remittance Man

I.

Now that I have introduced Julius Crabbe for a second time—the two instances nearly thirty years apart—it is proper that I finish the account of my family's first encounter with him in 1855.

That summer began to unfold very much as the spring had played itself out: my mother's health remained relatively strong; my health also remained strong; Julius, his hopes of securing a place in our family business kept in a perpetually delayed and probationary state by my father's fear of Ellsworth's silent reproaches, used his time in a manner of sly retribution for that delay, making reminders to my father of how his New World wealth and energies could better be used to further the Old World Crabbe family's cause and mission of philanthropy; my father—feeling guilty on two counts: one, for keeping Julius, because of Ellsworth's wishes, away from the family business; and, two, because Julius' suggestions about charity plagued his conscience—gave more and more of his time to entertaining his obliquely sinister nephew; and Ellsworth, even when our weaknesses seemed least threatening, maintained a vigilant campaign against these externally fostered sensations of guilt.

So long as the polarized stresses pulling on my father remained limited to the pushes and ingratiation of Cousin Julius and the canceling forces of Ellsworth, my father was able to maintain a degree of fragile stability. However, that balance was not to last in its pure and delicate state for very long. After Independence Day passed and the full, hot, stretch of the summer unfolded, my mother began to enter a period, albeit brief, of exceptional and radiant health unlike any I had ever seen her enjoy. This was, of course, regarded as a blessing by all of us, and Ellsworth took extra pleasure in believing that my mother's exceptionally good health would only assist him in maintaining, if not tipping in his favor, the contested state of our father. He was sure that my father, then free of the fear of any worry about his wife's health would only strengthen in his resolve against any threat to our well-established ways of material comfort. And my mother's brief state of glorious health may indeed have had that effect upon my father's mind.

However, whatever power my mother's transitory physical strength had for supporting Ellsworth's hopes was soon negated. My mother, via her own vain, special weaknesses of mind, substituted the threat she usually posed to our stability with a threat that was equally—if not arguably more—dangerous than any posed by her habitual cycles of consumption. In her brief bloom of complete health she used her time—fueled in part by some hitherto latent and shameful ill-regard she harbored for her native origins—used her time not only to spend as much energy as possible entertaining her British nephew, but in learning all she could of a land and way of life, which in the blissful first decades of courtship, marriage, and family, her husband had by aggressive omission convinced her needed not to be recalled nor honored.

Because she was by then made to feel secure of her place in our family, and because her seeming complete restoration of health also gave her a greater illusion of security than she had ever known in her adult life, she felt free to labor at eradicating one of her great insecurities—the hitherto unrevealed sense of humility that a childhood on a remote Long Island farm had implanted in her spirit. She wished to free herself of any last plagues of humility. She had none when dealing with our neighbors or fellow villagers of Pauktaug—even if they knew her original status as a farmer's daughter.

But she felt great humility in the presence of her English nephew. She wished to acquire his total lack of humility. If her husband would not tell her stories of place and station and condescending obligation from the old country, then surely this haughty young man could; and he could and would indeed. Thus in all its perversity she sought to see the completion of her ascent from farmer's daughter to seeming American royal lady by learning all she could of the Old World Crabbe's cause of Relief and Philanthropy.

My mother not only encouraged Cousin Julius to regale her with descriptions of how—until only recently—the British branch of the Crabbe family plied their shipping trade with magisterial aggression in ports around the globe, but also demanded that it was revealed how with the administration of manifold relief societies so much wealth was redeemed in charity and thus led to the redemption of the Crabbe legacy.

And in addition, my mother—in July—took to entertaining guests far more than we had ever seen before. Normally we lived in an affluent seclusion, in a wealthy, unbroken chain of indistinguishable days of paradise. In fact, in those days, nay decades, of isolation, my mother enjoyed a greater degree of station than she ever realized. But now she was possessed with a mania for demonstrating caste. And so, in the company of her nephew, she accepted invitations and tendered them—amidst my father's business circles in New York City—with the sole intention of finding avenues by which our wealth could be directed for the sake of supporting her growing lust for the condescension of rendering public service. My father and brother were hardly aware of the full magnitude of this threat, for it was only I—free of my tutors and nurses for most of that early summer—who accompanied my mother and cousin on these rounds. But my father and brother would learn of it at the same time that other, later, disasters revealed themselves—which magnified that threat beyond its component place in the full picture of disintegration that was to characterize the late summer of 1855.

And yet, before things became utterly disastrous for my family, they appeared to look even more stable and pleasant than normal. Though Julius cast his pall over my brother—and thus, too, my father—my mother's great health gave us a sense that we were finally entering the halcyon days as a quartet of a family in Pauktaug Village. And then came splendid news for Ellsworth—and thus again, too, by way of secondary reaction, for my father: my father's brothers had set things aright in the British shipping concerns of the English branch of the Crabbe family.

My English uncles and grandfather, but most particularly Julius' father, had need again for Julius in the home office of the company. My cousin was being recalled to England.

When that news arrived it was decided that Julius would depart in a month's time—near summer's end, at the conclusion of August. But just as that plan was made, and just as it was thus made certain that we would have one more month of intense and intimate exposure to our invading cousin, an entire series of circumstances conspired to dissolve the peace of my family forever.

The first element in that fateful conglomeration of circumstances was the sudden decline in my own health. Though this was not my first bout with consumption, it was—next to the instance that preceded and attended my journey west nearly thirty years later—to be one of my worst. Within days I went from a summer of social rounds with my mother and cousin, and from late afternoons and evenings in the company of my brother and his collections and his books, to confinement to my bedroom for nearly all hours of the day—including, after only a few days, even the dining hours.

Though my mother was never to surrender her fascinations with the tales of Julius—and of the golden, exulted condescensions such examples could lead to with her own, vast, American means—she did minister to me with all the maternal zeal she could muster. But soon, she, too—and this in the midst of an ugly, yellow, and torrid spell of August—was bedridden, appearing each day more and more like a prostrate alabaster statue that was increasingly hewn and overworked beyond the limits of its minimum widths and dimensions.

But even in this time she continued to have Julius share tales of the exulted heights that a claim to charitable altruism could achieve—my cousin completely aware of the mendacious reasoning; she however, one of the world's half-pitiable, half-execrable fools, for she did not fully grasp that the drive which compelled her onward in such a sly cause was primarily, in her case, fueled by nothing more than pernicious vanity. But, again, my cousin knew; he knew all right.

In the evenings, when Ellsworth and my father (and I briefly) would visit my mother, she would recount her new hopes for our family's fortune. I was merely a child, but blessed with great powers of recollection; Ellsworth, then, he would only appear increasingly angered and silent; my father, however—this was the start for him of the suppuration, unto an obscene intensity, of a lifetime's festering weakness.

My father would retreat from such scenes in fear of Ellsworth's scornful eyes. That scorn was leveled upon my father because Ellsworth was suggesting my father had failed to protect his family on all sides from a jealous invader. And that was just it; Ellsworth had sensed it perfectly. The threat from Julius was motivated by his envy of our way of life, and the more my father resisted—on my brother's urging—giving Julius a place in the family business, the more Julius would press with his suggestions to my mother of how our lives could be.

Had my father immediately placed this acquisitive and bellig-
erently lonely man in our family business, it is possible that Julius
would never have celebrated to my mother the English Crabbe's
call to form Relief Societies and Charities. But Ellsworth sensed
otherwise, and so he enjoined my father to keep Julius out of the
business, completely out of our private American paradise lest he
find, then, some new way for his avarice and belligerence to render
our quartet into scattered lonely pieces like himself. Thus Ellsworth
trusted my father to help him weather the consequences of not placing Julius into the business—weather Julius' subtle machinations
until he could be safely and permanently sent back to England.

But when Ellsworth learned that Julius had made such insid-
ious progress with our mother, he simmered and raged below his
normally contented but ponderous brow. With the announcement
of Julius' departure, however, for the end of that August, Ellsworth
made a crucial error. He assumed that not enough time remained
for any more damage to be done, so he did not escalate, at first, his
pressure upon our father. But Ellsworth maintained the looks and
levels of reproach he had already practiced.

And from that point the true disaster unfolded. As my father
would retreat, he would take solace in his imitative habit of feigning to read—feigning to read the great volumes of which Ellsworth
had truly made himself the master. And with all the passivity of
an average child, he would scan immense tomes by New England
essayists, and give no more focus to the print than that same average child would to engravings in books he only half wished to
hold in his lap on an indolent day. While he was in that posture,
in that vulnerable frame of mind, Julius would seek out my father
and have warm conversations, late at night in the library, and prey
upon my father's guilt—all this as my mother and I lay upstairs in
a continuing state of decline.

On those quiet nights in the library my cousin unearthed,
detected, the guilt in my father, detected it as only the most skilled

nocturnal predator can. What was the essence of that guilt? It was simple. In my father's rudimentary, childish, moral sensibilities, he felt guilty for hosting his nephew for some months, on the understanding that he was supposed to entertain a position for him in the family business on at least an active probationary basis—yet for reasons that were not clear to my father, he was forced by Ellsworth to defer constantly in this and thus, in essence, default on that promise. Therefore his guilt on that count—a count he would hold to, nevertheless, for he feared Ellsworth, and in a way thought him right (but did not and could not know why)—again, his guilt on that count made him vulnerable to making some concession to Julius on another level. Because my father would then avoid Ellsworth, and because Julius relentlessly then preyed upon my father in those late July and early August nights in the library, my cousin now pressed my father, successfully, on account of the old family cause. My father was too afraid of Ellsworth to establish suddenly a Relief Society or a Charity, but he was fool enough, was meek and pliable and utterly helpless enough to look down at one of the open volumes on his lap one night and to feel suddenly it was necessary to become *the* guiding force, *the* grand patron and benefactor and administrator and fool impresario of the resurrection of the Pauktaug Village Lyceum.

A splendid, a grand, a noble idea, confirmed our Cousin Julius on hearing this. Indeed!

But then, with this new resolution in play, a weakness of my father's mind that not even my nefariously perceptive cousin could ferret from the situation was also put in motion—a bizarre and disastrous way of thinking, born of years of cycles in my family, years before Julius had ever appeared in our lives. I have already expressed, in a much earlier part of this writing, what this unique and odd weakness and quality of my father's was. But now I must repeat what that was, and perhaps I should simply paraphrase my own words:

My father was weak in a critical way; he undertook the American experiment only so long as it was pleasant—yet he had never been tested by unpleasantness. Somehow, unlike hundreds of other barons, he had ascended without conflict. He had become wealthy without ruthlessness, and thus his deeper faith in the material world was limited—or his faith in its applications to the remedial was limited—especially when he felt unsettled in his mind and spirit, for he had done no real unsettled battle to gain or possess his riches. They had come as a matter of course. And so his tender, ongoing romance with my mother had somehow made him associate the means expended for use in the fight against her illness with the very illness itself, for he knew no other associations concerning means of wealth connected to conflicts. And thus he began to form dangerous and peculiar associations when she became well—as if her recoveries and the end of exorbitant financial and material hemorrhages were somehow united in a manner outside of traditional cause and consequence. Sometimes the relapse would follow the cure so quickly that while he was still paying the cure's bill the disease would reappear. He connected all of this in a strange way. It was as if he began to believe that removing the cyclic cure applied in a cyclic illness might prevent its recurrence.

My father loved my mother. But, again, a bizarre association had taken hold of him. This association, this perverse concept, one must understand. Because my mother was usually ill for so long, my father would almost forget that it was the start of a bout of illness that would begin the giant outpouring of money. When her recoveries came—months, sometimes years, later—he would only associate the final victory of health with the cessation of expenditure—as if the peace just after the signing of the treaty was what had won the war. He did not honor the power of his means, the power of the material. His was not a faith of the spiritual that he posed instead. His was a faith, perhaps, in chance, for that was how he had ascended and prospered—freakishly without conflict, with miraculous ease and luck. But his was a meek mind; I do not believe he had a credo. He was merely an ultimate kind of prey, fattened mindlessly without ever having wintered on its own—heedless, too, of the wisdom of his protector, but intensely vulnerable if that protector should ever let down his guard. If one had wished to credit my father at this point, one might have thought that he believed finally that my mother's care needed then the application of a new and abstract value system. But he had no replacement. And he simply had no faith in the escalated application of his limitless means. And what cure might he have found had he tested those means?

If one can understand the difference in my father's lack of policy, lack of faith, lack of worship and reverence for wealth, for the material, for what one can ultimately earn and touch and use for its force and tangible, if abrasive, influence; and then understand the regard for all such things that Ellsworth had been finishing slowly in himself since his mind began to work—since his mind had begun to graze freely on whatever had inspired him concerning security and robustness and earthy reliability and its glory—then one may already hold the skeleton key to all that I have yet to explain and tell. Please grasp firmly to that key; it will fit all the ostensibly locked doors that are yet to come.

Thus on choking yellow nights of August humidity and torpor, my cousin could see to it that as much revenge as a cold and malicious and jealous heart could realize was realized upon his American branch of the family.

Yes, my mother's basic comforts were seen to. Yes, a nurse was reengaged to minister to my mother and myself as we coughed our crimson and bloody way—and this from bodies as white as bleached powder horns—coughed to states nearer and nearer to death. But now that our states were worse than they had ever been, it appeared that no venerable and accomplished specialists from New York were to be called in (as they had been in the past); the village doctor would do. Even in former episodes of nearly comparable—but never as threatening—bouts of my mother's and sometimes my own consumption, the notion that we would all uproot out lives and seek refuge in some dry, southwestern climate, or subscribe to the treatments of some heralded new sanatorium that could also be found in a salubrious part of the country, were seriously entertained. But now our rooms and a single nurse would do. The means were there to travel the world in search of a cure; the means were at hand to bring the world to us, had that slight but still promising hope still been considered. But, again, our rooms—and simplicity—would now do.

Though my cousin's passage back to England for the end of August was soon arranged, there were the gestures now, inspired by him, that had to be realized. There was the restoration of the Village Hall's auditorium, a once mildly thriving venue on Long Island's humble Lyceum circuit; there was a committee to form for the administration and advertising of such a sound public service and forum; and, most importantly, there was the solicitation of fine and erudite speakers to fill out the forthcoming seasons of the revived institution.

In addition to all the perverse, all the weak and mad, reasoning that fueled this suddenly idealistic enterprise, this sudden new emergence of the Old World Crabbe's impulse in the New World, there was the crowning reinforcement of my mother's sympathy for the undertaking. And the more her sympathy in this cause was fed—and thus, one might imagine the more she might be able to summon some inner resource of yet unused strength for a rally—the more her health seemed to wane.

Again, my father did not neglect my mother or me in this time of our greatest illness, but he did refrain from anything but the ordinary measures that an affluent man of the mid-nineteenth-century would undertake. Thus, to outsiders—to any of my mother's visitors—she appeared, and I appeared, to be receiving the best of care. But Ellsworth knew better; and though I was but a child, and extremely ill and often in a profoundly removed state of mind, I knew better, as well. I cannot say that my father knew better, however. This chain of truly unique circumstances and peculiar influences had merely revealed an habitual weakness of philosophy, and a peculiar formation of familial shame and vanity to which he was utterly vulnerable—provided another, more belligerent, member of his English family was at hand. And a more subtly belligerent English Crabbe could not have presented himself to us at that time.

But Ellsworth was convinced that my father should have known better. And even though in my childish faith and need I still clung to my father without doubt and without wavering in love or esteem, there was still somehow some part of me that felt Ellsworth was correct—at least insofar as he felt that my father was liable for neglect of our mother. Curiously, perhaps because I was so small, it never occurred to me that I too might be a subject of neglected efforts in such a situation. But it occurred, of course, to Ellsworth; and thus, as the torrid, still, August nights pushed closer and closer to the end of that month, I could hear my brother rage against my father in the library below my own bed chamber. From time to time, I would muster the energy to descend to the library after these conflicts had subsided, and on peeking through the door would only see my helpless father taking refuge—with the assistance of Cousin Julius—in further planning the Pauktaug Lyceum's opening season for that autumn of 1855. And on some of those nights, after I would then look in on my mother, and see her wheezing and coughing bloodily through weaker and weaker nights of sleep, I would then peek into the doors of my brother's galleries and catch glimpses of him carefully packing his collections into trunks and shipping containers from my father's factory.

Ellsworth was sure that my father should have known better. He was also sure that Julius should have known better, as well—and because Ellsworth was certain that there was no trait which obtusely blinded our cousin (as there were weaknesses which blinded, and, as maddening as it may sound, allowed for small pardoning of my father), Ellsworth was certain that our cousin could *only* know better—could only know exactly what was happening. And thus, that part of our cousin which knew better—which, again, was all of him—that part was a murderer. He had already been a murderer of many intangible things in our father and in our family; it was now nearly certain that time would reveal him for a sort of actual murderer, as well, if things were to continue along their unchecked consumptive lines that August. And they did.

2.

Thus I must take one through the result of all that summer's conflicts—to a night in early September. It was a night that perpetuated the monstrous heat of that 1855 August in Pauktaug; but the weather would break before that night was over. It was to be a night of many departures.

I cannot be certain of the hour, but I think near midnight of a Sunday my mother's nurse roused me and encouraged me to dress—to tuck my nightshirt into my trousers. The nurse escorted me down the long hallway, and soon we were before the closed door of my mother's room. We entered after knocking, and there in a chair at my mother's bedside was Cousin Julius. He had my mother's hand in his; he was smiling after the manner of those who heartily give encouragement whilst listening in silence.

"Tell me, Julius, who is to be the first lecturer in October?" my mother asked.

Though we had knocked and had been beckoned inside by Julius, neither my mother nor Julius yet acknowledged the presence of the nurse or myself.

"I can't say I recall, Aunt Ellen, but Uncle Charles has not only secured the first speaker for the new Lyceum, but has almost completed subscribing an entire season of famous and instructive lecturers," answered Cousin Julius.

"Just think!" my mother exclaimed, with the limitations of very weak lungs.

My cousin's eyes flitted to my mother's nurse and to me at that moment; there was nothing clearly communicated in that glance, but the nurse saw no warning in it for us to keep our distance, so she moved me close to where Julius sat next to the bed. I was confused and frightened—and still sleepy (and sick myself, too)—but I recall thinking it strange that the nurse would look to Julius for any sort of permission. I also found it strange that Julius should be present there at that hour on account of the fact that he was due to leave in the morning—via a steamer out of neighboring Northport—for New York City. From there he would meet the ship on which he had secured passage for his return voyage to England.

As we came closer to my mother, it was clear to me that her eyes were closed. Julius had not spoken to us directly when we had entered for fear that my mother would have immediately summoned me to her side and thus dropped the course of their conversation. I could even tell that he feared I would speak too soon; but he was also too cowardly to command silence from me by the press of an arm or some other gesture. He had the good fortune, then, that I was still too young to overcome my own fears—too young to make sounds of reproach under such circumstances, and too uncertain about the importance of the scene. Had I known that I had been brought to take leave, that I was standing before what was soon likely to be my mother's deathbed, I surely would have made my presence known, if even solely from the sobbing that would have come with tears.

Even down unto his last moments in Pauktaug, Julius was intent on reinforcing the perverse course onto which he had set us; or perhaps it was not reinforcement by that time, but instead he engaged in labors that permitted him to savor the damage he had wrought. Yes, I think that was it; he was secure in his achievement; he simply wished to carry home with him as many memories as possible of the disintegration of our fragile paradise—even witnessing its most intimate literal throes.

"Is the hall, the auditorium, to be beautiful?" my mother asked after a gasp. Her eyes remained closed.

"Yes, Aunt Ellen. Uncle has spared no expense. I venture there is to be no finer theater or hall in this state—even considering New York City," answered Julius. He looked at me as he answered.

"The mahogany? Did you persuade your uncle to commit to mahogany?" my mother asked after another hideous, white, gasp.

"Yes, Aunt Ellen. Ours will be the finest furnishings of any on the Lyceum circuit," said Cousin Julius. That he had the outrageous audacity to use the word *ours* struck me, even then, as obscene. He continued to look at me with an ostensibly sympathetic smile—that kind that appears to be filled with pity for the very young—as he made each of his answers to my mother. The nurse saw these seemingly discreet gestures and was moved to squeeze my shoulders, to communicate to me what seemed a veritably senile respect for any cliché granted by a young gentleman. I knew better, and I quietly shrugged my shoulders so that her squeeze could have no subtlety of meaning, no seeming sympathetic reception from me.

I suspected I should have the right to despise him, but I was still confused that Julius had the sympathy of so many adults—my father, my mother, all of our visitors and all of our servants. There were times when I wondered if perhaps when I was adult I, too, would see as the majority and thus learn that perhaps that it was Ellsworth who was moved by the greater jealousy. I suspected that this was not the case, but I knew I would need the passing of time to meditate the evidence.

"To think!" my mother wheezed in red after a still more alabaster gasp. "To think! So many humble people, so many good country people—so many of the poor, as well—so many of my people, of the people that I originally came from, I should say—will hear the greatest minds, under circumstances and a setting of beauty that they are sure to know they never could have afforded but for my husband. They will be compelled, positively conquered, into gratitude."

"Into improvement, into elevation!" Julius assured my mother as he patted her hand in gentle correction as he looked intermittently at me—as if he were getting away with something, as if he were sure that he could expose his full intent to a child, using a wry smile that could not be fully translated by that child until decades would pass. But he was wrong, in part. I still knew better, for the most part, even though I was not entirely certain. I think he felt certain that he and I would never see one another after that night or the next day.

"Yes," my mother continued. "And just think!" she began, but I could not make out the next phrase of what she said, for at that instant an enormous roar and shout rose from the floors below. It was Ellsworth's voice—his powerful voice escaping from the closed doors of the library below—my brother's voice roaring in anger, in a rage, his voice shouting out of all bounds.

The nurse involuntarily squeezed my shoulders once more when the roar came to us. My mother had ceased speaking. I knew that breathing and speaking were difficult for her, but I did not believe her hearing had been compromised. However, she continued to lie quietly and silently after she finished her phrases which had over-lapped with the roar from below. Julius had perhaps communicated alarm to her through their clasped hands and had silenced her.

Julius continued to make no eye contact with my mother; he also continued to ignore the nurse altogether. But he did look to me. At first I took some solace in the fact that even Cousin Julius could be jolted by the new level of rage he had himself surely engendered in Ellsworth—and jolted by it even though it was muted by several layers of floors, walls, heavy rugs, and ponderous doors. But that was merely the jolt of a startled predator, for he soon regained his cold focus and returned the full, cryptic force of his eyes to mine. It was clear that because I was the sole, standing, American Crabbe to witness that very moment in my mother's bed chamber, I was to serve as a sort of vessel—as an empty bottle, into which his sinister figurative note could be rolled and enclosed (that note telling and at the same time decoding all his work since he had arrived on Long Island, and how it had all fully realized itself in that moment at my mother' bedside). And that note in a bottle was to be cast in a sea of time to be opened by me when it chanced to wash up on my middle-aged conscience, or at any time in decades hence when, he suspected, I might mistakenly pity him, but then discover via that figurative note that it was he who had wrought upon others the realization that they should pity themselves. He wanted it known that he had not succeeded in stealing by sharing the prosperity and place he had so envied in Ellsworth and myself, but he had indeed succeeded in redirecting all of that wealth, succeeded in scattering it to the abstract and speculative winds in the name of a good, charitable, but personally vindictive cause.

He wanted me, the witness who would presumably live the lon-gest, to know what he had done. I knew already in so many ways, but, again, in my childish confusion, in the haze of the formative years which can obscure even the deadest certainty, I stood there with a degree of boyish doubt and objectivity. But, really—ultimately—I knew. Julius stared at me for a long moment—with a look that the foolish nurse again took for some noble, manly, gentlemanly look of reassurance across generations within a family of breeding—stared at me for the purpose of quietly sealing, with the aid of a mild smile, the cork of that figurative bottle, with the hot wax of his belligerent satisfaction.

Just as this bottle was cast into its sea, the door of my mother's room opened without a preluding knock. Ellsworth stood there in the open threshold—his eyes appeared sore and red, either from anger or sleeplessness or tears. Perhaps it had been all there. Julius continued to look in my direction and glanced only mildly and briefly to Ellsworth as the door swung open. My mother remained still. The nurse turned to Ellsworth and gave him a look—as if to say, "If one had to confront an event so grim, was it not at least beautiful to walk in upon a scene of such tender solicitude surrounding it?"

I turned to Ellsworth and stared; I had to free myself from the nurse's grip in order to do so.

Ellsworth looked to me and then to the nurse. He did not look at my cousin directly save for one enraged glare. After looking at the nurse, Ellsworth astonished me by asking *me*—after he seemed to dismiss the idea of asking the old nurse—"What is this? What is going on here?"

I was too young to answer, of course, but somehow I was thrilled that he placed me before and above all. I was able to keep that in mind when he asked this question of the nurse after I could not answer.

"What is going on here?" he demanded of the nurse.

The nurse stepped back from the bed and moved toward the door; she did not speak.

After dropping my mother's hand, Julius stood up quietly. He, too, said nothing, but Ellsworth locked eyes with him, and the two young men held a seemingly interminable stare, a frozen duel of stance, a very long but silent expression of limitless contempt, one for the other. There was no need for figurative messages in a bottle between them. Their exchange was direct, targeted, and immensely in the present. Ellsworth only broke his stare when Julius' eyes moved beyond him and followed the entrance of two more figures into the room.

Even my father's weaknesses could not at that moment shake Ellsworth's focus from our invading cousin. Ellsworth's direct rage against our father had been sated for the time being, only a few minutes before in the library below. But that my father had then gone to the parlor to retrieve a man who had been waiting in the house, even during the time that father and son had been shouting in the library—a man whom Ellsworth had not even known was in the house—and that my father would bring this man to my mother's death chamber under the circumstances, was enough to madden Ellsworth so much against our father again, that a singular rage—one so powerful and intense that it could not bear division—engulfed *and* poured forth from him, unlike any rage I have ever seen before or since—singular again because it demanded, lived, exalted, in its craving for a sole target and focus, but somehow heightened because the scene demanded that he must rage at two uniquely guilty and reprehensible men. It demanded focus for its strength; but it somehow grew stronger, that rage, because Ellsworth was also denied that focus.

Ellsworth followed my cousin's eyes to the doorway, where stood my father and the quiet, pursy, and cloyingly humble Dr. Pierce, the oldest of the village doctors. When Ellsworth saw this man in our home, he exploded once more with supreme, vocalized passion.

"Outrageous! This is outrageous!" Ellsworth shouted.

To Dr. Pierce's credit, the simple country doctor, who had never been to our home before, replied with controlled indignation, "I beg your pardon, young Mr. Crabbe."

Of course, Dr. Pierce had up until then been only known to my brother and myself as a vaguely familiar and friendly village figure; he had never been known to us as a doctor we would ever summon or consult. And despite that fact, he had always greeted Ellsworth and myself in a kindly way. He had never been known at all to my mother or father, either socially or medically. Doctors for my family, again, up until that summer, were only exalted, expensive, and supremely learned figures who were summoned from New York City. Dr. Pierce had been invited by a conscience placed entirely in new directions—but wakened to the necessity of medical consultation when the extremity of death made any sort of further deferral, no matter how ostensibly high-minded the procrastination, a moral outrage. Thus, for the first time in our paradisiacal lives of comparative wealth and limitless resources my father was forced to summon a country doctor from Main Street.

"Outrageous!" This is an outrage!" Ellsworth shouted again, screaming the words with such force and in such proximity to my shaking father that I could see the trembling.

Ellsworth moved in my direction. The nurse stepped aside and removed herself to a corner. Julius took a step back toward the wall, and another to the side—so that he had retreated from the pathway to my mother and into the innermost corner of the room. I suspect that, even in this his moment of triumph, he would have retreated to the doorway, into the company of my father (my father, both his ally and victim), or at least to the corner where the nurse had taken refuge, but Ellsworth's approach was too swift.

Before reaching my mother's side, Ellsworth paused before me and lowered his voice—as if the lowering of voice was the necessary translation for a child ally's sympathetic mind—and he repeated yet again: "This is outrageous. This is an outrage, Campbell."

Ellsworth passed me, and he took up our mother's hand into his. From the instant he grasped her white, limp, hand, its coldness justified his rage maturing into a quiet, resolved, wordless fury. Our mother lay there as white, as bleached, as much an instant part of the limitless, dead, past as the intermittent buffalo or cow skull I would later see, decades in the future, on my ride west to the second Pauktaug. Ellsworth respectfully then dropped her hand as one might with one of those skulls, after cradling and weighing it in the palms for a respectful minute.

Ellsworth looked without uttering a word or sound, but looked with a dramatic system from Cousin Julius and then to my father. And though he had not left the room yet, he seemed to turn his back on them forever. Ellsworth took a step toward me, and he did not condescend or kneel—and I always remembered that and profoundly appreciated it—and he said to me, as if I were alone in the room, though I am certain the others could hear, "Look for our return."

What was one to make of that? Even, then, though I was but a six-year-old boy I did not take him to mean—and I still do not take it that he meant—that by the *our* he meant he would return with my mother somehow resurrected, somehow restored via an Egyptian-like certainty to her frail and familiar ivory life. Nor did I take him to be invoking a theatrical utterance of the Imperial We; his *our* did not mean that, I am certain. I am sure, rather, that his *our* meant him and me—*our* return, if not there in Pauktaug, then someday, somewhere. He meant that the Crabbes would return via us—the two American brothers—as soon as he could engineer the means and security to restore the way of life to which we had been born and in which we had invested all of our faith.

"Look for *our* return," also seemed to promise more than a restoration, but rather an effort that would surpass, exceed, its precedents—and make glorious and final war upon anything that threatened its idealized, ultimate, realization.

Ellsworth put his hands on my shoulders for a long moment, and then he strode from the room without another word. I do not believe that father and Ellsworth ever met again after that parting.

After Ellsworth was gone from the room, a difficult silence prevailed, but for no more than a quarter minute. After that time had passed, my father entered into the frame of mind that would characterize his public and private presentation for the rest of his years. He would proceed upon the model set forth by his nephew; Julius Crabbe had seen to it that all my father had kept at a distance via the moat of the Atlantic and by the virtue of his anonymity in a New World would still ultimately characterize him. He was from that point on the son of his father, the nephew of his uncles, the uncle of his nephew, rather than the father of his sons.

Despite all that I had successfully observed and recorded in my brain of the truth of that incident, I was still a very small boy, and by some irresistible instinct I ran to my father and sought his embrace. Fortunately for me, for I was in such a delicate state on so many counts, my father's new code not only welcomed my demonstrative emotional display but it also profited by gestures of reciprocation.

As my father took me in his arms we began our weeping for my mother. My father lifted me from the ground until my head rested upon his shoulders. He moved toward my mother's side, and as he walked I could look behind him to see the foolish nurse exulting in tears of her own—rejoicing at such a tender sight coming so quickly and mercifully on the heels of such an ostensibly wild and ugly display from the senior son of the American Crabbes.

My father put me down, and then he knelt at the side of my mother's bed. He began to sob—yet he did so, somehow, with control—and then he asked that I kiss my mother. After I did this I took a few steps back from her icy white form and pressed my shoulder blades against the wall. As my father continued to kneel upon the floor and quietly weep, I looked from time to time between the nurse and Julius, they standing in opposite corners. The nurse continued to smile upon me as much as she did upon the scene, with an obtuse pity for me and with a truly misconceived sympathy for my father. My cousin continued to smile gently upon me, as well. The nurse was touched by this, too—that he appeared to soften his aquiline and seemingly handsome features for my sake, that he appeared to smile with a benevolent understanding, a smile filled with pity and warm humanity for the young, the innocent, and the helpless. But, again, his smile was not a smile; it was a grin.

3.

Soon the nurse escorted me back to bed. I slept for a time, perhaps—or tried to sleep—but the sound of several sets of muffled footsteps above (coming from my brother's rooms of collections) absorbed my attention hours after midnight. I followed the sounds in my mind as they made their way about upstairs, and then made their way down to the second floor where all the bedrooms were, and then further still to the ground floor. I looked out of my door as the noises left the second floor, but in the darkness I could make out little more than one single, indistinguishable head as it descended the stairs—even though it moved slowly, as if it were at the back of a burdened pack train, making its way with very unwieldy cargo in hand.

Before I closed my door I looked to the rows of the other bedrooms—particularly to my father's chamber and to the guest room that had been given over to my cousin—and they seemed sealed and undisturbed as one would expect of them at that hour. That September night was cold, and I was quickly driven back into the warmth of my bed. I slept or tried to sleep for an indeterminate period of time.

Sometime later I rose and was compelled to look out of my window. My chamber was on the back side of the house, and so upon looking out across a fair expanse of ground I could make out the silhouette of the barn's side. On the right, near the entrance, appeared to be my brother, standing with folded arms. After watching closely, it seemed to me he had three of our servants with him, and Ellsworth directed and assisted them in moving at least a half dozen trunks into the barn. After that task was complete, all four men paused outside the barn for a brief time—as if in recovery of their breath—and then they all vanished again into the barn, this time each man with a large spade in hand.

I felt an inclination to go to Ellsworth, but some childish wisdom had already begun to work itself in me—some childish but wise instinct toward survival. Indeed, I wished to go to my brother, but at the same time I did not wish to do so and be discovered by my father—the last remaining figure I felt I might look to for any kind of imminent, predictable, security, however shallow that protection might be. Again, all my love and allegiance—and sense of justice and ultimate security—drove me to my brother, but something told me I should cling to my father for the immediate time. I went to bed once more.

Just after dawn I woke for a third time. Perhaps it was the sound of the maids rising in their attic chambers, or perhaps it was the sound of the three male servants Ellsworth had commandeered, they returning to their quarters, but in any event it was sound from above that woke me this third time. In this instance, however, I did not feel compelled to look into the hallway; I felt instead, moved to look out once more from my window.

But I had to hurry to the window, for as soon as I formed this resolution to rise, the sound of a horse at a gallop inspired me to fear that I might miss anything important that might be seen. As I reached the low sill upon which I could kneel, I was able to glimpse my father's finest riding horse, Leicester, moving to pass the house and make its way toward the village. Though covered in a dark hat and obscuring cloak against the cold early autumn air, atop Leicester was surely the figure of Ellsworth. I do not know where he was bound on that ride; he never returned.

As tired and as weak as I was, the nurse still came for me at the customary early hour. Before we went downstairs to breakfast, I noted in passing Julius's room that his things were gone and the room appeared empty. My father's room was also open for the day. He had gone to see our cousin off on the steamer from Northport to New York City.

My father returned for breakfast, however. He was not especially demonstrative when he entered, but he did run his fingers through my hair in a way that reassured me, and thus in my fatigue, illness, and grief I discovered the meager foundation upon which I would build, in the next decades, what security and dubious warmth I could find in the world. The nurse appeared touched by the simple scene between my father and myself.

The undertaker came later that morning. Though I did not see her body again that day, I recall thinking that the undertaker could not take away a rounded, healthy, aged old woman—one who had been fattened on life's pastures—but someone thin; pale, and unfinished.

PART V

Grass Freight

I.

The return trip to the new Pauktaug from the small railroad town passed without incident. It was, however, slightly delayed in getting started on the morning after the day we found our Cousin Julius. For in addition to seeing Julius Crabbe to town, we consented to lead two wagon loads of carpenters and two wagon loads of women to Pauktaug, as well.

I was only able to remain on horseback for about an hour before my sickness made it impossible to ride, but before I left Ellsworth and his men in the vanguard of our makeshift train and made my way to one of the men's wagons, Ellsworth assured me that the men in the wagons were merely carpenters who had answered his call to complete the realization of the new Pauktaug's Main Street and the ongoing task of fencing in his enormous range.

I had my ideas about the women, and Ellsworth's remark that they were a very fine and fancy band of sporting girls from Chicago, come to help pass the idle time for mostly Whisker's men in the long hot months before the fall roundups and before the arrival of Whisker's new herds, confirmed my suspicions.

I was compelled to lie down flat in a bit of spare space in the first of the two wagon loads of carpenters. Julius had been riding in the front of that same wagon, and when I needed to lie down, Ellsworth suggested I offer him my horse. With inward reluctance I consented to this—as much because I was suddenly too weak to offer any protest as because Ellsworth gave me a knowing but cryptic look when he made the suggestion to me. Ellsworth and Julius were soon riding ahead in each other's company at the head of our unusual train.

I would soon learn that the sight of English remittance men in the cow country was so common that I began to suspect—as painful and as mysterious as this reunion with Cousin Julius was—that my brother's petitioning for the loan of his capital and permitting his presence were perhaps unavoidable and even somewhat efficient necessities.

Julius helped to make this confirmation by treating me with only the mildest remarks of familial recognition, and that was, of course, more than fine by me. It even occurred to me that tangled issues of shared surnames and ancient English legacies may have made it, in the world of banking law and foreign investment, even less a bizarre coincidence that of all the British investors whom my brother may have sought or with whom he may have been saddled, Julius Crabbe should be the man.

My cousin looked older in his face, but his hair was still full, though by then quite gray. His manner—his display of character, I should say—was far simpler under the circumstances than in the past, for there was no affectation of familial love. The situation as it appeared—a foreign investor having come or having been summoned to observe the progress of his capital's growth in a new business experiment—permitted him to be simply what he was, a lone man actuated by profit.

But for my coughing—and the perverse vision of Ellsworth and Julius leading a wagon train on the northern American range—I slept for quarter hours at a time on that first day's ride, almost regularly.

The second day passed much like the first, and in the late afternoon we came into Pauktaug—my second entrance somewhat like my first, for my prostration from sickness reigned over the scene. However, in the second case I at least had the dignity of the wagon to carry and conceal me. The atmosphere prevailing in town upon my second arrival was completely different from that of the first, however.

Main Street was filled with men—cowhands from Whisker's ranch, coming and going from the two or three saloons, and from gambling halls that stood in the exact place and storefront locations of businesses that had other, more placid, functions in the old Pauktaug back East.

In the four days since I had left town, the spring roundups had concluded—both by Whisker and his men, and by the crews my brother had left behind. However, it would become more and more evident to me—on that evening, but especially so in the following days—that the crowds of cowpoke revelers in town were almost entirely from Whisker's outfit. Again, because Whisker had sold nearly his entire herd in the previous season, their spring roundup, with the assistance of men from Ellsworth's outfit, was a rather light concern. And until the two new herds from Texas arrived, Whisker's men had comparatively little to do in the way of summer duties. They had been paid and virtually laid off for a time, as often happened to many crews at the conclusion of roundups.

On getting out of the wagon I expressed an immediate desire—despite my weakness and coughing—to push on so that I could finally see and settle into the house Ellsworth had built for himself on his land.

"There'll be plenty of time for that later, Cam. I think this is as far as your health will permit you to travel for now," Ellsworth said as he—and then McCarthy, too, coming from the hotel—helped me to walk indoors.

"But, Ellsworth! The noise here!" I protested as I took exhausted steps forward and looked about at the crowds of cowhands. I thought it strange that he had pronounced so little caution on account of my health before I had made that request, but I withheld that challenging remark.

"Yes, sure is noisy!" said McCarthy. "I suspect the summer slows is upon us again—only more so this season. Ain't it so, Mr. Crabbe?"

Ellsworth did not answer, but he did smile with tolerance upon McCarthy as we made our way into the lobby.

"Good for business, for sure, though," added McCarthy when it was clear Ellsworth had no intention of answering.

"Yes, it will be," Ellsworth said as I was helped up the stairs, making our way to my same room from days earlier. "A lot of idle boys will be having some fun for quite some time. That's the way of things when the work slows down. I have other plans for them, this season, however."

"Really, now!" said McCarthy. "For until we get some reliable law in here, as nice as it is to have business after the spring and fall roundups is over, it would be nice to keep some order and sense over all the customers."

The sound of shots fired intermittently into the air, usually accompanied by cheering and laughter, had erupted throughout the course of my slow migration back to my hotel room—but the shots and other noise were coming from the other end of Main Street, closer to where dozens of idle Whisker men, aimless and out of work for a time, found diversion in the quick liquidation of their spring salaries. The sound, however, seemed to grow nearer with each subsequent uproar, until the crash of a shattering window followed hard upon pistol report—and then there was a scream of a horse, the scream of women, and then once more a chorus of laughter.

McCarthy and Ellsworth put me to bed. McCarthy was off to the restaurant and off to manage the front desk—both of which would soon be humming with business, he was sure, though he had remarked that business had strangely come to town a few days earlier than expected. He had thought that Whisker's boys would still be out driving in the small remaining herd of three-year-old steers that had been cut out for beef, driving them then to the railroad and to market. I said to McCarthy that we had not seen anyone driving anything to market as we had made our way back ourselves along the stage road to Pauktaug.

"Isn't that right?" I asked Ellsworth as he helped me remove my boots. He said nothing in reply.

However, he did say, when the laughter and gunfire got closer, "I think the boys down the way have got wind of the new ladies. I best get downstairs and see that the gals settle in before things in the street get out of hand. Come along, man."

"Yes, sir, Mr. Crabbe," answered McCarthy.

I had many questions, but I soon happily gave way to sleep, even though the hotel resounded with as much noise as a New York City depot until nearly dawn.

2.

A cycle of several days and nights would pass, just like the one recounted above, but I remained in my room for that time, encouraged by Ellsworth and served by McCarthy, so that my second emergence from that sick chamber might be in a state of better health.

During the morning of that Sunday when John Whisker was

supposed to arrive in town and discuss matters of the law, I went downstairs for the first time and took a late breakfast. Though it was nearing noon, the hotel restaurant and lobby were quiet.

I found my brother at lunch, in the company of two guests at his table. Ellsworth rose when he saw me enter.

"Cam! Are you sure you are well enough?" he asked.

"Yes," I smiled. And I was well enough, for I did not need to stifle a cough when I answered. "I am quite fit to rejoin the world."

My brother's guests had not risen from their places upon my entrance. Ellsworth gave them both a subtle look of reproach, not meant for me to witness. He continued to stand, and by his manner I could tell that he preferred I not yet seat myself.

After a few moments, the woman of the seated pair—who by subtlety of mannerism made it clear she was the superior of the two—affected to take it upon herself to rise. She was a comely woman of, perhaps, forty, still slender, but somehow weathered in her looks beyond her years—a kind of weathering that seemed due to some personal history and not due to the harshness of the prairie wind or dry air of the West. She cut a rather absurd appearance in that recreation of an Eastern hotel dining room of a Sunday morning, for she was attired in what appeared to me— from magazine engravings I had seen—to be a Parisian dress, gloves, and hat. But into her dress had been sewn the patterns of every ranch brand to which she and her doves had been of service. She sported an unopened whalebone parasol, of a construction familiar to me.

After she finally rose, the man in her company followed.

"Come, Professor," she said to the man. She only addressed him as *professor*. He was a tall, muscular man, in a rather fine suit—a suit only a bit weathered from the long wagon ride we had all recently endured from the railroad settlement. He certainly did not appear to me to be an academic. He seemed inattentive to the scene and itching to display some sort of unemployed power.

"Thank you for breakfast, Mr. Crabbe. I am sure you have other business to discuss." It was clear she had only recently arisen, as well. Ellsworth, however, I was certain, had been up since dawn.

"Thank you, Mrs. Morgan. I do in fact have other business," said Ellsworth.

He meant to reproach the pair for not rising in deference to me, but if they were rising then to depart so that my brother could be alone in my company, he would accept that gesture as a close second in his quest for a particular kind of etiquette where his family was concerned. At the same time, it never seemed to me, even had this Mrs. Morgan and her Professor remained, that Ellsworth had any intention of introducing the pair to me.

"Come along, Professor," Mrs. Morgan said to the tall, muscular man, once more. He said nothing in reply, but he followed the woman dutifully. "I should check upstairs after my daughters now," she added as they left the dining room.

"Daughters!" I thought as I took my seat at the table. This Mrs. Morgan had at least nine ostensible daughters.

McCarthy then appeared and brought me coffee. As he took my order for breakfast, neither he nor my brother paused as the Professor took a seat across the hall in the parlor and began to play "Woodman! Spare That Tree" upon its piano.

I was on the verge of forming words, of beginning to speak to Ellsworth when into the dining room strode Julius. On his arm was one of Mrs. Morgan's daughters—a blue-eyed young woman with elaborate cascades of blonde curls. She, like her ostensible mother, looked like she had dressed for an evening at the opera. Julius simply nodded to Ellsworth and to me and took another table.

Ellsworth had been on the verge of words himself just before the entrance of Julius, but he seemed to defer all he had to say—at least until I could finish my breakfast and be free to follow him to a place more private. Thus for an awkward interval, I sat opposite my silent brother as I ate, and Julius and his guest took their own luncheon nearby—all this to the strange accompaniment of the dubious professor in the nearby parlor.

As soon as I was finished, Ellsworth insisted that I rise and follow him. A second nod to Julius seemed unnecessary, and we left the hotel without a word to him or his companion.

Though the hotel had been quiet when I had first come down to the dining room, I was astonished at the amount of traffic there was in the street on that Sunday afternoon. Though I had come and gone from my window intermittently in those few days of my second convalescence, and had glimpsed an increasing flow of wagon traffic—especially on the day before my emergence—it was not until I stood in the street that I saw fully that a ceaseless chain of shipments had gotten underway, between the railroad and Pauk-taug during my second recuperation. On top of these countless buckboards were mountainous supplies of feed: various types of grain, but also and primarily a seemingly endless supply of hay. The wagons were using Pauktaug as a final stopover along a journey that was not to end until the supplies were delivered to specified points on my brother's range.

I asked Ellsworth about the endless train of loaded wagons—and about the empty wagons that were done with their deliveries and already bound back to the railroad, apparently slated to pick up more supplies of imported fodder—and his reply was simple:

"We're preparing against the possibility of bad winters," he answered curtly, as if my question required an obvious answer that only distracted him from his present thoughts. He seemed suddenly to sense the inappropriate character of his answer, and he reached over and patted my back as a sort of fraternal apology. He was spared having to say anything more, however, for nearly every quarter minute he was compelled to tip his hat or shout a hail back in answer to one of his men who were either driving one of the inbound or outbound buckboards. We continued to walk with speed, south along Main Street's board sidewalk, until we reached the end of the recreation of old Pauktaug (and the end of where old Pauktaug's Main Street buildings did, in fact, end back East), and then we continued farther south along the new Pauktaug's expanding Main Street, which consisted mainly of saloons.

We entered a district in which carpenters were engaged in the framing of no less than three new structures. Two of these structures were on the east side of Main Street; one was on the west, and next to the one on the west was a nearly completed, modestly sized building with a false front above its porch. Ellsworth had me stop in front of this place and made it clear that we were to enter, but not before he exchanged a silent nod and a few inscrutable glances with Pope Pope, who was positioned about fifty yards south, at the end of Main Street, where the street simply dissolved into the grasses of the range land. Pope was on horseback. He had stationed himself there to direct the traffic of buckboards and to check the invoices of each wagon's cargo.

We stepped into the newly completed structure. A beautiful desk sat in the front room, and on one of the walls was a locked gun cabinet with an array of fine new rifles. In the back area of the building was a set of sturdily constructed prison cells. Up a flight of stairs was a pair of chambers that could serve as living quarters.

After showing me the upstairs rooms Ellsworth said, "These I do not think you'll need. You can keep your place in the hotel as long as you like, and all of your meals will be taken care of there, too. I have rooms for you out at the house when we're finally ready to go out there."

We returned to the first floor. I was astonished by the sight of an enormous bull's head mounted on the front wall—a sight I had missed on entering because I had passed beneath it.

"I was sorry to lose him; he was one of our best. But he can serve now to remind you, in a way, of all you would be protecting," Ellsworth said when he saw me lost in thought before the great bull's head.

Then he walked to the desk and opened a drawer with a small key he produced from his vest pocket. From the drawer he pulled an immense ring of keys—keys both large and small, yet they all appeared shiny and new. He walked over to me and put the keys in my hand; then he reached into his vest pocket once more and pulled out a deputy marshal's brass star. This he placed in my other hand.

"Think about it, Cam. You've already done this kind of work back east. Whisker and I can take care of most of the trouble around here, but—"

I interrupted Ellsworth. "But I thought Mr. Whisker was coming into town to discuss this very thing."

"He is. But he will go with me on this when I tell it to him. I am going to go back to the hotel and wait for him. Stay here for awhile and think it over. It would be nice to have a little official help from time to time. And even I could use a little policing, I suppose."

He said that last line with a distracted air, and he reached up and touched the chin of the bull as he finished the phrase.

"When you make your decision," he continued, bringing himself from his brief reverie, "come on back to the hotel, and Whisker and I will draw up the papers and have you sworn in."

"Ellsworth," I asked, "are *you* to pay my salary?"

My brother seemed startled by this—startled that he had forgotten to mention something that would present him in clean standing. He relaxed after a moment of tension and replied, "No! No, it will be the taxes from Mrs. Morgan's daughters that will pay for your situation."

Ellsworth left me there, and I watched him from the window, with Pope Pope soon following close on his heels on horseback.

I took several steps back and leaned against the desk. Though my health had taken extreme turns in my brief time in the new Pauktaug, my spirits had remained hopeful. However, as I stood alone in the midst of the small office, I felt a despair come over me for the first time since my arrival.

Had I found a place in, had I even been summoned to, this new Pauktaug solely for the purpose of supporting and turning a blind eye to the dubious business of a man I perhaps hardly knew and for the purpose of merely enjoying myself in turn, via a superficial nepotism and the ease of an obscure sinecure—a sinecure that rested on a position that was meant, ideally, to bring the best of law and order and civilization to a new country? I began to fear so; I began to fear I *knew* so.

I was no cattleman, but what kind of prosperous cattleman does not sell a single animal for going on two seasons when he is reputed to have one of the grandest herds in all of that country? What to make, then, of the seemingly endless wagon train of imported fodder (in summer, mind!) when in addition to the nearly state-sized private range holdings my brother possessed, millions of free grass acres extended beyond the boundaries described in his deed? What to make of the death of Kettle? Would no one show any interest in the peculiar death of a stranger? What to make of Ellsworth's connection to the hotel's evident role as nothing more than a place of business for prostitution? Was I expected to be complicit in those undertakings? Apparently so, for my salary was to be raised as a consequence of Mrs. Morgan's enterprise in town. But, above all, was I expected to understand that one of the most powerful memories of my life—the memory of that summer long ago which had assured me Ellsworth knew Julius Crabbe for the brutally selfish scoundrel he was—needed to be put aside? Was a simple nepotistic ease the prevailing order of things in that case, as well? And, thus, did Ellsworth value his association with me no more than he did with a man like Julius Crabbe?

Beyond my normal illness and weakness, my despair suddenly brought a further sense of sickness—real, physical, sickness—to my body and conscience during those minutes I stood alone in that new deputy marshal's office. I looked down at the ground and then to my hands; in the one I held the great ring of keys; in the other I held the deputy marshal's star. Then I looked up again and out of the front windows—each window to the side and below the great bull's head—and that is when I saw the Indian.

3.

I had never seen a real Indian before, save for illustrations in magazines and newspapers. Yet something in his bearing made me sure that at one time he had known the true wild life—a life entirely removed from towns and white men's trade.

However, at the same time there was also a confidence in his manner on entering the town, as if he had become long accustomed to Main Streets, coins, and shod horses—and as if such things, in turn, had also become long accustomed to him.

My eyes followed him with fascination as he first appeared through the front window that afforded me the most significant view to the right, to the south. He had apparently come from the south, on foot, right off of the range and onto Main Street. He seemed new to the new Pauktaug, for he looked about—left and right, up and down—as a man does when he takes in a new place for the very first time. I was able to watch him for a bit through the right window, not only because of the angle but also because the wagon traffic seemed to have halted for a spell, perhaps because of the midday sun. But eventually he was nearly in front of the marshal's office and about to pass right in front of the office's door, and thus out of view of the right front window. As he disappeared, I shifted my position in anticipation of his coming back into view in the left front window. At the pace he had been walking, the time before he should have appeared from behind the eclipse of the front door and back into view in the left window should not have been more than a few seconds. However, after ten seconds he did not appear. I had the fear, then, that I would soon hear footsteps coming to the door—should he have turned and approached directly. But that did not happen.

I moved to the left window and looked out into the street to where the Indian should be had he stopped moving. He was there. He stood perfectly still; he had dropped a sack he had been carrying over his shoulder; he held his hands in the air and stared straight north. I looked left through the window and north along Main Street, as well.

There, about twenty-five yards from the Indian, and standing directly in his path, was Mitch Rutledge. His revolver was leveled at the Indian; its metal looked dull and black, like the cold nib of a sharp lead pencil, notwithstanding the glare of the midday sun. The left window had been left open a few inches, and I could hear everything that came from the street.

"Well, look at what we got here!" roared Rutledge.

Two of his underlings from Whisker's outfit were right behind him. All three appeared to be drunk—as did a larger group of Whisker men who gathered further north along the board sidewalk just outside of the saloon from which they had emerged.

Rutledge was drunk indeed; the long barrel of his revolver inordinately shook as he cocked the hammer with his trembling thumb. The gun sounded like iron knuckles cracking as the cylinder turned.

"So you think you can just rob and kill a couple of white men and then just walk into town to a have a look see, like you don't know nothing about it ? You red sons-a-bitches!"

The Indian muttered a few unintelligible phrases in broken English; he then inexplicably nodded from one side of the street to the other and then gestured with a nod toward his bag on the ground.

"Shut up, you murderin' son-of-a-bitch! Get down on your knees!" shouted Rutledge, as more of his men closed ranks behind him. The Indian just looked baffled and continued to stare straight ahead, in a careworn but rather innocent sort of manner.

"I said kneel, you son-of-a-bitch, or I'll paunch you!" shouted Rutledge.

He gestured with the barrel of his gun that the Indian should move to the ground. But when the Indian still did not move, Rutledge suddenly fired a shot. I cannot say if he intended to miss with such precision—I rather think that he did not (and could not, because of his condition)—but the bullet appeared to have passed through a narrow margin between the Indian's waist and a fold in his loose buckskin shirt. The Indian dropped one of his raised hands and checked after himself in a state of amazement that the bullet had hit no more critical mark.

It was when the report of the revolver made me clench my fists that I became aware again of the jabbing, but balled, points of the brass marshal's star in my hand. Somehow, all the suspicion and ambiguities that had been plaguing my mind just before the Indian appeared seemed easy, for the moment, to dismiss. In my other clenched hand, was the great set of keys, and by dint of great luck, the first of the smaller keys on the ring unlocked the gun cabinet. I pulled out a rifle and found a box of fitting ammunition on the lowest shelf of the cabinet. I loaded; I put more rounds in my pocket and then quietly opened the front door of the office.

Rutledge was by then just two yards or so from the Indian; he had also persuaded the Indian to kneel. Rutledge was in the midst of shouting the end of a phrase of intense obscenity and damning all Indians for red sons-of-bitches when I astonished myself and spoke.

"Back off, Mr. Rutledge. I can drop you easily from here, with one, easy, shot. Do as I say and back away."

Some of the men behind Rutledge laughed. Rutledge himself

eased his aim on the Indian and turned about in astonishment—but not because he was yielding to my warnings or relaxing his ultimate fixation upon his target.

"And what do we have over *here!*" he laughed with contempt. "Who done and gone made you a lawman, or made you someone that I or anyone else should have to answer to?"

I paused for just an instant. I had not been sworn in, but I was sure I could and would be if I wanted it, and I suddenly, earnestly, wanted it.

"The powers that be! That's all you need to know!"

I held my aim right at his temple. The men behind him began to back away, but they were all still so drunk that the only sounds they made were lazy chuckles and snorts. My eyes flitted about to check the scene to my left, north up Main Street. A crowd had started to gather, and I could not fail to glimpse Julius strolling casually up the west sidewalk toward the crowd. With indolence he held a burning cigar a few inches away from his face.

"The powers that be?" shouted back Rutledge with scorn. "And wouldn't the powers that be be happy if I finished off one of the red sons-a-bitches who sure as anything shot those men on the stage? Hell! You came in on that very stage!"

Julius was now close enough that I am certain he heard every word of this exchange.

"I think the powers that be would want it that a man can walk into town without his first fear that of being shot for no reason!" I shouted back as I kept the gun steady.

"Hell! No reason! You don't know this country at all, boy! No reason! No reason for this murdering son-of-a-bitch? Hell, the only powers that be for you right now, I bet, is your brother giving you something to do!"

"That may be," I replied (and I continued to amaze myself with my boldness), "but that next *something to do* will be to fire this rifle right at your skull if you don't put that sidearm away!"

"Really? Is that right? And if you do that then who'll be left to look after the other half of the town's interests? Unlike you, I ain't paid just to be kept busy. You may be Ellsworth Crabbe's brother, but you ain't no one's marshal, and I'm like a son to Mr. Whisker. And, hell, if I ain't planning to—"

"You'll do no such thing!" I shouted, but this last shout triggered a coughing fit that I could not control.

"Hell, the barrel of your rifle's shaking like a branch stuck in a creek. You're no better than a punkin' roller out here. Hell, I ain't going to listen to you. For you can't be a better shot right now than even a drunken man, and *I* am a drunken man!"

This remark earned a laugh from several in the crowd, and his men started to drift back into a supportive circle around Rutledge. But the laughter stopped quickly and the forward motion of the mob halted when a lone figure stepped through the crowd, and stopped right behind Rutledge and spoke.

"You don't have to listen to the new marshal—not yet, at least. But you'll have to listen to me—right now. Drop the gun!" The man cocked a revolver at the back of Rutledge's head.

"Mr. Crabbe!" muttered Rutledge without turning around to look. But he kept up his courage—and he kept up his stare, right upon the Indian, and kept his aim squarely at the Indian's.

"Mr. Crabbe," he continued coolly. "You saw what they did to the stage. You don't want this any less than I'm sure Mr. Whisker would want it!"

"Look, boy, John Whisker doesn't want murder on his account because of your foolish reasoning. We don't know anything about this man," Ellsworth said so that the entire crowd could hear, as he continued to aim the pistol to the back of Rutledge's head.

Rutledge raised his voice to match my brother's: "About this red son-of-a-bitch? He looks just right. He looks Cheyenne to me."

"That he does. But did you catch him doing something? Doing anything? Did you catch him trespassing on Whisker's land? Did you catch him trespassing on *my* land?" demanded Ellsworth. The manner in which he gave peculiar inflection to the latter question is beyond my powers of representation here. But I felt, then, that the inflection caused a strange vibration in the crowd on the street—but was soon lost in the swiftness of the unfolding event.

"Mr. Crabbe," Rutledge shouted back to Ellsworth while continuing to face the Indian, and while taking a small step closer to his target and confirming the precision of his aim, "I just came upon the red son-of-a-bitch that I know killed those men on the stage. Just by walking into this town he's tresspassin' against justice. I know—"

As Rutledge finished this phrase, his brow furrowed ever so imperceptibly, as even the most veteran gunman's brow will do just before he takes a deliberate shot. Though Ellsworth was behind Rutledge, somehow he sensed this furrowing of Rutledge's brow, and in the instant that followed—as Rutledge was distracted by the sound of several horsemen coming onto Main Street from the south range—Ellsworth shifted his grasp on his gun from the grip to the barrel, and with one swift but surely forceful blow, he struck Rutledge on the back of his head with the butt of the gun.

Rutledge fell to the ground in an insensible heap. Many of the same men who had laughed with Rutledge when he had taunted me and countered my demands, now laughed at his fall—but not the nervous laughs of turncoats. These were the laughs of accomplished drunks. This somehow reassured me when later I looked back at the early part of the standoff—when I had stood alone against Rutledge and his men's laughter.

Ellsworth ordered a few of Whisker's men to carry Rutledge into the new jail. Though my title was not yet official, I could still say that I had taken in my first prisoner—or at least my first disorderly citizen who needed to sleep off a spree. I collected his gunbelt and had a cell opened for him.

4.

The horseman who had caused distraction just long enough for Ellsworth to knock Rutledge out with his pistol butt had been Whisker himself with several of his hands in tow as escort. He had arrived in town as promised for the Sunday meeting concerning the appointment of a marshal, but had arrived just a moment too late to address the conflict between Rutledge and the Indian.

When I left the office and went into the street, I came upon Ellsworth and Whisker and several of Whisker's more sober men gathered around the Indian. Julius, I noted, had begun already to stroll back toward the hotel. He only looked back from time to time to reveal a wry raising of his eyebrows and the lazy tendrils of his cigar smoke.

When I reached Ellsworth and Whisker, Whisker was confirming the general summary of what had just transpired.

"You mean he wouldn't stand down when you ordered him to?" he asked my brother in a tone of confirmation.

"No. And he wouldn't stand down when the marshal ordered it either," added Ellsworth.

"Marshal?" asked Whisker, and he looked toward me as Ellsworth gave a nod in my direction.

"You don't say!" Whisker said after looking at me for a long moment. He then smiled; his thoughts were evidently elsewhere. I was disappointed, for I had hoped my appointment would merit more consideration. Whisker, however, seemed already to have accepted it as a matter of course.

"Your man Rutledge said you would have wanted this kind of thing," Ellsworth said, to force a conclusion onto the discussion of the incident.

"Wanted something like this? You don't say! Hell, the boy was drunk. He didn't know what he was talking about," replied Whisker with a scornful laugh.

"That's what I thought—" Ellsworth began to say, but Whisker could no longer contain the joy that fueled the smile he could not conceal.

"I've just had the damndest turn of easy luck, Ellsworth—never thought it would happen twice to me in this business. Yesterday I—" Now it was Ellsworth who felt obliged to interrupt.

"I'm eager to hear it, John. Let's just resolve this concern first," Ellsworth said, and he pointed to the Indian. The Indian still kneeled in the same place.

"Listen," Ellsworth said to the red man as he signaled for him to rise. "You'll have to pardon us here."

The Indian was silent. Ellsworth paused and then said, "Do you understand me? Do you speak American?" The Indian slowly nodded. "One of these boys is going to take you to get something to eat—maybe buy you a new shirt for your trouble. But we've had some things going on nearby, some trouble, so when you're done it's best for you to walk straight south, straight in the direction you came from—and not come back. Do you understand? And you're not to go north because that's where we've had some bad trouble. And you're not to go west—or east!—because you'll be trespassing on private land. Do you understand me?"

The Indian took a slow step toward Ellsworth, and then he placed both of his hands on my brother's shoulders and said, "I understand."

My faith in Ellsworth climbed back. I thought: What matter should some perhaps necessary ambiguities of the frontier—like the presence of Mrs. Morgan and her daughters—be to me? What matter? I grew at ease once more in the presence of what I felt to be Ellsworth's profound and seemingly constant objectivity.

Whisker was eager to take Ellsworth somewhere for a happy, more private conversation; so he stepped in at this moment:

"Ellsworth, my fellow here, Jake, will take this red fellow for food and rest and anything else he might need. I'm too happy to care that we're attending to an Injun!"

"Thank you, John," said Ellsworth, and he put some coins into the hands of this Jake before the cowhand took the Indian away.

"Hell," laughed Whisker, as Whisker and Ellsworth, with me encouraged to follow, made our way toward the hotel, "I'd have told you to have one of your own boys take the Injun away, but I don't see one damn one of them around here. You and your little brother faced off against my boys—alone—when my boys were at their worst. I'm sorry for that, Ellsworth."

"It was nothing," said Ellsworth, and from the casual tone of his remark, I was sure he meant it.

"Where in hell are all your boys, Ellsworth?" asked Whisker.

"Still working," was the answer.

"You don't say! Well, you see! I told my boys you'd have to be cutting out a fair share and sending to market by now. Your numbers must be enormous. When are you driving to the cars?"

Ellsworth smiled and seemed to be about to answer, but Whisker cut in as we neared the front of the hotel: "Hell, you don't even have to say—because no matter when it is supposed to be it will be too late for you to catch the good fortune I happened into. But, wait! Hell, what am I saying! It's possible your man Pope already told you about this. It happened yesterday."

"I've dealt with Pope today in town, but he didn't mention anything," Ellsworth said as we paused, on Whisker's lead, in front of the hotel.

"Hell," Whisker exclaimed as the obvious suddenly became evident to him. "What's all this wagon traffic about? Is this the freight you said you'd be expecting?" Whisker's eyes looked north along the stage road where one could see an almost endless line of incoming wagons making their way south toward town. Pope could be seen riding in with the frontmost wagons; he had apparently ridden out to stop the traffic when it was clear that trouble had started to stir on the south end of Main Street—that trouble turning out to be the standoff between myself, Ellsworth, and Rutledge.

"That's it. That's some of it," smiled Ellsworth.

"Well, hell, you must be getting a big herd out there for sure. You feeding whales or dragons out there too? Hell, don't answer that, Ellsworth." Whisker then smiled at me as Pope rode up to us. "Campbell, your brother's probably got some plan that'll put me out of business, and I'm too happy right now to worry about it."

Pope reached us and dismounted.

"Here's your man, Ellsworth!" said Whisker. "Well, here's Mr. Pope. Pope, I was about to tell Mr. Crabbe here of the good fortune you brought me yesterday. He says he doesn't know anything about it yet. But I'm glad; it'll give me the fun of telling him myself."

Ellsworth and Pope—as if by some agreement—restricted their eye contact. Whisker seemed to find nothing remarkable in anyone's manner. We proceeded into the hotel—with Pope Pope only slightly behind as he tethered his horse.

We passed through the noisy lobby and by the equally noisy parlor. The Professor still played upon the piano in the parlor. Both rooms were filled with Whisker's men—most, if they chanced to catch a glimpse of their employer, sent up cheers for him, as if he were responsible not only for putting the last of their spring pay in hand, but also for somehow arranging the special opportunities through which they could be disburdened of their heavy pockets. But some of his men, even when he directly passed, were either too drunk to notice anyone or too absorbed by the satin and perfume of Mrs. Morgan's daughters as they passed from man to man and whispered unheard things in the cowmen's ears.

"Hell, I'd forgotten Mrs. Morgan would have arrived now!" exclaimed the smiling Whisker as McCarthy led us to Julius' table in the dining room.

Julius stood up as we approached; by some remarkable instinct, he knew that the stranger to him in our group was a man of great significance in that country. One could see this register in his brow. The two had yet to meet in the West; and something made me sure they would not have met during Julius' first time in America back in the old Pauktaug. I am certain Ellsworth would not have introduced any of his friends to Julius at that time.

When we all reached the table, there was a moment of hesitation from Ellsworth. It was clear to all that the responsibility of introduction devolved to him, but he seemed unprepared with words with which he could properly present Julius to John Whisker.

With a kind of swiftness which remained civil but which left room for a very observant third party to wonder, Ellsworth said, "John Whisker, this is Mr. Julius Crabbe—" And then, after another brief pause, Ellsworth added, "Mr. Crabbe is a significant new investor in the my expansion."

Julius' natural coolness failed to register any distinct reaction to Ellsworth's brief introductions. Julius simply shook hands with Whisker, who seemed particularly gregarious, relaxed, and unobservant at that time. To Ellsworth and myself Julius gave a cool nod; between Julius and Pope Pope there was no exchange. Though I am certain that Julius was naturally indifferent to Pope, Pope had—by observation and instinct—formed an antipathy for and caution toward Julius, feelings that naturally had to be limited and suppressed in their expression. Despite the seeming indifference between them during the introduction, Pope Pope somehow made it clear to me that he regarded my cousin with suspicion.

McCarthy began to pull chairs out at Julius' table so that we could all sit. When he came to Pope, Pope quietly waved off the gesture and insisted to Ellsworth, Whisker, and myself, that he had to return to his duties with the freight traffic.

"You don't say!" exclaimed the smiling Whisker. "It seems I sure made the weaker choice in finding a foreman! And you're not likely to end up in a cell during your idle hours, Pope!"

Pope Pope only smiled and then left the hotel.

"Mr. Julius Crabbe!" roared the ebullient Whisker. "A real, live, remittance man! Now we've got one of our own, right here in Pauktaug! We really must be coming up in the world as a town! Don't you think so, Ellsworth?"

Ellsworth only nodded and smiled. It was clear that when Whisker was filled with joy, he could shout with indiscretion as other men do only when they are well on their way to drunkenness.

"What do you think, Mr. Crabbe," Whisker boomed to Julius, "of your cousin's outfit in this new country? Seems to be running it after a mighty strange fashion of late!"

Julius seemed eager to pursue this suggestion: "Yes, I am puzzled by the affairs of the ranch, of the company, of late. It seems, normally, to prosper, but my cousin assures me that his experiments—"

Julius could not finish; Whisker interrupted.

"Whatever experiments Ellsworth here is undertaking, you should follow along with them. He can be a secretive cuss with that kind of thing, even with me, even

when—"

Julius himself then interrupted: "But the scale of this experiment; there is no precedent, no real discernible cause, for a man refraining to sell—"

Whisker cut in yet once more: "You do what this man says and then see returns on your investment unlike any you ever dreamed, Mr. Remittance Man! Soon you won't have to be writing home for any money at all!" Julius evidently took exception to the levity and nickname, but held his tongue.

Whisker continued with the enthusiasm and gregariousness of a drunken man, though I am certain he had not been drinking.

"Just leave old Ellsworth to his notions. I learned myself to do that back in Texas! No! I had to learn to do that back in New York! No! Even before that! I had to learn to trust this friend even when he first persuaded me to leave Pauktaug and to go to New York with him to found our first business! I was the one with the money then. He had none, really, but he had the notions, the ideas. Soon I had doubled my investment, and Ellsworth here was on his way to becoming a rich man too! You've got to trust this man of business. Even now, everything I hear in town about his ranch this past year or more—and I've heard little (his men are sure loyal and silent!)— everything I hear runs counter, it seems, to all logic. But he knows what he is doing! He'll suddenly be shipping to Chicago again, and the rest of us will be run out of business by his new notions—and looking to him for jobs punching *his* steers into the cars to Chicago! But that's just it, too! He won't do that to *me*! He's a great man, a great businessman—and a greater friend. He doesn't forget his friends. He doesn't forget things. He'd carry me in on this idea of his, but only after he's tested it—makes sure it's safe. He assured me after risking my money, years ago, on that first investment, that he would never jeopardize or test my confidence. I trust the man completely! He's a brother to me—my family. I hope you won't take exception, Cam. And, then, there is this land—this new country!"

Whisker only paused here to place an order with McCarthy, who had been standing silently by since we had been seated. When Ellsworth and I began our own requests for food Whisker continued where he had left off with Julius.

"Again, Mr. Crabbe, this land, this country! You could not have made a more solid investment than in your Ellsworth's business here—not only because of the man himself, but because of this new country! Why, I can tell you that returns come out of this land even where you're not looking! Take this that I have to tell you all for example. (And, Ellsworth, if I didn't know you were engaged in your great experiment, I'd have to say you'd have to be envious of the luck I've just had in this!) But, then, again, maybe he wouldn't be—because this land is just that filled with luck and good fortune that it is just as likely that some wild bit of luck will be at Ellsworth's gate this afternoon!

"Just yesterday I rode out to the steers we had cut from the spring roundup so that I could look over the road branding. Granted it was a small herd, what with my good fortune of last year's sale! But, hell, you already know about that!

"Just as I arrived that fool, Rutledge—still, hell, he's a good foreman—he was branding the last steer and was almost ready to strike out for the railroad and the cars so as to ship 'em to Chicago. And just as I was about to send him and the drive boys on their way to the cars up rides your man, Pope, with a few of your boys. He said he had encountered a man here in town who was willing to pay a dollar more a head for the entire herd—a dollar more per head than in any contract I expected for that herd!

"You sure your man ain't told you about this?" Whisker asked again of Ellsworth.

Ellsworth merely raised his brow and shrugged as negative answer at the same time that McCarthy brought food to the table.

Whisker continued: "This unseen fellow wanted to buy outright, then and there—through your man, Pope—the entire mark and brand. Hell, has there ever been such a country? I ask you, has there ever been such easy luck? I've had this happen twice now! This year and last now! Hell, these fellows making their way to Canada make offers sight unseen and just drive 'em up there, I suppose. Your man never said who the buyer was, really. Hell, I don't care."

I asked, "Did you sell, Mr. Whisker? Is it customary out here for such things to happen?"

"Sometimes it can, and it just did for me for a second time! Hell! You bet I sold! There's always someone who thinks they can bargain better than you in the future and is willing to take on the drive themselves—or stock their range with your animals and build a new herd. He, whoever this fellow was, only made it a better deal for me—and easier on my boys. Hell, I was able to send those boys of mine right here to join my other boys in town, to start them in their summer fun. I've had to lay off as many men for the summer as I would, at times, in winter—but with some pretty generous severances. Hell, I'll have a nearly empty range—hardly any cows at all—until my two herds from Texas make it up here. That could be any time now. But until then, I don't have much for most of my boys to do. Good thing Mrs. Morgan's daughters are here!"

"You were paid by the buyer already?" asked Julius with mild concern.

"Hell! Of course! Ellsworth's man had the cash in gold right on him, and he had a few of your boys to drive them to the south boundary of your place where the buyer was to be met for his drive—to wherever he was off to."

"Who was the buyer?" asked my cousin.

"Hell, I told you! I don't know—and I don't care! Maybe some Texas drover on his way home who thinks he can make some deal with the army or another buyer before he makes his way back south again—or some Texas man on his way north hoping to sell to the Canadians. Again, hell, I don't know!"

"Ellsworth, you permit your men to partake in such transactions?" Julius asked Ellsworth as Whisker paused to dig into his food.

"Pope can do as he pleases so long as business runs smoothly. I did not even know he was gone yesterday; the wagon trains have been running so smoothly," Ellsworth answered.

It was clear that a sense of uneasy puzzlement ruled over Julius concerning Whisker's story; he also seemed angered by the oblique reproach Ellsworth had just delivered to him. It seemed that Julius was maneuvering himself into a position for what he was thinking was an apt time for his debut as an agent partner of Ellsworth's. He seemed bent on delivering an entire series of remarks when just at that moment Mrs. Morgan appeared and planted herself right on Whisker's lap.

"Johnny!" she exclaimed after she gave Whisker a long and theatrical kiss.

"Jenny!" he shouted, and then he looked at us all and let out a dismissive laugh that took the place of the embarrassed one I suspect he would have been obliged to give had we been back East. For some reason Whisker then put his focus upon me.

"Jenny, this is to be our new Deputy Marshal, pending the formality of the approval of the territorial governor," he said.

Mrs. Morgan affected a bow and a flourish with her head and hand and let out a strident laugh. I nodded back; Ellsworth and I exchanged a glance.

"Cam," Whisker continued, "just think, the business from Mrs. Morgan's girls will pay your salary, not money from us. That way you are free to know you should do what's right here in town no matter who you have to deal with—even us. We won't pay into that part of the tax at all—so your conscience can stay clear. Just think—a business you might be obliged to stop back East can help keep you honest out here!"

I nodded my ascent to the odd but true reasoning of this; Ellsworth then let out a nearly imperceptible laugh—a slight puff of air from out his nose—which also conceded the crass but sound logic of his blustering friend. Julius remained cool, and only moved so as to dissect the food that had just been placed before him.

"Enjoy that steak while you can, Mr. Crabbe," Whisker said to Julius. "With nearly all of my cows gone and with your cousin refusing to sell any of his, I venture there'll be little to have of that kind of thing soon!" Whisker laughed. He then turned his attention to me once again.

"So, Mr. Deputy Marshal of Pauktaug, what do you see as your first order of business now that, save for a few formalities, you are the law in town?"

A rise in the boisterous noise from the street at that moment seemed to hint he was asking about the trouble his men had been brining to town—not only in general since the close of his spring roundup and road branding work, but in particular because of Rutledge's confrontation with me that very day.

"I was thinking," I began tentatively, "of seeing to it that after I give the man who was just killed here a proper burial, I should ask around town to establish if anyone saw anything that can be connected to his death."

"You don't say!" exclaimed Whisker. "If that doesn't sound like quite a fine idea: burying him nicely! That's the kind of thing we need around here to really make a town out of ourselves, some real formality!"

McCarthy then surprised me: "But I'm afraid we couldn't continue keeping his body in the ice house. Two days ago we had to bury him. He was getting pretty bad like, so we had to get him underground, even before we could fashion a coffin for him."

I was unprepared to respond to this news.

Whisker was in the midst of laughing over some other remarks between Mrs. Morgan and himself as McCarthy spoke. Whisker pounded the table with his closed fist, to relieve his good humor. This sound caused only a mild jolt from Julius, who was engaged with his steak. Ellsworth had a steak before him, too—but he did not flinch at all when the blow upon the table from Whisker came. And he had not looked up, not even once, as I revealed my first intentions as Deputy Marshal. Mrs. Morgan, however, gave Whisker an absurdly long and indiscreet kiss after he struck the table. Then Whisker and she laughed loudly together.

At the end of the laugh, Whisker turned sober and looked straight upon me: "And what do you intend to do about my man, Rutledge?" he asked.

After all he had said about how Mrs. Morgan's taxes would allow me to act freely according to the law and according to conscience, I felt his question—or perhaps the intensity with which he posed it—to be somewhat threatening.

"I intend to let him sleep off his turbulence for at least a day of so," I said.

"That's fine. That'll do," answered Whisker, as if he were giving approval. This disturbed me. But what disturbed me quite a bit more was that though I seemed to have been tacitly approved for the job, I still had no sense that my role had been made binding or truly legal.

"But Mr. Whisker, nothing official has been done. There has been no swearing of an oath, no documents signed," I protested.

"You don't say! Hell, I'd have thought old Ellsworth here would have taken care of that already!" Whisker seemed relieved that my status as Deputy Marshal still hovered in a vague, unofficial confusion.

"I have the paperwork from the governor right here," Ellsworth said suddenly. He pulled a document from inside of his coat. "I can have you sworn in as soon as we are finished here," he added.

"That would be a good idea, I think. I have committed myself to the duty," I said, but no one seemed to be listening with any care. Whisker and Mrs. Morgan had resumed laughter over some whispered matter between them; Julius continued to dissect his steak, and Ellsworth, though looking up from his plate, seemed lost in some distant consideration.

"Come on, Johnny!" Mrs. Morgan exclaimed, and she rose up from Whisker's lap. "I'll be needing you to come upstairs with me for a spell."

"You don't say!" answered Whisker. "Well, you'll have to excuse me, gentlemen. For who am I to neglect the command of such a figure? When the mother hen of doves commands, I must obey."

She led him out of the dining room by the hand. "Meet me in my room at the head of the stairs, Johnny. I have to speak to one of my daughters first. She's pretty, but she don't have the slightest idea of how to avoid an obstruction."

5.

I was left, then, with Ellsworth and Julius. McCarthy brought me more food, and for a few minutes I applied myself in silence to the steak before me. Noise in the street—and in the hotel's lobby—rose and fell according to how near any group of Whisker's idling men happened to be.

I was astonished, when in reaction to a particularly rowdy crash outside of the hotel on the plank sidewalk, Julius addressed Ellsworth about me as if I were not present.

"Your brother here will have quite some time managing all of that, I daresay," Julius remarked.

Ellsworth put down his knife and fork and replied to Julius sternly.

"Campbell can deal with these men. But he won't have to. Many of John's boys will be idle until the arrival of his new herds from Texas, and I intend to hire them. I have work for them."

"Doing what?" asked Julius.

"Helping to manage the herd, and helping to finish the main fence," Ellsworth replied.

Julius looked puzzled. "It was my understanding that no cowhand will condescend to undertake work that is not performed on horseback."

"They'll take the work at the rates *I* will offer them," said Ellsworth.

Julius now looked shocked.

"Cousin Ellsworth," he protested, "the degree to which I am now invested in your ranch renders you, frankly, one of our weakest shareholders. We have discussed this before—to a degree of finality, I am certain. There is to be no more spending without my direction or approval. We are to concentrate all efforts on getting to market after the autumn roundup—if not sooner. Your surprising invitation to me to take part in this endeavor, some remarkable booster literature about this new country, and now Mr. Whisker's enthusiasms all support my continued confidence—despite the fact I have invested, nay risked, my entire share of the family fortune for the promise of the greatest returns. Again, we are to move all the three-year-olds to market as soon as possible."

I was appalled by Julius. The boldness of his tone with Ellsworth enraged me; but I was thrilled by my brother's response.

"You're an investor, Julius, that is certain. I'm pledged to see to it that your investment—"

Here Ellsworth paused a moment, a rare kind of pause for him, as if he were searching for the right word. He began again: "I'm pledged to see to it that your investment, your investment in our affairs, sees returns. But I run the ranch. I control the men; I rule the cows. I say when they come and go, when they stay and when it is time to cut them out!" Ellsworth said all of this slowly and sternly, and he leaned back in his chair and crossed his arms.

"Is that so?" returned Julius, and he too leaned back slowly in his chair.

Just as Julius finished that challenging question, Ellsworth uncrossed one of his arms and let it fall below the level of sight—to his waist, to his gunbelt.

"That *is* so," Ellsworth said simply.

Julius wore no gun at the table, though I had seen him wearing one when we first met him at the railroad. Julius leaned forward and righted his chair at the table; the tension created by Ellsworth's subtle motion had compelled Julius into a surrender of relaxation for the time being, and he resumed cutting the remaining pieces of his steak.

I looked involuntarily to Ellsworth's plate at that moment. He had not touched the meat at all, though he had been busy with his knife and fork for some time.

Julius spoke, then, as if he and Ellsworth were in accord. .

"We will proceed toward finalizing the Chicago contracts over the next two months, and then we will move a record sale to market. I must ask, however, that you fulfill your promise of showing me the range we command—and showing me the herd as soon as possible. I must also ask that I be permitted to inspect progress on the completion of the main fence."

"We can do that tomorrow," Ellsworth answered with little sign of any remaining outward hostility. "John Whisker expressed an interest in seeing the fence we have going up along the western boundary—near where the final gap will soon be closed. We'll ride out of town tomorrow morning, go south until we reach the gap in the fence where the work crews are, and then swing back north and east to see the cows."

I was surprised that Ellsworth tolerated Julius' use of the words *we* and *our* when speaking of the ranch. But Ellsworth never failed to limit his words, however, to *I* and *my* when speaking of his land and cows to Julius.

Julius rose and bowed mildly to my brother; Ellsworth remained seated.

"I will be ready to ride in the morning," Julius said coolly as began to walk out of the dining room.

"We'll leave at five," Ellsworth replied without turning his head.

"That will suit me," Julius said—he also not turning about.

Ellsworth told me he had some affairs to resolve and things to think about. He said that later that week he would take me at last out to the house, but for the time being that I should remain in town—settle into my office and position, and allow my returning health to shore up.

I rose and said I would go back to my new office for a bit. I hoped he would stop me and suggest that he should swear me in first, but he did not seem to sense my hesitation. Instead he only smiled, stood up so as to shake my hand and congratulate me on

214

challenging Rutledge earlier, and to assure me that he would call for me by mid or late week.

"Rest until then, Cam," he said. "All should be quiet until I return. The road traffic should let up in town tonight; all of Whisker's boys who are willing should be out on our land working, and the town should be as when you first walked into it last week—nearly silent. But today was quite a day for a Sunday."

We both endured an awkward pause as loud laughter from a group of Mrs. Morgan's daughters sounded from the parlor. The sound of the Professor at the piano was clear again, too. He had begun to play "Woodman, Spare That Tree!" once more.

"I'm going to wait here for Pope's return and then send him out to hire as many of Whisker's idle summer men as are willing," Ellsworth said.

I wanted to ask him at last why it was that he refrained from selling any stock for so long. But, again, I could tell he did not wish to speak further and wished to be there alone for a spell. I did not mind. That was often his custom, I recalled, even when I was a child, so I took its familiarity as reassuring. As well, I took immense pleasure that his range was *our* range when he spoke to me and not to Julius—though as a shareholder I had no money to contribute at all. So, with all those things in mind, I left my brother at the hotel.

Though I had not been sworn in, I chose to wear my star. The exalted idealism in which I approached the position—brought about as much by the romantic elevation I brought to the calling (from the innumerable dime novels I had read in my young manhood and even up until the last hours of my train ride west) as from the care with which I had undertaken my constable duties back in old Pauktaug—led to my confidence that no swearing in could outmatch the commitment I would bring to the star in my private heart. And in that commitment I was not capable of self-delusion. In my acceptance of the position, I felt that Ellsworth had heard me swear. Concerning the paperwork, however, I felt that Ellsworth was content, somehow, with ambiguity and deferral for the time being.

Though it was a Sunday afternoon, I was able to locate a carpenter willing to construct a coffin for Kettle. I felt that should be done, though he was already interred. The carpenter, in sight of the marshal's star on my lapel, asked to whom the billing would go.

"The marshal's office. I am the marshal," I said.

The man smiled. I had not met him in town before. "And who says you're the marshal?" he asked.

I should have said that the territory did *and* its governor. But because I had not taken the official oath I refrained from saying as much. Instead—and therefore compounding the ambiguity of my true independence as a lawman in town—I said, "Ellsworth Crabbe and John Whisker. They say so."

The man suddenly became apologetically earnest and said that he would get to work on the coffin as soon as the body could be disinterred and brought to him for measurements. I was pleased with his sudden deference; at the same time I regretted it.

I spent the rest of the afternoon settling into my office. From time to time I checked in on Rutledge, but he continued to sleep away the knock to his head without interruption. Through the late evening I sat under the front awning of the office and glanced at a few new law books of the territory and its neighbors while I watched the wagon train traffic dissipate until it altogether vanished at nightfall. I began to be curious as to the exact size of my brother's land holdings, for I discovered in my reading that night that it was against the law to errect fences on any government land, on any free grass.

At dinner time I went to the hotel and dined alone. I could have had company if I had accepted the aggressive interest of one of Mrs. Morgan's daughters, but I declined politely and left her to pursue one of the few of Whisker's men who still lingered about the hotel. Indeed, most of Whisker's men had vanished from town by that hour, it seemed—so had John Whisker and Pope Pope and Ellsworth. The latter two, McCarthy ventured, had ridden out of town with a group of Whisker men some hour or so before I appeared for my supper. He did not volunteer where Mr. Whisker was, or my cousin, and I did not ask.

After dinner I returned to the chair I had placed under the awning of the marshal's office. For a time I simply sat and dozed. A small bit of commotion woke me, however. Not far up the street—about fifty yards north and on the opposite side—I saw the Indian stumble from one of the restaurants in the newer part of town. He soon seemed firm on his feet; he had only stumbled as he emerged because he had been given a push out the front door—as if the man charged with feeding the Indian, feeling his duty had been more than fulfilled, suddenly felt an urgency to be rid of his responsibility.

The Indian stepped into the street. For a time I watched him as he weighed his options for the direction of his march out of town. Much to my relief, he seemed mindful of the warning that Ellsworth had given him—that he was to proceed due south in the direction whence he came—for soon he began to walk south. Wishing to remain out of sight, I remained seated in the shadows, against the wall, and I saw him pass as he made his way directly in front of the marshal's office. Soon he was obscured by the darkness. I believe I then slept again for a brief time.

I woke to the sound of the very angry Mitch Rutledge. I went inside and saw Rutledge running a foot of the cell's only chair against the bars.

"How long am I supposed to stay here?" he demanded.

"Twenty-four hours should suffice—long enough for you to cool down," I replied.

"A whole day! I have to be hogged down that long! Well, can't I even get something to eat?" he asked.

"I suppose so," I replied.

I was not sure of the procedure under such circumstances, but not wishing to exacerbate the feelings of a man with whom I was likely to be a fellow townsman, I thought some sort of civil gesture might be in order.

"Here, follow me," I said, and I proceeded to unlock the cell and let the man out—all the while making it clear in my posture that I wore a gunbelt and that he did not.

Rutledge seemed surprised by this gesture, as if, having perhaps been in a cell before, such a development seemed altogether new to him. It probably was, and I was probably unwise to make such a gesture. But the look of surprise did not seem to extend to a look that might be concealing any desire to take advantage, so I marched Rutledge across the street to the same place where I had seen the Indian emerge perhaps an hour before.

On our way across Main Street, Rutledge asked me who had the power to keep him in the cell.

"I do. I'm the deputy marshal now of this district," I answered.

"*You're* the marshal!" he laughed, as if he hardly recalled the exchange we had had during the standoff over the Indian earlier that day.

When we entered the little establishment, a pair of Whisker men—the only patrons in the place—tried to muster a cheer for their foreman. But in their drunkenness they succeeded only in raising a lazy blur of words, and even that mild noise caused Rutledge to cover his ears and to clinch his aching head. Rutledge ordered them to shut their mouths, and he took a seat. I told the proprietor to feed Rutledge but to serve him no liquor. The man nodded, and Rutledge muttered something foul under his breath. I ignored whatever it was that Rutledge had said and told him he had a half hour before I was going to take him back to his cell.

I then strolled onto the board sidewalk before the little restaurant, dragging with me one of the chairs from the tables within, and there I recreated the same resting posture I had adopted in front of the marshal's office. Feeling good about my charity toward Rutledge, the resolution of that day, and the continuance of my returning health (I had had only one coughing fit that day), I snoozed once more for an indeterminate time.

I awoke with a start, however, with that feeling one can have when they are unsure how much time may have passed during a nap. The street was altogether silent; also, there was no sound coming from within the restaurant where I had left Rutledge. I ran into the little dining room to find it deserted, save for the proprietor behind the counter. I demanded to know where Rutledge was.

"Easy, son," replied the man. "He's just out back, washing up."

Rutledge was indeed there when I went into the alley behind the restaurant. He knelt over a basin and was pumping cold water over his head from a well.

"Who was it that hit me like this on the back of the head?" he asked as he looked up at me from the basin.

"You don't remember?" I asked.

"No, but I think I know anyway," he replied, and then he gave a few more strong pumps on the well's lever. "The high and mighty, bull-headed, son-of-a-bitch!" he muttered to the noisy water, but I heard him notwithstanding.

Rutledge was compliant in returning to his cell. It is possible he viewed having to endure a night in jail as a sort of inconvenience with monetary benefit, for he was spared paying for a room if he had intended to stay in town.

After I had Rutledge safely locked away for the night I returned to the hotel. Though there was some moderate noise in the parlor betwixt some last remaining Whisker man and some of Mrs. Morgan's daughters, I found the hotel otherwise peaceful, and I went straight to bed.

Perhaps because I had napped excessively from time to time during the preceding evening, I found myself wakeful by an early hour, and after a fruitless interval of hoping to get back to sleep, I rose at four in the morning and thought I might enjoy my returning health with an hour's walk before breakfast.

Though Ellsworth had promised to take me to the house at the ranch by the week's close, I still felt a mounting curiosity to see a bit more than I had already of the land that was ours, so I walked across Main Street and made my way out to the road that led to the entrance of my brother's ranch. During the first light of dawn I crossed the fence, and then a quarter of an hour later I passed the place where I had found Kettle's body about a week earlier. No rain had fallen since my arrival, and the wind had been limited to powerless breezes. The ground was still marked with the peculiar signs that surrounded the precise place of Kettle's grisly passing. I did not linger there long.

I was resolved to begin my return to town when I saw in the east, at about a half mile's distance, what at first appeared to me to be a pair of quarrelling small dogs. As I came closer I could tell they were, instead, that species of small wolf, the coyote, common in that part of the country. As I came still closer I suspected my eyes were playing a macabre trick upon me in the early light. Thus I took out my revolver and fired two shots into the air above. The coyotes scattered, and so, too, did several birds that had gathered just outside the coyotes' ring of contention.

Soon I could see that my eyes had *not* deceived me, for lying on the open ground, just next to the road was a human body—that of an Indian. Though the coyotes and perhaps birds had already gone to work on the body, I could see that the man, just as in the case of Kettle, had been violently stabbed or impaled as if by a long implement of some kind. As in the case of Kettle, as well, the prints of one or more very large, unshod, animals surrounded the body. Mixed with the unshod prints was a set of prints from what appeared to have been a lone, shod, horse. All of the prints came and went from the main road of the ranch, where they then vanished into an array of comparably fresh prints from heavy traffic traveling to and from my brother's home.

Again, the body had already been mangled—not only by the stabbings that appeared to have delivered death, but also by the early feasting of the wild animals. However, from the clothes, and from the build and color and face of the man, I was certain that this was the same Indian who had just left town the night before. Apparently he had not made his way south, as commanded.

I returned to town and the hotel as soon as possible. The hotel was still, but I did find McCarthy already stirring in the kitchen, readying for the day. He said that Ellsworth, Whisker, Pope (they coming in from the ranches by roads I had yet to see), and Julius, had already ridden out as planned, perhaps a half hour before I appeared in the kitchen. McCarthy said he thought he had heard the two shots I had fired.

I convinced McCarthy to defer his preparation for the day until he helped me bring in the body of the Indian. With the use of a buckboard, we soon retrieved the Indian's body and placed it in the company of Kettle's disinterred body in the ice house behind the hotel.

I took a solitary breakfast, and before I left the dining room I asked McCarthy to keep the news of this latest killing to himself for a day. With all of Pauktaug's highest ranking citizens gone from town, I wished to meditate this compounding mystery of unusual deaths by myself.

I knew I should ask questions of Rutledge, even though it seemed unlikely (because of what I knew had been the only brief and improbable opportunity) he could have any knowledge of the death of the Indian. Still, I knew it could be a possibility, and further still, I had to concede to myself that such a possibility had come about because of my vanity—of my desire to appear generous to a man who would likely bear me and mine enmity no matter what overtures I made to him.

221

But before I could return to the marshal's office, I felt compelled to walk a bit more—this second walk to allow myself to
meditate the gruesome revelation provided by the first walk of the
day. The hotel was on the northern-most corner of the west side
of Main Street; on the northeast corner of Main Street there was
a large building indirectly facing the hotel. Of all the buildings in
my brother's recreation, it looked the least distressed by the rough
new environment in which it stood—which is to say it looked so
new that it appeared hardly a human hand had touched it since the
last carpenter had stepped away for the last time. In both Pauktaugs it was the opera house—serving, too, as a general theater and
meeting hall. In the old Pauktaug it was the space that my father
had refurbished so as to host his Pauktaug Lyceum Society when
it was founded in 1855.

Part of me was surprised that Ellsworth would recreate this
building—what with all the associations it surely had for him. Yet,
perhaps, without another model in mind, I wondered if he did not
indeed build it with the intention of filling it with entertainments
and diversions for the working men of the new country, as a likely
profitable business venture.

Yet as far as I could tell during my week in the new country,
the only entertainments Ellsworth and Whisker had imported to
Pauktaug for their men, and perhaps themselves, were Mrs. Morgan and her very large family of daughters.

That suspicion seemed confirmed as I climbed the steps.
Though the building had been carefully completed, even painted
in such a way that its resemblance to its model was astonishingly
close, the opera house appeared untouched, as if upon completion,
it had been condemned. Yet no dangers appeared to me as I walked
up and down the length of the board sidewalk before its central
entrance doors and the windows looking upon the lobby. As this
opera house was constructed after the typical manner of second
story opera houses of the day, there were two storefronts on either

side of the central lobby and entrance on the first floor. But these stores were empty and without tenants.

To my surprise, when I tried the doors of the opera house, they opened, and I entered the dark lobby and met the scent of freshly stained lumber and untouched, new, carpeting. I climbed the steps to the dark auditorium itself on the second floor, and was surprised to find that despite the finished exterior and lobby, the opera house's auditorium was bare and incomplete—as vacant of business prospects as were the two storefronts on the groundfloor of the building.

I took a chair on the edge of the empty stage and pondered the problems of Kettle and the Indian as I looked out into the empty hall, at once so familiar and at once so foreign. The vacuum of that space suggested the odd smoothness that bodies prepared for funerals often present—familiar in features and general outline but strangely free of hard-earned wrinkles and defining lines, oddly and slightly bloated, suggestive of restored youth to a degree but ultimately more disturbing than a true child's face or the customary, familiar, aged, face.

I had taken a chair in the near blackness on the edge of the empty stage, for both the balcony and the orchestra section had not a single seat in place. Only the empty floor ranged through those places, so that had I waded through their dark expanses I might not have been surprised to encounter buffalo grass springing up between the seams of the new but neglected flooring.

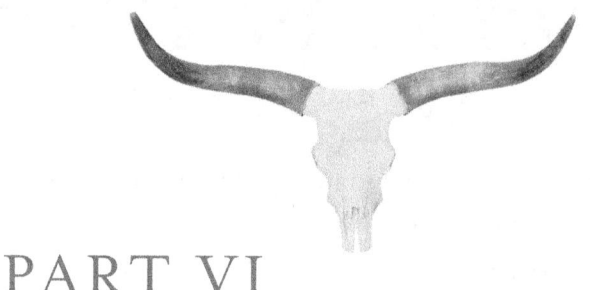

PART VI

The Concord Sonata

I.

Having been drawn into the opera house in the new Pauktaug—so eerily similar and eerily unlike its model in the East—I am reminded that I must return this history to earlier events in the old Pauktaug, to the time after my mother's death.

After Ellsworth left on that night in September of 1855, life began to proceed as if my brother had never lived. No word came from Ellsworth, and my father never spoke of him in any way.

Though my cousin had done his work very well—for my father's focus had settled completely upon the running of Pauktaug's Lyceum Society—a comfortable intimacy grew between my father and myself. Because of his unremitting new dedication to presenting the most celebrated and erudite speakers in the country—and sometimes the world—to our little industrial village and to its surrounding hamlets of remote farms and fishermen, and because of the passing of my mother and the disappearance of my brother, the life of comprehensive opulence that we had once known vanished forever.

However, my father retained some degree of his old generosity towards me when he realized that I was all he had left to him—and realized, too, that I was but a little fellow confronted with so much loss that surely it would strain our alliance if some semblance of the former life was not maintained. Thus, though in miniature when compared to earlier days, my father saw to it that at least one or two of my whims were always placated, and so it was—perhaps as much to keep the memory of my beloved absent brother alive as it was to keep part of my father's old self still living—that I delighted in encouraging the gifts of antique and modern weapons that my father permitted me as I aged into the habit of forming collections. As I entered late adolescence, I was also permitted to cultivate my skill in marksmanship, and this absorbed countless hours of my time in the woods and fields behind our home.

Though it strikes me with great melancholy now to think of it, for I became accustomed to being content, even overjoyed with only little gestures of attention, my father also attempted to pay heed to my emotions in ways that I do not think would have been his custom had the summer and autumn of 1855 not unfolded as they had. Though my father, as peculiar as it may sound, gave up all pretence to being a reader himself when he began to undertake the promotion of men of learning and abstraction, some of my happiest memories of those years were spent with him in our library. After a morning and possibly an afternoon still spent fulfilling his obligations to his partnership at the factory in the village—although as the years passed my father managed to give less and less time to the managing of his business—my father would spend long hours in the library engaged in correspondence concerning the burgeoning Lyceum. Even when attendance at the lectures was sparse and subscriptions went down, my father gave his attention and his powers of wealth to the cause. I would affect to engage in correspondence myself as my father worked in earnest at his desk across the room; and as I matured I assisted my father as a sort of secretary and amanuensis. During those hours my father would often look up from his work and regard me with a warmth that I always secretly hoped would break his devotion to managing and promoting the Lyceum.

This was my life with my father until I was about ten or eleven years old, until about the time of the beginning of the War. Up until that time I still enjoyed the care of a private governess and, when my illness chanced to return, a local and doting nurse. After my mother's death I never experienced a bout of consumption as severe as the wave I had shared with my mother in 1855. Though I was, of course, glad of that, I was always left with the disconcerting curiosity as to whether another descent into sickness, equal to the extreme of 1855, might truly wrest from my father his obsession with realizing the ostensibly selfless Lyceum cause. I was also left unsure, of course, if my father would then merely repeat the only passable medical gestures he had offered my mother and myself when my mother passed away. Such thoughts chilled the joy I felt in the paternal glances he offered. Thus I endeavored to revel in my comparative health and the untested truths it kept at bay.

Though I still had my own private teacher and sometimes a nurse, not long after my mother's death my father contracted to a great degree the size of our serving staff. Soon after the autumn of 1855, my father reduced the staff to two maids, two women for our kitchen, and just a single man to attend to all my father's other requests. Gone were the driver and the groomsman and the gardeners, as well as other very particular servants. Though this still left us—outside of the Whisker family—enjoying an extremely comfortable existence when weighed against our humble neighbors of the village, it is noted as evidence of the steps my father was taking to contract his expenses, not because our family had diminished in size, but because he wished to concentrate more and more of his monetary force upon his educative cause.

The only time I saw blazes of the old opulence rise up from time to time in our weathering and once grand manse, was when my father wished to ingratiate himself with someone who in some way might promote the Lyceum's notoriety—or better still, might somehow, if they be a feted guest in our home, be inclined to make a special effort to praise the work of my father. And this destructive praise generally came from lazy men of privilege—they too indolent to follow their fathers in any manner of a realization of Manifest Destiny; too mistrusted by their fathers to have any viable means to contribute to my father's cause; too indolent to be thinkers themselves after the manner of the lecturers they feigned to worship; but not too lazy to say just the perfect thing to inspire my father to continue unremittingly in his headlong efforts to further a cause that he neither had the intellect to support nor the ultimate means to prevent from descending into the crumbling spheres of the economically unsupportable. But onward and onward he went, hungry for this praise of his selflessness, and for every one hundred dollars he would sink into the enterprise, some mildly interested farmboy from Huntington might appear and offset the expense with the purchase of a nickel ticket to an arcane lecture.

As I have observed, up until my tenth or eleventh year, this round of concerns—and the general level of comfort through which I enjoyed these relatively lonely circumstances—remained rather stable. But sometime during the early part of the War, as my father became less and less involved with the factory in the village and even more preoccupied in bringing ministers of the abstract to Pauktaug's Lyceum, he suddenly discharged one of the maids and also my governess. He said that it was time for us, as so many others were endeavoring to do without in a time that tested principle over possessions, to give up what we did not need. Though I was still very young, I knew even then the degree to which this statement was more affectation, a perversion of reality, than a representation of the true case. My father wished to give up certain things, yes; but he only wished to redirect the means that were used to possess those things in favor of other things—for more sinister things. He did not really wish to favor principle over possession; he wished to buy more of the vanities that came with the profession of principle.

As difficult as my first months were in Pauktaug's schoolhouse, however, the rough company I was forced to endure soon became one of my refuges. When my father's limited affections were impeded or distracted by his work on the Lyceum, I took pleasure in fighting for a place of supremacy in the schoolyard against older boys who thought my withered appearance—and privilege—deserved attack. Much to my surprise—save for one or two instances which brought about genuine fear and peril—I enjoyed this rutting before and after the schoolbell, and I also found that not only was my then small frame more often than not up to the task of self-defense, but it also slowly gained muscle and a hale urge to fight the more I found myself engaged.

My father seemed to take little notice of my often happily distressed face or soiled clothes when I returned home from school each day; I am uncertain whether he had the confidence to ask what was customary for an American boy to experience in a common village schoolhouse, but he seemed eager to pay no notice so long as I did not complain, for then he was free from having to involve himself where he might have to commit some sort of practical hypocrisy against the appearance of his cause for my sake.

However, there came an afternoon in the spring of 1864, when, upon returning from a school day, I could see that my father had an intense but somewhat secreted interest in me—outside of the vaguely warm and solicitous smiles he would offer me as I wiled away the evening hours in the library with him. A letter had come for me from the city, from New York. It was from Ellsworth. Because my father did not have the courage to ask about its contents, I did not—because my father also never volunteered any interest in my days among the rough children of the villagers of Pauktaug—volunteer anything about the letter. Even before reading it I felt proud suddenly of the battles I had been waging in the schoolyard—proud of my unassisted endeavors to augment my strength and bulk by sheer effort against the rude mass of schoolboys. Somehow I felt I had earned the letter, even though it was certain that Ellsworth had had no notion of my progress or life for nearly nine years. Its contents were simple. Ellsworth reported that along with John Whisker, Jr. as a business partner, he and his friend had begun to make their way and fortunes as builders and real estate men in New York City. He also hinted at the prosperity that he and John Whisker, Jr. had met with as contractors to the government during the ongoing War. He said little about the full nature of his business affairs, but though he suggested that so long as I felt secure in Pauktaug I should remain, I should also know that from the time I received his letter and onward, he would be ready to receive me into his home and work at any time.

I cannot say enough concerning the secret thrill this letter gave me, and, again, I felt that with each battle I won among the bullies of the schoolyard, with each rough patch of earth rubbed into my skin by battle, I prepared for the day when I might accept Ellsworth's offer. Other letters followed, carefully timed it seemed, repeating very much the same message, but oftentimes reporting a change of address. I rarely, if ever, replied; but I carefully preserved each letter, and my father never spoke a word about them. I knew the letters preyed upon his thoughts; yet we seemed to arrive at a tacit agreement that the letters were my private affair—save for when my father had to announce that among his letters there was one waiting for me.

Though Ellsworth's letters gave me a secret pride, and a sense of ultimate refuge if needed, I must confess that for all the harsh observations I can now make in regard to my father, at the time I still clung to him with a simple and childish affection and dependence.

2.

About a year after I received my first letter from Ellsworth, one of the only instances wherein my father was witness to anything of my life as a Pauktaug schoolboy came about by chance. Though most of the rutting that took place between the contentious boys was held in the woods behind the schoolyard, one afternoon in late April a slightly older boy and myself took our battle to a large lot on the west side of Main Street. I remember the time of year and the month quite well, for the village was still dressed in celebration for the end of the War and in mourning for the death of the President.

During the latter half of this particularly rough struggle in which I was taking the worst of the beating, I chanced to look between a gap in our audience circle of schoolmates and saw my father passing on Main Street. He was conducting business in the village either on behalf of the Lyceum or the factory. Whether or not he knew that I saw him as I was in the throes of a tight head-lock I cannot say; I do not believe he was reacting to what might have appeared as a plea for help (and I had indeed made no such plea), but he suddenly made his way across the street, through the encircling crowd of cheering children, and right up to my opponent and myself.

As he came close and made me certain he was going to inter-cede a part of me felt a childish hope, a singular new thrill. Some-how I felt suddenly he intended to pull us apart and make living some tenet or principle that had come to him with force and power from one of the speakers he had engaged for the Lyceum. Here, I thought, would be a moment that would reveal some great, alter-nate, impetus to all his actions since the summer of my mother's decline and death.

Here, at last, would be some demonstration that gave proof to a hope I had never thought to foster before—that his efforts for the Lyceum were not merely to serve the reminders that had come from his nephew and which had terrorized him. Perhaps that had been so at first. But perchance by some living force of renewed will he would now purify the idealized words of the Lyceum speakers, purify them for me of their sinister emptiness, of their specious, brutal vanities. Perhaps his action would allow me to join in the praise of him without shame.

In part moved surely by the desire of a father to see that his son was unharmed, he had dashed to us both, we boys locked in a brawl of great violence but no ultimate danger. For a moment he had been driven by that impulse; of that I have no doubt. But surely there would be more; I was sure.

Whilst still holding to his fine cane, I was thrilled to see him, to a degree of physical animation and violence I had never seen from him, pull the older boy away from me. He pulled the dusty boy backward until he gripped him by the shoulders and held him tight to his chest. The sweaty, dirty, child stood astonished—framed by my father's normally soft grip and in relief against the perfectly tailored and pressed brown suit he wore. The boy yielded in his fright and his surprise. But then, after a permissible moment of transition and surprise, my father made it clear he would say nothing.

I stood astonished and silent and panting myself for an instant. And then I could see that in my father's eye he only held the larger boy so that I might continue the fight without handicap—and with handicap thrown utterly unto my slightly larger opponent. My father said nothing, but as clearly as if he spoke the words, his eyes and a nod beckoned me to pummel the boy with complete freedom. Several of the more rude children in the surrounding circle confirmed this for me, for they cheered at the astounding turn of events.

Then, just as clearly as his eyes and nod had just stated their encouragement to me to fight, they relented when they saw both my paralysis and my true bafflement—and even more my disappointment.

It should be understood that I was not disappointed in the call to violence. I was instead disabused of my sudden hope that there was some sincerity in his cause since my mother's death. The various professions of idealist philosophers did not interest me; but I had wished somehow that before that day of the fight he could reveal some degree of betrayal of that Lyceum cause that had driven him via his wild, meek, shame and vanity since that summer of my mother's death. But he said nothing of the sort. And yet he said, as well, nothing during the fight, said nothing that supported my hope that there was at least some philosophical sincerity in all his efforts for the Lyceum.

He said nothing as he stood there. Yet then with his eyes he said a great deal. He relented in his encouragement to promote the assisted fight. Then he looked hopeful a second time, as if I might reconsider when his plaintive eyes explained themselves. His eyes revealed no faith in the Lyceum cause but vanity; and that same weakest part of the man that had been pushed down that path by Julius Crabbe also begged that he be, whilst staying on his present path, allowed into the world that once was his with his sons.

I, for myself, was fighting my way back into the tangible world, the actual world of Manifest Destiny and the concrete. Might he be allowed back in whilst he still moved inevitably forward under the sinister inspiration and reminders of Cousin Julius? Though we had never spoken of Ellsworth's letters, might he rejoin me in that world—that world between his sons—that I seemed to be winning back for myself in my lonely schoolyard battles—they, those battles, surely shared (though they were not) in imagined response to my brother's letters to me?

No, he would not be allowed. He was not to be permitted.

I stormed away to the jeers of the boys that had wished to see the held boy pummeled. A little girl, Ellen Paw—a girl who thought she loved me—ran after me to praise me for abandoning the fight. I could not answer her, for she could never comprehend the nature of my disappointment. I ran off.

Had only little Ellen known. She thought she praised the sudden birth of a thinking pacifist. Had she only known how it burned me up to back away from leveling that boy's features whilst I had the chance, whilst my father held him for me.

My father and I never spoke of that incident.

3.

In the spring of 1866, my father arranged for the largest event he had yet held at the Pauktaug Lyceum. Somehow, through patient constancy in his correspondence, through flattery and unremitting persuasion, by fortuitous geographical alignment in the great man's schedule on his tour of the New York and New England Lyceum circuit—but in addition, too, it must be conceded, by the offering of an unprecedented fee for a venue of Pauktaug's size—my father convinced Gerald Larimer Dunstable himself to give a series of lectures in Pauktaug Village. Gerald Larimer Dunstable! He was said to be the great flint, dragging himself nimbly across the craggy New England landscape, he that gave the spark of fire and life to the best of speeches and tomes and generally repeated principles and aphorisms of the greatest of New England's Transcendentalists; to their mere kindling he brought a conflagration of excitement. He was said to be as a Ralph Waldo Emerson crossed with a Daniel

Webster; no, he was said to be as a Theodore Parker permitted the passions of a Henry Ward Beecher. He wedded the highest of the newest thoughts: born of nearly inscrutable German musings and given English phrase and flight—wedded these shapeless, volcanic, but lofty ideas and molded them into smarting, driving, carriage whips of words and speculations. He was a Transcendentalist unashamed to invoke the tone of his remembered Puritan hellfire heritage and origins; yet his listeners came away raised not to fear but as to a Heaven spread before them in American Nature—its limitless, vast, stands of trees, looming then before them as a forest of boundless representations. Ideas were as numberless to him as the acres of the frontier. Entirely new territorial governments and square-shaped future Western states might be formed in the minds of even the most wretched housewives and the farmhands deformed by labor—in so many, nay in all, who heard him!

He abstracted the spaces, the very venues in which he spoke, it seemed. Men did not seem to recall where they had heard him. "The theater itself had become abstracted, merely representative!" they shouted as they left their city's Lyceums. Men and women themselves he left abstracted. They departed as representations of better things. He lived for ideas and Ideas became higher than life. Abstraction, abstraction! Representation, representation! All matter was merely suggestive to him. No object was too high nor too low but that it would be eradicated of its weight, of its ostensible function, and made instead to be but an emblem. The shadow a man cast was the best, the most solid and ultimate part of the man. The shadow surely cast the man, he said.

In 1855, when Cousin Julius and my father cut the pages of Dunstable's early volumes for the first time and read them by the library fire, as my mother withered and faded in her chambers above, Julius understood the ideas. He was capable and keen, for with his sinister skill came a great deftness and Understanding, though his Reason was foul. Yet he did not need for himself the good of what he read, not at all. My father, he did *not* understand the ideas; he was neither capable nor keen. He abandoned the objects, the riches of the earth, and thus leaped in fear into the misty side of metaphor without the solid material spring still in place, and he wandered like a fool in abstractions and representations—his metaphors completely without the original objects to give them true life. He leaped away from all that could cast shadows. Thus he leaped into shadows that were without form, without definition; he merely leaped into darkness.

My father would give birth to shadows in his new work, in the hope of praise, without there first being men to live and die and be healthy and solid to cast them. He needed the good of ideas most of all, but, again, he was utterly incapable. His was the embodiment of a poisoned, sickened Idealism. He permitted his own inability to understand great ideas to foster a false understanding of the function and use of those ideas. I cannot say who was worse for all of this—Julius Crabbe or my father. I do not know if I knew when I was a child; I am not certain even now.

But, because of my childhood's unique pressures and bizarre alchemy, I knew that I hated the idea and the name of Gerald Larimer Dunstable. Of that fact I was certain. I had never read a word of his works; I have still not read him. Perhaps that is a pity, for I am certain there is something to the man. And I find it remarkable that though I have avoided the man of abstraction for all of my years, I still meet him unexpectedly in many solid places—the deceased man of abstraction, now if living only living as a ghost, but he congealed into so many busts and statues and solid reliefs in nearly every Carnegie Library I have ever entered, including now old Pauktaug's and Northport's. Again, I hope I can be pardoned when I say I have never read the man. But I did hear him speak once.

It was to be in June of 1866 that he was to give his lecture series. There was, however, a profound problem that had developed in my father's Lyceum. Its actual space, its hall, was beautiful, and it was enormous—enormous when measured against the pitiful size of the audience which my father and the Lyceum Society could manage ever to gather. My father maintained a full and unrelenting schedule for the Lyceum; it could not be said to have a season. With rarely a significant gap between offerings, the Lyceum Hall ran without rest all throughout the year. There was virtually no consideration given to the limited size of the audience our village or its surrounding villages and hamlets could muster.

Women of limited perception idolized my father for this cause, and the small audiences only caused him to be elevated further in their minds as a selfless champion of the eradication of ignorance. Many of them were as surely enamored of him for this as they were enamored of him as a worthy bachelor. But my father was not vain of the latter thoughts. He was, however, vain of the former—of the idea that he was as a hemorrhaging fire, acres wide, come to burn a few match sticks. He virtually reveled in the wasteful equation—of the bizarre volume of expense in ratio to effect, of effort in ratio to result. He reveled in the notion that the more he wasted the easier it was for the easily reached to offer the praise he needed for his sickly vanity. In fact, a greater success, a ratio of greater soundness, would have disconcerted him, otherwise the praise of his seeming indifference to gain in proportion to expenditure would be missed. His vanity burned and thrived to the degree his cause was an absolute paragon of business absurdity and earthly failure. The greater the inefficiency, the greater his satisfaction. And never did the wildest playboy of this present century take greater pleasure in spending fortunes on worthless objects as did my father in spending fortunes on worthy ideas that went almost constantly unheard. But, again, in his near madness, in his sickness of unique vanity, he depended upon this order of things. He was virtually a martyr who had to escalate constantly the subsidy of his own inquisition for fear it would dissipate. He had no persecutors, granted, but he thrived on the pity that led to praise in regard to the pearls he cast into empty barnyards—for it was impossible to even conjure ample audiences of swine.

Into this bizarre outpost of the Lyceum Circuit my father wished to bring Gerald Larimer Dunstable. But, as I have observed, there was a profound problem that had developed in my father's Pauktaug Lyceum by the year 1866—that problem not even described fully by the considerations I have presented above. Though I was not certain of it then—and nor would I be certain of this for several more years—I suspect that by the time of that very important set of lectures by Dunstable my father was already beginning to realize that he would soon have financial problems if he continued along the paths he was pursuing. But because he had no intentions of straying from those exorbitant and unremunerative paths, in the month before Dunstable's arrival, my father took steps that seem to me now to be indicative of his first awareness that he would require the assistance or investment of others to maintain the high level of the Lyceum and the impressions he was able to give via his managing and promotion of that venue.

In other words, he would need loans so the *he* could continue to give the impression that he selflessly subsidized an intellectually magnificent but monetarily disastrous concern. I do not think he had a plan for making it less monetarily disastrous, but I do feel that once he knew he needed to seek assistance he realized the vanity he derived from such a venue's attraction of a limited audience was something he would no longer be able to enjoy. His vanity had relented at least to the level that he would be pleased at that time if the Lyceum might survive and also begin to support itself. Yet, again, unlike thousands of entrepreneurs who have wrestled with the business crises of struggling theaters, my father merely changed his hopes at this point. Unwilling to change the attractions at his venue, my father merely hoped that the most famous intellectual speaker of the Lyceum circuit of the day might begin to change his business from one in which he took pride that it was neglected to one in which he could be certain that at least enough people recognized its quality so that it could maintain itself—and thereby survive as a reminder of its early days, of the time when the Lycuem supported my father's most perverse notions, his most egregious misappropriation of ideals.

Dunstable was to arrive in May of 1866, at the end of April, and three events occurred in close succession that made me later suspect my father's encroaching financial troubles. On the last Sunday of that April, my father was to receive his business partner, John Whisker Sr., for a supper at our home in the early evening. Such suppers had been quite common, even in the decade after my mother's death, but they became more rare during the latter years of the War and during the time leading up to 1866 as my father continued to escalate the opulence he poured into the Lyceum.

A strain had entered into the relations between my father and his business partner in the years since my mother's death. But John Whisker, Sr., a kindly man of nearly seventy by that point, maintained a degree of affection and tolerance for my father—even as my father neglected increasingly his business duties as the Lyceum grew in size and ambition. This affection and tolerance were due not only to Mr. Whisker's pity for my father's loss of his wife and the disappearance of his oldest son, but also to Mr. Whisker's ceaseless gratitude for my father having provided the initial capital, plan, and energy in founding the Pauktaug Stays Works. Mr. Whisker never forgot that his wealth came from my father's efforts many years before, when they were both young men—my father a rash yet intuitive English entrepreneur, new to America; Mr. Whisker the son of a Long Island farmer, the son of a man who had first fought the English before he could raise a son who might grow up to go into business with them.

This supper was the first of the three events in close succession I alluded to above. As was customary, I was in attendance. Mr. and

Mrs. Whisker were kind to me, I recall, as they usually were, but toward the end of the supper the tenor of the evening grew very strained. Somehow a tacit agreement had arisen between my father and Mr. Whisker that the affairs of the business could continue as they were so long as my father did not remove himself from the precarious balance of things any further than he had; Mr. Whisker could manage my father's distracted attention and the waning demand for whalebone items rather well. However, that evening my father violated that tacit agreement; but he did not violate it by distancing himself more from the business; he violated their understanding by instead asking that *Mr. Whisker* become involved in the Lyceum for the first time.

The Whisker family involvement had been limited up until that time to Mrs. Whisker's cautious but genial attendance at the lectures and receptions, but that was all. As the table was being cleared, however, my father broached this subject to Mr. Whisker and made the evening's tenor grow tense and cool; my father also raised the topic as he had suggested that Mr. Whisker and he adjourn to the parlor to smoke. However, as soon as Mr. Whisker took my father's meaning, he remained standing and stationary— and he signaled to his wife by some silent means that she should rise as if in sudden recollection of a need to depart.

My father had asked Mr. Whisker for money. My father had boasted of the imminent visit of Dunstable, and then he asked—in an odd and indiscreet and direct way—if his business partner could be relied upon to contribute a large and specific sum to support not only Dunstable's appearance, but also the entire season for the forthcoming year. Mr. Whisker merely smiled and then yielded to his wife's quick thinking. They had a Sunday evening caller whom they could not neglect to entertain.

My father had presumed upon Mr. Whisker's understanding of their tacit agreement in ways he did not even suspect. Not since their business had become profitable decades earlier had they ever even alluded to the manner in which the other disposed of his income. Again, though Mr. Whisker was forever mindful of my father's initially superior investment in the company, once all debts were paid and an even distribution of the profits was established, a curtain of privacy had fallen over their own personal choices of spending. My father might make it his business to spend on behalf of the public and strangers, but it was a presumption for him to ask the same of Mr. Whisker.

The Whisker family still lived nearly after the manner that my family had enjoyed before my mother's death. There were times when I was certain that Mrs. Whisker's kindness and pity for me were founded on her knowledge of this, but she, of course, never spoke of this to me—save, in effect, for when they presented me with a rare set of pistols for my collection upon my birthday or at Christmas.

My father's question of Mr. Whisker was also a gross imposition upon a very particular aspect of Mr. Whisker's generosity, an aspect that had never been acknowledged nor perhaps ever noted by my father. Mr. and Mrs. Whisker seemed somehow to have some notion of how it came to pass that Ellsworth had felt compelled to abandon his place in our family after my mother's death and during the final hours of Julius Crabbe's cruel invasion. They also seemed to have formed their own dark impression of Julius Crabbe, though I cannot say if it ever could have approximated the detail and degree of truth I was privileged sadly to witness. With all of those things in mind, Mr. Whisker had displayed a great deal of continued tolerance for my father after my brother disappeared. And he showed that tolerance in particular by never mentioning or acting upon the resentment he surely felt from Ellsworth's disappearance having inspired his own son to leave Pauktaug, as well.

Again, I learned through my brother's letters that John Whisker, Jr. was in business partnership with Ellsworth. John Whisker, Jr.'s departure for New York City had crushed his father's hopes that his son would enter business with him. Instead, as had Ellsworth Crabbe, John Whisker, Jr. had fled Pauktaug with what capital he could call his own and hoped to emulate the fathers, perhaps, insofar as in attempting to found a partnered company of his own. Insofar as emulation might have been their intention, Mr. Whisker was willing to forgive the departed boys. But he did bear resentment for Ellsworth for giving the inspiration; he did resent his son for being susceptible to the inspiration; and he did indeed resent my father for giving cause that there should ever have been need for the inspiration to have been formed at all. Though John Whisker, Jr. had had no falling out with his father before departing, he was compounding the one he had created by departing and by returning so infrequently.

Asking for money for the Lyceum convinced Mr. Whisker that my father did not at all recognize the generous tolerance he had been shown. Though their business relationship would continue awkwardly for another disintegrating decade, when Mr. and Mrs. Whisker left the house that evening it was for the last time. Their social connection with my father had vanished forever. I was pleased to see in their faces, however, that they regarded me as an innocent. I noted this should the day come when I might require their sympathy.

After the Whiskers left, my father and I went into the library.

4.

In the library I witnessed the second of the three events that occurred that day which would later allow me to suspect that at that time my father had already discovered he was spending beyond his means.

My father sat in silence for a time behind his desk. I sat at a small writing table and resumed the copying of letters I had started for my father earlier that day—pursuant to the promotion of the imminent arrival of Gerald Larimer Dunstable. Of a sudden my father rang for his personal man; when the man arrived my father asked that one of the two women who worked in the kitchen and one of the two maids be brought to him—whomever the man alighted on first was to determine the manner of making the selections. Soon one of the young women who served as a maid was present; a few minutes later one of the middle-aged women from the kitchen appeared. He credited them both for their excellent years of service—giving particular notice to the older woman from the kitchen who had been with us since before my mother's death—but confessed he no longer required such a large staff for the house. He used very much the same phrase when he had reduced the roster of our servants some years before. Both women cried but gratefully accepted the three month's pay he offered as severance.

The women left the room. I said nothing and continued to copy the letters. After an interval of silence my father began to speak, and what he said surprised me deeply. What we spoke of was the third of the three events that occurred that day to make me suspect that my father's monetary resources were starting to be strained. As I put down the pen and began to listen to my father, I suspected his halting, embarrassed, and cautious manner to be attributable to sentiment. Again, only later did I realize that the impetus for this exchange came from the threat of imperiled finances, and thus a threatened vanity.

"Campbell," my father began. "I have another letter for you here from your brother in New York."

I was astonished; my father had never—not once—alluded to Ellsworth since he had departed nearly eleven years earlier, not even when he was obliged to hand over one of his letters to me. I could not summon a single word, but some impulse compelled me to stand—as much from my normal instinct, born of affection for this wrecked man who was the only present representative of my family upon whom I could render my child's need to love, as from a sense in this particular instance that something remarkable, even momentous, was about to be said.

"Campbell," my father began again, "I, of course, know that you have been receiving such letters from your brother for some time now." He then paused. During that awkward silence I felt great pity for my father, for I was certain he was endeavoring to surmount great emotional obstacles in beginning to speak of this to me.

He looked disappointed that I did not begin to speak. I was not at that time old enough, however, to know to take the initiative of kindness when I saw a man faltering so.

Thus he stood up himself, as well, and endeavored to begin again for a third time: "Campbell, how is your brother? Is he well?"

I was still so astonished that I nearly forgot my obligation to answer, but after a long moment, during which I shifted my weight from one foot to another and put my hands in my pockets, I finally replied, "Yes." Though my manners were indicative of a diffident boy, a sudden shift took over me as my father was again silent. My pity for him gave way to a sudden flash of impatience for his lack of words, and I then felt it easy to remove my hands from my pockets and to stand evenly and easy upon both feet. The longer my father failed to speak, the more I thought again of the incident on Main Street where my father had intruded upon my fight with another, older schoolboy. In this instance I did not feel anger—or the excitement, of course—I had felt after the fight. In this case I felt calm, and the same sense came over me once more that my father was trying to intrude upon lost ground. But this time I not only felt calm, but I felt I had ascended to a place of greater age— or at least to a place of greater authority. This feeling came to me suddenly, for I realized that not only was my father's awkwardness due to his feelings about my brother, but he was wrestling with an entirely new set of difficulties he was facing concerning me.

Why did I suddenly feel older then? It was because I had the distinct feeling my father was approaching me as a man would an agent, or an owner of something important. I felt my father invoking his old style of business caution, but for the sake of his present, perverse, vanities. I had seen him, when I was a very young child, assume this cautious air of a bargainer when he dealt with the whale ship owners directly in Cold Spring Harbor. I had not seen that face for a long time, and I certainly did not expect to see it directed at me when I saw it again. But despite all these perceptions I still felt a bit of pity and affection for the old man, so I continued to stand respectfully before him in expectant silence.

"You say he does well for himself?" my father asked.

"I believe he is in good health, father," I answered innocently.

My father smiled and walked around to the front of his desk. "Campbell, to ask if a man does well for himself is to ask if he does well in business."

"I see," I replied, being too young to tell him that he had not asked as much with his original question. My ambivalence—whether I should feel pity for my father or caution about his desire to trespass upon territory he had surrendered and betrayed—increased as the seconds passed. I could see that my father continued to wish that I volunteer more to the exchange, but my continued surprise and fascination kept me quiet. Thus, my father, deciding that my terse answers came primarily from a youthful diffidence and callowness, resolved to be more rapid, plain, and direct in his questioning.

"Where is your brother living, Campbell?" And, if I may put the question to you again, does your brother do well for himself?" he asked rather forcefully.

"He lives in New York, father, and though I am not certain of his business, I believe he is doing well for himself, as you say," I answered.

"I am glad to hear of it. I am glad to hear that he is prospering," my father said quickly, and then he lapsed into a spell of his former cautiou and hesitation once more. He looked away from me for a moment, as if gathering courage, and then he stood up straight, ceasing his relaxed leaning against the front of his desk.

"Are you in the habit of answering these letters of your brother's?" my father asked. My feeling that his intrusion was about to grow to an unpardonable degree became suddenly intense; I became certain that he was going to ask me to write to my brother for money. I was appalled, but I said nothing.

"I don't answer all of them. He does not put questions to me. He just tells me of his life and his business and his business associates. I do not fully understand all of the details he gives about business," I said.

"I understand that, Campbell," my father interrupted, in an attempt to seize on a moment during which he might sound reassuring. I continued on, however.

"But I do answer them, but not regularly—and I say very little in them. He writes to me though I hardly write to him," I said. I was surprised how much I was willing to volunteer even though my father's intrusion angered me. I can only imagine that because of my youth and dependency I was also somewhat fearful of trespassing too far in anger upon my precarious relationship with my father. Though he was cautious, I could also tell he was too obtuse to sense my principal resentment. Something still told me to spare him if I could, protect my connection with him, *and* protect my developing though fragile correspondence with Ellsworth.

"Campbell, you know of the important series of lectures that the Lyceum will be hosting in May. I need not tell you that presenting Gerald Larimer Dunstable is quite a privilege for our village. You do know this?" he asked, so that I would confirm what he was already certain would be obvious to me.

"I do know this. Yes, sir," I replied.

"Under most circumstances I endeavor to remain indifferent as to the size of the public any of our speakers meet with here in Pauktaug."

Though my anger and resistance toward my father were tempered by a remaining childish sentiment and love for him, my anger and my desire for justice were fueled by the sudden steps my father seemed to be taking toward a confession of his consuming vanity concerning the Lyceum. I did not say a word but preferred to let him continue uninterrupted, for fear I might otherwise inhibit the oncoming concessions.

"I need for us to present Mr. Dunstable with a full audience. We must fill the hall of the Lyceum to capacity, Campbell," he said quickly, as if, had he said it with slowness and care, he might have checked himself before finishing the entire thought.

This was not the kind of vanity that had been proud to revel in making presentations that mainly went unnoticed by the local public—save for the ladies of his Lyceum Board who swelled his pride over that lack of notice, who fueled his vanity via praise of his ability to be so generous in the face of neglect and ignorance and ingratitude. This was, instead, a confession of a more simple kind of vanity, I believed. He wanted as much recognition and praise as possible in this instance. His old perverse vanity had to yield in part to a revision—had to accept change so that enough revenue might come in, if not to resurrect the patterns of his old vanity, then at least so that the venue could survive and support the terms of his new vanity. He was ready to meet the change if he had to, for he did not even have the strength to hold to the convictions of the perverse vanity that had fed him so well via the early history of the struggling Lyceum. His cause had then settled simply in keeping the Lyceum going at any cost. This confession was not quite as satisfying as one that would have conceded the warped and sick perspective of his original cause and vanity, but I was still somehow content with the things he was then saying, for they revealed an honest, emerging desperation, even though he spoke with as much confidence as ever. I must also say that I do not think my father could ever have been capable of understanding unto a level of spoken expression the full complexities of his original vanity. I said nothing, myself. Again, I merely endeavored to remain silent and permit my father to incriminate himself before me as much as possible—the only consequence of any incrimination being a verdict I could never express and unto which I could never attach or deliver a definite or even latent punishment.

"Campbell, would you write to your brother on my behalf? Or would you write to him and make a request for me though you might allow him to think the request comes from you?" my father asked.

I was eager to hear the nature of the request so I remained silent but tried to look receptive and encouraging.

"Campbell," my father began again after taking one last full breath before his final commitment, "I would like it if you would ask your brother to raise an audience for us for the Dunstable lectures, particularly the opening lecture. If your brother has become an accomplished man of business, surely he has acquired for himself a set of alliances from which he could produce a crowd for us. Attention from New York City could do much good for our cause here. I myself have neglected such connections, as I had there through business, in order to apply myself to our cause; yet now we keenly need those attentions," he said, and then he paused. "Would you do this for me, Campbell?"

There had been no direct request for money, though there was in this request a call for assistance to help the very cause that had eroded the bonds of my once happy family. I was certain that my father had related all the aspects of his request, for he stood before me then in nervous, expectant, silence. I was pleased and proud that I commanded that nervousness in him, though I was still astonished he had the strength and resolve to make the request. Along with my pride I was also able to muster pity for the man upon whom I depended, and with the anger I felt upon this intrusion into my shared world with Ellsworth I imagined I should also link some pity—for surely in this request there must be, I felt, some degree of veiled attempt to reach tentatively forth from a secretly penitent father to an alienated oldest son. Yet I was astonished that my father made no request of me in regard to style or sentiment in writing to my brother on his behalf. There was part of me, then, that suspected his request carried with it no ulterior purpose.

"I will write to Ellsworth, father, and put to him the request. I will write to him now in my room and post the letter today," I said.

This answer had come to me suddenly and easily, for I realized just before I spoke that I had not been placed in a position that challenged any of my feelings of intense conflict. Surely my brother would know, no matter how I made the request, that such a request could not really come from me, for in the little I wrote in my replies to Ellsworth I was sure that my contempt for the Lyceum's place in our lives was clear by the constancy of its omission from all of my descriptions of events and of my developing sympathies as a young man. And surely Ellsworth would refuse the request, and I would be free to continue my correspondence without allusion to our intruding and increasingly desperate father.

I posted the letter with confidence—sure that the reply would come with continued, uninterrupted relations of Ellsworth's business conquests in New York City and with solicitous questions after my interests and health, but with no reply at all to the impertinent and desperate request of my father. Thus it is difficult to express how surprised I was to find after a little more than a week passed that my brother's reply demonstrated how unfounded my confidence had been. The letter was short, but its answer was certain. Ellsworth asked that as many rooms be set aside at the hotel as possible; he also asked after the exact capacity of the Lyceum's hall. His brief letter ended by saying that he would endeavor to create as large an audience as possible for that first Dunstable lecture in May. He said no more; he seemed bent on keeping this letter separate from our usual correspondence, for soon after this letter arrived another letter came—a letter that continued the customary stream of remarks about his life in business and his traditional list of questions for me about my general thoughts and youthful philosophies. In the second letter there was no mention of the first. And in neither the first nor the second letter was there even the slightest suggestion that Ellsworth himself might appear in Pauktaug in May.

As we entered the final fortnight before Gerald Larimer Dunstable's arrival, I nearly forgot the strange request I had made of Ellsworth on my father's behalf, for not only had that second letter arrived but also two or three others from my brother to me which made no allusion to the event in May. Again, the letter that had answered the request was very brief, and it contained neither allusion to nor greeting for my father. Of course, when it arrived I told my father that my brother had pledged an audience for the first lecture. I told him, as well, of my brother's practical questions about the hotel and the hall. The answers were duly given, via my hand, and my father seemed relieved but at the same time slightly disturbed that I had no personal message to relate. He seemed to wait for and fear that I had such a message for just a moment, but then quickly passed onto other matters when it seemed likely I was holding nothing back, and I was not. I then put the lectures out of my mind. Again, my brother's subsequent letters gave me no feeling that he would soon appear or that anything would change in his relation to my father, and as the prospect of another set of lectures in the village was hardly a matter of note for me—no matter the exceptional notoriety of the particular speaker soon to be at hand—I did indeed cease to think of Gerald Larimer Dunstable until the night of his arrival, which was on the evening before the day of his first address to the Pauktaug Lyceum.

5.

On the night of Dunstable's arrival in Pauktaug, my father and a delegation of ladies went into the village to meet Dunstable at the steamer from New York, and to escort him to an evening reception and then to the hotel.

After some time alone in the house, the rich May air and its luminous new green and its accompanying, incongruous, colorful buds and perfumes—all of this, both color and scents all the more intense, somehow, under the critical and cool growing darkness of the twilight—compelled me to go walking.

Though I did not yet have the courage to speak to her about such things, there was a young lady from school for whom I had formed a strong attachment (the same young lady who had been so sympathetic to me during my schoolboy's fight on Main Street some time earlier), and it had become my custom to walk into the western hills near her home on the chance that I might see her. On that evening of Dunstable's arrival I set out on such a mission, and my walk took me, as usual, down to Main Street and past the hotel.

It was when I came in sight of the hotel, however, that I became aware once more of Ellsworth's reply to my father's request.

Before the hotel was a parade of traffic unlike any I had ever seen, outside of the mornings when an actual parade was held on Main Street. Buggies and wagons with hired drivers were coming to the hotel from the steamer at the dock, and an equal, great, volume of carriage traffic was also departing from the hotel. It appeared that the hotel was full for that night, and I watched as its proprietor—confronted with such a challenging windfall for the very first time—was compelled to send away any number of patrons which he would have been eager to accommodate, but for whom he simply had no room. As I passed this spectacle of Pauktaug's overflowing guests from New York City, I listened as they were directed to the hotels of the neighboring villages of Northport and Huntington; and as I walked on and watched these frustrated but determined admirers of Dunstable accept the prospect of a journey to other lodgings I smiled as still others passed them and me on their way to the hotel—many of these newest arrivals proceeding with haughty sureness even when they had been warned by drivers going the other way that the hotel had not a single vacancy.

I did not remain in the village long to watch much more of this spectacle for I did not wish to be on hand when my father paraded in with pride, escorting Dunstable to the one room that remained empty and waiting at the hotel. Nor did I linger on the west side of the village very long that evening in the hopes of catching a glimpse of the girl I wished to make a sweetheart. Instead, I returned home and retired early, for I felt strangely crowded in my own village, even though the hotel was outside of sight and sound of our family home, the house hidden on the eastern rise well above Main Street.

The day of Dunstable's lecture dawned and brought a clear, bright, May sky. My father was absent from the house for the entire day; he had gone to attend to any whims of his great guest and to see to it that the Lyceum's hall was prepared in every way to receive the first audience that would fill its auditorium to capacity. I resolved to pass the entire day at home, and I also had resolved to refrain from attending the lecture. Though I had taken, in my dependencies and my affections, to helping my father during many quiet hours in his vast correspondence concerning the Lyceum, it was tacitly understood somehow that whenever it pleased me, it was not necessary for me to attend the lectures themselves. Outsiders may have thought this strange, but I believe my father felt that what appeared to be my concessions over the correspondence left him indebted to me—even though those hours in his library were among the most pleasurable I spent with my father. Though I helped him labor over the cause that had destroyed my family's happiness, I could work in silence with him and at least enjoy the illusion of some warm, speechless, though limited understanding between father and second son. But he seemed to realize that demanding my presence at the Lyceum itself, especially when it was in use, would test too much what love and tolerance remained in me.

However, as the lovely evening of that bright, scented, May day revealed itself, I felt an urgency to leave the house and walk abroad again into the village. I imagined I had a premonition that Ellsworth would reappear in Pauktaug on that evening. It did not seem a hopeful premonition, or an imaginary premonition, which would be too hard to support, for indeed, with the affirmative but brief answer he had given to my father's request, and what with the evidence I had seen the evening before that he had fulfilled his pledge to create a full audience for the Lyceum, I thought it possible that he might make some sort of surprise and furtive visit to the village, perhaps if just for my sake. I had hopes he might use this event in which he had a hand as a pretense for catching a glimpse of me.

I was certain he had developed no sudden sympathy for my father's cause; nor did I suspect rekindled sentiment toward my father could inspire such a visit. Again, I was certain that if he did appear it would be for my sake For I had come to feel that he could not have assented to assist in this affair in any capacity had it not been that he felt it would assist in my comforts at home in some imagined way.

Perhaps I was foolish to imagine that he would come for this purpose. For he had already begun to hint that I could find a place with him in business and life when I felt ready and willing. (I was still uncertain what his business was in New York City.) But since I made no complaints in my letters, and since, too, he had never ventured to see personally to my safety and health at any previous time, I do not know why I felt he would use this event as an opportunity to seek me out. These doubts occurred to me even as I approached Main Street on that May evening. But notwithstanding such doubts, I felt very strongly that something about that evening might attract the actual presence of Ellsworth. I was certain, too, that even if I did not see him, that somehow he would be making an appearance in the village on that night.

When I arrived on Main Street, a lovely blue twilight was descending upon the village, and I recall the sound of small birds as they made their way betwixt the folding parasols of the ladies who made their way into the lobby of the Lyceum. Gentlemen in fine clothes walked parallel or behind the spectacular assortment of women.

As the rear of this crowd finished making their way into the hall from the Lyceum's lobby, I stood upon the board sidewalk and took in a few last breaths of the oncoming evening air before resolving to go inside and catch a glimpse of this Dunstable for myself. Two of the village women—two of my father's devoted admirers—had been taking tickets, but they, of course, let me pass without ceremony—though not without a warning that I would likely have to stand, for there was not a free seat remaining. I did not respond to this remark, for it was given with a jovial tone of satisfaction for my father's great cause; I also did not respond for I felt contempt for the expressions the women exchanged between themselves upon my appearance in the lobby—expressions of mawkish sentiment (as if my appearance there suddenly heralded the end of my childishly petulant resistance to my father's great works).

But as I took to the steps to climb to the first level of the Lyceum Hall (on the second floor of the building), I had to stop absolutely dead and listen. Though I was well inside the building by then, and though the sound of the enormous crowd in the hall's orchestra seating above made its way around a corner doorway and down half a flight of stairs to where I stood, there was no mistaking the sound of a steamer coming into the harbor. The high, airy, sibilant sound of its incoming whistle compelled me to note the time of day. The schedule for the steamer was limited and strict, and there had never, in my lifetime, been an extra steamer arriving from New York at that time or on that night of the week. I was certain of what I had heard, but upon looking behind me, I saw the two oblivious women who had been collecting tickets, closing but not locking the Lyceum's outer doors and then starting to make their way up the stairs themselves behind me. I did not wish for these women to overtake me, so I put thoughts of the unexpected steamer out of my mind and proceeded to the orchestra level.

Peeking into the concert hall from the front of the orchestra, I could see that there was indeed not a single seat left on that level. I then proceeded down a long hallway to the front of the building, a hallway that ran hidden from the full, sloping length of the orchestra's many rows—and I climbed the steps to the balcony and box level that wrapped around three full sides of the hall's auditorium. This space was full, as well, so I leaned against the back wall, resolved that I could make an easy escape after having my simple glimpse of Gerald Larimer Dunstable.

In addition to the two women he had appointed to the lobby for collecting tickets, my father had placed two of his admirers at the entrance to the orchestra—to stand there and serve as ushers. But as the hour for Dunstable's start neared, all four of the women who served as either ushers or ticket takers made their way to the balcony as I had, in the hope of finding a discreet place to stand so that one could catch an ubobstructed view of the famous lecturer and philosopher.

I looked about the hall as a hush fell over the eager crowd. Not only had I never seen the hall with so many people inside of it, but I never thought I would see it with every one of its seats taken. But this was not the end of the crowding; somehow an inordinate number of standing room tickets had been sold, as well. Behind the back rows in the entire balcony and behind the ring of seats that extended to the hall's upper sides until the boxes were reached, rows of standing people shifted their weight from one foot to the other as they gently asserted for themselves a place next to neighbors who were equally unsure of a place to be secure and balanced. I believe there was an equal crowd of standing patrons at the back of the orchestra, as well. Women in this part of the crowd had begun already to fan themselves.

Outside of how I was sure I felt about the Lyceum, my father's cause, and this Gerald Larimer Dunstable fellow, there was, I must concede, an excitement in seeing such an enormous crowd. But I believe my excitement did not come from sharing in the crowd's anticipation at the prospect of soon seeing such a great and famous man. No, my excitement came, instead, from the size and closeness of the crowd. I had never seen such a large assembly of living beings so densely assembled in one place. There were moments when there seemed to be no spaces between anyone in the hall. It almost appeared—for brief, illusory, moments—that the entire human assembly was one large vibrant block of conjoined matter. The crowd in the standing room was so close that even the shifting of weight seemed to stop; individuals after a time fell into relying upon their neighbors to support them—so that when someone did have to shift at all, the telltale squeak of the floorboard beneath their feet revealed their location precisely. Thus, as the hush fell over the crowd, even these squeaks were suppressed for fear of rudeness, and so it was that the illusion of the great, living, conjoined block seemed even greater.

Suddenly my father appeared on the stage from its wings, and he met with a considerable degree of applause. In that day, when reliable likenesses were more rare than they are now, I am certain that many in the audience thought that this might be Dunstable himself. My father's vanity swallowed this mild ovation completely. He made a few feigned gestures of resistance as he reached the podium, but then he yielded and accepted what came until a full half-minute was necessary for it to subside.

My father looked pitiable to me—pitiable because my contempt for him at that moment was so great that I felt at the same time a pity for the man who earned such enmity from me at the same time. I was glad at that moment that most thoughts can remain concealed and private. He also looked considerably older and more feeble to me—under the light of the stage—than I had yet realized.

Though he was responsible for establishing the Lyceum Hall, and its management and promotion for more than a decade, and the securing of its speakers—and in that case perhaps the most famous American lecturer then on the Lyceum circuit next to Ralph Waldo Emerson—I watched with particular scorn as my father made a last flourish unto his humble bow (made a few moments after the dying applause had ceased to justify it) to an audience that he could never have created for himself.

My father's meek voice failed to carry well as he introduced Dunstable, for as my father retreated from the lectern and Dunstable approached it, only a moderate applause ensued—as if the public, not wishing to be fooled twice by an imposter for the main attraction was content to settle in and be sure by the words of an actual lecture that they finally had *the* man of the hour at hand.

However, it was *the* man of the hour, and his fame and erudite reputation seemed, I must concede, instantly reinforced by the confidence, authority, and volume of his clear voice:

"Ladies, Gentleman,—Friends: I appear before you this evening after having made a wondrous and eventful trip south, to you here, from Boston. The wonders of our nation—its signs of industry, commerce, the marvels of improvements—are so many, so keen to overwhelm the senses, that I feel I came here this evening, at first, almost uncertain of my own theme. How easy it has become, how glorious, even—in this year of peace since the end of our Nation's great contest—to revel in our powers of mechanical reformation. Everywhere on my journey I behold the wonders of our machines. All Nature is harnessed to their teams. The traces and reins of industry are as a glorious web, pulling from all sides upon the face of creation. In each factory, each workshop, the latest signs of industry reveal our looking ahead. There is not a device that emerges from such places but reveals our great skill for reformulation. We are giddy with revision. In such places, as well, are made, too, the machines that in turn will be used in other factories to make still more machines for the great advancement, the great reformulations. There is at once so much production, so much delight in the material, that even the genius and principles necessary for the creation of such wonders seem veritably subsumed by the mass, by the bulk, of the productions themselves. It is as if the man in joining the horse to become the Centaur lost his reverence for mind and reveled in a beast that was horse's body, man's torso for Centaur's head, but decided to forgo his own head as part of that conflation. He makes something all body. We revel now not so much in power and creation, but worshiping best, perhaps, the end of that process and less so the shooting of the gulf—and least of all the genius and principles that give birth to such process. Will, at last, our creations take their way

without Mind and improve upon themselves—or perhaps even merely glory in the sheer escalation of their own mass? Perchance this will be, for on more than one occasion I am certain I saw less wood and iron go into a factory than now by some great spell seems to come out of it. Again, the horse of the Centaur seems day by day to overpower the man of the Centaur. Material reigns; matter has outrun thought."

The audience sat and stood utterly motionless for this abstruse opening of the great man's lecture. Still fascinated by the sheer mass of the audience itself, I did my best to follow at the same time Dunstable's theme, which I conceded to myself I found rather interesting. But whilst attempting to monitor both of these fascinations a third issue of interest subtly introduced itself at this very juncture in the earliest part of the lecture.

From where I stood I could see down into the orchestra to where its one open entrance door communicated with the outer hallway and the head of the stairs that led to the lobby. There, at that doorway, I could see several gentlemen and ladies crowded together, crowded close to one another for it seemed they were merely at the head of a great throng of people behind them who virtually compelled them to move forward. With no one in attendance at the door, a flow of new patrons for Dunstable's performance began an indiscreet attempt to enter discreetly the Lyceum's orchestra section. Judging from the reaction of audience members seated farther back in the orchestra, it was clear from their indignation that doors parallel to their rows had been opened and that a flow of new audience members was also entering along the entire length of the orchestra. One of the women my father had appointed to handling the tickets also saw this and made her way down from the balcony to address this flood.

My fascination was then divided between the lecture; the mass of the giant, ponderous, audience; and then the new stream of men and women—apparently arrived from the city on this latest, unscheduled, steamer—who seemed bent on catching what they must have felt was their own entitled glimpse and hearing of Dunstable. Yet these did not appear to be common people; nor did they appear to be crowds of artists. These new waves seemed to be from the same class as the throngs already filling the Lyceum's hall—a wealthy, privileged sort, who might account a hearing of Dunstable as they might account their view of any rarefied person or thing on a tour dearly purchased: as their easy right. They all had the air of entitlement mixed with ennui which made their crowding into the hall a singular, mindless, event. They felt sure of their place there; yet they pressed in with an air of indifference at the same time. They were a perfectly finished, elegant, dense, herd—shiny and fattened.

I endeavored to turn my attention to Dunstable's words once more. He did not yet seem distracted by the pairs who attempted to swell quietly the standing room crowd in the orchestra.

"Again, Material reigns in our age. The War only brought us newer and finer means by which to create our materials. It would seem: Material outruns the thoughts and principles that allowed for its greater, speedier, creation. Indeed, it seems that not merely a Centaur has become the symbol for our vigorous, wondrous, people, but a headless Centaur. That Centaur which is our emblem is as a mighty, thoughtless, beast which has bucked its rider's head but kept the rider's legs and torso; that Centaur has augmented and thus revels in a pure bodily power, a power that only acts reflexively on ideas of a thwarted and disenthroned mind.

"I must confess that as I made my way here—by the power of steam on land and sea—I could not help but thrill to our advancement as a people. I cannot help but be made giddy with the great power our national ingenuity has produced—again, a

power and a material result out of proportion, seemingly, to the amount of ideas and principles invoked in the starting of this great process. Why, in fact, on the train from Boston—whilst being pulled by that beast that the Red Man of our plains is said to call the Iron Horse—I was certain that the Iron Centaur at the train's head might eject its pilot's, its engineer's, head on a sharp curve but add his body to the fuel of the tender and continue without stopping to our ultimate destination. I would not have been shocked that such a headless Iron Centaur would create and throw ahead of itself new rails—make, somehow, miles of new track by some magic applied to the as yet untapped grandeurs in a lump of coal. In this country an embodied Erlkönig has overtaken our race, but steals instead our forms and rejects our spirits.

"But is it any wonder that we the Thinkers are drawn to the beasts and to matter so as to augment the power of our limited bodies? Does not the best race horse run faster if he has a jockey atop him to coax his thoughtless potential to greater speed? Is this not true? As I have conceded, I too have a wild sympathy with the alchemy that has bled from our Yankee peoples into our men of the West and even unto, I am certain, our returning friends of the South.

"But I endeavor to remind myself that in the glory of such unmatched and unprecedented enterprise is a seduction unto which we all must temper our complete submission. We must insist that this temptress yield something of herself, as well, if we are to join in this romance. We must ask for some domesticity from this Wild Woman before we beget out full family of Titans by Her. We must keep our heads upon the rider who is to be the exalted half of the new Centaur.

"Indeed, my friends of Long Island, your fields and your fishing nets cannot long escape the seduction that is coming. I do not entirely warn you away from the temptress. But do not yield all to her. Even here in this village, the bones of whales are made

to fit and broaden the skirts and to strengthen the parasols of our women. Into such a factory I am certain will soon come the seductress. What results will come if you are prepared when you come to meet her!

"Do not reject her; but do not let her altogether dominate you.

"It is for you to recall that the value or the true physical mass of matter, of an object, must remain in ever smaller proportion to the prospect of greater principles it projects. Matter must not beget matter; and I fear we are nearly on the precipice of such a skill. We must endeavor to recall that matter is the shadow of principle. Disaster lies in confounding what is the true shadow with the true projector. Ideas throw their shadows upon Creation, just as the First Creator through His shadow rendered a material Creation. It is for us to carry on this glorious impulse; but it is for us to keep matter, regardless of our material prosperity, as only the lesser outcome of our industrial endeavors. For each mile of new rail upon which runs the Iron Centaur let there be one hundred new Thinkers born for the cars it pulls to our greater and greater realization as a race."

Dunstable was still only in the opening minutes of his lecture, but my attention could not resist the patterns that were unfolding in the orchestra seating below. All of the standing room in the aisles in the orchestra—both house left and house right—were entirely filled, as was presumably the rear aisle behind the last row in the orchestra (concealed from my view below the balcony). Yet latecomers there, unable to find either seats or even adequate space in the aisles to claim as standing room, kept themselves in hushed, constant, indignant, and frustrated motion.

I was able to make out the ticket taker by this point, the woman who had left the balcony to attend to this unexpected overflowing of people, but she only seemed successful in preventing more people from entering at that one orchestra aisle door I could see from the balcony. She could do nothing about the immense, slowly circling, horde which had already trapped itself inside the hall. Nor could she, it seemed, do much about stopping that part of the crowd she had successfully blocked from entering the orchestra from following their impulse to climb to the balcony via its staircase. Even over Dunstable's great and powerful voice, I could hear the swish of approaching skirts, and the muffled tap of canes and closed parasols against the carpeted stairs as this unexpected new crowd from the latest steamer began its climb to the balcony.

Dunstable continued without a pause, perhaps aware of this bizarre circumstance but showing no sign of it in his manner. My father, however, I could then see peering with great anxiety from behind the gathered curtain on stage left. As there was no easy way to reach the orchestra from the stage during a performance—not without walking right across the sight of the performer—my father continued to stare helplessly out into the hall from behind the open curtain as the glory of a full house increased to the crisis of a tender bubble near its volume of disaster. I saw my father's eyes look up to the balcony as the pressure of the new crowd began to hunt for places there.

And, still, somehow Dunstable—as much a performer as a philosopher—continued. As my view of him began to be obscured by throngs of elegantly dressed but exhausted ladies and their men from New York, as all these struggled with me for the last remaining inches of emptiness in the balcony, I felt suddenly a great grin overtake my face. I now became possessed by the grand absurdity— no, the sheer grandeur—of such a space being so deftly though chaotically packed by human forms and their sartorial accoutrements. The space was so filled that I passed at once from the sense of impending threat that I imagine an unordered crowd should pose to feeling suddenly a jubilation in the wonderful, dense, pageant. There were, from moment to moment, fewer and fewer inches to spare, but the confident crowd continued to advance, each pair of that crowd sure that the fine box to which their sure individualized privilege entitled them must be just a few paces farther away. As the crowd continued to compact itself, I stood so close to so many fine gentlemen's ladies that it seemed the very substance of their perfume would surely crowd out the last spaces in the air through which Dunstable's words could travel. It seemed we were on a course for the opposite of a vacuum. As feet shifted on the balcony's floor, a chorus of identifying floorboard squeaks also made an antiphonal contest in the dwindling air.

Somehow I could still hear Dunstable.

"Friends, but it is pardonable that our race should strive so fiercely to create this new Centaur in modern times. For is it not so that even in our earliest, distinct, literature in this new Republic, we are given to celebrating its manifestations? Take, if you will, the dark, headless horseman in Mr. Irving's Sketchbook. *The author would have us think his headless horseman rides his nightly rounds, taking the heads of victims as he goes, in the hope of recovering the head he lost in life. Yet I do not believe this notion of the story and its character is what holds our minds in thrall. Nor do I think the simple interpreter, putting forth an adolescent alternative to this idea, is correct when he ventures that the horseman, hopeless in his aim of recovering his own, true, head, is merely spreading misery and pain by decapitating others. No. There is, rather, another way to regard this tale, and I would submit that the conception I now venture accounts truly for the growing appeal of Mr. Irving's legend. The Centaur of his fable is in fact no villain but a manifestation of an aggressive national hope. He, this headless horseman, exults in his headlessness. He is all Centaur—the strength of bodily man applied to the strength of bodily horse. Yet both parts—the horseman himself, and his horse in essence, for the latter is mere brute—are free of heads, of Mind. This muscular conflation exults in the*

strength of Nature without conscience, without remorse. It is straddled neither by the skittish fears of the beast's mind (for he has a controlling rider) nor the moral scruples of Man (for he is free of the seat of intellect). It exults, revels, in pure strength and power. And this headless horseman, this new Centaur of the New World, does not impart vengeance on his rides but the hope that all may share in his throes of shameless power. In that spirit, after a manner of generosity, does he behead others. He is as a second Founder; he is as a new signatory to a new type of Declaration. His fable bespeaks the strength of Man welded to Nature on this great new Continent of Wilderness; his fable bespeaks our will to exalt in giving way to strength without remorse. Perhaps it will astonish you, Friends, if I venture that it is not altogether a vile path that we follow in this regard. I have conceded that I, too, stand before factories and marvel as more of a product seems to emerge, in sheer volume, than raw material was put in to produce the result. Again, it would almost seem we live in an age wherein matter can beget more matter. Like a child, I sometimes stand in wonder and ask, 'Does the Earth grow heavier day by day as result of the works of Man, as a result of his increasing productivity?' This question seems to emerge from the same illogical but irresistible impulse that both horse and headless rider produce something greater, more powerful—larger, even—than that same horse and rider would produce if the rider still had his head. Again, I cannot fully reproach this impulse. For there would still be something of our great National will and spirit— all that comes from the head—even in that headless rider, even in our wildest, most astounding feats of ceaseless production and industrial improvement.

"But permit me, Friends—"

It was at this point in the lecture that I head the great crack— akin to the sound that attends the falling of an enormous but still healthy tree when it is either felled or vanquished by wind. I cannot say for how long Dunstable continued to speak after the last words I give above, but I heard a scream from below even before all the many people about me let out their own screams. From the inordinate weight the balcony then held, but had never been tested nor intended to withstand, an exquisitely complex but limited collapse commenced. Though enough of the structure remained in place to prevent anyone in the balcony from spilling into the orchestra, that part of the balcony that was parallel to the hall's back wall gave way to such a degree that everyone in that section tumbled forward and created a terrified, lowing, mass of men, women, canes, and parasols. Below the balcony an immediate flood of people moved from beneath the dangling threat and caused the start of a hurried, panicked, but not altogether disorderly emptying of the theater. As the balcony had collapsed several yards below its original position and lowered its front end to the greatest degree, I myself had managed to grab onto an elaborate but evidently strong sconce above my head which secured me from falling forward, unlike nearly everyone else in the balcony's standing room horde.

To the credit of several gentlemen in the balcony and several gentlemen from below, everyone in the balcony was ultimately removed without significant injury from the dangling wreckage of the hall's uppermost seating area. As I escorted a particularly frail woman down to the orchestra level and then ultimately down to the lobby and the street, I heard from her and nearly everyone within range of my hearing nothing but the bitterest complaints about the experience and the dangerous venue to which they had been drawn by the promise of seeing a great man—a great man whom one would never suspect had been secured as bait for a mere bumpkin business and deathtrap.

I knew my father still remained inside the Lyceum's hall at that point, presumably attending as best he could to the management of such an enormous disaster to his cause. I pitied my father, not because of the disaster—which after I had seen that it had caused no one any significant injury, gave me a sense of great, youthful, glee—but because the disaster revealed that not a one of the wealthy and enormously inconvenienced New York City patrons mentioned his name or thought to hold him responsible. This meant that since they did not have the knowledge to attach his name to the event when they had the greater human impulse to place blame, they surely would have entirely overlooked him had Dunstable's series of lectures gone on without incident. He was merely just another one of the bumpkins on hand.

As to where such an unfairly abused, cajoled and deceived mass of refined people could indeed place blame, it was clear that they were uncertain. Each party to which I listened—as they limped back to the hotel, or to buggies, or to the pier where the latest steamer still remained—seemed only able to blame another friend from their strata who had himself heard from some other friend of the novel expedition out east from New York that could not be missed. They had all seen Dunstable any number of times before, and in the velvet, palatial, comfort of New York. Who had persuaded them via some irresistible rumor of the irresistible allure of this foolish expedition to see him in such a remote place? For what purpose? For what cause? No one could say.

The chaos that ultimately brought no broken bones or slaughter, and the growing, blamable, mystery which these crowds felt had compelled them to attend such a disappointment, moved me to stand back at last in a shadowy corner with folded arms.

As the darkness wrapped itself about the village I walked down to the water's edge and watched as most of the passengers who had arrived on the latest, unexpected steamer, embarked again upon it only an hour or so after having arrived. I looked about the docks in the rich darkness, and I looked, too, from there, back toward Main Street—where, in more than one instance I felt I saw a man with folded arms, sitting on horseback, watching the scene of the steamer from a distance. I fancied, of course, that this was Ellsworth. It may have been, perhaps; but when I returned myself to Main Street the figure on horseback was gone: head, body, horse, and all.

As I continued away from the harbor along Main Street I looked back when the steamer sounded again its great whistle, as if in preparation for departure back to New York. However, I was surprised to see that it was not the steamer which had arrived during the lecture. It was, instead, yet another tardy vessel—another ship filled with an excess of wealthy patrons for the lecture that had already ended. But as the camel's back had already been broken, this was merely an extra straw cast upon an already excessive, demolished, heap, an addition to surfeit.

I looked about me one last time, hoping to share a distant smile with the unidentified man on horseback. But he was indeed gone— vanished into the night like Irving's Headless Horseman.

PART VII

Hush and Who

I.

I had found the Indian's body early on a Monday morning; I had been in the new Pauktaug for a day or two more than a week by that point. Later in the morning of that Monday I slept again for a time in my room at the hotel, but by early afternoon I made my way to the marshal's office with the intention of establishing myself fully.

That Monday was the first cloudy day I had experienced in the new country. A gray slate of clouds—interspersed with genuinely black tufts—spread from horizon to horizon. Remarkably—just as the dark, clear, evening light made spring colors seem more brilliant for me back East—the dark sky made the farthest details of the range's horizon perfectly reveal themselves in the new territory. I had thought that the days of unremarkable, comprehensive domes of blue sky and brilliant sun would have revealed the most detail. But not so. I paused as I made my way to the marshal's office and looked up the alleys between the buildings of Main, and then looked past the south and then back past the north end of Main Street itself and noted rolling details of the range I had never discerned before. The land seemed to be veritably filling itself. One might have thought that the emptiness of the range would have been happily compromised a bit by the then qualifying and emerging details, but it looked at the same time all the more an immense grassy vacuum to me.

It was not long after noon when I checked again on Rutledge in his cell and told him I would release him by three o'clock. He had asked where his horse had been stabled since he had been locked up, and I told him that Mr. Whisker had told me he himself had taken the animal—the prime horse in Rutledge's string from the allotment given to him by Whisker for the season. I told Rutledge that Whisker had told me to tell him that he would discuss such things with him in a few days—after Whisker and my brother returned from their inspection of the fence. The reminder about the fence seemed to disturb Rutledge, but the earlier news about his confiscated horse—the news of such a devastating cowman's reprimand—genuinely appeared to enrage him. I believe his rage was then so intense because for a man of such wild impulsiveness to grow so suddenly and so intensely silent and introverted, a great indignation had to be working a violent revolution within him.

I left the office for a brief time and returned with food for my prisoner. Rutledge accepted this with more of his disturbing, focused, silence. I then spent more than an hour poring over a set of territorial law books until sometime after two o'clock I could hear the sound of a horse at a gallop being driven right up to the marshal's office hitching post.

I rose to look out the window, but before I could reach it the front door opened. I was astonished to see that it was Julius who entered and then stood before me. I had never seen him move with such speed—neither in the time back east nor in the days since his arrival in the new Pauktaug. Though he made an effort to maintain his usual appearance of coolness and comprehensive social indifference, he was uncharacteristically breathless—as if he had as much a part in the galloping of his horse as had the horse himself. I looked past Julius and to the horse; it was dreadfully lathered and showed all the signs of being played out.

As I look back, this breathlessness and this uncharacteristic speed from such a deliberate man should have given me great pause. However, I was too distracted to register the importance of the details because of a nearly incredible third factor. Julius Crabbe suddenly and inexplicably affected a fine degree of deference to me! The suddenness and brevity of our meeting then, combined with my vain and naïve perception of what I took to be his regard for my new appointment, left me vulnerable to the simple request that he made. Again, I should note that Julius and I—outside of formal nods and very brief greetings and leave-takings—had almost never spoken to one another. Again, his sudden deference, no matter the seemingly simple nature of his request, should have put me on guard. I should have known how to spot a man suddenly too intent on surrendering his sense of superiority; I should have recognized a man desperate to get past the seemingly simple, last, hurdle that stood between him and his enormous realization or opportunity.

"Dear Cousin Campbell, I am back from the south range. Pardon me, I mean Marshal Crabbe," he said, and then he paused with an uncomfortable smile as he considered the qualification he had just made. He removed his hat. For another uncomfortable instant he rotated his bowler hat a quarter circle by pinching its brim between his nervous fingers.

"Cousin Cam," he continued, and I found it offensive that not only did Julius presume to use my brother's shortened version of my name for me but that he even knew this intimate title at all. "Cousin—Cam, may I see Mr. Rutledge? Is he still here?"

I was so astonished by the simplicity of this request that all my indignation and cautiousness were pushed aside—at least for the moment.

Julius was indeed a shrewd man, for seeing my surprise he began to make his way to the door that led to the back cells even though I could not muster a word in reply. I followed the force of his momentum and moved to beat him to the door so that I could unlock it. I was so steeped for a moment in an embarrassment over the defense I had thought to mount against any request he might make that I moved in a nearly involuntary manner of solicitude so as to cover my astonishment at the simple nature of what he had actually asked of me. Julius spoke to fill the silence as I found the key for the door to the back cells.

"I just came from the south range. Your brother and Mr. Whisker are still there. I thought it a waste for them to send back a hand who might be needed, so I volunteered to bring information from Mr. Whisker to his foreman—information he needs for when he is freed. He is to be out soon?"

"At three o'clock," I said, as I took the key back out from the lock.

"I won't be long in delivering the message," Julius said as he began to make his way to Rutledge's cell. Incredibly, the last look he gave me over his shoulder persuaded me to close the door and leave them to a private meeting, even though I do not think either party was entitled to such conditions.

I paced in the front room for a time. I could not make out what the two men in the back were saying at all, though from time to time I could hear individual words and suppressed exclamations coming from Rutledge. As I continued to walk back and forth before the open front door my indignation began to rise, for I realized more time was passing than the relation of any mere message would require. And as I continued to pace before the open front door, my eyes settled upon the exhausted, spread-legged, horse; it had been tethered so hastily and carelessly, that though it was free to wander, it did not. It had been ridden close to the edge of death; no mere delivery of a cowman's casual news would call for such treatment of an animal.

Just as my increasing anger had me resolve to go back to the cells, I heard a final, but in this case very clear, fit of words roar forth from Rutledge's distant cell:

"That no good son-of-a-bitch!" shouted Rutledge.

Only a few seconds later I heard a knocking at the outer door to the cells, and in answer I immediately opened that door for Julius. As the door swung open I heard a more intense, more sibilant, but less voluminous repetition from Rutledge of his last phrase.

Before my cousin exited the small cellblock he turned and called back to Rutledge (whom one could not see from that position): "Do try, Mr. Rutledge, to be patient. Save what you feel for just a bit longer," Julius said with condescension and finality, and then he nodded for me to close the outer door of the cells.

As I proceeded to lock that door several questions formed in my mind, but Julius must have anticipated this, so taking advantage of his ability to speak quickly, and my remaining sense of angry speechlessness and general bewilderment, Julius suddenly put an unexpected question to me.

"Cousin Cam, having just come from that part of the range where your brother is extending the fence, I did see a crew of men digging postholes who seemed hired just for that labor," he said.

I did not realize this was really a question. Thinking I might have further information about the statement he had just made he made a clear question out of it.

"If your brother did not hire nearly all of Whisker's idle summer men for work on the new fence—but instead has some crew in place just for that labor—can you tell me where he put Whisker's men to work?"

"I really couldn't say," I replied, but before I even finished this answer Julius was in the midst of putting another question to me.

"Again, at what hour do you plan to release Mr. Rutledge?" he asked quickly. As I began to answer, Julius interrupted and added,

"Rutledge said you said three o'clock? That would be quite soon, wouldn't it?"

"Yes, it would," I replied.

Before I could continue to form the many questions that were coming to mind, Julius put his bowler hat back on his head and walked out the door. I followed only as far as the front of the office, and I watched in perplexed silence as Julius made his way toward the hotel on foot. He had abandoned altogether the devastated horse, as if circumstances were about to change so comprehensively that he could afford not only to neglect an animal so egregiously but also neglect the prime resource it represented in that country—in a land where such behavior rendered anyone into a pariah.

Seeing that Julius had not only ridden one of my brother's top string horses nearly to death, but that he had discarded it as one might do with an empty bottle or a newspaper, I immediately loosened its saddle cinches to help it cool down, and then I led him slowly to the livery stable up and across Main Street so that someone could see to what remained of the beast.

As I walked back to the marshal's office, the sky darkened further, and there was yet more clarity to the distant undulations of the range in all four directions. It was nearly three o'clock when I entered the office, and I could hear Rutledge, now past his enraged silence, calling out my name angrily and demanding that he be freed.

Even as I began to open his cell, Rutledge continued to demand his release.

"It's three o'clock, Marshal!" he shouted with contempt—and he used the title *Marshal* with particular disdain. "It's three o'clock; I needs to be on my way."

"Easy, Mr. Rutledge, that's what we're doing right now," I said.

"Where are my things?" He demanded as we made our way to

the front office. "Where are my persuaders?" he asked as he looked about frantically and wrung his hands.

"First, why don't you tell me, what was the nature of your business with my cousin?" I asked him, knowing that even though I could not keep him any longer, I did not wish to surrender the impression that I would be seizing as many implied powers as I could appropriate. I did not wish to appear meek, to appear as if in letting Rutledge out on time I was yielding more to his reminder that he was to be released at three o'clock.

My brief time and experience as constable in a small Long Island village had not prepared me for the kind of response which Rutledge (I realize now) predictably made:

"The nature of my business is none of your damn business, *Marshal*." he hissed. "I ask again! Where are my damn smoke poles?"

I opened a drawer and tossed Rutledge his gun belt. Then from a shelf I retrieved his hat and spurs and boots. It was hard for me to give him back his gunbelt, I did not know at the time on what pretence I might make an effort to keep his guns. Rutledge quickly put on his gunbelt and his hat, and as he pointed at me with the hand that clutched his silver, gal-leg spurs, and as he backed his way out of the open front door he said again, "The nature of my business is none of your goddamned business."

And then, after he made his way onto the street he turned back one last time to repeat himself "My business here and now is none of your damn business, even if it is with your cousin—or with your brother!"

The final qualification did not give me concern at the time. Somehow, I felt he was referring merely to the past incident with the Indian and that he was demanding the chance and privacy to swallow his pride. I was foolish enough not to realize that he might be thinking prospectively in his reference to Ellsworth, and I was also foolishly relieved that another immediate confrontation between Rutledge and myself had not immediately presented itself.

I closed the office front door as a light rain began to fall. I sat down and reflected that it had not taken days but hours for visions from my beloved dime novel readings to become actuality for me after I was named marshal. I knew that it would take me some time before I could cite with confidence the details of local and territorial laws and ordinances, but I felt confident I was already an expert in my romantic conception and role as a frontier marshal. My lonely readings from dime novels had long fixed within me a code toward which I was compelled to grasp if, as fate and brotherly circumstance did at last ordain for me, I were named to a post of police authority somewhere on the frontier.

Because I was so expert in that romantic conception for myself, I sat at my desk for a time after Rutledge had left and lamented the fact that I was certain I had already fallen short of my code in the exchange with Julius and during Rutledge's parting from the jail. I was not sure what it was I imagined I should have done or should have said, but, again, I sat for a long spell and pored over memories in my mind of simple novels and their tenets whilst ignoring the indisputable territorial and state tomes that lay on the desk before me.

I do not know how long I sat there, idly recalling the romantic patterns I felt I had slighted. But as if to recall and compel me back into of my lawman's actual appointment, I looked up to see the front door of the office swinging open.

2.

There stood Pope Pope, his long slicker shiny from rain. I stood up as he entered and closed the door behind himself.

"Mr. Crabbe," he said, and then he added, very respectfully and sincerely, "Marshal, sir."

He embarrassed me out of my gloom and compelled me to start anew in my quest to realize an ideal of the frontier lawman. But though it was clear that Pope Pope would pay due heed to my title, it was soon evident he was then there to update me in an ongoing chain of events that had rhythms and tides that would swell over the presence and authority of anyone posted in my new position. He paid heed to my title because I was the marshal, however absurd the degree of my novitiate rendered me; but he had come to me as the brother of Ellsworth Crabbe and for no other reason. I feel that Pope liked my brother, and I feel that Pope liked me. I could not help liking him, as well.

He said that his time was short, that he would have to continue on in but a few moments. I insisted he remove his wet hat and slicker for the moment, however, and that he sit before my desk and pause if just for a moment. He did so.

"Mr. Crabbe—Marshal—has anyone come into town in the last several hours?" he began.

"No one new that I noticed. But, strangely, my Cousin Julius came off of the south range and into town alone and came right here," I answered.

"He came here?" Pope asked, and he leaned forward as if to have suspicions and fears confirmed.

"Yes, he rode, from the sound of it, straight here, and he nearly—or probably—doomed the horse from the ride. I've taken it over to the livery," I said.

Continuing to lean forward, Pope quickly pressed on with questions: "What did he say to you? What did he want?"

"It was very strange. He said almost nothing to me. He only wanted to see Mitch Rutledge," I said.

"He did?" Did he say why?" Pope almost demanded, and then he caught himself in the tone of demand and tempered himself by leaning back in the chair slightly.

"No, he didn't say," I replied, trying to hint by my tone that Pope could not overstep his bounds with me, especially where Julius was concerned.

"Did you let him?" Pope asked, returning to his eager leaning.

"I did. Shouldn't I have?" I asked.

I could tell that many things then passed through Pope's mind, but in deference to me as a Crabbe, and in very tolerant deference to my title, he concealed all of those thoughts. He did not answer my question.

"What did they speak about?" asked Pope.

"I can't say," I had to confess. "I was not in the back there as they met. But I could tell that Rutledge was angry—very angry—after my cousin left."

"Where did your Cousin Julius go to when he left?" asked Pope.

"He left on foot—again, his horse was all played out—and I think he made his way to the hotel," I said.

"I need for you to let me in the back to see Rutledge now, too," Pope said quickly, and he stood up as he spoke.

"I'm afraid that he's not there. I had promised to let him go by three o'clock, and I did," I said.

"How long ago was that?" demanded Pope.

"Fifteen minutes, perhaps a half hour—maybe more," I answered. I still did not know where Pope's alarm was leading precisely, but he had communicated to me a full sense of apprehension. "Can you tell me what's happening? Or what's about to happen?" I asked finally.

Pope held up his hand deferentially, but nevertheless it was to stop me from speaking.

"Do you know where he went? Did you give him back his guns?" demanded Pope.

"I can't say I know where he is. But I was told to tell him his string from Mr. Whisker had been taken away; he doesn't have a horse, any horse," I said.

"That doesn't mean that he didn't find one anyway. I can only hope he did, for otherwise he's still in town. But what about his gunbelt? Does he have it?"

"Yes. I am afraid I returned it to him," I confessed.

Pope paused and gathered himself for a moment, and then he said, "I'm hoping I am wrong about your cousin's conversation with Rutledge, but I fear I am not. I came here, back into town, hunting for your cousin, Marshal. But, I fear, the man I am after first is Rutledge. I must go."

"No, wait; you have to tell me what is happening," I insisted.

"Your brother and Mr. Whisker can't be more than a half hour or less behind me on their way here. I don't have much time if I'm to find Rutledge—*and* perhaps your cousin—before they arrive," Pope countered, and he turned to open the door as he began to put on again his hat and slicker.

"Mr. Pope," I exclaimed as I took hold of his arm," I implore you, since this seems to involve my family, that you tell me what is happening."

Then I took a deep breath and prepared myself to face the condescending tolerance that I knew must surely seethe in Pope but which he would never show overtly—that embarrassing tolerance a consequence of what I would say next.

"And, Mr. Pope, I insist, as Marshal, that you tell me what is happening."

The slightest trace of a sigh came from out of Pope's nose; the slightest sign of either a gentle smile or a fatigued grimace flashed nearly imperceptibly from the corners of his mouth and the muscles of his chin. Pope then held up his hand respectfully to signal me to wait for just a moment. He stepped out into the now heavily raining day, but remained beneath the office's awning as he took a long careful look to the south.

The view to that horizon—to the direction whence he feared my brother and Whisker and their men would appear too soon—must have satisfied him that it was for the time being free of anyone's approach. He then looked briefly to the north along Main Street, and as, of course, neither Julius nor Rutledge were plainly to be seen, Pope was able to heed my command for a time, even against his nervous conscience. He stepped back inside, but he did leave the door ajar; and he would pause from time to time as he told me of the morning's events—pause and look south from outside on the board sidewalk before the office.

3.

"In the late morning, around ten o'clock, we had all reached the southernmost reaches of the new fence posts," Pope began. He was uncharacteristically frank in his references to Julius and my brother as he continued: "The trip, as I think you know, was for your cousin's sake as an investor—so that he could see the evidence of the new fence. Your brother, sir, built this entire place up; he shouldn't have to prove anything to anyone—no matter who it is, or what their investment may be. I beg your pardon, Marshal, for my plainness."

"No pardon is necessary—especially in this case, Mr. Pope," I replied.

"I see. I do appreciate that, Marshal," Pope answered with a knowing look, as if confirming that I knew he was really defending something much greater than one of the most ambitious ranches on the northern plains. What that greater something was I could not guess; nor could I say for certain if that knowing look I saw in Pope's face was really there or merely projected by my rising hopes that any coming conflict be supported by some elevated sense of reckoning.

Pope continued after glancing out the window into the intensifying rain: "I was pleased to see, however, that the trip was used to show Mr. Whisker our fence, as well, with the idea that we were really there to allow him to consider fence for his own range. I fear the fence is what is coming to this country.

"Your cousin started to ride at a distance from us. No one spoke to him, and he did not seem interested in speaking to anyone. He was always fifty to a hundred yards behind us. After we reached the southern camp where the boys who are digging the postholes are situated, we all had coffee. But soon your cousin drifted back to where he had picketed his horse, some half mile from the camp, I think. And there I believe he just lay down and slept for a time."

Here Pope paused again and stepped out onto the board sidewalk and looked south. After a quick look north again, as well, he came back in and resumed his report. But he still left the door ajar. The sound of the heavy rain was now a pronounced hiss.

"What happened next, Mr. Crabbe—Marshal, sir—is both remarkable and not remarkable, if you recall all that I have told you since you came to this country. It is remarkable if one remembers that I have never seen a man in control of a bull unless by whip, rope, or gun. It is not remarkable—though I have never seen the like before, and likely will not ever again—if one remembers that your brother took it upon himself to care for one of our finest English bulls when it was a newborn and its mother died and when no other cow would nurse it. Your brother abandoned all to his care of the animal. With bottles in hand he nursed it himself, raised it until it was weaned. Yet even then that bull seemed to remember it all; I've never seen the like. That bull seemed to remember it all, as if it were a grateful dog. Your brother could call to it and it would come. He could whistle and it would back down. It turned, all right, as bulls do; but it never turned on your brother.

"As your brother and Mr. Whisker walked south from camp about a hundred yards to look at the newest holes the boys were digging, I remained in camp and took some lunch from the chuck wagon. The camp cook asked if something should be offered to the sleeping man—your cousin. As the cook dished out a plate of beef and beans for me to take to him, I noticed a small group of cows—no more than five or six, and perhaps a bull—making their way to the fence line from the east, from your brother's range.

"As I began my walk toward your cousin with the food in hand, I looked south and saw Mr. Whisker making his way back into camp, likely coming in for beef and beans himself. He was walking slowly along the new fence line, on the inside side of your brother's land. Your brother remained with the boys who were digging, but from the looks of things they, too, seemed almost ready to come into camp to eat."

Pope showed an impulse to check outside so he could look south and then north along Main Street, but he could not stop at this point from finishing the report of the morning's strange events.

"When I was closing in on your cousin—about ten paces from him—I heard shouting from camp. I turned to look back, but I could hear that this noise also woke your cousin and compelled him to look about, as well. A bull was attacking, was goring at Mr. Whisker, and the animal had Mr. Whisker trapped against the southernmost piece of fence. Men in camp were already aiming at the bull with their guns, but none fired for fear of hitting Mr. Whisker.

"Your cousin ran to me and watched. Your brother, sir, did not draw his gun, but instead he ran to within yards of Mr. Whisker and the bull. When he reached them he put his fingers to his mouth and let out the most peculiar, intense, whistle—and then he shouted some strange call. The bull suddenly stopped its attack and stood still. Your brother, sir, moved forward and took a place next to Mr. Whisker, who was then kneeling on the ground by the fence; and after your brother then made a remarkable set of gestures or signals to the bull, the animal backed away, suddenly content to return to its cows. It continued back east and north and vanished over a roll in the range.

"I was then astounded, Marshal, to hear your cousin speak up.

"'Astonishing! I have never seen anything like it,' your cousin said. I answered, yes. Then he said, 'To see a man able to call off, to control, a dumb brute, a bull with rare and hot blood—a bull of all things—with merely a few signals!'

"I then started to make my way toward the camp and to this scene, and it was then that I am sure I heard your cousin add, 'And to think that he likely started the animal with signals of his own, as well.'

"I stopped and turned around. 'Sir?' I said. 'I beg your pardon! What cause would there be, would he have, for such a foul action?'

"'He might have much to gain from such a supposed accident. There might be any number of causes,' your cousin suggested.

"'Sir?' I said again. But this time he said nothing in reply. He only smiled, I think. I then made my way to camp and then to your brother and Mr. Whisker. Mr. Whisker was then out cold, and his arm had been broken, but he was in no other apparent danger. Your brother and several other men were kneeling about Mr. Whisker when I reached them.

"'We'll take him into town and have the doctor look over him. He'll likely need to have his arm set. It appears broken, Pope,' your brother said. 'We'll be behind you in an hour or so. We'll come in slowly. But I want you to go after him and find out what he's up to.' I looked up and north to see that by *him* your brother meant your cousin. He was off at a hard pace toward town. I did not believe he would drive his horse that hard; but that's how he got so far ahead. And the weather came on me before I reached town."

"What's to be done?" I asked as Pope, having completed his story, made his way for the door for a final time.

"I have to find Rutledge first. You could help me by looking as well. It won't be easy to bring him back in here until we can get Mr. Whisker to speak to him," said Pope.

"Why do we need Rutledge?" I asked.

"Because I am sure your cousin just told him your brother tried to murder Mr. Whisker," Pope answered quite plainly as he buttoned his slicker.

"Are you really certain?" I asked.

"I can't be. But I am nearly sure. We have to find him before your brother reaches town. And we should bring in your cousin, too, Marshal, if I may suggest it—and if we are lucky enough to find him."

"Then let's go," I said as we moved north up Main Street into the rain.

"You're not a cowman, sir. But you could do with a slicker in this country for times like these."

I did not answer that statement. I hardly noticed the pelting rain, though I well remember now how heavy it was. "Why would Julius do such a thing?" I muttered loudly enough for Pope to take it as a question for him.

He paused deferentially for a moment, and then he said, haltingly and with sincere modestly: "It is not for me to say or guess, sir, really. But I would venture that something that happened to your people, long before they came to this territory, might account for it. You would know better than I, sir."

We began our search of the town, and we would no sooner enter a place and find no one there than Pope would lead us in a run back to the outside, or quickly to a window to look out into the street, for more than once the lighting and thunder that was then passing overhead suggested the flash and reports of gunfire.

PART VIII

Corn Freight

I.

It may seem strange that I should pause here, so close to giving the conclusion of my strange fortnight of history in what is now known as the Old West. But I feel it is necessary to chronicle my last stretch of time I spent in old Pauktaug and how it impelled me, at last, to seek out my brother. As well, I am one of those strange men who longs after past times which—though marked by ostensible gloom, loneliness, and uncertainty—hover in the mind as lovely, unique, and mysteriously blessed because of their quietness, their formlessness, their remove, and humility.

My father's Lyceum did not survive. By the early seventies the enterprise was abandoned, and the building fell into disrepair. In 1874 my father sold the building, and it was then refurbished modestly for use as a venue for minstrelsy.

With the end of the Lyceum, I had imagined my father might muster his energies to resume the duties of his role as partner in the Stays Works. But when that did not happen—and after my father dismissed the last of our servants in 1875—I took it upon myself to pay a call upon Mr. Whisker, Sr. Though I had occupied my time all those years assisting my father as a secretary, not until the money from the sale of the Lyceum building was exhausted in 1875 did I realize fully the extent of my father's and my destitution. And not until I paid my call upon Mr. Whisker, Sr. did I realize my father had not been a partner in the Pauktaug Stays Works since 1864! He had sold all his shares in the company for the sake of the Lyceum and our own increasingly meager expenses.

So instead of returning from a meeting in which I had expected to persuade Mr. Whisker, Sr. to encourage my father not only to return to his earlier business affairs but to avail himself also of the income such activity would surely inspire him to increase—and also the income that was accruing, I hoped, in an account from his neglected partnership—I learned that my family had not even been connected to the Stays works for more than a decade. But I did not return from that meeting without restoring some connection to the company my father had founded so many decades earlier.

Mr. Whisker, Sr., long knowing my predicament though I did not know it fully myself, kindly offered me a clerkship in his office—despite the surely remaining resentment he maintained for my father on account of Ellsworth having lured John Whisker, Jr. away from the family business and Pauktaug seemingly forever.

By 1875, when I took this position so as to support my father and myself in our decaying manse, I was spared having to reveal to my father the nature of the work I performed and the melancholy source of my income. By that time my father's health had begun seriously to decline. Though his body was still limber—he performed pedestrian feats nearly every morning and evening—his mind had begun a descent into feebleness not long after the Lyceum's balcony beams had fatefully cracked and failed. At first he seemed only to forget the foreground details of any given present day, but after a few years a true regression began. By 1875 his mind reveled in his walking routines and deluded anticipation of the return of Ellsworth and my mother from a journey he was sure they had taken to my mother's childhood farm in Commack.

Father would return each evening from his walks to find me preparing our supper, and he would declare, "Why, Campbell! How is it you can be so tall? We must stand you up against young Ellsworth when he returns with your mother."

He would then sit at a small table in our kitchen and stare as I finished cooking, yet sometimes, after remarking on my height and thinking surely of my older brother as still a little boy he would manage to exclaim, "But how? But how could—?"

However, Ellsworth was never again to be a part our lives in the old Pauktaug.

But if it had been Ellsworth in fact who had brought such voluminous crowds, and thus brought via the balcony's collapse such humiliation to my father at that lecture of Dunstable, then I was glad of it. Ellsworth and I never alluded to that event in the very intermittent letters we continued to send to one another each year. I would have made efforts, in fact, to conceal it from him if he did not in fact know the outcome of that lecture. For after my father's humiliation, when neither reform nor defiance came from him in answer or retaliation to the lesson that my brother may have delivered; but when only an enfeeblement and a gentle, sad, regressive mist fell over my father, I no longer suffered my old ambivalence toward him. I lapsed into a simple sense of protectiveness and pity, and I made the easy gestures that permitted him to support his illusion that we were still a thriving young family of four—still an aggressive family, unapologetic in our prosperity in a tempered wilderness.

By the late sixties my father had ceased to be able to augment my weapons collection. But sometime in 1876—I recall it was the summer of the centennial, with its exhibition in Philadelphia—he returned from one of his walks and proudly presented me with my first dime novel.

Our library of ponderous tomes and classics had long gone neglected and had begun to molder—in fact we had contracted our lives in the great house down to the kitchen on the first floor, and our two bedrooms on the second (all else went to dust and darkness). But my father, who had never seen me do much reading, made me a gift of a dime novel one day, as if such books had the importance to me that my gun collection had.

"Here, Campbell! I will start you a new collection. It will complement your weapons," he said after he slumped into his chair and then made his daily remark about my astonishing height.

The little book did have a gun depicted on its cover—in the hand of a masked bandit, who in his other hand clutched a distressed woman in a lurid scene of abduction. I dutifully read aloud from this book for my father each evening in his bedroom until I completed it. I read aloud at times to my father in the kitchen, as well, but I do not think he listened. Instead he would watch the clock I had moved into the kitchen and suddenly remove himself to bed at seemingly appointed but random hours. When I finished the book, however, he must have noted it, for every time I finished a dime novel he presented me on the next day with a new one, and our odd but stable reading sessions after supper would begin anew.

As the years passed, the kitchen began to fill with them. After a time I moved the collection into the adjacent dining room. I never discarded any of them; eventually a seeming little city of stacked books filled the room in which so long ago Julius and my brother had first begun their long, agonized, enmity and opposition. My reading became part of my father's illusion of security; my reading for me, however, ostensibly for my father's sake, ostensibly carried out as a salve against the damage of an irretrievable past, was instead filling me secretly with half illusion, half code, those two halves to serve for an unexpected future vengeance against the wrongs of that seemingly forgotten time that had begun in that very same dining room where the dime novel towers grew.

Of course, it was with pocket money that I had given to my father that the books were purchased. But they seemed genuinely to come from him when he made the presentation. I could never have bought them myself—many compunctions would have prevented me from doing that—yet I came to depend upon them and the ritual that attended them with an almost desperate joy. I use the phrase *desperate joy* with great care, for I know no time in my adult life that was more characterized by the true threat of penury and instability yet at the same time recalled both the dream *and* the actuality (in a strange, limited, way) of the bounties of my childhood.

During all this time Ellsworth and I continued to exchange about two to three letters a year. Though it surprised me that I had developed such a degree of protectiveness and discretion concerning my father late in his life, I did not find it difficult to conceal the details and true state of our affairs from Ellsworth when I wrote to him. He seemed content to have it confirmed by me that I was well and that I remembered his offer of safe harbor and reunion (reunion, provided I went to him) always stood firm. He also seemed content that though I gave him fewer and fewer details of my quiet and meager life with our father on Long Island, he felt free to give me clear reports of his standing in business, his locations as he moved, and from time to time, as well, telling details of his personal life.

Not long after the disastrous Lyceum lecture of Dunstable in 1866, my brother's letters ceased to originate from New York. In the late sixties and early seventies the letters began to arrive instead from Texas. The Austin and sometimes San Antonio postmarks resounded silently at all times in my mind as places of great, suggestive, mystery and size but also as strange reminders of places of refuge. For every thirty or so of the dime novels I piled in the dining room there was also a letter that would arrive from a town that was often the actual setting in the books. Though I was oddly and sadly content in my routines and life with my father amidst scenes of lush decay and comforting and familiar obscurity, I built at the same time my strange collection of my symbols of refuge and rescue. Though the books were wilder and more fantastic in their promises, they created such a reassuring heap; though the letters were thin and simple, they promised, in my mind, a ponderous resource of might and imagined mass so great that at times I fancied that single letter placed on a balance could lift and show equal to a carefully stacked pile of dime novels on the other side, in the opposite pan. But the books were still my greatest comfort and my great private love of those years. My family's penchant for collecting finally and truly had demonstrated itself through me toward perhaps the most tawdry and ephemeral of collectible objects. But, once more, it had to be my father who procured them, though with my own money. Had I bought even one myself, the spell they granted may have been broken.

Yet, too, Ellsworth's letters continued to arrive, usually one or two in the spring and often one in the autumn. My brother and John Whisker, Jr. had begun their interest in Texas after Appomattox via some connection to the government contracts they had obtained during the War. Speculation in beef supply to the army in Virginia had led to their interest after the War in the natural, unhusbanded, proliferation of that Texas miracle, the Longhorn. My brother recounted his and Whisker's early involvement as investors. By the early 1870s they were themselves owners of land and herds in Texas, and later the two men sent great harvests north through the Indian Territory to the cowtowns of Kansas, such as Dodge. A careful rereading of these letter would recount my earliest introductions to some of the names I would ultimately encounter in the new Pauktaug. One letter recounted the fortitude displayed by a rising hand in one of Whisker's outfits—a story of a young, surly, Texas boy or man (with seemingly no history behind him) by the name of Rutledge.

In another letter that arrived one spring from a town in north Texas came the astonishing news that my brother had married. Both Whisker and Ellsworth had, in fact, found wives and had been married at the same time. They wed a pair of young and beautiful twin daughters of a fellow Texas cowman. As a sort of reverse dowry, they, Ellsworth and Whisker, had each presented their mutual father-in-law with a fine English bull by which the stringy bloodlines of his vast Longhorn herds could be improved.

Yet in the autumn of that same year a letter came reporting that both new brides had been killed in a great storm whilst visiting their father and mother. The entire family had been killed, in fact. There was mention that Rutledge had been present and felt he deserved credit for the efforts he had made to save the women. Somehow, from Ellsworth's letter it appeared that Whisker was able ultimately to accept this disaster with equanimity, but though my brother said little more of how he himself had been affected by the loss, I could sense that the death of his young wife and the loss of his brief marriage had particularly and peculiarly grieved him. Again, he said very little more of this, and very little of a personal nature through his years of letter writing. But from time to time he would offer a singular personal remark which would compel one to recall all of his writings as personal, though, again, principally they were not. For instance, at the close of the autumn letter that detailed his bride's death, he noted—perhaps only in the postscript—that he thought it odd to have so soon looked twice into the same minister's eyes: at his wedding and then during the officiation of his wife's burial. He recorded the minister's name. It was Pope.

As a material result and gain of such a disaster of the heart, both Ellsworth and John Whisker came into the entire estates of their wives' families. As the two men began to divide their shared inheritance, their brief shared time as brothers-in-law came to a close. But in continued alliance on many other counts they left north

Texas and struck north, across the Indian Territory and Kansas and Nebraska, and made their way into the great grasslands of eastern Dakota and western Montana—into a new free grass empire: born, cleared, and patented by the placental strains of Custer's and Sitting Bull's mutual descent.

In the late seventies my brother's letters slowed, and not until 1881 or 1882 did I ever receive a letter with a consistent postmark. In 1882 when I received a letter with a Pauktaug cancellation I was delivered quite a jolt. Not before I read the letter could I be sure that my brother had not taken up residence once more on his native Long Island, though the weather and traveled appearance of the envelope should have been a hint to me of otherwise.

As I have observed before, I shared little personal information with Ellsworth. I told him nothing of our father's declining powers, and I volunteered nothing—in light of Ellsworth's sad, short marriage—of my own brief and always moribund romances.

My family's descending station in Pauktaug Village made my calls upon the village's only suitable young ladies impossible affairs (though Ellen Paw seemed to remain fond of me), and the quiet and sad dignity of my time with my failing father precluded my conscience from permitting more tawdry and common prospects.

Because my gun collection had also impelled me to develop my powers as a shot, the village did turn to me one last time upon my remaining station as a Crabbe, however, before my father's death. As a last act of pity, perhaps, before John Whisker, Sr. passed away in the summer of 1882, I was appointed town constable. Mr. Whisker's power and his pity for me accounted for my appointment and the small honorarium that I would receive with the position. Even then I knew the truth behind my election; but, once more, I tried to fancy that their need for a policeman upon whom they might rely as a marksman had won me their consideration—even though my elderly predecessor had never been known to carry, own, employ, or ever hold a weapon in his life as Pauktaug's constable. In fact, I had never known him in all my then more than thirty years to be called upon for any service but to settle the mildest of disputes—disputes held between Main Street idlers as to who was the prettiest woman in the village.

But I was happy to have this work in addition to my clerk position at the factory (the latter under the direction of one of Mr. Whisker, Sr.'s younger sons). I reveled in the night rounds I was obliged to make—during which I checked that doors were locked. I reveled in my happy melancholy, as a man prepossessed too early by personal retrospection and how the humble dramatic stage of the village and the panoply of Nature that brooded and loomed over it gave a sense of fable to my life. And in the other half of my imaginative existence the dime novels informed every notion of the heroic conduct I would be sure to employ during the grand conflicts I could be certain would never occur in Pauktaug Village. I am sure I was the butt of many an old codger's joke—as the only man who saw fit to bear a revolver along his night rounds in the alleys behind the stores of Main Street.

My appointment as constable had another strange overtone, for as the summer of 1882 yielded to the autumn, my family's chronic affliction began to rear itself once more in me with increasing violence. My coughing and feeble breathing became as much a harbinger of my approach on constable rounds as did my testing and rattling of back doors.

My father managed to escape the threat of consumption throughout his life, but in October of 1882, as the beeches turned as yellow as dark corn, my father finally ceased his long morning and night walks and began a final sedentary descent that resulted in his death that November. By the time he passed he was nearly free of all memory, and he expired contentedly on a cot I had installed for him in our vast and once grand dining room—he content in his forgetfulness, forgetful of all that he had squandered. And how easy it was for him to keep his forgetfulness clean and pure, for he expired amidst a wealth of book piles! It was no matter that the piles represented no more amassed wealth than stacks of dimes; they were solid, dense, piles, formidable in their closeness and compactness and height.

2.

My father's passing brought a small alleviation to my finances. But it devastated my routines. There was no one to buy new dime novels for me, and I had not the means to repair the disintegrating manse, much less to fill it once more with the fine things I would have permitted myself to buy had I the resources. I slipped into a despair of stasis and steady decline. The village of Pauktaug—even its most humble members—continued, for the most part, to prosper and gain. I could only manage to bear witness to dissolution.

And then came the news in January that Mr. Whisker, Sr.'s successor at the Stays Works had no intention of keeping me on in any respect at the factory founded primarily by my father. To a degree, I was happy to lose that situation, for I was certain that the era of working in whalebone was passing.

But in respect to survival, my situation was growing serious. As my health continued to deteriorate at the close of 1882, the prospects of finding work that I could perform became increasingly dim; none of the stores or businesses in the village were hiring, and my intensifying consumption made the notion of applying for manual labor both hopeless and dangerous.

With all these considerations conspiring together, an old

image I had conjured returned to me, one of my brother's letters poised on one pan of a balance and my collection of dime novels somehow all piled together in the pan on the other side of that same imagined scale. However, the balance ceased to weigh these two loads evenly in my imagination. My brother's letters—particularly their constant offer of refuge—suddenly boasted the most heft, and so on the first of the year in 1883 I wrote my brother that I would finally accept his offer. I had been hinting to him about this possibility for nearly six months. I wrote that I would do my best to get my affairs in order in Paukatug—mainly by closing up the old house—and would hope to reach him by mid to late spring.

I began my preparations by selling nearly all my family's furniture and remaining possessions—including my elaborate collection of weapons. Though it pained me to part with many of those latter pieces, the money they brought in secured me the resources I would need for the long and arduous train travel I knew lay ahead, and I knew I would need to travel in enough comfort and style to make my health survive the journey. I sold all of the guns, save for a few modern ones that I resolved to keep as bartering pieces (in more than one respect) should my cash run out before the journey's end or in case I met with some other unforeseen circumstances.

My books, however, I resolved proudly to keep. So it was that as the spring of 1883 approached, I contracted my living space in the old family manse down to the kitchen and dining room. I smile now to think of my protectiveness of the books. No one would have bought them, I think, had I even thought I could part with them. It would have been hard to have given them away, for I cannot think of the wife or mother in that proper village who would have permitted them to go to husband or son. So they remained my prized yet altogether unthreatened possessions; they remained the last legacy of a father who had betrayed his original fatherly impulses but had recovered them in part through giving me mountains of cheap books. But then his mind betrayed the memory of his meager recovery, and I was left alone to cherish their meaning, even whilst my father still lived.

As I continued my preparations—selling all I could and boarding up the house—I continued my constable duties up until the completion of the evening of the day before my departure. I finished my rounds of Main Street and returned to the house for one last night after turning over a few things to my successor as constable.

It was a May evening, and I resolved to nail shut the final open doors and windows of the house; I would sleep in the hotel that night and begin to gamble my means on living as comfortably and easily as I could until I could reach my brother. As I stood on the back porch with my few trunks and a carpet bag at my side, I was driving the last nails into the back door when a neighbor's boy came running to me and called out, "Mr. Crabbe! Mr. Constable, sir!"

He had come from the east—from playing in the woods beyond my family's barn. I smiled at first as he called to me, despite the genuine fear in his voice, for he was familiar to me, and I was to him; it sounded comic for him to address me as *Mr. Constable.*

He ran up to the base of the back porch steps and then caught his breath for an instant. Between pantings he said, "Mr. Constable, sir! Come quick! I heard gunshots coming from inside your barn!"

"I've been out here for quite some time, and I have heard nothing," I said to the boy, and I knelt down so as to catch my own breath; I had been hammering at the door vigorously for the previous five minutes.

"You probably couldn't hear it from all the hammering you've been doing! Come on! There's someone in your barn, firing off a gun. You'd better bring *your* gun. Come on!"

The boy then ran back in the direction of the barn. The boy had been in such earnest that I removed my leg holster and the revolver

I had sported on my constable's rounds from the carpet bag. After strapping them on I jogged with concealed good humor through the lovely and fragrant spring air. Just as I noted how full the air seemed with the sound of birds I came upon the boy crouching behind a pile of moldering, neglected, hay bales. The run had really been beyond my capacity in my state of health, and I knelt down next to the boy in the middle of a terrible fit of coughing. The run had been fueled by a strong surge of sentiment, a strong wave of affection that rose up for all the natural details of the setting to which I had yet to take formal leave.

The boy shushed me, but it was a good half minute before I could stifle my long and bloody cough: "Quiet," the boy insisted, "they'll know you're out here."

To oblige the boy I lay there silently behind the rotting bales of hay for several minutes. I was confident that we would hear nothing but the scented spring breeze and its birds.

In the previous weeks I had sold our animals—our last horses and our single remaining cow. The carriages, the buggies, all the gear of livery had been sold, as well. The barn was an empty void, but as I lay there I chanced to think of the treasure that might still be buried beneath its floor; yet I could not be certain, for perhaps I had only imagined that my brother had buried his trunks of collections in the barn. Perhaps he had shipped away his things. Perhaps I had indeed dreamed all I had believed I had witnessed from my window on that night then twenty-eight years in the past. It was when I was deepest in thought about these things that an astounding bang brought me completely into the present.

"Do you hear? Do you hear?" the boy hissed.

"I do indeed," I whispered back, for indeed the sound was as powerful as any gun's report. I unholstered my revolver nervously and checked the cylinder. There was one bullet inside, as I had thought, and I rolled the cylinder until the bullet was in the proper position for use.

I remember thinking of the great towers of dime novels that remained in the house—patiently waiting there in dusty piles for me should I ever return from my then imminent journey to Ellsworth—and then I took a deep breath and stood up.

"You must stay here," I insisted to the boy. I covered my mouth as another painful cough came on, and I moved forward. The bales of old hay behind which we had been hiding had afforded an oblique but clear view of the closed south doors of the barn. From there I had also seen clearly along the full length of the undisturbed west side of the barn. I resolved to investigate the east side, and then to make my way carefully along that side to the unseen north doors of the barn. It was possible, I thought, that I had left one or more of those doors open as I carried a few last things from the barn on the night previous.

I reached the east wall. As I crept along its undisturbed length, I peered into the woods to the east. They appeared undisturbed, as well, though the evening light was coming on. But as I neared the northeast corner of the barn another profound bang resounded from within. I cocked the hammer of the revolver and looked around the corner to the north face and saw that its doors were indeed open.

I crept behind the easternmost open door and paused. Perhaps fear and excitement had suppressed my inclination to cough. I was safe on that count. But then I thought of the towers of dime novels once more. I then resolved to call out.

"Hello!"

There was an immediate third bang—loud and fierce, and also seemingly very, very, near on account of my standing so close to the open entrance to the barn's interior.

I checked my revolver again and did my best to remain steady. Yet again I thought of the dime novels.

I called out, "You are trespassing! You have no call to be firing rounds in there! I am the constable of Pauktaug!"

I had no plan for such a situation. I then astonished myself with my impatience and called out, "I will count to three, and then I will enter!"

The proclamation sounds suicidal in retrospect, but that is what I said, and that is what I did. I counted to three and then moved swiftly around the edge of the door and leveled my revolver at the center of the barn's interior. Another loud bang sounded forth, but this time it caused little reaction in me but a smile and a sigh—and the sudden freedom to cough without fear. I called to the boy for him to come and look.

Standing outside of her closed stall was my family's cow, Leslie. The neighbor to whom I had sold Leslie had apparently left his corral gate open, and Leslie, as the evening fell, simply made her way across the woods and our pasture, back to her old barn. Finding the stall closed, however, this cranky cow of habit had repeatedly kicked at the stall door with her hind quarters. Her violent kicks against some peculiarly aged and oddly constituted and disposed timbers made for the great sound that was so much like the report of a gun. I paid the boy to return Leslie to her new home, and I closed the barn doors securely for a final time.

By the next morning I departed old Pauktaug, bound for its new incarnation in the west. Several weeks of difficult travel lay ahead of me along with several long stops during which I idled as I waited for increasingly remote connections—the most remote of which was the Pauktaug spur itself, which ran southwest from the Northern Pacific. The layovers and the travel would not have been particularly arduous had it not been for my declining health and the omnipresent threat of my dwindling finances.

My money had nearly exhausted itself in fact when I reached the end of the Pauktaug spur of the Northern Pacific. There, as has already been related, I sold my remaining guns for a ticket on the stage to the new Pauktaug. It was on that ride, as has also been told before, that I encountered the desperate and touched Mr. Kettle. Though I suspected him to be a bit mad, I was glad of his company on that stage ride and glad, at the time, of his ostensible knowledge of the range. The driver, Buckle, and his shotgun man, Reggie, kept mainly to themselves as I made the final stretch of my journey in search of my brother.

It was on the second day of driving in the coach that we crashed violently as consequence of suddenly losing a wheel. It was during that crash that I suffered my cracked ribs. Two of the horses suffered broken legs as a result of the wreck. They had to be shot immediately. As evening fell, Buckle was preparing one of the two remaining horses as a mount for Reggie—so that the latter could return to the last stage depot and report our plight—when he, Buckle, first caught sight of what he was certain were Indian fires.

Kettle insisted that we escape, then, to the south, in the direction of our destination. Buckle and Reggie called that madness and insisted that we remain—not only on account of the dangers looming from the supposed Indians but also on account of the great distance that lay ahead of us that we proposed to traverse on foot by night, and then followed by what should certainly prove a brutally hot and waterless day.

Somehow Kettle convinced me to follow him. Though his plan was mad and unwise by all reckoning of that country and terrain, had I remained with the coach I would have perished as surely as did Buckle and Reggie. Kettle and I departed from the coach before nightfall. On the second day of walking, Kettle insisted on a cross-country route. Despite my fears of being left utterly alone on the completely open plain—without water, food, strength, or much hope—I refused to part from the stage road. On the evening of the third day I reached the new Pauktaug. Thus there is now no part in the circle of this tale—of this full history—that is not joined. It only remains for me now to render its conclusion.

But before I do so, let me remark that when I look back upon my arrival in the new Pauktaug itself, I do not often recall the arduous journey that preceded it; rather, for some inexplicable reason,

I think first of the night before I left the East and then immediately of the end of my journey—as if all that happened in between were negligible or somehow of no importance. Not only do I think in those terms now, but also when I awoke in the hotel in the new Pauktaug for the first time, I thought at once of that strange last night in the old Pauktaug— when Leslie filled the darkening, sweet, spring air with the sounds of her false, impatient, gunfire.

PART IX

The Pauktaug Sonata: The Descendentalist

I.

The sound of false gun reports continued to fool Pope Pope and myself as we scoured the town for Rutledge and Julius. However, as the storm passed over, the thunder claps ceased, and Pope and I stepped back into the middle of the empty, muddy, Main Street.

"They could not have left town," said Pope. "I do not think they would do that. They must still be here. I'm going to look over at the hotel again. Would you please see to the south entrance of town, Marshal? Mr. Crabbe and Mr. Whisker should be coming in from that direction any time now."

We parted. I made my way south, but did not go all the way to Main Street's end before stopping into my office to pick up another gun. I had been carrying my revolvers during our search of town, but I wanted a rifle, as well, should any long range shooting present itself.

It was just after I retrieved my rifle and emptied nearly an entire box of ammunition into my pockets that I heard the voices on Main Street. I stepped out onto the board sidewalk, and there to the south, to my right, in the center of the street stood Rutledge, with both of his six guns drawn. His left hand was aimed at me—or rather I walked right to the spot to which he had anticipated would be wise to aim with his weak hand, that spot a few paces just outside of the Marshal's door. His right hand was aimed straight north along Main Street. It was easy to make out the precise bearing of the barrels as the sun emerged from behind the departing clouds.

Rutledge's right hand was aimed straight at my brother, who stood alone in his place on the street. Somehow Ellsworth must have entered town from the side, perhaps approaching from the east, so as to move directly on the back entrance of the town's doctor's office. Whisker was likely in that office already. I think Rutledge saw me enter the scene, but he only acknowledged me by keeping his left hand steadily trained on the spot in which I stood. I stood still; I had neither revolver drawn nor rifle leveled. I felt any move from me would cause Rutledge to fire.

"What's this about, son?" Ellsworth called out to Rutledge.

I would venture that Ellsworth stood at a distance of about thirty yards from Rutledge. I was about ten from Rutledge myself; about twenty from my brother.

"I ain't your son! If anything I'm as near a son to John Whisker as a man can get. And I hear tell that you just about succeeded in murdering my father!" shouted Rutledge.

"No such thing happened, boy! You'd best just settle down and put your persuaders away," said my brother.

"I told you I ain't your boy—not anyone's boy. But I'm just about John Whisker's son! I've earned that place!" shouted Rutledge.

I looked slowly to my left at this point, down the long board sidewalk, all the way to where it concluded in front of the hotel.

I could see Pope there. His rifle was trained on Rutledge. He was more than a seventy-five yards away. I could sense that Rutledge could see him there and had already assessed that threat.

"What cause would I have to do harm to John Whisker?" Ellsworth called back to Rutledge, and at the same time he took a step boldly closer to him.

"To take from him what has yet to be willed to the true and rightful inheritor: he who is as much a son to him as if he were a son in fact," shouted Rutledge. I was impressed by Rutledge's ability to fashion such a phrase. He had nursed it for a very long time—or, perhaps the phrase had been given to him.

"Not only is John Whisker quite alive, I am sure he has no intention of bequeathing anything to anyone," said Ellsworth, and then he took yet another step and added in address to Rutledge, "—boy!"

Rutledge shook and shivered with rage. "You're one for words and your own peculiar notions and ways, Mr. Crabbe. But you're a liar on that count!"

"That's a big accusation," my brother answered. "But I'm telling you the truth. And I'm also telling you the truth when I say you might clip me, boy, but you won't get out of this alive if you do start shooting." Ellsworth said this with remarkable calmness, even with a slight smile.

I had been so transfixed by Rutledge and my brother, that somehow I had not seen John Whisker step out into the street. He emerged from the east side, from the alley adjacent to the doctor's office. He stood about five yards behind Ellsworth, but slightly closer to the east side of the street. Again, I was on the west side of Main. It was possible that my view of all the precise positions was somewhat distorted.

After Ellsworth finished his last phrase, and just as his face broke into its latent smile, Rutledge formed a hard grimace as his eyes flitted between my brother, the distant Pope, myself perhaps, and the new arrival who made his way, in Rutledge's line of sight, to somewhere to the rear of Ellsworth's left shoulder.

Rutledge squinted, and then he fired one shot from his right revolver. As he moved his left hand into play, into the same direction as his right hand, a shot came my way from the left gun but only made contact with one of the posts which supported the office awning; answering shots came from Pope's distant rifle. Rutledge fell back in the mud upon his back. The firing was over.

Pope entered the street and ran toward Ellsworth. When he reached him, I was already at my brother's side, as well. We three, with Whisker moving slowly behind, made our way to Rutledge and then stood around him. In the still and humid air, a stagnant tendril of gunsmoke still hovered over the spot where Rutledge had fallen. He was still quite alive, but it was also clear he was fading.

When Whisker reached our circle, he fell to his knees. At first for an embarrassed and shocked moment, I imagined that Whisker had fallen in grief. But then, as one looked to where Whisker was clutching his waist, one could see a rich and bright stain of new and flowing blood coming from a gunshot wound. The sole shot Rutledge had fired from his right hand had hit Whisker.

(Later, I heard it speculated that Rutledge had decided to give that first shot to Whisker—this upon finding him still alive and clearly standing in sympathy at my brother's back, and also as wild reciprocation for Whisker's seizure of his string of horses. But I had my doubts about this. I think he did aim for Ellsworth but missed.)

As Whisker involuntarily knelt before Rutledge, Pope made a move to assist Mr. Whisker, but Whisker waved him off.

"You're a fool, boy!" the dying Whisker said to his dying foreman. "Let me tell you before you go, boy, that the only man who would ever come into my holdings as the son I do not have because he is as a brother to me is—" Here Whisker paused and looked up. "—Is you, Ellsworth."

My brother nodded one of those inimitable sure nods of men, best and most beautiful when a crisis might seem to call for so many words.

"You don't say," muttered Rutledge as he stared into the sky and met no one's eyes with his own fading sight.

"Listen, Rutledge. Who told you I made a play after Mr. Whisker? Who told you that?" Ellsworth asked.

"Your Cousin. Your Cousin—that son-of-a-bitch," hissed Rutledge. Those were his last words.

"Yes, that son-of-a-bitch," echoed Whisker, and then he took to his haunches and began to lower himself into the mud.

"Indeed, the son-of-a-bitch!" said Pope, too, as he forced his ministrations on the fading Whisker.

"The son-of-a-bitch, indeed!" exclaimed my brother calmly.

I looked over to him, imagining I would see his eyes gently looking down on Whisker as he joined in this union of imprecations upon my Cousin Julius. But Ellsworth's back was turned away from the scene. Though his utterance was in solidarity with the other men, it was also meant as an exclamation of discovery—for my brother had turned and spotted Julius Crabbe himself atop a fresh, stolen horse, making his way at full gallop off of the north end of Main Street and out onto the range. He seemed to be heading northeast—perhaps making a desperate play for the stage road, or perhaps in confusion and fear instead making a run for the road that led to my brother's ranch house and headquarters.

With the speed of a man who had finally received every mark of freedom and permission he had ever sought from circumstances, Ellsworth broke into a run—evidently making his way to where his first string horse had been left in the alley of the doctor's office. I noted that it was the same alley in the western Pauktaug as the corresponding one back East in which my father had interfered with my fight with another schoolboy so long ago.

Before he began to run, however, he had turned to me and

rendered a look of leave-taking that was so rich in ambiguity I did not at first know how to answer or interpret it. The look was followed by the same sort of definite manly nod he had only just moments before delivered to John Whisker, Jr. Then he was off on a run to his horse. But the look of ambiguity somehow encompassed the elation he could not suppress at the prospect of his imminent hunt of Julius; it, that ambiguous look, also seemed to beckon me to join him in that ride of reckoning; but it also seemed to express regret that I might yield to that invitation— seemed to express that regret whilst gently regarding the star pinned to my vest.

2.

As Ellsworth vanished into the alley, and as one then heard him atop his horse commence the violent pursuit of Julius which he had been orchestrating (or waiting for) for well beyond a quarter of a century, I stepped back several paces from the small group that was kneeling about the dying body of Whisker—McCarthy and other men from the businesses of Main Street were assisting by then—and I afforded myself a moment to think.

And yet I hardly even required that moment I granted myself; all became clear to me in a telling, forceful, instant. I looked at the body of Whisker as it was carried off gingerly. No, indeed, my brother had had no intention of harming this lifelong friend by means of setting that singular, shrewd, trained, bull of the Crabbe ranch upon Whisker. He had not set the bull upon him at all; that was all merely chance and misfortune.

But because I was the marshal, and a marshal formed as much by conscience as by the romance of a library that remained stored in dusty, little, towers in an abandoned dining room by the shore, nearly two-thousand miles away, I had been endeavoring constantly to meditate the recent deaths of Kettle and the lonely Indian. Had anyone else given those deaths much thought? After seeing my brother's command over the remarkable bull that morning, had anyone thought that Ellsworth Crabbe must be responsible for the deaths of those two relatively innocent men? Perhaps they had; perhaps they had not. Trespassing was an offense that was met quite often in that country with a casual death sentence, and with tacit permission and a clear conscience from the law for the executioners. If the other men of Pauktaug had even thought my brother responsible for those two deaths, responsible because the two men had trespassed in the common sense and he then retaliated, I do not think they would have believed it worth mentioning. It was common for a man to be permitted to protect his land, his stock, his property without question in that country.

But I knew in that instant that Ellsworth was actuated by another motive. He was protecting his property not for its own sake—not in the sense of the traditional remuneration it might one day yield. No, he was protecting the life of every cow, every steer, every calf, every bull, for the sake of a grand design beyond mortal husbandry—a grand design meant to assist ultimately in the realization of a perfect and questionable mortal vengeance, but also a grand design that may have grown benignly beyond that vengeance. His manifest revenge may have grown into a manifest destiny, a greater dream for Man against the voids. I was suddenly certain my brother had killed Kettle and the Indian, but he had not killed them as common trespassers. If he had, I would have permitted the acts as implied powers of property owners of the range—especially as he had given due, even excessive, warning. Of his lesser vision, his vision of manifest revenge, he had warned me—and even his target, Julius—over the course of a lifetime. But he had warned no one of his manifest destiny, of his greater dream.

It was not just that Kettle and the Indian should have perished on account of ignorance of *that* kind of law. Thus the common man that I was that had been made a new deputy marshal—the common man who would be obligated to make his arrests and carry out his enforcements based upon the texts of territorial and state codes *and* the customs of a country defined by such great size that it almost tacitly empowered its individual citizens as sheriffs and marshals themselves—would not have gone after Ellsworth Crabbe to make an arrest. But the man who knew his brother, knew the story, and, most of all, in years of romantic loneliness had embraced his dime novels in almost supernatural preparation against this unforeseeable day—that man could be counted on not to look the other way because the malefactor was a brother, but relied upon to retain his focus and pursuit with unremitting conscience. The star on my chest had risen to an orbit that shone on a firmament far more exulted and rare than any over the range of mere rustlers and bar fights.

How odd, I thought, as I made my way to my horse, that books my father had bought me so long after my mother's death should place the star on my chest so far above the calling of the law I was obliged to uphold. And how odd—and yet how touchingly like him, perhaps—that it should have been Ellsworth who pushed for my appointment as marshal. He was to be commended. That appointment was no gesture of common nepotism. It was instead a rarefied nepotism that insured that there might be one man to stop him should his experiment, his metamorphosing vengeance, grow beyond his ability to maintain justice whilst realizing the vision.

Thus I knew which part of my brother's last ambiguous expression most to trust. Pursue and stop him as a killer of innocent trespassers upon his dream; but pursue slowly, gently, so that he could, at last, vanquish the truly guilty.

Thus I went to the livery stable and mounted the magnificent horse my brother had bequeathed to me as if for this moment, this pursuit. I had him saddled and readied quickly, and I was off on the horse that, because of circumstances, I might have reined in whilst I at the same time spurred.

I took a last look at Main Street—and the people who had emerged once it was clear that the storm and the gun play had passed—took a last look at those who would not have known of my brother's wider, deeper, visions, and would not have cared if the protection of those visions also fought against the minor sort of infraction, the trespassing, that they could understand. But I rode on, for I had to care. The dime novels and my star made how and why I cared compulsory. Those things had held most fast for me in my years of thought and isolation: symbols of romantic principle. I rode on. My dude's fantasy had become a necessity of principle.

I do not think Cousin Julius knew which road was the coach road back to the railroad, or I think he would have taken it for his flight. I followed my brother's tracks and Julius' along the road to the ranch headquarters—nearly due east from the new Pauktaug. I noted the sites where I had found the bodies of Kettle and later the Indian, but I pushed on.

After twenty minutes of hard riding I reached a crest on the plain, and at that point the realization I had experienced suddenly back in town was augmented by a massive scene of explanation, of reinforcement, a scene of manifest clarity I had forgotten to suspect.

There in the mild valley of the plain below was what is called a line camp. But this was no common line camp; nor was this line camp after the fashion of some Texan, he hoping to inspire fable by producing, for one time only, a feat of vastness for the sake of a bold stunt. Here was the near end of a line camp that visibly and densely stretched, as if just part of a circle conceived on a plane-tary scale, from north horizon to south horizon. And, again, those horizons seemed to bend eastward as they vanished, suggesting a circle so large that one was almost certain it might be visible from the moon, as the moon's crater circles are visible from the Earth. This line camp was defined by intermittent posts of countless tents surrounding countless busy chuck wagons; it was further described by dozens of mounted cowpokes who filled the intervening spaces on horseback; and in between *those* spaces were the hundreds of wagon loads of hay and feed that had so recently been shipped into town. On top of those wagons stood countless cowhands with pitchforks in their hands—but standing idle and baffled and looking to the east.

As I came closer to this supernaturally engineered corral or belt, I could see that it was not only manned by every hand I had ever seen in my brother's employ, but by scores of men I had never seen before—men who had not yet had leave in town during my time in the new Pauktaug. But in addition to this enormous count of steady Crabbe men were all the men of Whisker's outfit who had just been hired by Ellsworth, much to the chagrin of Cousin Julius.

I finally reached the point in this great circle where it intersected with the road running east to my brother's house and headquarters. A cowhand who was familiar stopped me as I tried to cross the line. "I wouldn't keep on in that direction, Mr. Crabbe," the man insisted.

My horse was almost as keen to pursue as I was, for he remonstrated at our halt. He was nearly out of control. But I was more shocked when the cowhand presumed to reach for the bridle.

"Mr. Crabbe, the herd—a herd so big you and no one has ever seen the like—is in there. You'd think the buffalo were back—but doubled in their return. It's breaking my oath to your brother to say this, but I'm telling you the ground ahead is brown with living hides."

"Let me pass," I insisted, and my horse backed away from the cowman's uncharacteristic reach for another man's bridle.

"You don't understand, sir. A man passed through here not long before, cut right into the herd and kept on east. Then Mr. Crabbe himself appeared and kept on after him. But then a bull in the herd took after both and started the whole bunch moving east. You can't go in there. There's the makings of a stampede like no one's ever seen."

"Let me pass!" I shouted a final time, and I pulled my coat's lapel aside and revealed my badge. The cowman muttered, "Yes, Marshal," and he stepped aside.

"But, Marshal, what does this all mean? Damn me for breaking my oath to Mr. Crabbe, but why are we keeping and building this giant herd? What is this all about?" the cowman pleaded as I began to ride on.

I paused. "It's likely the material world finally rejecting and fighting the presumption of ghosts and vacuums," I answered. "It's about the spaces between things," I said, and I rode away from the baffled hand.

"Can you stretch that plainer?" he called back. I did not answer.

Into the monstrous corral I went. All along the road, from this point on—and from horizon to horizon on my left and right, and on up ahead—were interminable reeking piles of cow chips, as if left by a concentration of animals long confined to a restricted space. Into the tight but enormous belt of living beef I rode, but still I had not seen a single cow. Into that singular corral of my brother's private vision but public cause I rode.

I rode on to the top of another rise, and from there I beheld it all.

The hoarders are the unwitting poets who go unrecognized for the fight they wage for us against ghosts, the intangible, all that is praised as abstract but which is merely a void.

Below me, encompassing the mild valley to all the compass points, was a comprehensive conglomerate of matter, of consciously collected living flesh—thousands upon thousands of desperate animals moving in two great wings, split asunder in the center by some force, but driving still, notwithstanding that narrow cleft up the middle, as if to one central point. They were being flung like a giant mace's head against the voids of the plains and the sky above.

If it had been Ellsworth who had orchestrated the genteel melee surrounding Dunstable's oration at the Pauktaug Lyceum in 1866, the result of that orchestration was merely my brother's mute answer to the lecture. But this herd, this was Ellsworth's own address, his own speech. Here would be his answer to my father and my cousin—to the meek follower and the sinister initiator. Here would be the joys of the material, the halcyon time of our mother's early, beautiful, days of maternity made living and vital once more—but on a scale that could not be eroded, could not be disintegrated by false ideals or sinister charity.

I halted at that crest and stared in wonder at the prospect before me. But I was not so appalled and astounded during that brief pause that I failed to realize that though it might delay my apprehension of Kettle's and the Indian's killer it would also per-mit Ellsworth's final and grand prosecution of Cousin Julius. For another instant I paused and compelled my horse to regain his wind—though seemingly against that great runner's will. I paused and gloried that whilst I had merely attempted to strike back at the sinister abstractions and vacuums fostered in my family's dining room so long ago by filling it with the pulp matter of dime novel stacks, Ellsworth had endeavored to push back against that same threat with a living mass of matter so great it seemed to multiply and grow virtually from its sheer surfeit, even in that seemingly inexhaustible open space of the free grass's greatest ranges.

I spurred my horse forward, but it was unnecessary; he wished to run forward at a greater pace than I would have dared to demand. He ran as if by instinct toward the great cleft in the two converging wings of the ceaseless herd. The herd was moving at a run toward a central point a mile away. That point was a house on the crest of the distant, opposite slope. That house was the ranch house, my brother's house. But it was indeed *our* house, for it was an exact replica of our manse back east. Even from that distance I could not only confirm it as a perfect, loving, replica, but I could attest to its soundness and newness—its paint gleamed in the unremitting Western light of afternoon, in the light after the storm.

At the center of the great cleft I was then entering, up ahead by about a half mile, was my brother, as sympathetic matador and Paul Bunyan—urging his horse at top gallop toward the house ahead. In front of him was the bull I suspect I had heard and wondered after so much since Pope's tale had been told of that strange morning. And in front of that bull was Cousin Julius, he nearly to the house—his horse nearly played out.

I became aware suddenly of a threat to myself and my horse. The great cleft was closing on my end—and up ahead, as well—but with the greatest speed closer to my location. I halted my horse, and he then seemed agreeable to the stop, as if he sensed this danger, as well. We took refuge on a small elevated knoll that preceded the final climb up to the plateau of the house. From there we watched as the cleft seemed to close all along the line of its course, uniting the great herd into one, seamless, unbroken, mass.

Surely, I thought and feared, if Julius had only just made it to the house before this great suture had contracted and formed then my brother and his horse had been swallowed by the stampede that continued to recede from me.

But then, a wonder to behold! I saw Ellsworth not astride, but standing atop the back or backs of part of the herd, being carried with thoughtless certainty toward the perfect replica of our Long Island manse. Both of his arms he held up to balance himself it appeared; on second glance and suspicion, however, it was clear his forearms were crooked straight up, displaying a revolver in each hand, the long barrels glinting in the sun—giving the impression that he had assumed that posture not only to display readiness of his guns but also to suggest the appearance of a pair of steer's horns shining in the critical light around his head.

Then for a time he vanished. The great herd cleft again as it reached the house and vanished over the plateau. To my astonishment I suddenly descried Cousin Julius on the roof of the house—apparently in the spot to which he had taken ultimate refuge at the end of the pursuit. He stood on the southernmost end of the roof. One could make him out to be gesticulating wildly, gun in hand, and shouting and pointing to the other side, to the north end of the roof.

There, on that north end stood Ellsworth, pointing back with his two guns in his hands. He, too, shouted, nay likely screamed, imprecations, recriminations, and a lifetime's ponderous, just, contempt. He, too, also gesticulated wildly with his arms—as if for a moment to insist that one take in first the empty prospect that was then all about my side of the house on the west and then the living mass that was concealed from me on the other side of the slope. All of this, of course, played itself out to me in complete silence, just as it does today in the motion pictures.

The two men then began to step towards one another. One final volley of unheard, shouted, rage was exchanged between them, and then Cousin Julius fired a shot. My brother fell to his knees, but he was not yet out of the fight. Rather than return fire he wildly pointed once more to the east, to the opposite side of the plateau that I could not see.

That was the last time I looked to them and the roof. The herd had turned, and it was returning west now, in a continued if not escalated stampede. In this instance they did not split asunder as they reached the house. They went through it. From out of the front doors, front windows, even somehow from the upper story windows—but especially from the large spaces afforded by the first story's set of bay windows—steers came crashing through the house, almost as if they had been born inside and finally burst (like maddened, massive, butterflies escaping from cocoons)—out into the challenging vacuums presented by the free grass range.

The herd kept coming on back west, back in my direction. I remained in my trance on the knoll, watching as the house began to fall, and then to burn as reckless animals overturned lamps or spread red ashes of neglected fires. Ellsworth and Julius were gone; they had vanished.

My horse then began to panic. Either inspired by the oncoming herd, or terrified of it, he champed at the bit to run west back toward town as well. I dismounted and slapped the horse on its rump. He galloped off—faster and freer without my weight—and I never saw him again.

On the western edge of the knoll was a slight badland outcropping under which I crawled; there I hoped to weather and survive the oncoming wave.

Though I could have continued to breathe, when the herd hit and passed overhead—and it took no less than a full quarter hour for the largest mass of beef ever assembled on the plains to pass—I intermittently held my breath. This was not only because of the great clouds of mud and new dust the herd formed though it had just rained but also because it seemed the mass of cows, the consolidation of matter that they represented, was so dense, I feared that if I tried to take a breath my lips would meet no open space and would taste only hair and hide. It was as a living nightmare in which one chokes upon solid beef. I saw the brands of both my brother and Whisker pass overhead; it had been my brother who had bought every cow that Whisker was willing to sell.

It had been Pope Pope who had engineered the secret purchases, he never understanding, likely, the full purpose of building such a herd. But he was my brother's perfect lieutenant. He understood things, suspected things, to an exquisite level, but he also refrained from asking ultimate questions.

Thus Pope Pope, a former shepherd of the flock, became instead a foreman of an actual herd, and served a master he both revered yet prevented himself from reproaching. I do not believe, however, that Pope Pope ever realized, as I did, that my brother was the agent force behind the deaths of Kettle and the Indian. I alone knew all the tenets of my brother's strange orthodoxy.

After a half hour passed, I dared to venture from my shelter. I began to walk back toward town. After a half hour of walking I reached the site of the western curve of the immense line camp and feeding circle. It lay in ruins. It lay pushed ahead for hundreds of yards beyond its original line—the detritus of the site had been thrown ahead as if by a brutal high tide. No living men remained anywhere nearby.

Though it seems strange now, I paused then and rested. Miraculously, a kettle of beef and beans, in the bed of a chuckwagon, had survived the great herd's passing. Perversely, I gorged upon this meal, and I relished it. Then I slept for a time in a surviving buckboard.

As evening came on I woke, but I woke to a great light burning in the west, spiting the stars that shone clearly overhead. I walked toward this light. After a time, as I got closer, it was evident that this light was the new Pauktaug burning to the ground. What parts of town that had not been razed when the stampede had reached town were now being finished in fire. Bewildered cowmen, tradesmen, and clutches of Mrs. Morgan's doves stood about in a silent, impromptu village north of the vanishing town. Using cowman's tarps and cavalry tents, a small tent city had been erected along the stage road; the army detachment for which my brother had wired, because of the Indian raid on the stage, had only just arrived. There was not a living cow in sight, just the one above that the old Greeks thought they could see in the constellations; the herd had scattered to the west, into the last stretches of unfenced free grass—they at liberty, for a time, to be as the largest assembly of mavericks ever to pass lazily a summer night beneath the sky. But there was nothing to keep them together; without innumerable steadying hands, the great herd had no more chance to remain bound than a house of cards left abandoned on the plains in a wind.

I spent the night alone, nearly fifty yards from the nearest cowman's tarp tent as the town burned away. The town no longer exists; I would say it is now one of the ghost towns of the West; but what greater degree of ghostliness has a ghost town reached when even its buildings have altogether vanished? It is a phantom ghost town, I think.

As the fire burned through the night, I smiled when I heard an unknown cowman and McCarthy reflecting on the fate of a few cows that must have perished whilst crashing through the hotel. The fire was then roasting their bodies, and didn't they smell awfully good, they said.

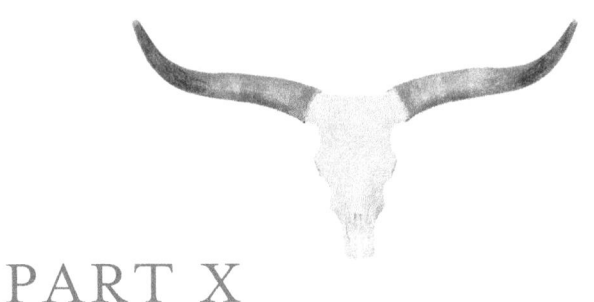

PART X

Epilogue

This history of my strange fortnight in the cow country is complete. With the help of Pope Pope, the great herd and lands that came to me via inheritance from Ellsworth Crabbe and John Whisker were sold as I made my way back east.

It is now 1925, autumn. I have lived a long and comfortable and happy life in my family's restored manse on account of that inheritance. Because of my sudden but unexplained affluence upon my return to Long Island's Pauktaug, I enjoyed partial restoration of my family's standing in the old village. I married well (the Paw girl, Ellen) and had a family. I now have a grandson. From time to time I take him to the site of the old Lyceum which now operates as a house for motion pictures. Sometime I take him to a Western picture there, but he does not know of my time in the territories.

My sons built their own homes closer to Main Street. One of them works in the law book publishing house that occupies the former site of the Stays Works. He was instrumental, upon the centennial of the Stays Works' founding, in soliciting from me a donation for the town's fund for the Pauktaug Girl statue—a monument to the industry that had characterized our village through so much of the nineteenth-century, and a monument to the young women who had performed so much of the company's manual labor. My grandson and I often visit this statue when we walk through the park before going to the movies. It stands very close to the piers where the steamers from New York used to dock.

Also of note in our village's transition into the twentieth-century is our mildly famous Sunken Cemetery. For many years, a burial ground on the west side of the village, tucked along a slope touching the harbor, it was a safe and beautiful place to inter loved ones—from the late seventeenth-century to the late nineteenth (when, at the latter time, a hurricane washed over the cemetery and its land and placed nearly half of it graves permanently under water via intense erosion). At extreme low tide, the stones that had been claimed by the new shoreline can still be seen. My father's stone is among them. His grave is both safe yet always threatened. His stone is covered by a beard of seaweed, as rough and thick as buffalo grass, and circled by horseshoe crabs at high tide. My mother's grave, however, is utterly safe. It lies on the older, higher, slope—never touched by the tide. My grandson and I often visit the cemetery after we see a motion picture. He is thrilled on the rare occasions when he catches a glimpse of his great-grandfather's headstone.

"A Crabbe covered by crabs," we often say together.

I say again: My writing of this heretofore unreported family history is indeed complete. Also I must say again my sons prefer to live closer to the village. My wife is dead; the house is too large for me. Later today a man is coming, one of the Gourds. He is going to buy the house and convert it into a funeral home. In the future when I return to this house, I will visit as a customer. Then I plan to join my mother on the high slope of the Sunken Cemetery. For the time being I hope my older son means his welcome to me in the village house. There I can see my grandson each day—and we can make our walk to the movie house with ease.

I mean to take one last walk around the old grounds before this man Gourd comes to finalize the sale. I mean to take one last look at the barn. For there something occurred upon my return to the old Pauktaug in late summer 1883 that I must record before this history is truly finished.

When I returned it was September, and I set right to work taking the boards from off the windows and doors of the house. The house had a look of beautiful dilapidation that is not brought about strictly by neglect. I looked up and thought the eaves of the house looked like books laid flat to mark their reader's place; I was ready to take them up again. On the third day of my working at this the same boy who had come to me in alarm that spring came to me in the same manner one evening with the same warning.

I told him I was no longer a constable—nor a marshal (though he was puzzled by my last remark). But in good humor, and in celebration of the health that had been returned to me so thoroughly, I consented to follow him towards the empty barn. I remarked to myself that what had been such a beautiful night of spring on our last approach to the barn was now an equally beautiful infant autumn evening. The night in the spring had been filled with birds; this night was filled with crickets, singing their frost-fear song.

The boy again insisted he had heard a gunshot. This was no cow kicking against a stall, he assured me. I smiled, but then I was stunned when I, too, heard what seemed a real gunshot as we approached the barn from the same path as we had used in the spring. Again, as in the spring, I told the boy to stay put.

I repeated my same motions of approach until I was again hiding behind the mysteriously open north doors of the barn. I shouted that I was unarmed but that trespassers were unwelcome. Then, hearing no reply and no further shots, I boldly announced I was about to enter. I stepped around the door and into the barn.

There was no one there—no man, no cow. But there was a gleaming, abandoned, spade lying against one of the stall doors. And in the center of the barn, next to an enormous pile of freshly heaped earth, was a great hole, in which still remained the impressions of trunks that had lain in the earth for years.

I sent the boy home without giving him a look into the barn. But I again gave him a coin for his keen ear and his work—even though I had no cow for him to lead back to its proper corral. I do not know who it had been that had disinterred the trunks that had been buried in the barn. Perhaps, I imagined for a moment, it had been the uncaptured band of renegades who had attacked the stage back near the new Pauktaug. But perhaps it had been someone else. We go to our graves suspecting things.

After the boy left I walked down to the old family beach. The gazebo my father had built for my mother had long before gone to ruin. But I walked along the edge of the shore, and imagined I could still see Julius, my mother, and my father strolling near the gazebo on that summer evening when my cousin had first arrived. And I imagined, too, that I could see my young self and Ellsworth as we played at the edge of the water, shoveling against the sea.

As it was then late summer, many small boats were still moored in clusters not far from the beach where I walked. If one listened carefully, above the sound of the coming autumn breeze and the crickets, one could hear the gentle ringing of all the buoys and chains out on the water, sounding like the bells of so many cows wandering in the darkness, looking for their barns.

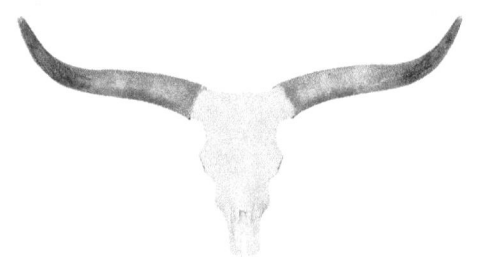

Appendices

*The above papers of my grandfather, Campbell Crabbe
(1849–1930) were willed to me by my father. My
father never told me of these events. I do not believe
he ever read these papers. Is this to be believed?*

—Thomas Crabbe, 1966

*I, too, have read these papers of my great-grandfather.
I will pass them on to my husband, Lawrence. I think
he will find them interesting as local history.*

—Lisa Crabbe Hare, 1999

Remarkable. Might we serialize this in our press?

—Lawrence Hare, Editor,
The Pauktaug Press, 2000

*As much as I would like to honor the wishes of my late
employer and friend, Lawrence Hare, how can I make use
of this? Is it a history? Is it a fiction?* The Pauktaug Press
*cannot survive whilst it still entertains literary submissions
and dubious local history. We hardly survive on local news
as it is. Again, is this a history? I do know the house here
in town of which he writes. I will ask Port Gourd, who
still lives and works there. The barn there still stands.*

—Rex Shell, Editor,
The Pauktaug Press, 2006

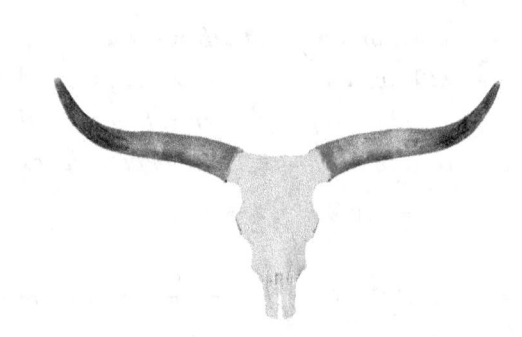